The Vampire Hunters' Casebook

The Vampire Hunters' Casebook

Edited by
Peter Haining

BARNES
&NOBLE
BOOKS
NEW YORK

1997 Barnes & Noble Books

ISBN 0-7607-0470-8

Printed and bound in the United States of America

97 98 99 00 01 M 9 8 7 6 5 4 3 2 1

QF

Contents

Acknowledgments

The Editor and publishers are grateful to the following authors, their publishers, and agents for permission to include copyright stories in this collection:

Seabury Quinn, "The Man Who Cast No Shadow." Copyright by *Weird Tales*, 1927, and reprinted by permission of Arkham House Publishing. Sydney Horler, "The Bloodsucker of Portland Place." Copyright by Hutchinson Publishers Ltd, 1935, and reprinted by permission of Random Publishing Group. Manly Wade Wellman, "The Last Grave of Lill Warran." Copyright by *Weird Tales*, 1951, and reprinted by permission of Frances Wellman. Peter Haining, "The Beefsteak Room." Copyright by Peter Haining, 1996 for this collection. Jeff Rice, "The Night Stalker." Copyright by Pocket Books and Simon & Schuster Inc., 1974, and reprinted with their permission. Karl Edward Wagner, "Beyond Any Measure." Copyright by *Weird Tales*, 1982, and reprinted by permission of the author. Robert Bloch, "The Undead." Copyright by Robert Bloch, 1984, and reprinted with his permission. Anne Rice, "The Master of Rampling Gate." Copyright by Headline Publishing Group, 1985, and reprinted with their permission. David J. Schow, "A Week in the Unlife." Copyright by David J. Schow, 1991, and reprinted with his permission. Peter Tremayne, "My Name Upon The Wind." Copyright by Peter Tremayne, 1996, and reprinted by permission of A.M. Heath Literary Agency.

Introduction

The vampire hunter is one of the most courageous figures to be found in the pages of horror fiction. A man who ventures into the world of the Undead armed only with a crucifix, a wooden stake, a bottle of holy water and some garlic. And his own bravery, of course.

The most famous of these stalwarts of the night is certainly Professor Abraham Van Helsing of Amsterdam, who first appeared in the pages of Bram Stoker's novel *Dracula*, and has since become an icon in print, films, on radio and television, and even in comic strips.

The late Peter Cushing, who will forever be remembered for his appearances on the screen as Van Helsing, said the role gave him great personal satisfaction, and he had no doubts as to the secret of the man's appeal.

'To me, he is the essence of good, pitted against the essence of evil,' Peter told me when I visited him while he was filming *The Satanic Rites of Dracula* in 1973. 'I think the Dracula films have the same appeal as the old morality plays with the struggle of good over evil, and good always triumphing in the end. Van Helsing is *such* an intriguing man – dedicated and determined, not to say brave in the face of great danger.'

Peter had thoroughly acquainted himself with the role of the vampire hunter long before he went on the set by carefully studying Stoker's novel. Interestingly, he felt that it was almost fate that he should have been cast to play the role in the first Hammer *Dracula* in 1958.

'I suppose in a way it is possible that I was pre-ordained to play the part of Van Helsing,' explained the gentlemanly actor, whose death in 1994 was keenly felt. 'Although I am not a religious man, I do try to live by Christian ethics and I believe in the truth as set forth in the New Testament. I can see so many of the elements of good and evil in life, and this seemed to give me added strength for my screen battles with the powers of darkness.'

Peter, of course, was well aware that others had preceded him in the role of Van Helsing – in particular Edward Van Sloan, who had co-starred with Bela Lugosi in the classic Universal version of *Dracula* made in 1931 – but his has certainly been the benchmark performance against which his successors have been measured. Even such classical actors as Lord Olivier, who played the vampire hunter opposite Frank Langella in the 1979 John Badham version of the story, and Sir Anthony Hopkins, who was Van Helsing in Francis Ford Coppola's 1993 production, *Bram Stoker's Dracula*, which co-starred Gary Oldman, were compared to Cushing by several reviewers.

Such, though, has been the success of the Coppola version that a sequel is planned, *The Van Helsing Chronicles*, in which the vampire hunter will take centre stage with Sir Anthony again playing the part of the intrepid Dutch professor. It will provide him with an opportunity to add a further dimension to the character he described in a light-hearted moment during the filming of the earlier picture as 'part mystic, part charlatan, like one of those travelling snake oil doctors in the westerns'.

Hopkins, like Peter Cushing, is a quietly spoken and rather shy man who puts an equal amount of hard work and concentration into recreating the legendary character who is already familiar in one way or another to most people. So how does he see Van Helsing?

'He is a great eccentric, a man who loves life, loves to eat and drink, and yet is capable of destroying Dracula,' he says.

Van Helsing – like Dracula himself – is now one of the immortals of the horror genre. But the fact remains that he was not the first vampire hunter in fiction – nor has he been the last. Indeed, a quarter of a century before Bram Stoker wrote *Dracula*, a certain Baron Vordenburg had been busy staking vampires in Austria in Joseph Sheridan Le Fanu's story, 'Carmilla', and a year before the publication of the book, readers of the monthly periodical *The Ludgate Magazine* were enjoying the exploits of an English nobleman-turned-occult investigator, Lord Syfret, as he tackled a voluptuous psychic vampire in a series written by a now-forgotten feminist author, Arabella Kenealy. Both of these landmark stories are represented in the pages of this collection – along with the other rivals of Van Helsing who followed in his dogged footsteps through pages of increasing bloodshed and terror as the nineteenth century gave way to the twentieth. The casebook is, I believe, filled with surprises in which the stake and an agonizing death await the vampires who are being pursued. Or *does* it?

I invite you then to step into the world of the vampire and study the case histories of those who have dared the impossible. Who have sought to end the existence of those who are already dead – yet live . . .

PETER HAINING, December 1995

Preface

The Way of the Vampire
PROFESSOR ABRAHAM VAN HELSING

There are such beings as vampires; some of us have evidence that they exist. Even had we not the proof of our own unhappy experience, the teachings and the records of the past give proof enough for sane peoples. I admit that at the first I was sceptic. Were it not that through long years I have train myself to keep an open mind, I could not have believe until such time as that fact thunder on my ear. 'See! see! I prove; I prove.' Alas! Had I known at the first what now I know – nay, had I even guess at him – one so precious life had been spared to many of us who did love her. But that is gone; and we must so work, that other poor souls perish not, whilst we can save.

The *nosferatu* do not die like the bee when he sting once. He is only stronger; and being stronger, have yet more power to work evil. This vampire which is amongst us is of himself so strong in person as twenty men; he is of cunning more than mortal, for his cunning be the growth of ages; he have still the aids of necromancy, which is, as his etymology imply, the divination by the dead, and all the dead that he can come nigh to are for him at command; he is brute, and more than brute: he is devil in callous, and the heart of him is not; he can, within limitations appear at will when, and where, and in any of the forms that are to him; he can, within his range, direct the elements: the storm, the fog, the thunder; he can command all the meaner things: the rat, and the owl, and the bat – the moth, and the fox, and the wolf; he can grow and become small; and he can at times vanish and come unknown.

How then are we to begin our strife to destroy him? How shall we find his whereabouts; and having found it, how can we destroy? My friends, this is much; it is a terrible task that we undertake, and there may be consequence to make the brave shudder. For if we fail in this our fight he must surely win; and then where end we? Life is nothings; I heed him not. But to fail here, is not mere life or death. It is that we become as him; that we henceforward become foul things of the night like him – without heart or conscience, preying on the bodies and the souls of those we love best. To us for ever are the gates of heaven shut; for who shall open them to us again? We go on for all time abhorred by all; a blot on the face of God's sunshine; an arrow in the side of Him who died for man. But we are face to face with duty; and in such case must we shrink? For me, I say, no; but then I am old, and life, with his sunshine, his fair places, his song of birds, his music, and his love, lie far behind. You others are young. Some have seen sorrow; but there are fair days yet in store.

Well, you know what we have to contend against; but we, too, are not without strength. We have on our side power of combination – a power denied to the vampire kind; we have resources of science; we are free to act and think; and the hours of the day and the night are ours equally. In fact, so far as our powers extend, they are unfettered, and we are free to use them. We have self-devotion in a cause, and an end to achieve which is not a selfish one. These things are much.

Now let us see how far the general powers arrayed against us are restrict, and how the individual cannot. In fine, let us consider the limitations of the vampire in general, and of this one in particular.

All we have to go upon are traditions and superstitions. These do not at the first appear much, when the matter is one of life and death – nay of more than either life or death. Yet must we be satisfied; in the first place because we have to be – no other means is at our control – and secondly, because, after all, these things – tradition and superstition – are everything. Does not the belief in vampires rest for others – though not, alas! for us – on them? A year ago which of us would have received such a possibility, in the midst of our scientific, sceptical, matter-of-fact nineteenth century? We even scouted a belief that we saw justified under our very eyes.

Take it, then, that the vampire, and the belief in his limitations and his cure, rest for the moment on the same base. For, let me tell you, he is known everywhere that men have been. In old Greece, in old Rome; he flourish in Germany all over, in France, in India, even in the Chersonese; and in China, so far from us in all ways, there even is he, and the peoples fear him at this day. He have follow the wake of the berserker Icelander, the devil-begotten Hun, the Slav, the Saxon, the Magyar. So far, then, we have all we may act upon; and let me tell you that very much of the beliefs are justified by what we have seen in our own so unhappy experience.

The vampire live on, and cannot die by mere passing of the time; he can flourish when that he can fatten on the blood of the living. Even more, we have seen amongst us that he can even grow younger; that his vital faculties grow strenuous, and seem as though they refresh themselves when his special pabulum is plenty. But he cannot flourish without this diet; he eat not as others. Even friend Jonathan, who lived with him for weeks, did never see him to eat, never! He throws no shadow; he make in the mirror no reflect, as again Jonathan observe. He has the strength of many in his hand – witness again Jonathan when he shut the door against the wolfs, and when he help him from the diligence too. He can transform himself to wolf, as we gather from the ship arrival in Whitby, when he tear open the dog; he can be as bat, as Madam Mina saw him on the window at Whitby, and as friend John saw him fly from this so near house, and as my friend Quincey saw him at the window of Miss Lucy. He can come in mist which he create – that noble ship's captain proved him of this; but, from what we know, the distance he can make this mist is limited, and it can only be round himself. He come on moonlight rays as elemental dust – as again Jonathan saw those sisters in the castle of Dracula. He become so small – we ourselves saw Miss Lucy, ere she was at peace, slip through a hairbreadth space at the tomb door. He can, when once he find his way, come out from anything or into anything, no matter how close it be bound or even fused up with fire – solder you call it. He can see in the dark – no small power this, in a world which is one half shut from the light.

Ah, but hear me through. He can do all these things, yet he is not free. Nay; he is even more prisoner than the slave of the galley, than the madman in his cell. He cannot go where he lists; he who is not of nature has yet to obey some of nature's laws – why we know not. He may not enter anywhere at the first, unless there be some one of the household who bid him to come; though afterwards he can come as he please. His power ceases, as does that of all evil things, at the coming of the day. Only at certain times can he have limited freedom. If he be not at the place whither he is bound, he can only change himself at noon or at exact sunrise or sunset.

These things are we told, and in this record of ours we have proof by inference. Thus, whereas he can do as he will within his limit, when he have his earth-home, his coffin-home, his hell-home, the place unhallowed, as we saw when he went to the grave of the suicide at Whitby; still at other time he can only change when the time come. It is said, too, that he can only pass running water at the slack or the flood of the tide. Then there are things which so afflict him that he has no power, as the garlic that we know of, and as for things sacred, as this symbol, my crucifix, that was amongst us even now when we resolve, to them he is nothing, but in their presence he take his place far off and silent with respect. There are others, too, which I shall tell you of, lest in our seeking we may need them. The branch of wild rose on his coffin keep him that he move not from it; a sacred bullet fired into the coffin kill him so that he be true dead; and as for the stake through him, we know already of its peace; or the cut-off head that giveth rest. We have seen it with our eyes. Thus when we find the habitation of this man-that-was, we can confine him to his coffin and destroy him, if we obey what we know!

BRAM STOKER
DRACULA (1897)

The Strange Investigator

JOSEPH SHERIDAN LE FANU

Vampire hunter: Baron Vordenburg
Locality of case: Styria, Austria
Time: Mid-nineteenth century
Author: Irish periodical editor and novelist, Joseph Sheridan Le Fanu (1814–73) is today held to be one of the most innovative writers of supernatural fiction, while his serial story 'Carmilla' (first published in *The Dark Blue*, 1871–2), from which this episode is taken, has been described by Everett F. Bleiler, the historian of supernatural fiction, as 'probably the best vampire story of all [and] important in establishing the vampire theme in the higher levels of modern English literature.' According to Jack Sullivan in his *Encyclopedia of Horror and the Supernatural* it was also 'an important (and acknowledged) influence on Stoker's *Dracula*.' The staking scene in 'Carmilla' is probably the most gruesome moment in all Le Fanu's work – not to mention a great deal of other vampire literature, too! The vampire hunter, Baron Vordenburg, is the latest member of the Vordenburg line to devote his life to pursuing the undead, and his father was the author of 'a curious paper to prove that the vampire, on its expulsion from its amphibious existence, is projected into a far more horrible life.' The Baron is clearly well aware of what lies ahead . . .

One of the strangest-looking men I ever beheld, entered the chapel at the door through which Carmilla had made her entrance and her exit. He was tall, narrow-chested, stooping, with high shoulders, and dressed in black. His face was brown and dried in with deep furrows; he wore an oddly-shaped hat with a broad leaf. His hair, long and grizzled, hung on his shoulders. He wore a pair of gold spectacles, and walked slowly, with an odd shambling gait, with his face sometimes turned up to the sky, and sometimes bowed down toward the ground, seemed to wear a perpetual smile; his long thin arms were swinging, and his lank hands, in old black gloves ever so much too wide for them, waving and gesticulating in utter abstraction.

'The very man!' exclaimed the General, advancing with manifest delight. 'My dear Baron, how happy I am to see you, I had no hope of meeting you so soon.' He signed to my father, who had by this time returned, and leading the fantastic old gentleman, whom he called the Baron, to meet him. He introduced him formally, and they at once entered into earnest conversation. The stranger took a roll of paper from his pocket, and spread it on the worn surface of a tomb that stood by. He had a pencil case in his fingers, with which he traced imaginary lines from point to point on the paper, which from their often glancing from it, together, at certain points of the building, I concluded to be a plan of the chapel. He accompanied, what I may term his lecture, with occasional readings from a dirty little book, whose yellow leaves were closely written over.

They sauntered together down the side aisle, opposite to the spot where I was standing, conversing as they went; then they began measuring distances by paces, and finally they all stood together, facing a piece of the side-wall, which they began to examine with great minuteness; pulling off the ivy that clung over it, and rapping the plaster with the ends of their sticks, scraping here, and knocking there. At length they ascertained the existence of a broad marble tablet, with letters carved in relief upon it.

With the assistance of the woodman, who soon returned, a monumental inscription, and carved escutcheon, were disclosed. They proved to be of those of the long lost monument of Mircalla, Countess Karnstein.

The old General, though not I fear given to the praying mood, raised his hands and eyes to heaven, in mute thanksgiving for some moments.

'Tomorrow,' I heard him say; 'the commissioner will be here, and the Inquisition will be held according to law.'

Then turning to the old man with the gold spectacles, whom I have described, he shook him warmly by both hands and said:

'Baron, how can I thank you? How can we all thank you? You will have delivered this region from a plague that has scourged its inhabitants for more than a century. The horrible enemy, thank God, is at last tracked.'

My father led the stranger aside, and the General followed. I knew that he had led them out of hearing, that he might relate my case, and I saw them glance often quickly at me, as the discussion proceeded.

My father came to me, kissed me again and again, and leading me from the chapel said:

'It is time to return, but before we go home, we must add to our party the good priest, who lives but a little way from this; and persuade him to accompany us to the schloss.'

In this quest we were successful: and I was glad, being unspeakably fatigued when we reached home. But my satisfaction was changed to dismay, on discovering that there were no tidings of Carmilla. Of the scene that had occurred in the ruined chapel, no explanation was offered to me, and it was clear that it was a secret which my father for the present determined to keep from me.

The sinister absence of Carmilla made the remembrance of the scene more horrible to me. The arrangements for that night were singular. Two servants and Madame were to sit up in my room that night; and the ecclesiastic with my father kept watch in the adjoining dressing-room.

The priest had performed certain solemn rites that night, the purport of which I did not understand any more than I comprehended the reason of this extraordinary precaution taken for my safety during sleep.

I saw all clearly a few days later.

The disappearance of Carmilla was followed by the discontinuance of my nightly sufferings.

You have heard, no doubt, of the appalling superstition that prevails in Upper and Lower Styria, in Moravia, Silesia, in Turkish Servia, in Poland, even in Russia; the super-stition, so we must call it, of the vampire.

If human testimony, taken with every care and solemnity, judicially, before commissions innumerable, each consisting of many members, all chosen for integrity and intelligence, and constituting reports more voluminous perhaps that exist upon any one other class of cases, is worth anything, it is difficult to deny, or even to doubt the existence of such a phenomenon as the vampire.

For my part I have heard no theory by which to explain what I myself have witnessed and experienced, other than that supplied by the ancient and well-attested belief of the country.

The next day the formal proceedings took place in the Chapel of Karnstein. The grave of the Countess Mircalla was opened; and the General and my father recognized each his perfidious and beautiful guest, in the face now disclosed to

JOSEPH SHERIDAN LE FANU

view. The features, though a hundred and fifty years had passed since her funeral, were tinted with the warmth of life. Her eyes were open; no cadaverous smell exhaled from the coffin. The two medical men, one officially present, the other on the part of the promoter of the inquiry, attested the marvellous fact, that there was a faint, but appreciable respiration, and a corresponding action of the heart. The limbs were perfectly flexible, the flesh elastic; and the leaden coffin floated with blood, in which to a depth of seven inches, the body lay immersed. Here then, were all the admitted signs and proofs of vampirism. The body, therefore, in accordance with the ancient practice, was raised, and a sharp stake driven through the heart of the vampire, who uttered a piercing shriek at the moment, in all respects such as might escape from a living person in the last agony. Then the head was struck off, and a torrent of blood flowed from the severed neck. The body and head were next placed on a pile of wood, and reduced to ashes, which were thrown upon the river and borne away, and that territory has never since been plagued by the visits of a vampire.

My father has a copy of the report of the Imperial Commission, with the signatures of all who were present at these proceedings, attached in verification of the statement. It is from this official paper that I have summarized my account of this last shocking scene.

I write all this you suppose with composure. But far from it; I cannot think of it without agitation. Nothing but your earnest desire so repeatedly expressed, could have induced me to sit down to a task that has unstrung my nerves for months to come, and reinduced a shadow of the unspeakable horror which years after my deliverance continued to make my days and nights dreadful, and solitude insupportably terrific.

Let me add a word or two about that quaint Baron Vordenburg, to whose curious lore we were indebted for the discovery of the Countess Mircalla's grave.

He had taken up his abode in Gratz, where, living upon a mere pittance, which was all that remained to him of the once princely estates of his family, in Upper Styria, he devoted himself to the minute and laborious investigation of the marvellously authenticated tradition of vampirism. He had at his fingers' ends all the great and little works upon the subject. 'Magia Posthuma', 'Phlegon de Mirabilibus', 'Augustinus de curâ pro Mortuis', 'Philosophicæ et Christianæ Cogitantiones de Vampiris', by John Christofer Harenberg; and a thousand others, among which I remember only a few of those which he lent to my father. He had a voluminous digest of all the judicial cases, from which he had extracted a system of principles that appear to govern – some always, and others occasionally only – the condition of the vampire. I may mention, in passing, that the deadly pallor attributed to that sort of *revenants*, is a mere melodramatic fiction. They present, in the grave, and when they show themselves in human society, the appearance of healthy life. When disclosed to light in their coffins, they exhibit all the symptoms that are enumerated as those which proved the vampire life of the long-dead Countess Karnstein.

How they escape from their graves and return to them for certain hours every day, without displacing the clay or leaving any trace of disturbance in the state of the coffin or the cerements, has always been admitted to be utterly inexplicable. The amphibious existence of the vampire is sustained by daily renewed slumber in the grave. Its horrible lust for living blood supplies the vigour of its walking existence. The vampire is prone to be fascinated with an

JOSEPH SHERIDAN LE FANU

engrossing vehemence, resembling the passion of love, by particular persons. In pursuit of these it will exercise inexhaustible patience and stratagem, for access to a particular object may be obstructed in a hundred ways. It will never desist until it has satiated its passion, and drained the very life of its coveted victim. But it will, in these cases, husband and protract its murderous enjoyment with the refinement of an epicure, and heighten it by the gradual approaches of an artful courtship. In these cases it seems to yearn for something like sympathy and consent. In ordinary ones it goes direct to its object, overpowers with violence, and strangles and exhausts often at a single feast.

The vampire is, apparently, subject, in certain situations, to special conditions. In the particular instance of which I have given you a relation, Mircalla seemed to be limited to a name which, if not her real one, should at least reproduce, without the omission or addition of a single letter, those, as we say, anagrammatically, which compose it. *Carmilla* did this; so did *Millarca*.

My father related to the Baron Vordenburg, who remained with us for two or three weeks after the expulsion of Carmilla, the story about the Moravian nobleman and the vampire at Karnstein churchyard, and then he asked the Baron how he had discovered the exact position of the long-concealed tomb of the Countess Millarca? The Baron's grotesque features puckered up into a mysterious smile; he looked down, still smiling, on his worn spectacle-case and fumbled with it. Then looking up, he said:

'I have many journals, and other papers, written by that remarkable man; the most curious among them is one treating of the visit of which you speak, to Karnstein. The tradition, of course, discolours and distorts a little. He might have been termed a Moravian nobleman, for he had changed his abode to that territory, and was, beside, a noble. But he was, in truth, a native of Upper Styria. It is enough to say that in very early youth he had been a passionate and favoured lover of the beautiful Mircalla, Countess Karnstein. Her early death plunged him into inconsolable grief. It is the nature of vampires to increase and multiply, but according to an ascertained and ghostly law.

'Assume, at starting, a territory perfectly free from that pest. How does it begin, and how does it multiply itself? I will tell you. A person, more or less wicked, puts an end to himself. A suicide, under certain circumstances, becomes a vampire. That spectre visits living people in their slumbers; *they* die, and almost invariably, in the grave, develop into vampires. This happened in the case of the beautiful Mircalla, who was haunted by one of those demons. My ancestor, Vordenburg, whose title I still bear, soon discovered this, and in the course of the studies to which he devoted himself, learned a great deal more.

'Among other things, he concluded that suspicion of vampirism would probably fall, sooner or later, upon the dead Countess, who in life had been his idol. He conceived a horror, be she what she might, of her remains being profaned by the outrage of a posthumous execution. He has left a curious paper to prove that the vampire, on its expulsion from its amphibious existence, is projected into a far more horrible life; and he resolved to save his once beloved Mircalla from this.

'He adopted the stratagem of a journey here, a pretended removal of her remains, and a real obliteration of her monument. When age had stolen upon him, and from the vale of years he looked back on the scenes he was leaving, he considered, in a different spirit, what he had done; and a horror took possession of him. He made the tracings and

JOSEPH SHERIDAN LE FANU

notes which have guided me to the very spot, and drew up a confession of the deception that he had practised. If he had intended any further action in this matter, death prevented him; and the hand of a remote descendant has, too late for many, directed the pursuit to the lair of the beast.'

We talked a little more, and among other things he said was this:

'One sign of the vampire is the power of the hand. The slender hand of Mircalla closed like a vice of steel on the General's wrist when he raised the hatchet to strike. But its power is not confined to its grasp; it leaves a numbness in the limb it seizes, which is slowly, if ever, recovered from.'

The following Spring my father took me on a tour through Italy. We remained away for more than a year. It was long before the terror of recent events subsided; and to this hour the image of Carmilla returns to memory with ambiguous alternations – sometimes the playful, languid, beautiful girl; sometimes the writhing fiend I saw in the ruined church; and often from a reverie I have started, fancying I heard the light step of Carmilla at the drawing-room door.

A Beautiful Vampire

ARABELLA KENEALY

Vampire hunter: Lord Syfret
Locality of case: Argles, Southern England
Time: Late nineteenth century
Author: English novelist and writer on medical and ethical subjects, Arabella Kenealy (1862–1938) gave up the profession of a GP because of a severe attack of diphtheria, but following the publication of *Dr Janet of Harley Street* (1893) she enjoyed a successful career as a novelist as well as writing a number of early feminist works including *Feminism and Sex-Extinction* (1920). Her occult investigator Lord Syfret was introduced to readers in *The Ludgate Magazine* in a series of cases under the heading 'Some Experience of Lord Syfret'. The nobleman's first encounter with a vampire was published in May 1896, just a year before the appearance of Professor Van Helsing in *Dracula*.

There was a flutter indeed in the little town of Argles, when it became known that Dr Andrew had made an attempt upon the life of Lady Deverish. Andrew was a youngish, good-looking fellow, junior partner in the firm of Byrne & Andrew, the principal doctors in the place. Everybody liked him. He was as clever as he was kind. He would take equal pains to pull the ninth child of a navvy through a croup seizure as he would have done had it been heir to an earldom. Some people thought this mistaken kindness on the doctor's part – the navvy's ninth could well have been spared, especially as the navvy drank, and in any case was unable to provide properly for eight. Some went so far even as to assert that Andrew was flying in the face of Providence – to say nothing of the ratepayers – when he brought this superfluous ninth triumphantly through its fifth attack of croup. Otherwise, he was as popular as a man may be in a world wherein flaws and scandal lend to tea and bread-and-butter a stimulating quality denied to blamelessness and good repute.

'The butler says he heard raised voices,' it was whispered over dainty cups, 'and then Lady Deverish shrieked for help, and he ran in and found the doctor clutching her round the throat.'

'And only just in time. Her face was perfectly black!'

'Isn't it awful? Such a kind man as he has always seemed. Is there any madness in the family?'

'It is not certain. They say his mother was peculiar. Wrote books, and did other extraordinary things. Always wore very large hats with black feathers. Quite out of fashion, Mrs Byass tells me. She knew her.'

'What have they done with him?'

'That is the strangest part of it. She wouldn't charge

ARABELLA KENEALY

him – said it was all a mistake. So he just got into his carriage, and continued his rounds.'

'Gracious! Strangling everybody?'

'Oh, I believe not.'

'Her throat was bruised black and blue. Old Dr Byrne went at once and saw to her. He got a new nurse down from London. They say it was a nurse they quarrelled about, you know.'

'Well, they won't get anyone to believe that, my dear.'

'No, because she was as plain as could be. And Lady Deverish's groom told cook that Dr Andrew scarcely looked at her.'

'And I never heard that he admired Lady Deverish.'

'Ah! well, most men do.'

'I don't see what she wants a nurse at all for. She's the picture of health.'

'She says she suffers from nerves.'

'If all of us who suffer from "nerves" were to have trained nurses looking after us, there wouldn't be enough trained nurses to go round.'

'No, but all of us are not widows with the incomes of two rich dear departeds at our bankers, my dear.'

Now, knowing both her charming ladyship and Andrew, I was naturally interested as to why he had put hands about her beautiful throat in anything other than loving kindness. Therefore, I made a point of drinking tea with a number of amiable and gracious persons of my acquaintance during the week following this most notable attempt. All the information I got for my pains has been condensed into the foregoing gossip, and since it was insufficient for my purposes I set about seeking more. I called early at the Manor. I did not entirely credit rumour's whisper concerning the victim's mangled throat, but I knew Andrew's muscular lean hands, if he had been in earnest, would, to say the least of it, have rendered prudent her retirement for the space of some days, so that I did not expect to see anybody but her companion, Mrs Lyall.

'Gracious, how ill you look!' I could not help exclaiming, as she entered.

I had known her some months earlier as a buxom matron. Now she was a haggard old woman. Her features worked and twisted. She slid into a chair, her hands and members shaking like those of one with palsy. For several minutes she could not speak.

'You must have been sadly troubled,' I said.

She was a mild and somewhat flaccid person, one of those plump anaemic women who give one the impression that their veins run milk. But as I spoke her face became contorted. She struggled up and brandished a trembling, clenched hand.

'If he had only done it!' she cried passionately, 'if by some mercy of Providence he had only done it!'

She was transformed – distorted. It was as though some mild and milky Alderney had suddenly developed claws. She slid trembling again into her chair.

'My dear Mrs Lyall,' I remonstrated, 'if he had only done it, the world would have lost a beautiful and accomplished member of your sex – and poor Andrew's career would have come to a summary and lamentable end.'

'No jury would have convicted him,' she protested, '*not when they knew.*' She dropped her voice and searched the room with apprehensive eyes. Then she whispered, 'She is a devil.'

Now I was aware that some plain and very good women are in the habit of regarding every comely member of their sex as allied in one or another way with the Father of Evil, but it was clear that some sentiment stronger than general principles was moving Mrs Lyall.

My interest was roused. But she had come to the end of her remarks. She glanced round timorously.

'For Heaven's sake, Lord Syfret, do not mention a word of this,' she stammered. 'I am sadly unnerved. I scarcely know what I say. Poor Lady Deverish has been rather trying.' She shut her weak lips obstinately. I assured her of my discretion. I expressed sympathy, and went my way.

Byrne had nothing to tell. 'Andrew will not say a word,' he said. 'He was over-taxed. Been up several nights. She must have exasperated him somehow. Shouldn't have thought he had it in him. He has always been the kindest of fellows.'

'What does she say?'

'Laughs it off, though she don't seem amiable. Looks as if she don't want things to come out.'

'You don't mean—?'

'My dear fellow, whatsoever I mean, I do not say.'

It has always been my habit in life to take the bull by the horns whensoever circumstances have rendered this feat at the same time possible and prudent. I determined to attempt it now. Andrew, after all, was a very mild and tractable bull, despite his recent outbreak.

'I will not disguise the object of my visit,' I informed him. 'You know my weakness. Anything you tell me will go no further. The ball of Argles' scandal will get no push from me. But I like to probe human motive; and you must admit the situation is suggestive.'

He smiled – a nervous smile. I had never seen him so careworn. He shook his head. 'She has tied my hands,' he said. 'If they had let me I would have strangled her.'

'I do not wonder you are hard hit,' I adventured,

watching him. 'She is certainly a siren of the first water.'

He burst out laughing. 'Great Scott!' he said. 'Is that what they say? Do they think I am aspiring to the Deverish's hand and acres? No, no; I am not altogether a fool.'

At this moment somebody ran up the stairs and after a preliminary knock, burst into the room.

'Please, doctor, come quick,' a page-boy blurted. 'There's Lady Deverish's nurse has fallen down in the road, and they says she's dying.'

The same change came over Andrew that had come over Mrs Lyall. His face became contorted. He held a clenched fist in the air. 'Damn her!' he cried, and rushed out.

Now this ejaculation had every appearance of applying to her ladyship's nurse, and would point to an amount of callousness on Andrew's part – considering the moribund condition of that unfortunate young person – whereof I am sure he was incapable. I hasten, therefore, to inform the reader that it was intended solely and absolutely for her ladyship's bewitching self. It was as fervid and whole-souled a fulmination as I remember to have heard. It left no doubt in my mind whatsoever as to the fact of her ladyship owing her life to that timely advent of her butler. My interest was not abated. I followed Andrew out. In the next street a knot of curious persons were assembled.

'Stand back,' the doctor called as we went up. 'Give her air.'

The circle widened, disclosing the figure of a young woman in nursing dress, lying senseless on the pavement. Her upturned face was curiously pinched, though the conformation was young, and her hair fallen loose about her cheek hung in girlish rings.

'She does not look strong enough for nursing,' I remarked to Byrne, who came up at the moment.

'Strong enough,' he echoed testily. 'A week ago she was sturdy and robust. The Deverish takes care of that. Can't stand sickliness about her.' He added half to himself, 'Must be something wrong with the house. Ventilation bad or something. One after another they've gone off like this.' The girl now began to show signs of consciousness. She opened her eyes, and seeing Andrew, smiled faintly. Presently she sat up.

'When you feel equal to it, my dear,' Dr Byrne said, 'we will help you to my carriage, and you can drive straight back.'

'Back,' she repeated wildly, 'where?'

'Why, to the Manor. You must—'

She interrupted him; she caught his hand. 'No, no,' she gasped, 'not there, never there. I cannot stand another hour of it.'

'The beautiful Deverish must be something of a vixen,' I reflected, seeing the expression in the girl's face.

Andrew was helping her to her feet. 'Don't be afraid,' he said quietly, 'I will see that you do not go back.'

She looked into his face. 'What is it?' she whispered, with white lips. 'Do you know?'

'Yes, I know,' he answered, meeting her look.

I had an inspiration. Among my clientele I numbered several trained nurses. I called at the post office on my way home and wired for one. In less than two hours she was with me. I despatched her to the Manor. 'Say you have been sent from Heaven or Buckingham Palace, or any other probable and impressive source, and keep your eyes and ears open,' I enjoined her, with that utter disregard for truth and scrupulousness which I have found the greatest of all aids to me in my researches.

She returned in an hour. There was anger in her eyes. The gauze veil streaming from her bonnet fluttered manelike to the offended toss of her head.

'You did not stay long,' I said.

'My lord,' she returned, 'I did not have the opportunity. Lady Devilish – I believe you called her Devilish – just came into the room and gave a little cry, and turned her back on me as if I'd been an ogre. "Oh, you would never suit," she said, "I must have someone young" – my lord, I am twenty-six – "and plump" – I weigh ten stone – "and healthy" – I have never had a day's illness. "Send someone young, and plump, and healthy," and she marched out.'

'I suppose that would not be difficult?' I commented.

'Not at all,' she said resolutely, 'a little padding, a touch of rouge, and some minor details are all that are needed.'

'You mean to go yourself, then?'

'Yes, I mean to go,' she returned. 'If there is anything to find out she may be sorry she wasn't more civil,' she added meditatively.

'Would she not recognize you?'

I admire grit. I admired the uncompromising and superior disdain with which she met my question. She turned and left without condescending a word. In fifteen minutes she came back, or, rather, somebody did whose voice was all I recognized. Her disguise was perfect. Before, she had certainly looked neither youthful (despite her assurance as to twenty-six), nor plump (despite her boasted avoirdupois), nor healthy. Now she was plump, and young, and rosy. She had been dark; now a profusion of rich red hair rippled from her brows. I wondered why she did not always go about disguised. She explained.

'In most houses, my lord,' she said, 'there are sons, and brothers, and husbands. A woman who has her living to get by nursing can only afford to sport cherry cheeks under exceptional circumstances.'

When she had gone I dipped my pen in coloured ink and

entered her name in my diary. Whether or not she succeeded with Lady 'Devilish', she was a capable person. And capable persons are red-letter persons in a world where incompetency rules seven days out of most weeks.

II
Nurse Marian's Story

She received me with open arms. 'You are just what I want,' she said effusively. 'I loathe sickliness. There was a gaunt, haggard creature here an hour ago. Ugh!' she shuddered, 'I would not have employed her for worlds.'

I may be prejudiced, but after her remark I confess to feeling somewhat antipathetic to her ladyship. She has a curious way of staring. I suspect her of being short-sighted and shirking glasses for the sake of her looks. Certainly I have never seen anybody so brilliantly beautiful.

Upstairs I was introduced to her companion, Mrs Lyall. She did not strike me as being altogether sane. She has rather a grim smile.

'You'll soon lose those fine cheeks,' she said the moment she saw me.

'I trust not,' I returned, with some amount of confidence. (I had only just opened a new packet.) 'Is Lady Devilish rather a trying patient, then?' I asked.

She broke into a laugh. 'What did you call her?'

'I understood her name to be Devilish,' I said.

'No, it's her nature,' she retorted, looking furtively about. 'Her name has an "r" instead of an "l".'

Her ladyship was plainly no favourite of Mrs Lyall's. Indeed, everybody in the house seemed to be in mortal terror of her. The servants would not, if they could help it, enter a room where she was.

From the unhealthy faces of the household I came to the conclusion that the house was thoroughly unsanitary. I determined to investigate the drains. Whatsoever there might be that was unwholesome it did not affect the mistress. Her energy was marvellous. She never tired. When after a long day picnicking or a late ball, everybody looked as white as paper, she was as fresh and blooming and gay-spirited as possible. It seemed a mere farce for her to employ a nurse. But she had a fad about massage, and insisted on being 'massed' morning and night.

'You don't look tired,' she remarked in a puzzled way, at the end of my first night's operations. She was staring curiously at my rouged cheeks. Strangely enough I was feeling actually faint. Strong-nerved as I am, I fairly reeled.

'Whatsoever I look,' I answered her, a little irritably, 'I certainly feel more tired than I ever remember feeling.'

I thought she seemed pleased. Certainly I had said nothing to please her. No doubt she was thinking her own thoughts.

Her engagement to be married again was announced the day after my arrival. She had been already married twice. The young man – the Earl of Arlington – was, with a number of other persons, stopping in the house. He was handsome and pleasant-looking. I was told he had thrown over a girl he had cared for and who had cared for him for years in order to propose to Lady Deverish. He did not look capable of it. But, to all appearance, he was head over ears in love. He could not keep his eyes from her. He sat like a man bewitched, and neither ate nor rested.

'Poor young gentleman! He'll go the way of the others,' Mrs Plimmer, the housekeeper, confided to me.

'You don't suspect Lady Deverish of poisoning her husbands?' I returned.

'It isn't my place to suspect my betters, Nurse,' she said with dignity, 'All I say is there's something terrible mysterious. Why does everybody who comes to the Manor fail in health?'

'Drains,' I suggested.

She tossed her ample chin. 'Why did her two young husbands, as likely men as might be, sicken from the day she married them, and die consumptive? Was that drains, can you tell me?'

I thought it might have been, but having no evidence, did not commit myself.

Mrs Plimmer tossed her ample chin again, this time triumphantly. 'And why,' she proceeded, 'did Dr Andrew, as kind a gentleman as walks, try to strangle her?'

I braved her scorn and ventured 'jealousy.'

She eyed me witheringly. 'The doctor's no lady's man,' she said, 'and besides if he was, it's no reason for strangling them.'

I was unable to find any fault with the drains. I began to grow interested. I myself felt strangely out of sorts – a new experience for me.

Lord Arlington's infatuation amounted to possession. He sat staring at her in a kind of ecstasy of fascination. He was pale and moody and obviously unhappy. I was told he had lost health and spirits markedly since his engagement. Probably his conscience troubled him about the other woman. At breakfast one morning he unwrapped a little packet which had come by post for him, without, it is to be supposed, observing the handwriting. As he undid it mechanically there dropped from the wrappings a ring, a knot of ribbon, and a bundle of letters. He seemed stunned. Without a word he gathered them together and quitted the room. I met him later pacing the garden like a madman.

Poor man! His love-affair was short-lived.

A week later I was involuntary witness to a curious scene. I was sitting late one evening in the garden. Lady Deverish would not need me until bedtime, when her massage was due. Suddenly he and she, talking excitedly, came round the shrubbery.

'I have been mad,' he exclaimed, in a hoarse, passionate voice. 'For God's sake let me go free. They say her heart is broken.'

She put her two hands on his shoulders, and lifted her face to his.

'I will never let you go,' she said, with a curious ring as of metal in her voice. She wound her arms about his neck and kissed his throat. 'And you love me too much,' she added.

'Heaven only knows if it is love,' he answered, 'it seems to me like madness. I had loved her faithfully for years.'

'And now you love me, and there is no way out of it,' she whispered. She leaned up again and kissed him. Then with a little cooing laugh she left him.

He remained looking after her. 'Yes, there is one way out of it,' I heard him say slowly.

That night he shot himself.

Now, although I had known her but a fortnight, I had known her long enough to believe her superior to the weakness of being very deeply in love. Yet the night he died I was inclined to alter my opinion. He had bidden her a hasty goodbye, saying he was summoned to town. He took the last train up.

During the night I was called to her. I found her sitting up in bed, her face ashen pale, her eyes distended, her hands clasped to her head. She was gasping for breath. She seemed like one stricken; her features were picked out by deep grey lines. She did not speak, but pointed with an insistent finger to her right temple. I put my hand upon it. Then I called quickly for a light; for my fingers slipped along that which seemed to be a moist and clammy aperture, moist with a horrible, unmistakable clamminess. But when the light was brought there was neither blood nor aperture, only a curious, blanched spot, chill to the touch.

I gave her brandy, and put hot bottles in her bed. She was shaking as with ague. She clutched my hands, holding them against that ice-spot in her temple till I was sick and faint. Soon she seemed better. Some colour returned to her.

'My God, he is dead!' she said, through chattering teeth. Then she crouched down in the bed, a shuddering heap.

Next morning the news came. In that same hour he had put a bullet through his right temple. She was ill all that day, nerveless and almost pulseless. She looked ten years older. I never saw so singular a change. I sent for Dr Byrne, who attributed it to the shock of bad news. Why it developed some hours before the news arrived he did not explain. He only said: 'Tut, tut, Nurse, life is full of coincidences;' and prescribed ammonia.

Next day she was better, and suggested getting up, but changed her mind after having seen a mirror. 'Gracious!' she said, with a shudder, 'I look like an old woman.' She broke into feeble weeping. 'He ought to have thought of me,' she cried angrily.

She demanded wine and meat-juices, taking them with a curious solicitude, and carefully looking into her mirror for their effect. But she saw little there to comfort her.

'Do you think it might be my death-blow?' she questioned once through quivering lips. I shook my head. 'Ah, you don't know all,' she muttered.

In the afternoon she asked that the gardener's child

should be brought to her. He was a chubby, rosy little fellow, whom everybody petted. 'I must have something to liven me,' she said. I had never supposed her fond of children. But she held her arms hungrily for him, and strained him to her breast. Her spirits rose. Her eyes brightened: she got colour. Soon she was laughing and chatting in her accustomed manner. The child had fallen asleep, but she would not part with him. When at last she let him go, I was horrified to find him cold and pallid. He was breathing heavily, and quite unconscious. I concluded the poor little chap was sickening for something. Later, I was surprised to receive a note from Dr Andrew, whom I did not know. I dismissed him as I had done Mrs Lyall, and probably Mrs Plimmer, as not altogether sane. 'I have been called in to attend Willy Daniels,' the note ran. 'For Heaven's sake, do not let her get hold of any more children.'

Next day she was better. She seemed to have forgotten Arlington and talked only of her health. She asked again for the boy. I told her he was ill. She broke into a curious laugh which seemed uncalled for. 'Thank goodness, I haven't lost my power,' she said a minute later. But she did not explain the saying.

She was in high spirits all the morning, talking and singing and trying on new laces and bonnets. She still complained of pain in the right temple. After her massage she turned peevish, protesting that it did her no good. 'If you hadn't such a colour I should not believe you healthy,' she said crossly.

She had the parson's children to tea. It would amuse her, she said, to see them eat their strawberries. They seemed afraid of her, and eyed her from a distance. When she attempted to take the little one, it clung to me and shrieked.

But she persisted, and it soon fell asleep in her arms. On presently taking it from her, I found it chilled and breathing stertorously and quite unconscious. I thought of Dr Andrew's injunction. Heavens! what had she done? Was she a secret poisoner? I dismissed the notion forthwith. I had not left the room a moment during the time the child was with her, nor had it taken anything to eat or drink.

'What is the matter?' I demanded.

Her eye avoided mine. She answered nonchalantly: 'What does one expect? Children are everlastingly teething or over-feeding or having measles.'

Next morning I was called up at daybreak. Dr Andrew was waiting to see me. I threw on my things and went down. He was stalking up and down the drawing-room. He stared.

'You seem to have resisted her,' he muttered, looking at my cheeks. I have a long memory, and had not forgotten my rouge. He told me a wild and incredible story. He wound up by handing me a small bottle.

'Give her that dose so soon as she wakes,' he said. The man was probably a better doctor than he was an actor. His manner paraded the nature of the dose. I took out the cork and smelt it. It was as I suspected. I walked across the room and emptied its contents out of the window. 'Pardon me,' I said, 'but you are exceeding your duty.'

'Is she to be allowed to go on murdering people?' he protested. 'Do you know I have been up all night with that unfortunate baby? Do you know Willy Daniels is not yet out of danger? Good Heavens! if I am willing to take the consequences, how can one who knows the circumstances hesitate?'

'I have a safer and more justifiable plan,' I said. 'If what you say is true the remedy is simple, and poison is uncalled for. After all, Dr Andrew, your story would sound lame enough in a lawcourt. By my plan you run no risks.'

I laid it before him. He seemed interested. But he would not, after the manner of men in their dealings with women, permit me to take too much credit to myself.

'It might work,' he said lukewarmly, 'and as you say it would certainly be safer.'

I went to my room and opened a further packet of rouge. I applied it lavishly. I began to see that the health tint on my cheeks had an important bearing on the situation. I put vermilion on my lips. Then I carried my patient her breakfast.

She seemed restored and lay in her rose-pink bed, a smiling Venus. She fairly glowed with beautiful health. I thought of that poor little sick boy. 'Goodness!' I said with a start, 'how ill you look!' She ceased from smiling. She leapt across the floor, her draperies clinging round her pink flushed toes. She fled to the glass. She turned on me peevishly. 'Why did you tell me?' she protested. 'I should have thought I looked well.'

I went and stood beside her. 'Compare yourself with me.'

She was pale enough indeed by the time she had done so. 'Am I losing my power after all?' she muttered. 'Heavens! shall I grow old like other people?'

Suddenly she flung herself upon me. She pressed her lips and cheeks against my throat and face.

'Give *me* some of it,' she cried ravenously. 'You have so much vitality. Let me drain some of that rich health and colour.'

I nearly fell. It seemed as if she were actually sucking out my life. I reeled and sickened. Then with a tremendous effort I pushed her away and stumbled from the room. Was

Andrew's story indeed true? Was she a monster or merely a monomaniac?

Years ago he had said she was dying of consumption. So far as physical signs could be trusted, she had not a week to live. Suddenly she began to recover. She made flesh rapidly, gained health, and came back to life from the very jaws of death. Meanwhile, her sister, a schoolgirl, whom she insisted on having always with her, sickened and died.

Then a brother died, then her mother. By this time she had grown quite strong. Since then she had lived on the vital forces of those surrounding her. 'The law of life,' he said, 'makes creatures inter-dependent. Physical vitality is subject to physical laws of diffusion and equalisation. One person below par absorbs the nerve and life sources of healthier persons with them. Many old, debilitated subjects live on the animal forces of the cat they keep persistently in their chair, and die when it dies. Wives and husbands, sisters and brothers, friends and acquaintances: there is a constant interchange of vital force. Lady Deverish has to my knowledge been the actual cause of death of a dozen persons. Besides these she has drained the health of everybody associated with her. And in her case – a rare and extreme one – the faculty is conscious and voluntary. She was living on Arlington. The man was powerless. She paralysed his will, his mind, his energies. She robbed him of strength to resist her. The sequel is interesting, psychologically. She being for the time charged with his vitality, his sudden death, by some curious sympathy, affected her in the way you have described. She was all at once and violently bereft of the source whence she was drawing energy. But she will soon, if she be allowed, find some other to prey on. For some years I have studied her closely. She is the arch-type of a class of persons I have long had under observation. I find such power depends largely on force of will and concentration. If she can maintain these there is no reason why she should not live to be a hundred. There will always be persons of less assertive selfishness to serve as reservoirs of vital strength to her. At present her confidence is shaken, her power – therefore her life trembles in the balance. In the interests of humanity and justice she must not be allowed to regain her confidence. She lives by wholesale murder.'

III

I drank a glass of port and went back to my patient. She lay panting on her bed.

'Fie!' I said; 'that was a bit of hysteria. Come now, take your breakfast.'

She looked me in the face. A terror of death stood in beads on her skin. 'I have heard of transfusion,' she said faintly; 'if you will let me have some of the rich red blood run out of your veins into mine I will settle £500 a year on you.'

I shook my head.

'A thousand,' she said. 'Fifteen hundred.'

'I should be cheating you,' I insisted, 'even were I willing. The operation has never been really successful.'

She broke into raving and tears.

'I cannot die,' she said; 'I love life. I love being beautiful and rich; I love admiration. I must have admiration! I love my beautiful, beautiful body and the joy of life! I cannot, cannot die!'

'What nonsense!' I said. 'You are not going to die.'

'If I could only get it,' she raved, 'I would drink blood out of living bodies rather than I would die.'

An hour later she summoned the housekeeper. She had

been cogitating with a fold between her brows; her teeth set like pearls in the red of her lower lip.

'Plimmer,' she said, 'give all the servants a month's wages and an hour's notice to quit. I cannot endure their sickly faces. Get in a staff of decently healthy people. These cadaverous wretches are killing me.'

Plimmer left the room without a word. At the door she cast one look toward me and threw her hands up, as one who says: 'The Lord have mercy on us!'

I followed, and bade her stay her hand. Whether Andrew's theories were true, or whether my lady were but a person with a mania, there was no doubt but that her convictions played an important part in the case.

I threw on my things and expended a half-sovereign at the chemist's. I came back the possessor of sundry packets. These I distributed among the household with explicit directions. Her ladyship was not well; her whim must be humoured.

It is surprising what a little rouge will do. In a few minutes the servants' hall was a scene Arcadian. Even the elderly butler reverted to blooming youth. Then I said to her cheerfully:

'You are making a mistake about the servants. For my part I am struck with their healthy looks.'

'Since I have been ill?' she faltered.

She lay quiet, breathing hard through her dilated nostrils. 'Send some of them in,' she said presently.

By the time they had gone she was as white as paper. 'Good Heavens!' I heard her mutter, 'I have lost my power. I am a dead woman.'

Then she flung out her arms and wept. 'Get me healthy children,' she cried; 'I must have health about me.'

Dr Byrne, who was attending her, assented in all

innocence. 'Why, of course,' he said; 'it will be cheerful for you. Get in some cherry-cheeked children to amuse her ladyship, Nurse.'

I nodded – in token that I was not deaf – not at all in acquiescence. Food and wine I supplied in plenty, but neither children nor adults. I isolated her *in toto*. I allowed her maids only to come near her long enough to dust and arrange the room. I have seen her fix them with a basilisk stare, straining her will. She had undoubtedly some baleful hypnotic power which set them trembling and stumbling about in curious, aimless fashion. They would seem drawn, as by some spell, to stand motionless and dazed beside her bed. Then I would turn them face about and parading their roseate tints, scold them for idleness and dismiss them. She would stare after them in a despair which, under other circumstances, would have been pitiful. The sense that her power was gone robbed her actually of power. She raved and cursed her self-murdered lover for involving her in his death.

Whether Dr Andrew and I were justified in that we did I sometimes wonder now. Then I had no room for doubt. In face of the horrible facts it did not occur to me to question it. If that she believed were true, we were assuredly justified; if not, that we did could not affect results.

Andrew's theory of those results is that she had lived so long on human energy that food in the crude state stood her in little stead. Certainly, though she was fed unremittingly on the choicest and most nourishing of diets, she was an aged and haggard woman in a week. Nobody would have recognized her. She shrivelled and shrank like one cholera-stricken. One day her dog stole into the room. She put out her hand and clutched it voraciously. I took it an hour later from her. It was dead and stiff.

How I myself, and a nurse I had called in to help me, kept life in us I cannot say. I had been an abstainer. Now I drank wine like water. All round her bed was an atmosphere as of a vault, though outside it was sunny June.

She raged like one possessed. 'You are murdering, murdering me,' she cried incessantly.

Dr Byrne thought her mind wandering. I knew it centred with a monstrous, selfish sanity. He sent for one of the first London consultants. After a lengthy investigation the great man pronounced her suffering from some obscure nervous disease. 'Nothing to be done,' he said. 'I give her three days: most interesting case. Hope you will succeed in getting a *post mortem*.'

Once she fixed me with her baleful eyes, how baleful was seen now that their fine lustre and the bloom beneath them were gone.

'I have had ten years more of life and pleasure than my due,' she chuckled in her shrivelled throat – the throat now of an old, old woman.

Then she broke into dry-eyed crying. 'I thought I could have lived another ten.' She begged once for a mirror. I thank Heaven that with all my heat of indignation against her, I was not guilty of that cruelty.

Dr Andrew called daily for my bulletin. Everything science afforded in the way of food and stimulant, he scrupulously got down from London.

'We must give her every chance,' he said, 'every justifiable chance, that is.'

After a few days I was again single-handed. My nurse-colleague succumbed. I felt my powers failing. I could scarcely drag about. I prayed Providence for strength to last so long as she should. Even in the moment of dissolution, such was her frenzied greed of life, that I believed should some non-resistant person take my place, she would struggle back to health.

Once when I arranged her pillows, she seized my hand, and before I could withdraw it she had carried it to her mouth and bitten into it. I felt her suck the blood voraciously. She cried out and struck at me as I wrenched it away.

She died in the third week of her isolation. I saw the death change come into her shrivelled face. Then in the moment wherein life left her she made one supremest effort.

It seemed as though my heart stopped. My head took on my chest, my hands dropped at my side. Then I swayed and fell headlong across her bed. They found me later lying on her corpse. I am convinced that had she been a moment earlier, had she nerved her powers the instant before, rather than on the instant life was leaving her, she would be alive to this day, and I— As it was, I did not leave my bed for a month.

'If I were to write that story in the *Lancet*,' Dr Andrew said, 'I should be the laughing-stock of the profession. Yet it is the very key-note of human health and human disease, this interchange of vital force which goes on continually between individuals. Such rapacity and greed as the Deverish's are, fortunately, rare; but there are a score such vampires in this very town, vampires in lesser degree. When A. talks with me ten minutes I feel ten years older. It takes me an hour to bring my nerve-power up to par again. People call him a bore. In reality he is a rapacious egotist hungrily absorbing the life-force of anyone with whom he comes into relation – in other words, a human vampire.'

Aylmer Vance and the Vampire

CLAUDE ASKEW

Vampire Hunter: Aylmer Vance
Locality of case: Blackwick Castle, Scotland
Time: 1913
Author: The son of an English clergyman, Claude Askew (1878–1917) began to write whilst a pupil at Eton but did not enjoy commercial success until after his marriage in 1900, when his wife, Alice, became his collaborator on many of his subsequent books, serials and short stories. Their first collaboration, *The Shulamite* (1904), was dramatized and produced at the Savoy Theatre in 1906, bringing their names to a much wider public. In all, the Askews are said to have produced about 100 books before their tragic death together at sea in October 1917. Aylmer Vance made his debut in *The Weekly-Tale Teller* in July 1914 just days before the advent of the First World War, and the horrors of the ensuing conflict in Europe undoubtedly gave readers other things to worry about than the cases of the resourceful Vance, which are today undeservedly forgotten.

Aylmer Vance had rooms in Dover Street, Piccadilly, and now that I had decided to follow in his footsteps and to accept him as my instructor in matters psychic, I found it convenient to lodge in the same house. Aylmer and I quickly became close friends, and he showed me how to develop that faculty of clairvoyance which I had possessed without being aware of it. And I may say at once that this particular faculty of mine proved of service on several important occasions.

At the same time I made myself useful to Vance in other ways, not the least of which was that of acting as recorder of his many strange adventures. For himself, he never cared much about publicity, and it was some time before I could persuade him, in the interests of science, to allow me to give any detailed account of his experiences to the world.

The incidents which I will now narrate occurred very soon after we had taken up our residence together, and while I was still, so to speak, a novice.

It was about ten o'clock in the morning that a visitor was announced. He sent up a card which bore upon it the name of Paul Davenant.

The name was familiar to me, and I wondered if this could be the same Mr Davenant who was so well known for his polo playing and for his success as an amateur rider, especially over the hurdles? He was a young man of wealth and position, and I recollected that he had married, about a year ago, a girl who was reckoned the greatest beauty of the season. All the illustrated papers had given their portraits at the time, and I remember thinking what a remarkably handsome couple they made.

Mr Davenant was ushered in, and at first I was uncertain as to whether this could be the individual whom I had in mind, so wan and pale and ill did he appear. A finely-built, upstanding man at the time of his marriage, he had now acquired a languid droop of the shoulders and a shuffling gait, while his face, especially about the lips, was bloodless to an alarming degree.

And yet it was the same man, for behind all this I could recognize the shadow of the good looks that had once distinguished Paul Davenant.

He took the chair which Aylmer offered him – after the usual preliminary civilities had been exchanged – and then glanced doubtfully in my direction. 'I wish to consult you privately, Mr Vance,' he said. 'The matter is of considerable importance to myself, and, if I may say so, of a somewhat delicate nature.'

Of course I rose immediately to withdraw from the room, but Vance laid his hand upon my arm.

'If the matter is connected with research in my particular line, Mr Davenant,' he said, 'if there is any investigation you wish me to take up on your behalf, I shall be glad if you will include Mr Dexter in your confidence. Mr Dexter assists me in my work. But, of course—.'

'Oh, no,' interrupted the other, 'if that is the case, pray let Mr Dexter remain. I think,' he added, glancing at me with a friendly smile, 'that you are an Oxford man, are you not, Mr Dexter? It was before my time, but I have heard of your name in connection with the river. You rowed at Henley, unless I am very much mistaken.'

I admitted the fact, with a pleasurable sensation of pride. I was very keen upon rowing in those days, and a man's prowess at school and college always remain dear to his heart.

After this we quickly became on friendly terms, and Paul Davenant proceeded to take Aylmer and myself into his confidence.

He began by calling attention to his personal appearance.

'You would hardly recognize me for the same man I was a year ago,' he said. 'I've been losing flesh steadily for the last six months. I came up from Scotland about a week ago, to consult a London doctor. I've seen two – in fact, they've held a sort of consultation over me – but the result, I may say, is far from satisfactory. They don't seem to know what is really the matter with me.'

'Anaemia – heart,' suggested Vance. He was scrutinizing his visitor keenly, and yet without any particular appearance of doing so. 'I believe it not infrequently happens that you athletes overdo yourselves – put too much strain upon the heart—'

'My heart is quite sound,' responded Davenant. 'Physically it is in perfect condition. The trouble seems to be that it hasn't enough blood to pump into my veins. The doctors wanted to know if I had met with an accident involving a great loss of blood – but I haven't. I've had no accident at all, and as for anaemia, well, I don't seem to show the ordinary symptoms of it. The inexplicable thing is that I've lost blood without knowing it, and apparently this has been going on for some time, for I've been getting steadily worse. It was almost imperceptible at first – not a sudden collapse, you understand, but a gradual failure of health.'

'I wonder,' remarked Vance slowly, 'what induced you to consult me? For you know, of course, the direction in which I pursue my investigations. May I ask if you have reason to consider that your state of health is due to some cause which we may describe as superphysical?'

A slight colour came to Davenant's white cheeks.

'There are curious circumstances,' he said in a low and earnest tone of voice. 'I've been turning them over in my mind, trying to see light through them. I daresay it's all the sheerest folly – and I must tell you that I'm not in the least a superstitious sort of man. I don't mean to say that I'm absolutely incredulous, but I've never given thought to such things – I've led too active a life. But, as I have said, there are curious circumstances about my case, and that is why I decided upon consulting you.'

'Will you tell me everything without reserve?' said Vance. I could see that he was interested. He was sitting up in his chair, his feet supported on a stool, his elbows on his knees, his chin in his hands – a favourite attitude of his. 'Have you,' he suggested, slowly, 'any mark upon your body, anything that you might associate, however remotely, with your present weakness and ill-health?'

'It's a curious thing that you should ask me that question,' returned Davenant, 'because I have got a curious mark, a sort of scar, that I can't account for. But I showed it to the doctors, and they assured me that it could have nothing whatever to do with my condition. In any case, if it had, it was something altogether outside their experience. I think they imagined it to be nothing more than a birthmark, a sort of mole, for they asked me if I'd had it all my life. But that I can swear I haven't. I only noticed it for the first time about six months ago, when my health began to fail. But you can see for yourself.'

He loosened his collar and bared his throat. Vance rose and made a careful scrutiny of the suspicious mark. It was situated a very little to the left of the central line, just above the clavicle, and, as Vance pointed out, directly over the big vessels of the throat. My friend called to me so that I might examine it, too. Whatever the opinion of the doctors may have been, Aylmer was obviously deeply interested.

And yet there was little to show. The skin was quite intact, and there was no sign of inflammation. There were two red marks, about an inch apart, each of which was inclined to be crescent in shape. They were more visible than they might otherwise have been owing to the peculiar whiteness of Davenant's skin.

'It can't be anything of importance,' said Davenant, with a slightly uneasy laugh. 'I'm inclined to think the marks are dying away.'

'Have you ever noticed them more inflamed than they are at present?' inquired Vance. 'If so, was it at any special time?'

Davenant reflected. 'Yes,' he replied slowly, 'there have been times, usually, I think perhaps invariably, when I wake up in the morning, that I've noticed them larger and more angry looking. And I've felt a slight sensation of pain – a tingling – oh, very slight, and I've never worried about it. Only now you suggest it to my mind, I believe that those same mornings I have felt particularly tired and done up – a sensation of lassitude absolutely unusual to me. And once, Mr Vance, I remember quite distinctly that there was a stain of blood close to the mark. I didn't think anything of it at the time, and just wiped it away.'

'I see.' Aylmer Vance resumed his seat and invited his visitor to do the same. 'And now,' he resumed, 'you said, Mr Davenant, that there are certain peculiar circumstances you wish to acquaint me with. Will you do so?'

And so Davenant readjusted his collar and proceeded to tell his story. I will tell it as far as I can, without any reference to the occasional interruptions of Vance and myself.

Paul Davenant, as I have said, was a man of wealth and position, and so, in every sense of the word, he was a suitable husband for Miss Jessica MacThane, the young lady who eventually became his wife. Before coming to the incidents attending his loss of health, he had a great deal to recount about Miss MacThane and her family history.

She was of Scottish descent, and although she had certain characteristic features of her race, she was not really Scotch in appearance. Hers was the beauty of the far South rather than that of the Highlands from which she had her origin. Names are not always suited to their owners, and Miss MacThane's was peculiarly inappropriate. She had, in fact, been christened Jessica in a sort of pathetic effort to counteract her obvious departure from normal type. There was a reason for this which we were soon to learn.

Miss MacThane was especially remarkable for her wonderful red hair, hair such as one hardly ever sees outside of Italy – not the Celtic red – and it was so long that it reached to her feet, and it had an extraordinary gloss upon it so that it seemed almost to have individual life of its own. Then she had just the complexion that one would expect with such hair, the purest ivory white, and not in the least marred by freckles, as is so often the case with red-haired girls. Her beauty was derived from an ancestress who had been brought to Scotland from some foreign shore – no one knew exactly whence.

Davenant fell in love with her almost at once and he had every reason to believe, in spite of her many admirers, that his love was returned. At this time he knew very little about her personal history. He was aware only that she was very wealthy in her own right, an orphan, and the last representative of a race that had once been famous in the annals of history – or rather infamous, for the MacThanes had distinguished themselves more by cruelty and lust of blood than by deeds of chivalry. A clan of turbulent robbers in the past, they had helped to add many a blood-stained page to the history of their country.

Jessica had lived with her father, who owned a house in London, until his death when she was about fifteen years of age. Her mother had died in Scotland when Jessica was still a tiny child. Mr MacThane had been so affected by his wife's death that, with his little daughter, he had abandoned his Scotch estate altogether – or so it was believed – leaving it to the management of a bailiff – though, indeed, there was but little work for the bailiff to do, since there were practically no tenants left. Blackwick Castle had borne for many years a most unenviable reputation.

After the death of her father, Miss MacThane had gone to live with a certain Mrs Meredith, who was a connection of her mother's – on her father's side she had not a single relation left. Jessica was absolutely the last of a clan once so extensive that intermarriage had been a tradition of the family, but for which the last two hundred years had been gradually dwindling to extinction.

Mrs Meredith took Jessica into Society – which would never have been her privilege had Mr MacThane lived, for he was a moody, self-absorbed man, and prematurely old – one who seemed worn down by the weight of a great grief.

Well, I have said that Paul Davenant quickly fell in love with Jessica, and it was not long before he proposed for her hand. To his great surprise, for he had good reason to believe that she cared for him, he met with a refusal; nor would she give any explanation, though she burst into a flood of pitiful tears.

Bewildered and bitterly disappointed, he consulted Mrs Meredith, with whom he happened to be on friendly terms, and from her he learnt that Jessica had already had several proposals, all from quite desirable men, but that one after another had been rejected.

Paul consoled himself with the reflection that perhaps Jessica did not love them, whereas he was quite sure that she cared for himself. Under these circumstances he determined to try again.

He did so, and with better result. Jessica admitted her love, but at the same time she repeated that she would not marry him. Love and marriage were not for her. Then, to his utter amazement, she declared that she had been born under a curse – a curse which, sooner or later was bound to show itself in her, and which, moreover, must react cruelly, perhaps fatally, upon anyone with whom she linked her life. How could she allow a man she loved to take such a risk? Above all, since the evil was hereditary, there was one point upon which she had quite made up her mind: no child should ever call her mother – she must be the last of her race indeed.

Of course, Davenant was amazed and inclined to think that Jessica had got some absurd idea into her head which a little reasoning on his part would dispel. There was only one other possible explanation. Was it lunacy she was afraid of?

But Jessica shook her head. She did not know of any lunacy in her family. The ill was deeper, more subtle than that. And then she told him all that she knew.

The curse – she made use of that word for want of a better – was attached to the ancient race from which she had her origin. Her father had suffered from it, and his father and grandfather before him. All three had taken to themselves young wives who had died mysteriously, of some wasting disease, within a few years. Had they observed the ancient family tradition of intermarriage this might possibly not have happened, but in their case, since the family was so near extinction, this had not been possible.

For the curse – or whatever it was – did not kill those who bore the name of MacThane. It only rendered them a danger to others. It was as if they absorbed from the blood-soaked walls of their fatal castle a deadly taint which reacted terribly upon those with whom they were brought into contact, especially their nearest and dearest.

'Do you know what my father said we have it in us to become?' said Jessica with a shudder. 'He used the word vampires. Paul, think of it – vampires – preying upon the life blood of others.'

And then, when Davenant was inclined to laugh, she checked him. 'No,' she cried out, 'it is not impossible. Think. We are a decadent race. From the earliest times our history has been marked by bloodshed and cruelty. The walls of Blackwick Castle are impregnated with evil – every stone could tell its tale of violence, pain, lust, and murder. What can one expect of those who have spent their lifetime between its walls?'

'But you have not done so,' exclaimed Paul. 'You have been spared that, Jessica. You were taken away after your mother died, and you have no recollection of Blackwick Castle, none at all. And you need never set foot in it again.'

'I'm afraid the evil is in my blood,' she replied sadly, 'although I am unconscious of it now. And as for not returning to Blackwick – I'm not sure I can help myself. At least, that is what my father warned me of. He said there is something there, some compelling force, that will call me to it in spite of myself. But, oh, I don't know – I don't know, and that is what makes it so difficult. If I could only believe that all this is nothing but an idle superstition, I might be happy again, for I have it in me to enjoy life, and I'm young, very young, but my father told me these things when he was on his death-bed.' She added the last words in a low, awe-stricken tone.

Paul pressed her to tell him all that she knew, and

eventually she revealed another fragment of family history which seemed to have some bearing upon the case. It dealt with her own astonishing likeness to that ancestress of a couple of hundred years ago, whose existence seemed to have presaged the gradual downfall of the clan of the MacThanes.

A certain Robert MacThane, departing from the traditions of his family, which demanded that he should not marry outside his clan, brought home a wife from foreign shores, a woman of wonderful beauty, who was possessed of glowing masses of red hair and a complexion of ivory whiteness – such as had more or less distinguished since then every female of the race born in the direct line.

It was not long before this woman came to be regarded in the neighbourhood as a witch. Queer stories were circulated abroad as to her doings, and the reputation of Blackwick Castle became worse than ever before.

And then one day she disappeared. Robert MacThane had been absent upon some business for twenty-four hours, and it was upon his return that he found her gone. The neighbourhood was searched, but without avail, and then Robert, who was a violent man and who had adored his foreign wife, called together certain of his tenants whom he suspected, rightly or wrongly, of foul play, and had them murdered in cold blood. Murder was easy in those days, yet such an outcry was raised that Robert had to take to flight, leaving his two children in the care of their nurse, and for a long while Blackwick Castle was without a master.

But its evil reputation persisted. It was said that Zaida, the witch, though dead, still made her presence felt. Many children of the tenantry and young people of the neighbourhood sickened and died – possibly of quite natural causes; but this did not prevent a mantle of terror settling upon the countryside, for it was said that Zaida had been seen – a pale woman clad in white – flitting about the cottages at night, and where she passed sickness and death were sure to supervene.

And from that time the fortune of the family gradually declined. Heir succeeded heir, but no sooner was he installed at Blackwick Castle than his nature, whatever it may previously have been, seemed to undergo a change. It was as if he absorbed into himself all the weight of evil that had stained his family name – as if he did, indeed, become a vampire, bringing blight upon any not directly connected with his own house.

And so, by degrees, Blackwick was deserted of its tenantry. The land around it was left uncultivated – the farms stood empty. This had persisted to the present day, for the superstitious peasantry still told their tales of the mysterious white woman who hovered about the neighbourhood, and whose appearance betokened death – and possibly worse than death.

And yet it seemed that the last representatives of the MacThanes could not desert their ancestral home. Riches they had, sufficient to live happily upon elsewhere, but, drawn by some power they could not contend against, they had preferred to spend their lives in the solitude of the now half-ruined castle, shunned by their neighbours, feared and execrated by the few tenants that still clung to their soil.

So it had been with Jessica's grandfather and great-grandfather. Each of them had married a young wife, and in each case their love story had been all too brief. The vampire spirit was still abroad, expressing itself – or so it seemed – through the living representatives of bygone generations of evil, and young blood had been demanded as the sacrifice.

And to them had succeeded Jessica's father. He had not

profited by their example, but had followed directly in their footsteps. And the same fate had befallen the wife whom he passionately adored. She had died of pernicious anaemia – so the doctors said – but he had regarded himself as her murderer.

But, unlike his predecessors, he had torn himself away from Blackwick – and this for the sake of his child. Unknown to her, however, he had returned year after year, for there were times when the passionate longing for the gloomy, mysterious halls and corridors of the old castle, for the wild stretches of moorland, and the dark pinewoods, would come upon him too strongly to be resisted. And so he knew that for his daughter, as for himself, there was no escape, and he warned her, when the relief of death was at last granted to him, of what her fate must be.

This was the tale that Jessica told the man who wished to make her his wife, and he made light of it, as such a man would, regarding it all as foolish superstition, the delusion of a mind overwrought. And at last – perhaps it was not very difficult, for she loved him with all her heart and soul – he succeeded in inducing Jessica to think as he did, to banish morbid ideas, as he called them, from her brain, and to consent to marry him at an early date.

'I'll take any risk you like,' he declared. 'I'll even go and live at Blackwick if you should desire it. To think of you, my lovely Jessica, a vampire! Why, I never heard such nonsense in my life.'

'Father said I'm very like Zaida, the witch,' she protested, but he silenced her with a kiss.

And so they were married and spent their honeymoon abroad, and in the autumn Paul accepted an invitation to a house party in Scotland for the grouse shooting, a sport to which he was absolutely devoted, and Jessica agreed with him that there was no reason why he should forgo his pleasure.

Perhaps it was an unwise thing to do, to venture to Scotland, but by this time the young couple, more deeply in love with each other than ever, had got quite over their fears. Jessica was redolent with health and spirits, and more than once she declared that if they should be anywhere in the neighbourhood of Blackwick she would like to see the old castle out of curiosity, and just to show how absolutely she had got over the foolish terrors that used to assail her.

This seemed to Paul to be quite a wise plan, and so one day, since they were actually staying at no great distance, they motored over to Blackwick, and finding the bailiff, got him to show them over the castle.

It was a great castellated pile, grey with age, and in places falling into ruin. It stood on a steep hillside, with the rock of which it seemed to form part, and on one side of it there was a precipitous drop to a mountain stream a hundred feet below. The robber MacThanes of the old days could not have desired a better stronghold.

At the back, climbing up the mountainside were dark pinewoods, from which, here and there, rugged crags protruded, and these were fantastically shaped, some like gigantic and misshapen human forms, which stood up as if they mounted guard over the castle and the narrow gorge, by which alone it could be approached.

This gorge was always full of weird, uncanny sounds. It might have been a storehouse for the wind, which, even on calm days, rushed up and down as if seeking an escape, and it moaned among the pines and whistled in the crags and shouted derisive laughter as it was tossed from side to side of the rocky heights. It was like the plaint of lost souls – that is the expression Davenant made use of – the plaint of lost souls.

The road, little more than a track now, passed through this gorge, and then, after skirting a small but deep lake, which hardly knew the light of the sun so shut in was it by overhanging trees, climbed the hill to the castle.

And the castle! Davenant used but a few words to describe it, yet somehow I could see the gloomy edifice in my mind's eye, and something of the lurking horror that it contained communicated itself to my brain. Perhaps my clairvoyant sense assisted me, for when he spoke of them I seemed already acquainted with the great stone halls, the long corridors, gloomy and cold even on the brightest and warmest of days, the dark, oak-panelled rooms, and the broad central staircase up which one of the early MacThanes had once led a dozen men on horseback in pursuit of a stag which had taken refuge within the precincts of the castle. There was the keep, too, its walls so thick that the ravages of time had made no impression upon them, and beneath the keep were dungeons which could tell terrible tales of ancient wrong and lingering pain.

Well, Mr and Mrs Davenant visited as much as the bailiff could show them of this ill-omened edifice, and Paul, for his part, thought pleasantly of his own Derbyshire home, the fine Georgian mansion, replete with every modern comfort, where he proposed to settle with his wife. And so he received something of a shock when, as they drove away, she slipped her hand into his and whispered:

'Paul, you promised, didn't you, that you would refuse me nothing?'

She had been strangely silent till she spoke those words. Paul, slightly apprehensive, assured her that she only had to ask – but the speech did not come from his heart, for he guessed vaguely what she desired.

She wanted to go and live at the castle – oh, only for a

little while, for she was sure she would soon tire of it. But the bailiff had told her that there were papers, documents, which she ought to examine, since the property was now hers – and, besides, she was interested in this home of her ancestors, and wanted to explore it more thoroughly. Oh, no, she wasn't in the least influenced by the old superstition – that wasn't the attraction – she had quite got over those silly ideas. Paul had cured her, and since he himself was so convinced that they were without foundation he ought not to mind granting her her whim.

This was a plausible argument, not easy to controvert. In the end Paul yielded, though it was not without a struggle. He suggested amendments. Let him at least have the place done up for her – that would take time; or let them postpone their visit till next year – in the summer – not move in just as the winter was upon them.

But Jessica did not want to delay longer than she could help, and she hated the idea of redecoration. Why, it would spoil the illusion of the old place, and, besides, it would be a waste of money since she only wished to remain there for a week or two. The Derbyshire house was not quite ready yet; they must allow time for the paper to dry on the walls.

And so, a week later, when their stay with their friends was concluded, they went to Blackwick, the bailiff having engaged a few raw servants and generally made things as comfortable for them as possible. Paul was worried and apprehensive, but he could not admit this to his wife after having so loudly proclaimed his theories on the subject of superstition.

They had been married three months at this time – nine had passed since then, and they had never left Blackwick for more than a few hours – till now Paul had come to London – alone.

CLAUDE ASKEW

'Over and over again,' he declared, 'my wife has begged me to go. With tears in her eyes, almost upon her knees, she has entreated me to leave her, but I have steadily refused unless she will accompany me. But that is the trouble, Mr Vance, she cannot; there is something, some mysterious horror, that holds her there as surely as if she were bound with fetters. It holds her more strongly even than it held her father – we found out that he used to spend six months at least of every year at Blackwick – months when he pretended that he was travelling abroad. You see the spell – or whatever the accursed thing may be – never really relaxed its grip of him.'

'Did you never attempt to take your wife away?' asked Vance.

'Yes, several times; but it was hopeless. She would become so ill as soon as we were beyond the limit of the estate that I invariably had to take her back. Once we got as far as Dorekirk – that is the nearest town, you know – and I thought I should be successful if only I could get through the night. But she escaped me; she climbed out of a window – she meant to go back on foot, at night, all those long miles. Then I have had doctors down; but it is I who wanted the doctors, not she. They have ordered me away, but I have refused to obey them till now.'

'Is your wife changed at all – physically?' interrupted Vance.

Davenant reflected. 'Changed,' he said, 'yes, but so subtly that I hardly know how to describe it. She is more beautiful than ever – and yet it isn't the same beauty, if you can understand me. I have spoken of her white complexion, well, one is more than ever conscious of it now, because her lips have become so red – they are almost like a splash of blood upon her face. And the upper one has a peculiar curve that I don't think it had before, and when she laughs she doesn't smile – do you know what I mean? Then her hair – it has lost its wonderful gloss. Of course, I know she is fretting about me; but that is so peculiar, too, for at times, as I have told you, she will implore me to go and leave her, and then perhaps only a few minutes later, she will wreathe her arms round my neck and say she cannot live without me. And I feel that there is a struggle going on within her, that she is only yielding slowly to the horrible influence – whatever it is – that she is herself when she begs me to go, but when she entreats me to stay – and it is then that her fascination is most intense – oh, I can't help remembering what she told me before we were married, and that word' – he lowered his voice – 'the word "vampire"—'

He passed his hand over his brow that was wet with perspiration. 'But that's absurd, ridiculous,' he muttered; 'these fantastic beliefs have been exploded years ago. We live in the twentieth century.'

A pause ensued, then Vance said quietly, 'Mr Davenant, since you have taken me into your confidence, since you have found doctors of no avail, will you let me try to help you? I think I may be of some use – if it is not already too late. Should you agree, Mr Dexter and I will accompany you, as you have suggested, to Blackwick Castle as early as possible – by tonight's mail North. Under ordinary circumstances I should tell you as you value your life, not to return—'

Davenant shook his head. 'That is advice which I should never take,' he declared. 'I had already decided, under any circumstances, to travel North tonight. I am glad that you both will accompany me.'

And so it was decided. We settled to meet at the station, and presently Paul Davenant took his departure. Any other details that remained to be told he would put us in possession of during the course of the journey.

'A curious and most interesting case,' remarked Vance when we were alone. 'What do you make of it, Dexter?'

'I suppose,' I replied cautiously, 'that there is such a thing as vampirism even in these days of advanced civilization? I can understand the evil influence that a very old person may have upon a young one if they happen to be in constant intercourse – the worn-out tissue sapping healthy vitality for their own support. And there are certain people – I could think of several myself – who seem to depress one and undermine one's energies, quite unconsciously, of course, but one feels somehow that vitality has passed from oneself to them. And in this case, when the force is centuries old, expressing itself, in some mysterious way, through Davenant's wife, is it not feasible to believe that he may be physically affected by it, even though the whole thing is sheerly mental?'

'You think, then,' demanded Vance, 'that it is sheerly mental? Tell me, if that is so, how do you account for the marks on Davenant's throat?'

This was a question to which I found no reply, and though I pressed him for his views, Vance would not commit himself further just then.

Of our long journey to Scotland I need say nothing. We did not reach Blackwick Castle till late in the afternoon of the following day. The place was just as I had conceived it – as I have already described it. And a sense of gloom settled upon me as our car jolted us over the rough road that led through the Gorge of the Winds – a gloom that deepened when we penetrated into the vast cold hall of the castle.

Mrs Davenant, who had been informed by telegram of our arrival, received us cordially. She knew nothing of our actual mission, regarding us merely as friends of her husband's. She was most solicitous on his behalf, but there was something strained about her tone, and it made me feel vaguely uneasy. The impression that I got was that the woman was impelled to everything that she said or did by some force outside herself – but, of course, this was a conclusion that the circumstances I was aware of might easily have conduced to. In every other aspect she was charming, and she had an extraordinary fascination of appearance and manner that made me readily understand the force of a remark made by Davenant during our journey.

'I want to live for Jessica's sake. Get her away from Blackwick, Vance, and I feel that all will be well. I'd go through hell to have her restored to me – as she was.'

And now that I had seen Mrs Davenant I realized what he meant by those last words. Her fascination was stronger than ever, but it was not a natural fascination – not that of a normal woman, such as she had been. It was the fascination of a Circe, of a witch, of an enchantress – and as such was irresistible.

We had a strong proof of the evil within her soon after our arrival. It was a test that Vance had quietly prepared. Davenant had mentioned that no flowers grew at Blackwick, and Vance declared that we must take some with us as a present for the lady of the house. He purchased a bouquet of pure white roses at the little town where we left the train, for the motorcar had been sent to meet us.

Soon after our arrival he presented these to Mrs Davenant. She took them it seemed to me nervously, and hardly had her hand touched them before they fell to pieces, in a shower of crumpled petals, to the floor.

'We must act at once,' said Vance to me when we were

descending to dinner that night. 'There must be no delay.'

'What are you afraid of?' I whispered.

'Davenant has been absent a week,' he replied grimly. 'He is stronger than when he went away, but not strong enough to survive the loss of more blood. He must be protected. There is danger tonight.'

'You mean from his wife?' I shuddered at the ghastliness of the suggestion.

'That is what time will show.' Vance turned to me and added a few words with intense earnestness. 'Mrs Davenant, Dexter, is at present hovering between two conditions. The evil thing has not yet completely mastered her – you remember what Davenant said, how she would beg him to go away and the next moment entreat him to stay? She has made a struggle, but she is gradually succumbing, and this last week, spent here alone, has strengthened the evil. And that is what I have got to fight, Dexter – it is to be a contest of will, a contest that will go on silently till one or the other obtains the mastery. If you watch, you may see. Should a change show itself in Mrs Davenant you will know that I have won.'

Thus I knew the direction in which my friend proposed to act. It was to be a war of his will against the mysterious power that had laid its curse upon the house of MacThane. Mrs Davenant must be released from the fatal charm that held her.

And I, knowing what was going on, was able to watch and understand. I realized that the silent contest had begun even while we ate dinner. Mrs Davenant ate practically nothing and seemed ill at ease; she fidgeted in her chair, talked a great deal, and laughed – it was the laugh without a smile, as Davenant had described it. And as soon as she was able to she withdrew.

Later, as we sat in the drawing-room, I could feel the clash of wills. The air in the room felt electric and heavy, charged with tremendous but invisible forces. And outside, round the castle, the wind whistled and shrieked and moaned – it was as if all the dead and gone MacThanes, a grim army, had collected to fight the battle of their race.

And all this while we four in the drawing-room were sitting and talking the ordinary commonplaces of after-dinner conversation! That was the extraordinary part of it – Paul Davenant suspected nothing, and I, who knew, had to play my part. But I hardly took my eyes from Jessica's face. When would the change come, or was it, indeed, too late!

At last Davenant rose and remarked that he was tired and would go to bed. There was no need for Jessica to hurry. We would sleep that night in his dressing-room and did not want to be disturbed.

And it was at that moment, as his lips met hers in a goodnight kiss, as she wreathed her enchantress arms about him, careless of our presence, her eyes gleaming hungrily, that the change came.

It came with a fierce and threatening shriek of wind, and a rattling of the casement, as if the horde of ghosts without was about to break in upon us. A long, quivering sigh escaped from Jessica's lips, her arms fell from her husband's shoulders, and she drew back, swaying a little from side to side.

'Paul,' she cried, and somehow the whole timbre of her voice was changed, 'what a wretch I've been to bring you back to Blackwick, ill as you are! But we'll go away, dear; yes, I'll go, too. Oh, will you take me away – take me away tomorrow?' She spoke with an intense earnestness – unconscious all the time of what had been happening to her. Long shudders were convulsing her frame. 'I don't know why I've wanted to stay here,' she kept repeating. 'I hate the place, really – it's evil – evil.'

Having heard these words I exulted, for surely Vance's success was assured. But I was to learn that the danger was not yet past.

Husband and wife separated, each going to their own room. I noticed the grateful, if mystified glance that Davenant threw at Vance, vaguely aware, as he must have been, that my friend was somehow responsible for what had happened. It was settled that plans for departure were to be discussed on the morrow.

'I have succeeded,' Vance said hurriedly, when we were alone, 'but the change may be a transitory. I must keep watch tonight. Go you to bed, Dexter, there is nothing that you can do.'

I obeyed – though I would sooner have kept watch, too – watch against a danger of which I had no understanding. I went to my room, a gloomy and sparsely furnished apartment, but I knew that it was quite impossible for me to think of sleeping. And so, dressed as I was, I went and sat by the open window, for now the wind that had raged round the castle had died down to a low moaning in the pinetrees – a whimpering of time-worn agony.

And it was as I sat thus that I became aware of a white figure that stole out from the castle by a door that I could not see, and, with hands clasped, ran swiftly across the terrace to the wood. I had but a momentary glance, but I felt convinced that the figure was that of Jessica Davenant.

And instinctively I knew that some great danger was imminent. It was, I think, the suggestion of despair conveyed by those clasped hands. At any rate, I did not hesitate. My window was some height from the ground, but the wall below was ivy-clad and afforded good foothold. The descent was quite easy. I achieved it, and was just in time to take up the pursuit in the right direction, which was into the thickness of the wood that clung to the slope of the hill.

I shall never forget that wild chase. There was just sufficient room to enable me to follow the rough path, which, luckily, since I had now lost sight of my quarry, was the only possible way that she could have taken; there were no intersecting tracks, and the wood was too thick on either side to permit of deviation.

And the wood seemed full of dreadful sounds – moaning and wailing and hideous laughter. The wind, of course, and the screaming of night birds – once I felt the fluttering of wings in close proximity to my face. But I could not rid myself of the thought that I, in my turn, was being pursued, that the forces of hell were combined against me.

The path came to an abrupt end on the border of the sombre lake that I have already mentioned. And now I realized that I was indeed only just in time, for before me, plunging knee deep in the water, I recognized the white-clad figure of the woman I had been pursuing. Hearing my footsteps, she turned her head, and then threw up her arms and screamed. Her red hair fell in heavy masses about her shoulders, and her face, as I saw it in that moment, was hardly human for the agony of remorse that it depicted.

'Go!' she screamed. 'For God's sake let me die!'

But I was by her side almost as she spoke. She struggled with me – sought vainly to tear herself from my clasp – implored me, with panting breath, to let her drown.

'It's the only way to save him!' she gasped. 'Don't you understand that I am a thing accursed? For it is I – I – who have sapped his life blood! I know it now, the truth has been revealed to me tonight! I am a vampire, without hope in this world or the next, so for his sake – for the sake of his unborn child – let me die – let me die!'

Was ever so terrible an appeal made? Yet I – what could I do? Gently I overcame her resistance and drew her back to shore. By the time I reached it she was lying a dead weight upon my arm. I laid her down upon a mossy bank, and, kneeling by her side, gazed intently into her face.

And then I knew that I had done well. For the face I looked upon was not that of Jessica the vampire, as I had seen it that afternoon, it was the face of Jessica, the woman whom Paul Davenant had loved.

And later Aylmer Vance had his tale to tell.

'I waited', he said, 'until I knew that Davenant was asleep, and then I stole into his room to watch by his bedside. And presently she came, as I guessed she would, the vampire, the accursed thing that has preyed upon the souls of her kin, making them like to herself when they too have passed into Shadowland, and gathering sustenance for her horrid task from the blood of those who are alien to her race. Paul's body and Jessica's soul – it is for one and the other, Dexter, that we have fought.'

'You mean,' I hesitated, 'Zaida the witch?'

'Even so,' he agreed. 'Hers is the evil spirit that has fallen like a blight upon the house of MacThane. But now I think she may be exorcized for ever.'

'Tell me.'

'She came to Paul Davenant last night, as she must have done before, in the guise of his wife. You know that Jessica bears a strong resemblance to her ancestress. He opened his arms, but she was foiled of her prey, for I had taken precautions; I had placed That upon Davenant's breast while he slept which robbed the vampire of her power of ill. She sped wailing from the room – a shadow – she who a minute before had looked at him with Jessica's eyes and spoken to him with Jessica's voice. Her red lips were Jessica's lips, and they were close to his when his eyes were opened and he saw her as she was – a hideous phantom of the corruption of the ages. And so the spell was removed, and she fled away to the place whence she had come—'

He paused. 'And now?' I enquired.

'Blackwick Castle must be razed to the ground,' he replied. 'That is the only way. Every stone of it, every brick, must be ground to powder and burnt with fire, for therein is the cause of all the evil. Davenant has consented.'

'And Mrs Davenant?'

'I think,' Vance answered cautiously, 'that all may be well with her. The curse will be removed with the destruction of the castle. She has not – thanks to you – perished under its influence. She was less guilty than she imagined – herself preyed upon rather than preying. But can't you understand her remorse when she realized, as she was bound to realize, the part she had played? And the knowledge of the child to come – its fatal inheritance—'

'I understand,' I muttered with a shudder. And then, under my breath, I whispered, 'Thank God!'

The Broken Fang

UEL KEY

Vampire hunter: Professor Arnold Rhymer
Locality of case: Blankborough, southern England
Time: *c.* 1915
Author: 'Uel Key' was the pseudonym of a mysterious
English writer, Samuel Whittell Key (1874–?) who is
believed to have practised as a doctor in Sussex for many
years, augmenting his salary by writing the occasional
novel and short stories for the popular magazines during
the years between the two World Wars. The first cases
featuring Professor Arnold Rhymer MD, student of psychic phenomena and a man upon whom Scotland Yard
frequently called for assistance, appeared in *Pearson's
Magazine* during the closing years of the 1914–18 War.
Some were later collected as *The Broken Fang and Other
Experiences of a Specialist in Spooks* (1920) while the
following year Dr Rhymer became the first vampire hunter
since Professor Van Helsing to feature in a full-length
novel, *Yellow Death*, in which he attempted to decipher a
message from a dead man. Today all of the stories about
Rhymer are of considerable rarity.

'Sorry to trouble you, sir, but can you help to clear up a mystery which, I'm bound to own, is baffling us?'

The individual thus addressing Professor Arnold Rhymer, MD – the young and distinguished *savant* in psychical phenomena – was a big, finely-built man. He placed his hat and stick on the table and deposited his frame in an easy chair, to which the professor motioned him.

'My name is Brown,' he explained, 'Detective-Inspector Brown of the CID, Scotland Yard. My chief has put me on to a case which doesn't seem quite – well – normal, you know. These sort of problems are in your line, I believe; or else I shouldn't have bothered you.'

'What's the nature of your case?'

'The Blankborough murders. Surely you've read about these mysterious crimes committed near the country town of Blankborough?'

'Yes,' Rhymer admitted, 'but the papers don't give much detail.'

'I know, for we've suppressed details to disarm the criminal, until we've got hold of some sort of clue towards identification. That'll be no easy matter, though, I dare bet. Will you help us, sir?'

'I'll give you what assistance I can,' he replied, 'but I shall want some details first, for I know nothing more than the newspapers have outlined, and, as you admit, that amounts to very little.'

'I'll be frank with you,' the detective affirmed; 'but what I've to tell you is confidential.'

'I shan't say a word.'

'The police-surgeon,' Brown continued, 'laid emphasis upon two points of deduction. The first was that he did not believe – judging from the appearance of the corpses – that the victims had succumbed as a direct result of the mutilated condition of the bodies.'

'That was certainly the impression I gathered from the reports,' Rhymer volunteered. 'Three healthy young men murdered in one week, in the same locality – close to a peaceful country town, and their bodies mutilated with some sharp instrument.'

'Just so,' Brown acquiesced, 'only the surgeon held a different opinion, since he discovered two punctures in the neck of each victim, and he was convinced that death was primarily due to a loss of blood from these incisions. His second deduction was that these wounds were inflicted with something sharp and wedge-shaped, and that the identically same thing was not used in wounding the third victim – or possibly the first – since the end was found broken off and embedded in the neck of the second victim.'

Rhymer seemed puzzled as he mentally absorbed these details.

'Were the wounds in the necks small?' he queried.

'Quite.'

'Merely incisions, not gashes?'

'Yes.'

'Then it seems improbable that the victims rapidly bled to death from these wounds alone?'

'That's what struck me at the time; but I've yet to add that the surgeon's opinion was that death supervened in each case from haemorrhage, probably due to suction, as though a small vacuum pump had been applied to the incisions.'

'Or the mouth of some living creature?' Rhymer hazarded with a significant glance.

'Good heavens! that never occurred to me,' the detective cried.

Rhymer pursed his lips and his brow contracted as he asked:

'What was the broken piece like, found in the wound of victim number two?'

For reply, Brown searched his waistcoat pockets and produced a small metal box. This he opened and handed to Rhymer.

The latter took it and, glancing within, suddenly stifled an exclamation, for that which he beheld revealed a supposition more horrible than he had previously contemplated.

'Don't mislay that piece of evidence, whatever you do,' he enjoined, handing the box back to the detective. 'This is going to prove a complicated case,' he added, 'but it'll furnish us with interest and excitement as well, I'll be bound.'

'I guessed it would be in your line, sir, for I've heard tell that you're OK on abnormal problems, and this one's creepy enough for anything.'

Later on in the day Professor Rhymer left his flat in Whitehall Court and, meeting Inspector Brown, by arrangement, at Charing Cross station, they boarded an evening train for Blankborough, arriving there an hour later. They at once proceeded to the best of the several inns which the little town afforded. This house – quite a superior hostelry of its kind – was known as the King's Arms Hotel. Brown had previously taken up his quarters there when recently visiting the scene of the murders. After a frugal war-meal, Rhymer proposed a quiet stroll, where they might be free from interruption or chance eavesdroppers. Accordingly they sauntered out into the old-fashioned town – the detective leading his companion along several back streets and alleys, which eventually brought them into a lonely country lane.

'Now we are free to talk without much fear of being overheard,' Rhymer remarked, 'and there are several things I want to ask you.'

'Fire away, then, sir.'

'I take it you've viewed the bodies of the victims.'

'Yes,' replied Brown, 'I saw them yesterday.'

'Did you happen to notice if each body was mutilated in a similar manner?'

'I noticed that the mutilations were alike in this respect – the bodies appeared to have been ruthlessly hacked about with a keen-bladed weapon of sorts. It resembled the work of a fanatic more than a responsible person.'

'So the police-surgeon thought these poor fellows weren't killed by violence as their remains seemed to suggest?'

'He intimated as much.'

'Then how on earth did he account for their mangled condition?'

'Oh, he put that down to the assassin's endeavour to create a false impression, that its victims had been killed in that way; or possibly to lessen the chance of identification. He was, however, inclined to favour the former theory, since the corpses were not so badly disfigured as to cause any difficulty in the latter direction.'

'Were the victims robbed?'

'No; they were all respectable young fellows, of the artisan type, who don't usually carry valuables about; but their pockets, containing some treasury notes and loose silver – being pay day – were intact. A solid gold watch was discovered on one of the bodies – evidently a presentation, from the inscription it contained. So robbery is entirely out of the question.'

'One thing's very evident,' Rhymer remarked, 'these murders were not committed by an ordinary individual. They're not a bit like common crimes done for revenge or robbery: there's evidently a far deeper motive than external appearances present.'

'Not unlike the old "Jack-the-Ripper" tragedies,' Brown remarked.

'Yes, there is some similarity, only his victims were women,' Rhymer observed, 'but in this case they are men, and it's significant to note that they were young and active as well.'

'Which looks as though the murderer possessed considerable muscular strength, and audacity into the bargain—'

'Hulloa! What's this?' Rhymer suddenly interrupted, coming to a standstill and gazing straight in front of him.

Brown hurriedly glanced in the same direction, where he beheld a blurred figure rapidly approaching them along the narrow lane. It was about fifty yards ahead. The midsummer twilight was rapidly fading, so it was difficult to see clearly at that distance. Its general aspect, however, was so forbidding, that Rhymer grasped the detective sharply by the arm and dragged him into a gap in the hedge, at the same time motioning him to silence.

They were only just in time, for a moment or two later the object was alongside their hiding-place, thus enabling them to obtain a clearer vision of it without being observed themselves.

This transitory view, as the figure shot past them, was far from reassuring. As they crouched there, an unaccountable sense of chilliness was prevalent. Brown afterwards owned up to an uncontrollable feeling of nausea as he beheld the figure. The unearthly face conveyed features devilish in their cold and pitiless cruelty, lifeless in their immobility, vacant in their utter lack of human expression – lifeless, yet living. The eyes were lack-lustre, yet wide open and round. The figure resembled that of a male, judging by its height and build. It was hatless and enveloped in a long cloak, from the folds of which an emaciated hand protruded – grasping a long, gleaming knife.

As the Creature swept past, a fetid, pungent smell was evident – horribly nauseous and corrupt.

Almost directly after the Thing had passed their place of concealment, Rhymer sprang into the lane.

'Come along,' he urged in a loud whisper, 'as quietly as you can. We mustn't lose sight of it.' Then, setting off after the retreating figure, beckoned Brown to follow.

The detective was middle-aged, stout and out of training, whereas Rhymer was lean and agile. As a consequence, he soon outdistanced the former, resulting in him and the object of his chase shortly being hidden from the detective by a sharp bend in the lane.

A few moments later, Brown was alarmed by the sudden report of a shot, followed by a hoarse cry for help. Redoubling his efforts he was soon round the afore-mentioned bend, and there, a few yards in front, he beheld two figures sprawling in the middle of the lane.

As he hastened to the spot where they were struggling, his ears were assailed by a sound like that of a ferocious animal when worrying its prey. Then the figure that was uppermost in the scrimmage suddenly sprang up, and turning upon the detective a ghastly face, distorted with the fierce passion of blood-lust, revealed the repulsive features of the Creature they were pursuing. With an indescribable, sickening, voiceless wail – which, somehow, seemed to give expression to anguish born of ungratified desire – it sprang, with one frenzied leap, over the hedge and disappeared.

Quickly approaching the other figure, which lay in a motionless heap upon the road, Brown beheld the limp form of the professor. Gently raising him, he was infinitely relieved to see him open his eyes.

He sighed audibly, and then stared with a dazed expression. In less than a moment, however, full consciousness returned. A flashing light of comprehension shone in his eyes as he regarded his rescuer.

'Have you collared it?' he cried.

'If you mean the thing that's just attacked you, I haven't.'

'You don't mean to say that devil's given us the slip?'

'I'm sorry, sir, but the brute was one too many for both of us; it jumped clean over the hedge before one could say "Jack Robinson"; but I hope you're not seriously hurt?'

'I shall be all right in a few minutes; but it's a confounded nuisance that "freak"'s got away,' said he, looking far more annoyed than injured. Raising his hand he placed the tips of his fingers upon his neck for a moment, and as he withdrew them Brown observed they were smeared with blood. Glancing with a thrill of apprehension at Rhymer's neck, he observed two small incisions from which a slight stream of blood was slowly oozing.

'Good heavens!' he exclaimed, 'your injury's similar to those of the three Blankborough victims; only, thank goodness, you've escaped with your life and any, more serious, wounds.'

'Your arrival, undoubtedly, saved me from a loathsome death, and butchery as well,' he replied as he took a white silk handkerchief from his pocket and deftly bound it round his neck, adding, 'Then you didn't come to grips with that fiend?'

'No, for the beggar bolted directly it saw me, before I had a chance even of attempting to seize it. What was the shot I heard?' he added.

'The report of my automatic pistol, and the strange thing is, I plugged the beggar at close quarters, clean through the body – impossible to have missed at such a close range – just as it tackled me – the moment I rounded the bend in the lane, where it had apparently halted.'

'Didn't attempt to stab you with that knife it carried?'

'That's the remarkable thing about it,' he replied. 'The Creature – who possessed abnormal strength – made one spring and floored me, at the same time dropping the knife, which fell with a clatter upon the road. Then it pinned me firmly down with its hands and knees and bent its face close to mine. I was quite helpless in its grasp. It bared its fangs with a snarl, and deliberately bit me in the neck. I was speechless for the moment with horror, but by a supreme effort I succeeded in raising a cry for help, though the exertion proved too much and I lost consciousness.'

'It's evident you've narrowly escaped the fate of those other poor fellows. Great Scot, it was a near shave! Here, take a pull at this,' he added, producing a flask from his pocket.

The stimulant rapidly revived Rhymer.

'Thanks,' he exclaimed, returning the flask. 'That's better. Now we must be getting on, for there's no time to be lost if we are to follow up this clue.'

'Anyhow, we've had a glimpse of the criminal we're after, that's very evident,' Brown asserted, 'and we shall both be able to swear to its identity, since I, for one, shall never forget the features of that monstrosity, if I live to be a hundred. Besides, since you say you've lodged a bullet in its carcase, it's not likely to travel far. We had better search over the hedge yonder.'

'You're free to search to your heart's content, but I'm going straight back to the hotel to cauterize and dress this bite in my neck.'

Brown looked askance at this remark, which was uttered with a trace of petulance.

'This thing cannot be dealt with by the customary CID methods,' Rhymer went on to explain, 'for I'm convinced that neither powder and shot nor even cold steel will have any effect in the ultimate capture of this Living-death, which you vainly hope to find over that hedge. Neither would your steel bracelets have any purchase upon its wrists. We're up against something abnormal here, and we must cut our coat according to our cloth.'

Brown at first appeared a trifle crestfallen, after listening to these disparaging comments upon his latest suggestion. The extraordinary circumstances sorely puzzled him, but he had the intuition to realize that some influence outside the usual rut of criminal investigation was facing them, and being previously assured of Rhymer's experience in such matters, was content to be guided by him, at any rate for the present.

'I'm blessed if I can follow the hang of the thing,' Brown grumbled, 'for I had labelled your assailant as a dangerous lunatic at large. Your last remark, however, puts quite another complexion on the matter.'

'You detectives are such a hidebound crowd,' Rhymer remarked with an indulgent smile, 'you try to handcuff clues as well as criminals. Give me plenty of scope when hot upon a clue, then I can forge ahead unencumbered.'

'Have you any definite clue, sir, to follow?'

'Yes, Brown, I've three. First, there are the incisions in my neck; secondly, there is this,' and displaying the palm of his right hand, exhibited a fragment of dark cloth, which, from its frayed appearance, had evidently been torn from some garment in the recent struggle. 'And here is the third,' he added, betraying a note of triumph, as, taking a few steps, he stooped and picked up an object lying at the side of the road.

'Ah! the assassin's knife,' Brown exclaimed.

'Precisely, and it's probably the identical weapon with

which those poor chaps' bodies were so hacked about, so it's an important link in our chain of evidence.'

'And a deucedly significant one, too,' Brown added.

There was the twinkle of a smile in Rhymer's eyes as he enquired:

'Are you still inclined to search for your escaped lunatic over the hedge, or shall we return to our quarters?'

The detective stiffened as he replied:

'It's my duty as an officer of the law to let no chance slip by, my professional credit's at stake, remember; but I am quite willing to be guided by you – especially as I asked for your assistance.'

'And you are welcome to it, Brown, as well as all the official credit, if success crowns our efforts. But I must ask you to act upon the lines that I point out. Is that agreed?'

'Quite, sir, and with your acumen you will be certain to find out something further that will help us to bottom this mystery after all.'

'Hope I may, Brown, I'm sure; so let's turn in for the night. I'm feeling a bit fagged after my wrestling-bout with that anaemic-looking blighter.'

'Hope you're feeling no worse, sir, after last night's experiences,' the detective enquired the following morning when he and Rhymer met at breakfast.

'I'm as fit as a fiddle, thanks,' said he; 'a good night's rest works wonders. It takes a lot to keep me awake long, when once I'm between the sheets.'

'How's your neck?' the detective added, glancing at a neat strip of sticking-plaster covering the injured part.

'Oh, just a trifle sore, that's all. The incisions weren't deep. I cauterized them last night, so don't contemplate any trouble in that direction.'

After breakfast they adjourned to the privacy of Rhymer's bedroom in order to map out future plans. During their discussion he produced the incriminating knife, and, handing it to Brown, remarked:

'Quite an antique, eh?'

The latter examined it with keen interest.

'Evidently,' said he, 'but its age doesn't lessen the cutthroat appearance of the engraven blade, set in its massive handle. A remarkable tool, I must admit, resembling, more than anything I've ever seen, a Kukri, the Gurka fighting weapon. One thing's evident, though—'

'What's that?' Rhymer interrupted.

'Why, that it belongs to the ugly brute we fell foul of last night.'

'Sorry to disagree with you,' said Rhymer, 'but we have yet to discover the real owner of this piece of cutlery, and until that's accomplished we're a long way off a solution of the mystery.'

Brown, unconvinced, shook his head.

'Well, it's beyond me even to guess what you're driving at. Anyhow, the weapon was owned by that individual temporarily – we can both swear to that – and possession is nine points of the law.'

'I shouldn't try and guess, if I were you,' Rhymer advised. 'Guessing is always destructive to logic. Far better observe small facts upon which large impressions may depend.'

'Then *you* haven't any idea as to whom else this knife may belong?'

'Not the vaguest.'

'And yet you refuse to believe it belongs to the creature who dropped it?'

'That's my opinion.'

'It's all an insoluble mystery to me,' said Brown, 'it

gets thicker instead of clearer.'

'On the contrary,' Rhymer contradicted, 'it clears every instant.'

'Then, hang it all, sir, can't you help me out of the fog?'

'That's what I'm trying to do.'

'How?'

'By taking steps to discover the owner of the knife, of course. I wonder if our landlord has an up-to-date copy of the local directory? I'll go and find out.'

Subsequent enquiry produced a recent edition of this book, and for the next few minutes they were poring over its pages.

It contained the customary list of private and commercial residents. Among the former, one name attracted Rhymer's attention:

'Ludwig Holtsner. The Gables.'

'An enemy in our midst,' he exclaimed, pointing it out to Brown. 'That fellow ought to have been interned.'

'He's bound to be naturalized,' the detective replied.

'All the more suspicious and dangerous. If I had my way, all Boche-born individuals residing in this country – notwithstanding their naturalization – should be interned. Boches will be Boches, and a mere scrap of paper, identifying them as naturalized British subjects, won't wipe out the inherited taint of *Kultur.* I don't trust the breed, and when I come across a male or female Boche my suspicions are instantly aroused.'

'We keep a sharp enough eye upon any suspicious characters of that sort,' Brown affirmed a trifle aggressively – so Rhymer thought.

'I'm not casting any slur upon the efficacy of the police in their dealings with aliens, but even they have been gulled by the Hun, over here, more than once.'

'I didn't suggest you were, sir, but we often get blame we don't deserve, so we are bound to drop an occasional word of protest.'

'I'm not contesting your rights in that direction, Brown.'

'All right, sir, but I like to justify my assertions, so I'll just slip round to the police station and hear what the local superintendent has to say about this Ludwig Holtsner. He won't have failed to make full enquiries, I know.'

'An excellent idea, Brown, only take care not to say a word about our adventure last night, since secrecy regarding our actions – for the present – will best promote our chance of ultimate success.'

'Very good, sir.'

Half an hour later Brown returned, having achieved his visit to the police station.

'Well, obtained any useful information?' Rhymer enquired.

'Not much in support of your suspicion, anyhow, regarding this Mr Holtsner,' he replied. 'The superintendent told me that he took out naturalization papers many years ago, and is quite all right. A man of local influence – he hastened to assure me – a wealthy bachelor and occupying a large house which he purchased.'

'Any other particulars?'

'Nothing of much importance, I imagine.'

'Did the superintendent say how Holtsner occupied his time?'

'Oh yes, he studied science a lot and was quite a keen Egyptologist.'

Rhymer's eyes sparkled as he heard this last piece of information. Instantly his faculties were on the alert.

'They are all quite all right until they're caught red-handed. And then – well – there's the very devil to pay. But, at all events, you've brought back one valuable piece of evidence in support of a theory I've already broached.'

'Oh! What's that?'

'My dear Inspector, do try a little analysis yourself,' he enjoined with a touch of impatience. 'I've already given you some broad hints as to my methods. Now it's up to you to apply them.'

Brown looked distinctly piqued.

'Very well, sir, as you choose to put it in that fashion. I've nothing more to say—'

'Which will afford you a better opportunity for mental analysis,' Rhymer chipped in with an apologetic smile. 'And may I give you a golden rule which I was taught by a famous detective?' He paused for a reply.

'Get on with it, then.'

'Well, when you have worn out the possible, whatever is left, however impossible, comes mighty near the truth.'

No place can be more productive of local information than the bar-parlour of a country town hotel. Brown was keenly alive to this fact, and that was why he got Rhymer to join him in the bar of the King's Arms later on in the day.

'We may pick up some useful information here, sir, if we keep our eyes and ears open.'

'A suggestion full of possibilities, Brown, so let's pledge our success in a drop of dry ginger. Can't make it anything stronger, if I'm to stand treat. It's forbidden by D.O.R.A. – And you are one of her guardians.'

They had been silently smoking for some little time, when two men entered the room, which was fairly full. They sat down at a vacant table next to that at which Rhymer and Brown were seated.

Having called for some liquid refreshment, they opened

a brisk conversation. Their general appearance plainly iden-
tified them as men-servants, who had dropped in at their
favourite house of call for a friendly chat over the cup that
cheers and loosens the tongue.

'Well, Alf,' the taller of the two was heard by their
neighbours to remark, 'how's your governor been treating
you of late?'

'Not 'alf, Jim,' was the reply. ''E's balmy, 'e is. I tell yer
it's fair getting on my nerves.'

'Why, wot's 'e been a-doing of now, Alf – anything
fresh?'

'Fresh!' he reiterated disdainfully. 'Not much – same old
row, blaming me for things I 'ain't done. That's all.'

'Wot 'aven't yer done?'

'Nothing. It's 'im 'as done it. Gone and lost a bloomin'
old knife that belonged to some 'eathen wot lived 'undreds
of years ago – says it's worth pots of money, and because 'e
can't find it, swears I've pinched it. I like 'is cheek.'

At this point their conversation was interrupted by the
arrival of a third man who joined them, and a few moments
later, after draining their glasses, they left the bar together.

Rhymer casually arose and, strolling across to the
counter, addressed the barmaid behind:

'Can you tell me, Miss, who those two men were, sitting
at the table next to ours? They've just left with a friend.'

'Yes, sir,' she replied with a glance of slight enquiry, 'the
short one was James Smith, a footman at Sir William
Doone's, and the other Alfred Ball, valet to Mr Holtsner.'

'Thanks,' said he, 'then I'm mistaken. One of them
reminded me of a servant that left me some years ago,' he
mendaciously added, to ease her mind of any faint suspicion
he might have aroused as to the real reason of his enquiry.

A few minutes later, Rhymer and Brown were again

closeted in the former's bedroom.

'We're progressing like a house on fire,' the former affirmed, rubbing his hands. 'You overheard what that fellow said about the knife? Well, the barmaid confirmed my suspicion that he was a servant of Holtsner's, so now it's pretty evident to whom the knife belongs.'

'Quite clear,' said Brown, 'and you were right after all. We may also take it that the knife was stolen from The Gables by that blooming chump we met in the lane, and without Holtsner's knowledge, too.'

'That's more than probable, and I'll go a step further in suggesting that Holtsner's not entirely ignorant of this Creature's presence in the locality, although he may not be actually aware it was the thief, since then he would scarcely have blamed Alfred Ball for his loss. Still, it must be remembered that a man, being acquainted with anything abnormal haunting his premises, usually wants to hush it up, since it gives the place a bad name.'

'Quite so,' said Brown. 'Yet there's something more beneath than meets the eye; although I admit the fog's clearing a bit.'

'Suspicions are becoming certainties, you mean,' Rhymer added. 'But, look here, we mustn't lose another minute. It's now six-thirty,' consulting his watch, 'and we've got to visit this German fellow as soon as possible, under cover of some pretext or other. Our episode in finding the knife is a good enough excuse for calling, even at this hour, in order to restore it to him.'

'That will also place him under an obligation,' said Brown, 'which may help matters forward a bit.'

'That's quite probable.'

'Do you know whereabouts his house is?' Brown enquired after a pause.

'Yes, I asked the landlord when returning the directory. It's not more than a quarter of an hour's walk, so let's get off.'

'We shall need extra caution at this stage,' Rhymer remarked, as they were hurrying along the lane which they had traversed the previous night. 'I'm positive it would be wiser for me to call on Holtsner alone, until I discover how the land lies; so I hope you won't mind waiting for me outside. We must avoid exciting this man's suspicion, and if we both arrive together he might suspect the real object of our visit.'

He spoke with a seriousness which gave authority to his words.

At first Brown seemed inclined to protest, but after a little consideration, fell in with the proposition.

'I'm sure I am advising you for the best,' Rhymer remarked as he halted opposite a pair of massive, iron gates guarding a long and tortuous drive. 'This is The Gables, I expect,' he added. 'If I should fail to return within – say – half an hour, you'd better call for me.'

With this parting injunction he entered the drive and soon disappeared round a curve in the shrub-lined avenue.

Arriving at the house, he was admitted by a man-servant whom he recognized as Alfred Ball.

'I've called to see Mr Holtsner,' said he, presenting his card, 'kindly inform him it's a matter of business.'

'I'm not sure if the master's at home, sir,' was the non-committal reply, 'but I'll enquire if you'll please step inside.'

He then conducted him to a small room at the further end of the hall.

A few minutes later the door opened, and a tall, middle-aged man entered, of fair complexion with closely-cropped hair and a bristly moustache.

He was inclined to obesity and wore a pair of gold-rimmed spectacles fitted with powerful lenses, which accentuated the prominency of his protruding eyes.

He bowed to his visitor, exclaiming in a deep, guttural voice – as he glanced at the visiting card held between his podgy thumb and forefinger:

'Professor Rhymer, I presume?'

'That is my name, Mr Holtsner,' he replied as he mentally sized up the fat German. 'I must apologize for this late call, but I've found an article which I believe you've had stolen,' handing him a brown-paper parcel.

Holtsner took it with a look of blank enquiry, and proceeded to remove the paper, exclaiming:

'Something I've had stolen – what can it be – er – where did you find it?'

'In the lane outside your drive.'

'In the lane—' Holtsner reiterated, pausing all of a sudden – arrested by the discovery of the knife which the parcel now disclosed.

'Well – how on earth—' he continued with an apparent effort, but the remainder of his speech died away upon his lips as he glanced suspiciously at the professor.

Rhymer met his look squarely with a well-feigned expression of innocent surprise, as though at a loss to account for his hesitation.

'You were going to say, Mr Holtsner, "how on earth did I guess that this interesting antique belonged to you?"' he suggested with a frank smile. 'Well, I can soon satisfy you upon that score, for I chanced to overhear some one casually remark that you had lost a valuable knife, and as I had previously happened to stumble across one in the lane, whilst enjoying a stroll, I thought I'd call and enquire if it was yours. If it's not, then I'd better leave it at the police station.'

This assumption of candour seemed to reassure Holtsner.

'Yes, this belongs to me; it was stolen from my museum,' he acknowledged somewhat reluctantly; 'but who did you overhear say I'd lost it?'

'Excuse me, sir, but it would hardly be fair for me to say, since the information was not intended for my ears. I only overheard it by chance.'

Holtsner was on the verge of resenting Rhymer's refusal to satisfy his enquiry, but he evidently thought better of it, apologetically exclaiming:

'Quite so, I oughtn't to have asked. I'm a keen collector of antiques, and was put out at losing this valuable relic of a lost Egyptian art. Its sudden recovery flustered me, so pray accept my apologies and thanks as well, for what you've done. By the way,' he added with assumed unconcern, 'you don't happen to have mentioned the matter to the police?'

'No,' said Rhymer.

'Ah! it's just as well you didn't,' said he, with an involuntary sigh of relief. 'You see, I suspect one of my servants of the theft, and I've no wish to prosecute. The police are so officious in these matters – I'm sure you'll understand?'

'Perfectly,' was the response.

It was evident to Rhymer's keen sense of observation that Holtsner's apparent agitation was not solely due to the cause he so lamely advanced. There was something he was anxious to hide. The man might be a collector, in fact, the local superintendent of police had informed Brown that such was the case; but the loss of a valuable antique and its subsequent restoration by a stranger, who had simply picked it up upon the road, would hardly account for its owner appearing as disturbed as Holtsner seemed to be.

His very attitude invited suspicion, but Rhymer was cute

enough to conceal any trace of his conviction that Holtsner was playing a deep game; so, assuming an attitude of nonchalance, said:

'I'm awfully glad I've found your knife, since it's afforded me the privilege of making your acquaintance, and being a scientist and collector myself, it's a pleasure to meet others with similar tastes.'

Rhymer's diplomatic reply seemed to set the German's suspicions at rest, for he enquired:

'Are you staying long in the neighbourhood?'

'Only a few days. I've run down with a friend from town to make a geological survey.'

Rhymer invented this excuse on the spur of the moment, since he judged it would avert further suspicion that might arise in Holtsner's mind, should he come across him and Brown roaming about the vicinity.

'An attractive branch of science,' said Holtsner, 'and it may interest you to know that I have some geological specimens found in the neighbourhood, which I'd like to show you in my museum.'

That was just what Rhymer desired. He didn't care a rap about the specimens, but he did want to get into the museum. So, without displaying any sign of the satisfaction he felt, replied:

'Thanks, I *should* like to see these specimens; but I fear I can't stop now. I'm overdue to join my friend at our hotel, but as he is also keen on geology, may I bring him along as well? Shall we say tomorrow?'

'By all means. How would the morning suit you? I'm a man of leisure, so my time's at your convenience.'

'That'll do admirably,' he replied, and, bidding his host goodbye, took his departure, rejoining Brown a few minutes later in the lane.

'Thought you were never coming,' was the detective's greeting. 'I was going to call for you in another minute. You've exceeded your time-limit and I was beginning to get anxious.'

'It's fortunate you didn't; as it was, I had some difficulty in getting away when I did, and if you had suddenly turned up we should have been in the deuce of a mess. So far I've fixed things up all right. The man acknowledges he's the owner of the knife, and though he seemed suspicious at first, I think I succeeded in blinding him as to the purpose of my visit. Told him I was down here with a friend to make a geological survey. He seemed to swallow the fable readily enough, and invited me to look at a museum he has on the premises. I'd have liked to go, there and then, but the event of your sudden appearance upon the scene – as requested – precluded my doing so. I got him, however, to ask the two of us to see the museum tomorrow morning.'

Brown pondered a few moments.

'That's top hole,' he at length exclaimed, 'for now we may be able to pick up some evidence in that place.'

'Exactly what I hope to do, for he let out that the knife was stolen from it.'

'Then in all probability the assassin will have left some traces there – finger marks or similar clues,' Brown hazarded.

'I hope to find something more tangible than that.'

'Hang it all, sir, what more could you find without you knocked up against the actual criminal?'

'Nothing whatever.'

Brown stared at his collaborator, and was on the point of making some further remark when he suddenly remembered the professor's former tip – 'Try and do a little analysis yourself' – so he tried and relapsed into silence.

'By the way,' Rhymer presently enquired, 'do you know

anything about geology?'

'Well – yes – a trifle. I studied it a little in my school days; but I've only a very hazy recollection of the subject now.'

'No matter, all I want you to do is to make out you're keen on the thing when we visit Holtsner tomorrow morning.'

In due course Rhymer and Brown turned up at The Gables, and were courteously received by Holtsner. Without wasting any time, their host led them into the museum – a large and lofty apartment built off from the house, though connected by a short passage with a door at either end.

Brown no sooner entered this apartment than he experienced a sensation of vague, unaccountable horror. A conviction of some eerie presence gripped tight hold of him. He advanced into the centre of the room, still oppressed with this novel sensation, which increased rather than diminished. He was no coward, neither was he superstitious, so the horror which obsessed him was all the more apprehensive.

Suddenly his gaze was attracted by a row of mummy cases which stood on end in a long showcase – fitted with glass doors – extending the full length of one end of the building.

He stared, awe-inspired, at the row of garishly-painted wooden boxes, containing their human relics of a bygone age. The lid of one was open, disclosing a swathed and bandaged form. Its lofty cheek bones, massive jaw, and aquiline nose depicted power and diffused a subtle influence – a latent force which was indefinable.

'My Egyptian mummies seem to interest you, sir,' Holtsner exclaimed, mistaking the keen attention Brown bestowed upon these curiosities as indicating admiration rather than horror.

'They're apt to give one the creeps,' he replied with an effort to hide his uneasiness, 'but that object in the open box seems to be in good condition—'

'What on earth do you know, Brown, about the condition of mummies?' Rhymer suddenly interrupted, giving the detective a warning look, unobserved by Holtsner. 'Geology is more in your line, so, for goodness' sake, stick to it and don't air your views upon matters you know nothing about.'

'What do you know about mummies?' Brown retorted.

'Not much,' said Rhymer, flashing him another significant glance, 'but sufficient to convince me the Egyptian lady or gentleman in that box is as old as Adam and not any better preserved than the majority of its class.'

'Professor Rhymer is quite right,' Holtsner was quick to assert, with what appeared to Rhymer undue emphasis; 'all these mummies date back to a remote Egyptian dynasty; but,' he added with precipitancy, 'as you and your friend are keen on geological specimens, if you'll look at this case over here, you'll find some fossils of local interest.'

'Ah, that's more in our line, Brown, isn't it?' said Rhymer as he moved towards his host, followed by the detective.

The specimens indicated were mainly echinoderms, lamellibranchs, and gasteropods, which were neatly labelled and displayed in glass cases. While they were inspecting these, Holtsner moved away in another direction in order to pick up some object off a table, apart from where they had all been standing.

Rhymer seized this opportunity to whisper into the detective's ear:

'For heaven's sake, man, don't allude again to those

mummies, but do try and feign some sort of enthusiasm over these blessed fossils.' Then, raising his voice for Holtsner's benefit, exclaimed:

'What a topping specimen of the *Tritonium corrugatum*! Observe the fusiform shell – the elongated spire and the slightly curved anterior canal. The gasteropods are very beautiful. Well, I fear we must be making a move if we are to get to town in time for that lecture tonight, and I don't want to miss it. I've some letters to get off, too, before we leave by the afternoon train.'

Holtsner overheard these remarks, as Rhymer intended he should, and as he again approached his guests, a look of satisfaction overspread his features.

'Jolly fine collection of yours, Mr Holtsner,' Rhymer enthusiastically observed, 'sorry we must be going – awfully obliged to you for showing us round. Quite envy you the possession of such a museum.'

'Pray don't mention it, sir; only too delighted, I'm sure. It's a pleasure to show one's things to those who can appreciate them. Hope you and your friend will drop in again, when you've more time at your disposal.'

'I can promise you that much,' was Rhymer's unspoken comment, 'only the visit will be a strictly private one, as far as your knowledge is concerned.' Then aloud he exclaimed:

'Many thanks, some day we may, I hope, have another look round.'

As soon as Rhymer and the detective had left The Gables, the former exclaimed:

'By Jove! But you made an unfortunate remark about that mummy, and, unwittingly – I presume – stumbled nearer the truth than you had any idea of. Holtsner, too, pricked up his ears. You kind of "put the wind up him", as the "Tommies" say. However, I doubt if any real harm's done, since he appeared somewhat reassured after I'd chipped in with my contradictory remark.'

'Whatever are you driving at?' Brown exclaimed, apparently nettled.

'Wait till you and I have got into that museum alone – which we must do tonight by hook or by crook – and then you'll know. We've got to fix up a private view of those mummies. I've made it pretty clear to the Boche, our professed intention of going to London this afternoon, and though he's still inclined to suspicion, I think we've managed fairly to mislead him with regard to our interest in his mummies. Anyhow, he won't be expecting us back in Blankborough until tomorrow, and that's a feather in the cap of our plan.'

After lunch Rhymer and Brown left the hotel for the station, with a handbag apiece, in order to convey the impression they were off for the night. Upon their arrival at the booking-office, Rhymer loudly demanded two tickets for Charing Cross. Having entered a first-class smoker and finding themselves alone, Brown remarked:

'You seemed anxious to let everybody know where we were going, sir, by the way you yelled out for the tickets.'

'Not every one, Brown – only Ball, Holtsner's servant, whom I spotted spying upon us – as he imagined unobserved – from behind a barrow piled up with luggage. I warned you that the Boche was still suspicious. Now he'll soon be posted up with the information that we have cleared out, with our kit, for a night in town.'

As the train approached the next station – three miles from Blankborough – Rhymer abruptly signified that it was to be their destination. A few minutes later they were out on the platform. Then, without any further word of explanation, Rhymer set off at a leisurely pace along the road, in the direction from which they had just come, with Brown – looking annoyed and puzzled – following in his wake.

The former volunteered no explanation until they arrived opposite a stile, where he suddenly halted.

'We'll take it easy for a bit here. Hope you've brought your pipe, Brown? Then let's light up, for on no account must we turn up at Blankborough again before dusk.'

The museum attached to The Gables had two entrances. One leading from the house, through which Holtsner had conducted his visitors that morning, the other giving access from the garden.

Outside the latter entrance – in the evening – Rhymer and Brown, concealed behind a thick bush, were watching the door, which was slightly ajar.

Suddenly the former slipped from his hiding-place – motioning the detective to remain where he was – and advanced on tiptoe towards the entrance.

Upon arriving there, he glued his eye to the chink between the hinges, intently observing something within. His inspection appeared to afford him satisfaction, judging by his expression when he subsequently returned to the seclusion of the bush.

'Sure enough, we're on the right track,' he whispered. 'Pay careful attention to what I'm going to say now.'

'I'm listening, sir.'

'At any moment a figure may slip out of that door, closely resembling the freak we saw the night before last. Follow it, only keep at a safe distance, to avoid being seen if possible.'

Brown stifled an exclamation, and as a ray of moonlight

struck his face, forcing its way through an aperture in the bush, Rhymer detected an expression akin to fear. Then with a challenging glance the former asserted:

'I'm no coward, sir, and I've yet to meet the crook I wouldn't tackle – provided it's human – but to stand up against a fiend like the one that went for you the other night – well – it's a bit more than I bargained for.'

'Don't blame you either, but so far my investigations give me confidence in assuming that as long as you don't directly impede this Creature's progress, it won't attack you. Follow at a safe distance and watch, that's all I ask you to do. I don't think *I* should have been mauled the other night had I not mentally registered a determination to go for the brute. My intentions were apparently conveyed by telepathy to the Creature's system of comprehension, hence the "scrap", which proved a "knock-out" for me.'

A creaking sound in the direction of the museum caused both men to turn round sharply, and there, illuminated by a ray of light from the now wide-opened door, a figure glided into the moonlight without.

'Quick!' Rhymer exclaimed with bated breath, 'don't lose sight of it.'

With a sharp intaking of breath, Brown started in pursuit, keeping his distance as directed, while Rhymer, with one rapid glance around, slipped through the open door of the museum.

Within the threshold he halted, as his eyes fell upon a recumbent figure stretched on a couch, over which a shaded electric lamp was burning, suspended from the vaulted ceiling.

Approaching on tiptoe, he recognized Holtsner. The German appeared to be in a deep sleep. A closer examination, however, revealed the man to be in a sort of trance, for his breathing was imperceptible. But for the faint trace of colour in his face, he might have been dead.

Rhymer then produced a small pocket mirror, and, placing it close to the man's nostrils, observed a slight blur on the surface. With a nod of satisfaction he replaced the glass in his pocket and was about to make a further inspection of the apartment, when his attention was suddenly arrested by the sound of stealthy footsteps in the passage that connected the museum with the house.

In a flash he surveyed his surroundings, and, spotting a curtained recess in the wall nearest him, slipped within. He had barely covered his retreat when the door slowly opened and some one entered whom he recognized – through a small rent in the curtain – as Alfred Ball.

The latter carefully closed the door behind him and locked it. Next he cautiously approached the couch upon which his master lay, as if anxious to avoid disturbing him. Bestowing a cursory glance at the sleeper, he fetched a small table from another part of the room, placing it by the couch. Going to a cabinet he produced two stoppered bottles and a graduated glass measure, which he laid on the table by Holtsner's side. Then he crossed to another cupboard from which he took a coil of stout cord. Retaining this, he placed a chair close to the outer door – which was still slightly ajar – and sat down, with his head thrown forward, in an attitude of alertness.

About ten minutes later, without any warning, the door was violently flung back, and in rushed a figure which Rhymer recognized to be the one he and Brown had previously seen leaving the museum.

Its eyes were lit up with a fierce passion. The lips and chin daubed with blood – fresh blood – hardly yet dry. It made straight for the couch upon which Holtsner was lying, and in another moment, would have reached him, had not Ball sprung up and whisked the cord – which was fitted with a running noose – neatly over the Creature's head, fetching it, with a smart jerk, sprawling on the floor.

Simultaneously with the crash occasioned by the falling body, Holtsner languidly raised himself, stretching his arms; and, as he moved, the monster – struggling violently on the floor, hampered by the coils of the lasso – became motionless – a horrid, inert mass of bone and sinew.

Holtsner wearily dragged himself into a sitting posture and, leaning towards the table, poured out a few drops of liquid from each of the two bottles into the glass measure, and, with a trembling hand, tossed the stuff down his throat.

'That's better, Otto,' he gasped. 'These frequent trances are beginning to take it out of me.'

'Number two has strafed another enemy of the Fatherland,' the servant vehemently asserted, his features fairly distorted with 'Hate'. 'Look! there's the blood of some pig-swine on its lips.'

The two wretches were conversing in German, a language with which Rhymer was well acquainted. He was not a little surprised to discover that Ball was a Boche, for his cockney accent and speech, when recently in the King's Arms, were so perfectly assumed. But, when he gathered, from their recent remarks, that another murder had undoubtedly been committed, he became intensely anxious about Brown; and keen though he was to see what else Holtsner and his accomplice were up to, he inwardly raved to get away and find out where the inspector might be.

'Must stick where I am for the present,' he soliloquized, 'until those two devils clear out. Confound it all! I do hope poor Brown's all right.'

UEL KEY

Meanwhile, Holtsner and Otto (to give the latter his correct name) set about a very revolting performance. A basin of water and a sponge were first produced, with which Otto, kneeling on the floor, carefully removed the bloodstains from the jaws of the motionless Thing lying there.

He then approached the large case with the glass doors – in which the mummies were stored – and, lifting out one of the tawdry Egyptian death-boxes, which was empty, laid it, with Holtsner's assistance, upon the floor. Opening the lid, they proceeded to place the inanimate Creature within, having first removed the lasso. Shutting down the hinged lid, they locked it, and, lifting the case between them, deposited it in its former place. Crossing the apartment to a small steel safe let into the wall, Holtsner unlocked the door, taking from within a leather notebook. Opening it he made an entry with a fountain pen.

He then put it back in the safe and began a rapid conversation with Otto, but their voices were so low that Rhymer was unable to hear what they said.

However, he was not kept much longer in suspense, for after stowing away the several articles they had been using, and carefully scrutinizing the apartment to make sure nothing incriminating was left about, they left the museum by the door communicating with the house, having first switched off the electric light.

Rhymer lost no time in quitting his cramped quarters. Noiselessly crossing the floor, he slipped back the latch of the garden door, opened it, and, as he bolted out, suddenly found himself confronted by a figure.

'Great Scot! How you startled me, Brown,' he exclaimed, upon discovering he had barged into the burly figure of the detective, 'how long have you been here?'

'For some little while, and I've seen what's been going on inside there, through a chink in the door. But where on earth have you been? I didn't see you in the place.'

'I was there right enough, concealed behind a curtain, where, like you, I could see without being seen. I'm glad you saw this sickening spectacle, since a witness will be useful. Why didn't you follow up the Thing as I asked?'

'I did my best, but It was too much for me. I couldn't keep up the pace. Lor'! how the Thing did scoot. Lost sight of it at the high boundary wall – topped with broken glass – which encloses the grounds. It scaled this with perfect ease, though it was too high for me to attempt. There I remained on the look-out for about a quarter of an hour, when I suddenly spotted it again doubling back on its original tracks. So, quickly hiding behind the trunk of a tree until it had passed, I followed it back here again. Had it not been for the bright moonlight, I couldn't have done as much as I did – but preserve me from ever seeing a sight like that in the museum again.'

'Quite Teutonic, wasn't it?'

'Teutonic? Why, I call it diabolical.'

'The same thing,' Rhymer observed. 'Anyhow you did your best, but I fear we shall shortly hear of another of these wretched murders as a result of tonight's work. You've got your electric torch and some skeleton keys, haven't you?'

'Yes, I have.'

'Good, then we'll proceed without delay. There's some more evidence I'm anxious to secure in there,' he added, nodding in the direction of the museum. 'I daren't switch on the light, as they might see the reflection from the house. There's a safe inside we must investigate. Quite an ordinary affair, I imagine, so one of your skeleton keys should fix up the job.'

It transpired as Rhymer had predicted. The safe was soon opened and the notebook produced. With the aid of Brown's torch they examined the contents. It proved to be a ruled manuscript, only just commenced. Some brief instructions, written in a German fist, occupied the first two or three pages.

Brown didn't know any German, but Rhymer was able to read the contents. It only took him a few minutes, and as he proceeded, first bewilderment, and then horror gripped him. Turning, at length, to Brown, he exclaimed:

'It's almost incredible! However, we've no time now to go into details. We must get away as quickly and quietly as possible. Every moment increases the risk of discovery.'

He then replaced the incriminating document in the safe and locked it.

Silently the two men left the chamber of mystery by the garden door, closing it carefully behind them. As they were walking to the inn, Rhymer suddenly exclaimed:

'It's amazing to think what fiends these Boches are. They'll stick at nothing. That book in the safe yonder contains some documentary evidence revealing one of the most revolting plots that could foul the imagination. Nothing short of *Kultur* – with a capital K – could hit upon such a conspiracy. Thank goodness, it's been our good luck to knock up against the thing in time, before these murders became wholesale, which, judging from the evidence, might shortly have been the case.'

'Good heavens! Do you mean to say that these Blankborough murders are part and parcel of a Boche conspiracy?'

'Undoubtedly that's the bald state of affairs, due, of course, to the tolerance of a naturalized enemy in our midst. And if we are to nip in the bud a scheme devised by demons in human form, we must lose no time in acquainting the authorities with our discovery. Yours is a name to conjure with at the "Yard": could you possibly get me a personal interview with your chief first thing tomorrow morning?'

'Then you believe Holtsner to be responsible for these murders?' Brown asked, evading the other question.

'Undoubtedly so; and for a good deal more besides.'

'Then he must be, somehow, employing demoniacal agencies?'

'That's more than probable, after what we've both witnessed.'

'Well, I'm jiggered! Can't understand it even now, but I can believe anything of the Boche, and though you've not yet told me all the details of the plot revealed in that book, I'm willing to phone to my chief and ask him to receive you as early as possible tomorrow morning.'

'Thanks,' was Rhymer's brief, but grateful response.

Brown's chief didn't appear very favourably disposed towards Rhymer as the latter was ushered at 8 a.m. the following morning into his sanctum at the 'Yard'.

'This is an extraordinarily early hour to fix for an interview, sir,' he curtly announced, as he motioned Rhymer to a chair. 'Your business must be correspondingly urgent, I presume.'

'Couldn't be more so.'

'Humph! Then I hope you'll waste no time in getting through with it. I'm up to my ears in work, and had it not been for Inspector Brown's urgent call upon the phone, I shouldn't have been here to meet you. I'm for ever being rung up to listen to matters of so-called "national import-ance" from unofficial quarters, which usually result in the discovery of a mare's nest.'

'I don't think you'll find my communication to be one of

that sort, I only wish you might; besides, Inspector Brown can corroborate it.'

'So I understand. Please proceed, Professor Rhymer.'

Without further preamble he began to relate all that had occurred at Blankborough since his arrival there in Brown's company, including the evidence he had obtained from the notebook in Holtsner's safe.

The official listened attentively as Rhymer continued his narrative. He never once interrupted until the report was completed.

Then abruptly turning towards the professor, he exclaimed:

'This is indeed a serious matter, if you are correct in your allegations, but I can hardly believe it.'

'Surely, sir, nothing the Boche might do is beyond your powers of credibility?'

'Under the circumstances, I admit you have acted judiciously in reporting the matter so promptly,' said he, ignoring Rhymer's last remark, 'but it's scarcely comprehensible.'

'Anyhow, I've clearly stated the facts, sir.'

'I know, and I'm quite aware there's something out of the ordinary rut in these Blankborough crimes, and though I'm not predisposed to place much faith in psychological phenomena, you have certainly impressed me with your view of the matter.'

Just then the telephone on the chief's desk rang up. He picked up the receiver and held it to his ear, thoughtfully replacing it a few moments later.

'These crimes are decidedly getting ahead of us. I've just received intimation of another murder last night at Blankborough, so your inference, sir, has been corroborated.'

Rhymer exhibited no surprise at this statement.

'It's only what I expected,' said he, 'and it supplements my plea for immediate and drastic measures.'

The official regarded him meditatively.

'May I make a suggestion?' Rhymer ventured.

'By all means.'

'Then, for goodness sake, sir, do use your influence to set the machinery in motion. Issue a confidential communication to every police centre throughout the British Isles, with instructions to furnish fresh reports relating to any naturalized Boches residing in each locality; especially ear-marking those engaged in scientific pursuits, and noting whether they are in possession of any Egyptian mummies. It would be well to insist upon all cargoes, shipped through neutral ports, being searched, and if any of these embalmed specimens are found on board, have them instantly confiscated as contraband. That would effectually put a stop to these atrocities.'

'I can see no difficulty in adopting the first part of your suggestion, but the latter might meet with serious obstacles.'

'Well, all I can say is that the safety of hundreds of human lives depends upon it.'

The chief fell to brooding again.

'Upon my word,' said he, 'I believe you're right, and I'm half inclined to try it – as far as it lies in my power; but others in authority will have to be consulted first.'

'I realized that from the commencement, but surely no responsible person in his right senses would hesitate to take prompt measures to quell a serious menace like this, for, should the German Intelligence Department get an inkling that we are on their tracks, all evidence would quickly be effaced by them.'

'That's very evident, but we must arrest this Holtsner fellow first.'

'Exactly: and if you'll give me a free hand, I'll undertake to catch him red-handed. Then you can more easily effect a wholesale arrest of naturalized Boches throughout the country on a charge of conspiracy, once their leader is safely under lock and key.'

'I'm relying a lot upon your assurances, Professor, and if you have made a blunder, then there'll be the deuce of a row.'

'I assure you I've made no mistake.'

'Well, I'll risk it.'

'And you'll let me have Brown's services for a little while longer at Blankborough?'

The chief pondered, and then with a look of resignation, said:

'Quite irregular, you know, since this case is officially in Brown's hands. It'll be creating a precedent, too. But the circumstances are exceptional, so I suppose I must agree.'

'Then Brown may return with me to Blankborough with a warrant for Holtsner's and Ball's arrest, and act under my directions?'

'Since you urge it, yes,' he reluctantly replied.

He pressed an electric push at the side of his desk, a plain-clothes officer shortly making his appearance.

'Tell Detective-Inspector Brown I want to see him.'

In a few moments the latter arrived.

'Professor Rhymer's officially assisting in the Blankborough murder case. You will return with him and work together until further notice.'

After leaving Scotland Yard, Rhymer and the detective entered the first small restaurant they came across.

'We can discuss some breakfast here, and our future plans into the bargain, for we appear to be the sole occupants,'

Rhymer remarked as he sat down at a small table.

'Not a bad idea either, sir, a journey before breakfast gives one an appetite.'

'Our case is almost complete,' Rhymer affirmed after the waitress had departed with their order, 'but even now we mustn't err on the side of over-confidence.'

'I'm quite alive to that fact, sir.'

'I don't propose returning to Blankborough till later in the day. Then we'll hire a car and arrange to be dropped within easy walking distance of The Gables. After breakfast I want you to phone to the local superintendent at Blankborough, and get him to send two plain-clothes men to meet us at some convenient spot, which I'll leave you to fix up.'

'Very good, sir.'

'Be sure you warn the superintendent to make all arrangements strictly on the Q.T.'

'I'll take care of that.'

'Well, now – I think – we've fairly staged the scene for Holtsner's final appearance, so it only remains for you to ring up the Blankborough superintendent – the curtain must wait till tonight – while I go and secure a car.'

'What time do you propose starting from town?'

'We don't want to reach our destination before dusk, so if we leave about seven-thirty, that will get us to our rendezvous by nine o'clock.'

'Then I had better mention that to the superintendent when phoning?'

'Of course. Tell him nine or thereabouts; better make it rather before than after.'

'Where shall we meet, sir?'

'Oh, at my flat in Whitehall Court – you know the number. Come early and we'll have a bite of something before start-ing.'

'Thanks, I'm much obliged.'

'So long then, Brown – don't forget your warrant for arrest.'

Shortly after dusk four men silently approached the garden door of Holtsner's museum: Rhymer, Brown, and two stalwart fellows from the local police force; the latter having met the car, containing the former, at a prearranged spot on the outskirts of the town.

'Conceal yourself with the two men behind that bush, Brown, while I manoeuvre the enemy's camp,' Rhymer enjoined as he crept up to the door. He found it shut. Bending down he peered through the keyhole. The inspection appeared to satisfy him, for he turned and beckoned to the others. They all three approached, led by Brown, and assembled in a group at the threshold. Rhymer then inserted a skeleton key in the latch. Cautiously opening the door he peeped within, and, pointing to the curtained recess, said:

'Inspector Brown and I will hide in there, and you two will return to your former place of concealment. Take this,' he added, giving the foremost of the two the skeleton key, 'but don't attempt to use it under any circumstances, unless you hear two loud blasts of a whistle. Then enter sharp – understand?'

'Yes, sir.'

'Remember not to stir before the given signal.'

The two men saluted and returned to their allotted post, whereupon Rhymer immediately entered the museum with the detective, noiselessly latching the door behind them.

'Now then, quick!' he exclaimed, slipping across the apartment and raising the curtain which covered the recess. A moment later they were both hidden behind its folds.

They were only there about ten minutes – which seemed to them as many hours – when the door communicating with the house suddenly opened. Glancing through a couple of slits in the curtain, they distinguished, in the dim light, Holtsner and his servant Ball entering the room. The former switched on the light, and together they approached the large case with the glass doors. Opening this they lifted out one of the mummy cases, which Rhymer observed was not the same as that they had replaced the night before.

'It's number three's turn now,' Ball remarked with a malicious grin.

Holtsner grunted some unintelligible reply. Then they propped up the box on end against the wall. Holtsner produced a key and unlocking the receptacle of death, threw back the lid, exposing the effigy within.

A gaunt, shrivelled, parchment-like freak was exhibited. The emaciated neck and head surmounted by a shock of tousled hair. The bulbous, moist-lipped mouth leering with vapid expression. Then Holtsner, with a deep sigh, stretched himself upon the couch, while Ball, crouching over him, passed his hands backwards and forwards across the recumbent man's face.

He had not made more than a dozen 'passes' before his body became perfectly rigid, and at the same moment Rhymer observed a distinct tremor passing through the mummified figure occupying the open case.

The Thing appeared to be suscipient to some mysterious endowment of life and motion. Brown evidently observed this manifestation as well, for he laid a trembling hand upon Rhymer's arm, as if to draw his attention to the abnormal change. The Creature's lips were now puckered with a sucking motion, relaxing into a diabolical grin. Then the nostrils dilated, as though about to renew their former function of breathing – and – then – two shrill screams pierced the horrible silence. Rhymer could stand it no longer. He had seen enough.

'Brown,' he cried as he replaced the police whistle in his pocket, 'get your pistol ready,' and smartly drawing back the curtain, the rings rattling along the rod supporting it, discovered himself and his companion to the other occupants of the room.

The effect of this dramatic stroke was instantaneous, for Holtsner immediately awoke, and leapt off the couch. Simultaneously the flicker of returning animation left the mummified corpse, while Ball and Holtsner – their features distorted with uncontrollable fury – sprang, with one accord, towards the intruders.

Their action, however, was abruptly checked by the gleaming barrels of their adversaries' pistols. Then the sound of a key grating in the latch of the garden door caused the two Boches to wheel round in that direction, only to find their retreat cut off by the entry of two more men similarly armed.

'Hands up! Herr Graf Friedrich von Verheim and Otto Krupp of the German Secret Service,' cried Rhymer, 'attempt any resistance and you'll be shot at sight as dangerous spies. The game's up, let me tell you.'

The two men instantly obeyed, unadulterated 'Hate' written broadcast on their faces. Turning to Brown, Rhymer added:

'Search these men for any weapons they may have concealed.'

The subsequent examination only produced a sheathed knife, found on the pseudo Alfred Ball.

'What's the meaning of this unwarrantable outrage?' Von Verheim blustered with a forced expression of outraged innocence. '*Himmel*! but I'll have the law upon you for forcing your way into my house.'

'It's no use, Von Verheim, we've nabbed you red-handed, and Detective-Inspector Brown, here, from Scotland Yard, has a warrant for your arrest, so you'd better come quietly.'

'Bah! What evidence have you?' he sneered with a cunning look of effrontery.

'Sufficient to have you both convicted and hanged for conniving in the act of wilful and premeditated murder.'

At this retort a vague look of relief illuminated the crafty face of the Boche.

'So!' he hissed with unbridled derision, 'you think, then, you clever pig of an Englishman, that one of your juries will convict me and my comrade of murder, committed by some madman running riot about the country, and whom your clever policemen are incapable of arresting.'

'No, Von Verheim, it won't be necessary for a jury to convict on that score, for we've a far graver charge to bring against you and your accomplices than murder – in the ordinary sense of the word.'

Von Verheim arrogantly raised his eyebrows.

'The contents of a notebook in your safe over there—'

'*Mein Gott*!' he gasped, interrupting Rhymer as the latter produced this trump card. His face underwent an appalling change. From a semblance of arrogance and bravado, it assumed a deathly pallor. '*Ach Himmel*!' he spluttered. 'So! you've been to that safe – Otto, what did I tell you? I suspected these English pigs were thieves. *Donner und blitzen*! What will the All Highest say?'

Then, in a burst of frenzy, turning his twitching face towards his confederate, he cried:

'The elixir – quick, Otto – I'm faint – the bottle – it's in the drawer there!'

The servant made a move in obedience to Von Verheim's demand, but was quickly arrested in the act by a sharp command from Rhymer:

'Move another step,' he cried, 'and you're a dead man. I'll get the bottle.' And, motioning Brown to keep an extra watchful eye on Otto Krupp, he quickly approached the table indicated by Von Verheim. The latter made a sly movement as though to intercept him, but was promptly pulled up by the detective.

'Remember you're covered by the police officers behind you,' he barked, 'and they've instructions to shoot.'

The threat was effectual, and Rhymer reached the table without further interruption. Opening the drawer, he produced a small though businesslike bomb, quite big enough to have blown the whole place to atoms.

'So this is your bottle of elixir, Von Verheim?' he queried with sarcasm, regarding the Boche with a gleam of triumph in his eyes. 'An effective dose, too, for strafing the safe and its contents, ourselves into the bargain. I suppose that wouldn't have been of any account, provided you were able to obliterate all evidence of your Hunnish plot.'

Without giving Von Verheim the opportunity of replying to this indictment, Rhymer nodded to the officers behind, who promptly seized both the Boches and handcuffed them.

So expeditiously was this accomplished that the prisoners were afforded little, if any, opportunity of resistance.

'Now,' he exclaimed, 'Inspector Brown will read the warrant.'

While this formality was being discharged, Von Verheim and his accomplice maintained a forced attitude of indifference, and not until the two officers began to lead them away, did either of them evince any further sign of protest.

Then, with a look of malignant 'Hate', Von Verheim, turning towards Rhymer, shouted:

'I hate your country! I loathe your government! Let them murder me and my comrade. What do we care? Bah! We defy you, even now. Kill the body – yes – and you release the spirit to live and effect a greater vengeance – inflamed by the unquenchable fire of eternal "Hate".'

A casual observer might have construed this furious tirade as nothing more or less than an outburst of rage proceeding from a man baffled in the pursuit of a long-prepared scheme of revenge. But to Rhymer it conveyed an extremely subtle threat, beneath which lurked an element of significance, far deeper than anger alone could account for. However, he made no comment, beyond a significant motion of his head directing the instant removal of the prisoners, which was promptly effected through the garden door.

Then turning to Brown he abruptly exclaimed:

'We mustn't lose a minute, for there's no knowing who may be lurking about this place, though I believe we have taken these spies completely by surprise. Lock both doors, please, and be ready for any emergency.'

Brown did as he was requested, after which Rhymer opened the safe again with his skeleton key, and securing the notebook, placed it in his pocket.

'Now,' said he, 'as soon as we get back to our hotel, I'll acquaint you with all the facts I've collected during the last few days. But, before we leave this unhallowed spot, I want to search for another piece of evidence.'

He approached the open mummy case, where it stood propped up against the wall, closely examining the gaping mouth with its row of discoloured teeth. A few seconds later he turned to the inspector, his eyes sparkling with satisfaction.

'Have you got that little box,' he cried, 'you showed me at our first meeting?'

'Yes.'

'Let me have it, then – quick!'

He almost snatched the box from Brown's hand as he produced it from his pocket, and opening the lid took out a tiny piece of some discoloured-looking substance, pointed at one end, carefully placing it between the leering lips of the mummy.

'The exact counterpart!' he cried, a moment later, in a tone of triumph. 'Look, Brown, don't you see what it is?'

'Well, I thought it was a piece of bone,' he ventured with indecision, 'which the surgeon took from one of the victims' necks.'

'Of course it's a piece of bone, or rather ivory, and what's of more consequence still – a piece of one of the *canine* or eye-teeth of this preserved corpse. Don't you see it fits the broken stump, and must have previously been snapped off? It's a BROKEN FANG! Doesn't that suggest a clue?'

'Great Scot, sir! Why, the brute must have bitten that poor fellow, and broken off one of its teeth in the effort! Good heavens! Surely the Thing's not a vampire?'

'That's what I've suspected it to be all along.'

'But I always regarded vampires to be purely mythical,' said Brown.

'When you become acquainted with the contents of this book,' patting the incriminating article in his breast-pocket, 'you'll alter your opinion. However, let me point out something else relating to this Thing here. Look at the skull. Do you see those two small holes?'

Brown signified assent.

'Well, you can't deny that they are bullet holes; therefore the natural inference is that this nondescript Creature met its death, originally, by shooting, which summarily rejects Von Verheim's assertion that it is the corpse of an ancient Egyptian. Firearms weren't used in those remote times.'

'But don't you remember,' Brown hazarded, 'shooting at the Creature in the lane – mightn't that account for the bullet holes in the skull?'

Rhymer regarded the detective for a moment with a half-suppressed look of amusement.

'By Jove, Brown,' he cried, 'you're waking up at last to the psychological probabilities of the case,' and slapping him on the shoulder, added:

'So now you begin to realize that this corpse, like the other we saw, is not quite so defunct as normal conditions would infer. But don't be too cock-sure yet. You've fallen into one error, for I told you I shot that other 'freak' *through the body,* and there is no corresponding bullet mark in the abdominal region of this corpse.'

Brown scratched his head in evident perplexity, then, with a bantering smile, observed:

'When I passed a remark in front of Von Verheim, the other morning, upon the apparently well-preserved condition of these mummies, you promptly shut me up.'

'I admit the charge,' Rhymer responded, 'but I had a good reason for doing so, as you will soon realize. But come,' he continued, 'let's examine a few more of these grotesque coffins before we make tracks.'

Two or three were accordingly wrenched open (they were all fitted with modern locks) and their occupants exposed. An exceptionally hideous specimen was eventually uncovered, which, upon closer inspection, revealed a small hole in the abdomen, with a corresponding bullet flattened firmly against the spinal column behind.

'Now, Brown, what do you think of that? Seems as though more than one agent was employed in these crimes, eh?'

'Looks uncommonly like it.'

'Holloa! What's that?' Rhymer suddenly exclaimed, as his keen glance happened to fall upon a long, dark cloak suspended from a peg in the corner. With a few strides he reached it, and taking it down examined the garment. A moment later his hand was in his pocket, and out came a letter-case, from which he produced a small piece of cloth, and comparing it with the cloak, exclaimed:

'Here you are, Brown, another piece of evidence.'

'What's that?' the inspector enquired as he crossed over to where Rhymer was standing.

The latter, by way of reply, spread out the cloak, exhibiting a gap in the hem from which a piece of the material had been torn.

'See that?' he enquired.

'By Jove! Yes, and you've got the missing fragment?'

Rhymer triumphantly waved aloft a small piece of frayed cloth, exclaiming:

'This is the identical piece I found in my hand after my "scrap" the other night with the vampire.'

'And it matches the ulster.'

'Perfectly.'

'Well, I'm—'

'No, you're not yet,' Rhymer hastily interrupted, 'but let's get out of this, or there's no saying what might happen. It's a confoundedly rum spot,' and buttoning up his coat, he switched off the light, and followed by the inspector, made his exit through the garden door.

'It is quite evident,' said Rhymer in the course of a conversation with the detective later the same night, 'that any one who investigates the phenomena of psychology, will, at some time or other, come across complicated influences devoid of explanation by common or garden theories. Now the case we have in hand seems to be one of these. Of course you've heard of the widespread and ancient belief in vampires – bodies which the earth has rejected, and, therefore, do not properly decay?'

'Yes, but as I recently remarked, I only regarded them as fairy tales.'

'Well, as I said before, I think you'll alter your opinion, if you haven't done so already, when you've heard all I have to tell you. To begin with, vampires are accredited with sucking the life-blood from their victims, and, as you have already told me, the police-surgeon attributed the death of the Blankborough victims as primarily due to some blood-sucking process—'

'Yes, by Jove! But you'd never get a judge and jury to accept such a theory, let alone convict on it.'

'I've no intention of asking for a conviction on that count; but do let me get on with what I have to say. This manuscript contains sufficient evidence to convict both our prisoners as dangerous spies, without introducing these murders or any psychical proof at all. Von Verheim is a distinguished German scientist and psychologist, so I fished out when in London, whose decease was falsely reported many years ago, and who has been residing in this country all the time, unsuspected.'

'Then he was naturalized under the name of Holtsner.'

'Naturally, and being employed by the German Secret Service, was supported by them in his deception.'

'That shows the war has long been contemplated by the Huns,' said Brown.

'There's no doubt about that. But, confound it all, what a chap you are to interrupt. Well, so much for Von Verheim, and now we come to Otto Krupp. He was an old pupil of the former, and a qualified chemist. A shrewd fellow, too, who has obtained a complete mastery of the English language—'

'That's very evident,' said Brown, 'for he took us both in, pretty neatly, at the King's Arms the other evening, with his Cockney speech and accent.'

Rhymer, ignoring the interruption, continued:

'There is a very brief but sufficiently clear record in Von Verheim's notebook, of a monstrous scheme for the importation over here of the corpses of German soldiers killed in battle: these bodies having previously been immersed in some special preparation – discovered by him – for definitely arresting decomposition—'

'Now I see why you wanted the chief to have all cargoes examined, coming through neutral ports.'

'Exactly, for these bodies were to be sent over, camouflaged as Egyptian mummies, and delivered at the private residences of various naturalized Germans. These wretched aliens are described by Von Verheim as "mediumistic" and capable of freeing, at will, the spirits from their bodies, and then, by "possessing" these preserved corpses, convert them into vampires, "controlling" them to commit any atrocities their Teutonic imaginations might devise.'

'Then that's what Von Verheim was up to in the museum when we interrupted him.'

'Undoubtedly, and by means of this demoniacal agency, they hoped to commit wholesale murders with little chance of discovery.'

'What on earth did they hope to achieve by such a course?'

'An expansion of the Boche mania for "frightfulness", I imagine; although the written evidence reveals that only fit men of military age were to be attacked by these vampires. This looks as though they were plotting to diminish the strength of our fighting units as well.'

'Then the mutilating business was evidently a cunning attempt to conceal the vampire element?'

'Exactly.'

'The whole thing seems too horrible,' Brown exclaimed, aghast, 'it's barely credible.'

'I repeat, nothing is incredible where the Boche is concerned; we've already had sufficient proof of that.'

'I wonder why Krupp made that convicting admission about the missing knife at the King's Arms the other night?'

'Presumably with the hope that some one might have chanced to pick it up, and overhearing to whom it belonged, would promptly return it to him or his master.'

'He little thought that it would lead to their ultimate detection.'

'No; but they were on the alert. The figure you followed last night hadn't a knife, so they evidently abandoned the mutilating "stunt" as too risky. I've also ascertained that the fourth victim, murdered last night, was not mutilated.'

'But do you believe this scheme could have been extensively worked?'

'Most decidedly. The assassinations would have spread broadcast, and these vampires, whose strength – when possessed with temporary life – is prodigious, would have played the very deuce, if once the evil had got a firm hold. For though the Boche has yet to be born whom any average Britisher would fear to tackle, and knock out into the bargain, still, there is a limit to all human endurance: and even the bravest amongst us would look askance when faced with a supernatural menace like this.'

'That I readily admit.'

'Exactly. Well, vampires are invulnerable, and unless unearthed and literally dismembered or burnt, when in a condition of inactivity, they cannot be suppressed. So the only effective remedy for the evil is that which we are adopting, in discovering the whereabouts of the living fiends who are "possessing" these vampire bodies, and forcibly removing them out of harm's way.'

'It'll be a difficult job to find the others,' said Brown.

'I think not, for Von Verheim was the head and moving spirit in the entire scheme, and by now he and his accomplice will be safely under lock and key. The notebook, remember, contains a list of those aliens over here concerned in the conspiracy, as well as an entry of the four Blankborough victims – we saw Von Verheim enter the last – which I shall send to your chief. In addition, documentary evidence here proves that Von Verheim and Krupp have been involved in conveying important information to the enemy, which has been puzzling the authorities for some time past. This evidence, alone, is sufficient to convict them. However, unless I'm much mistaken in your chief, the remainder of the gang will soon be interned or even more efficiently disposed of.'

'It's a good job I sought your assistance when I did, sir,' Brown exclaimed with an expressive nod of his head, 'for though we shan't be able to satisfy the public as to who the perpetrators of these atrocities are, we have, undoubtedly, knocked on the head a very grave menace to the country. A great pity the B.P. won't know this, since they'll be sure to blame us police for apparently failing to bring home these crimes to the real culprits.'

'Never mind,' said Rhymer, 'console your official mind

with the knowledge that you, your chief, and I have learned the truth, and we shall shortly get our own back in the satisfaction of knowing that Von Verheim and his gang have got their deserts.'

'After all, that's some recompense,' Brown admitted – still hankering after public recognition.

'Some? – A great deal, I call it, since a widespread catastrophe has narrowly been averted. And our job, after all, is to serve King and Country, and if we've done that to the best of our ability, "then," say I, "hang public opinion."'

The Man Who Cast No Shadow

SEABURY QUINN

Vampire hunter: Jules de Grandin
Locality of case: Harrisonville, New Jersey
Time: 1927
Author: The American lawyer and expert in medical jurisprudence, Seabury Grandin Quinn (1889–1969), combined his literary energies to become the most popular contributor to the legendary pulp magazine *Weird Tales* whilst acting as the editor of the trade journal for undertakers, *Casket and Sunnyside*! A man of prodigious output, Quinn contributed over 150 stories to *Weird Tales* between 1923 and 1952, as well as countless tales, essays and articles for other periodicals such as *Thrill Book* and *Young's Magazine*. He had apparently become fascinated with horror stories after reading *Dracula* as a teenager, and not surprisingly vampires featured in many of his subsequent tales. His most famous character is the egotistical French-born investigator Jules de Grandin, whose adventures are chronicled by his friend Dr Trowbridge. Although both men and the town in which they live are wholly imaginary, Quinn gave de Grandin his own middle name. Vampires featured in a considerable number of the Frenchman's 93 cases which his author poured out over a quarter of a century – the very first of these being 'The Man Who Cast No Shadow' which appeared in *Weird Tales*, February 1927.

'But no, my friend,' Jules de Grandin shook his sleek, blond head decidedly and grinned across the breakfast table at me, 'we will go to this so kind Madame Norman's tea, of a certainty. Yes.'

'But hang it all,' I replied, giving Mrs Norman's note an irritable shove with my coffee spoon, 'I don't want to go to a confounded tea party! I'm too old and too sensible to dress up in a tall hat and a long coat and listen to the vaporings of a flock of silly flappers. I—'

'*Mordieu*, hear the savage!' de Grandin chuckled delightedly. 'Always does he find excuses for not giving pleasure to others, and always does he frame those excuses to make him more important in his own eyes. Enough of this, Friend Trowbridge; let us go to the kind Madame Norman's party. Always there is something of interest to be seen if one but knows where to look for it.'

'H'm, maybe,' I replied grudgingly, 'but you've better sight than I think you have if you can find anything worth seeing at an afternoon reception.'

The reception was in full blast when we arrived at the Norman mansion in Tuscarora Avenue that afternoon in 192–. The air was heavy with the commingled odors of half a hundred different perfumes and the scent of hot-poured jasmine tea, while the clatter of cup on saucer, laughter, and buzzing conversation filled the wide hall and dining room. In the long double parlors the rugs had been rolled back and young men in frock coats glided over the polished parquetry in company with girls in provocatively short skirts to the belching melody of a saxophone and the drumming rhythm of a piano.

'*Pardieu*,' de Grandin murmured as he viewed the dancers a moment, 'your American youth take their pleasures with seriousness, Friend Trowbridge. Behold their faces. Never a smile, never a laugh. They might be recruits on their first parade for all the joy they show – ah!' He broke off abruptly, gazing with startled, almost horrified, eyes after a couple whirling in the mazes of a foxtrot at the farther end of the room. '*Nom d'un fromage*,' he murmured softly to himself, 'this matter will bear investigating, I think!'

'Eh, what's that?' I asked, piloting him toward our hostess.

'Nothing; nothing, I do assure you,' he answered as we greeted Mrs Norman and passed toward the dining-room. But I noticed his round, blue eyes strayed more than once toward the parlors as we drank our tea and exchanged amiable nothings with a pair of elderly ladies.

'Pardon,' de Grandin bowed stiffly from the hips to his conversational partner and turned toward the rear drawing room, 'there is a gentleman here I desire to meet, if you do not mind – that tall, distinguished one, with the young girl in pink.'

'Oh, I guess you mean Count Czerny,' a young man laden with an ice in one hand and a glass of non-Volstead punch in the other paused on his way from the dining-room. 'He's a rare bird, all right. I knew him back in '13 when the Balkan Allies were polishing off the Turks. Queer-lookin' duck, ain't he? First-class fightin' man, though. Why, I saw him lead a bayonet charge right into the Turkish lines one day, and when he'd shot his pistol empty he went at the enemy with his teeth! Yes, sir, he grabbed a Turk with both hands and bit his throat out, hanged if he didn't.'

'Czerny,' de Grandin repeated musingly. 'He is a Pole, perhaps?'

His informant laughed a bit shamefacedly. 'Can't say,' he confessed. 'The Serbs weren't asking embarrassing questions about volunteers' nationalities those days, and it wasn't considered healthful for any of us to do so, either. I got the impression he was a Hungarian refugee from Austrian vengeance; but that's only hearsay. Come along, I'll introduce you, if you wish.'

I saw de Grandin clasp hands with the foreigner and stand talking with him for a time, and, in spite of myself, I could not forbear a smile at the contrast they made.

The Frenchman was a bare five feet four inches in height, slender as a girl, and, like a girl, possessed of almost laughably small hands and feet. His light hair and fair skin, coupled with his trimly waxed diminutive blond mustache and round, unwinking blue eyes, gave him a curiously misleading appearance of mildness. His companion was at least six feet tall, swarthy-skinned and black-haired, with bristling black mustaches and fierce, slate-gray eyes set beneath beetling black brows. His large nose was like the predatory beak of some bird of prey, and the tilt of his long, pointed jaw bore out the uncompromising ferocity of the rest of his visage. Across his left cheek, extending upward over the temple and into his hair, was a knife- or saber-scar, a streak of white showing the trail of the steel in his scalp, and shining like silver inlaid in onyx against the blue-black of his smoothly pomaded locks.

What they said was, of course, beyond reach of my ears, but I saw de Grandin's quick, impish smile flicker across his keen face more than once, to be answered by a slow, languorous smile on the other's dark countenance.

At length the count bowed formally to my friend and whirled away with a wisp of a girl, while de Grandin returned to me. At the door he paused a moment, inclining his shoulders in a salute as a couple of debutantes brushed past him. Something – I know not what – drew my attention to the tall foreigner a moment, and a sudden chill rippled up my spine at what I saw. Above the georgette-clad shoulder of his dancing partner the count's slate-gray eyes were fixed on de Grandin's trim back, and in them I read all the cold, malevolent fury with which a caged tiger regards its keeper as he passes the bars.

'What on earth did you say to that fellow?' I asked as the little Frenchman rejoined me. 'He looked as if he would like to murder you.'

'Ha?' he gave a questioning, single-syllabled laugh. 'Did he so? Obey the noble Washington's injunction, and avoid foreign entanglements, Friend Trowbridge; it is better so, I think.'

'But look here,' I began, nettled by his manner, 'what—'

'*Non, non,*' he interrupted, 'you must be advised by me, my friend. I think it would be better if we dismissed the incident from our minds. But stay – perhaps you had better meet that gentleman, after all. I will have the good Madame Norman introduce you.'

More puzzled than ever, I followed him to our hostess and waited while he requested her to present me to the count.

In a lull in the dancing she complied with his request, and the foreigner acknowledged the introduction with a brief handclasp and an almost churlish nod, then turned his back on me, continuing an animated conversation with the large-eyed young woman in an abbreviated party frock.

'And did you shake his hand?' de Grandin asked as we descended the Normans' steps to my waiting car.

'Yes, of course,' I replied.

'Ah? Tell me, my friend, did you notice anything – ah – peculiar, in his grip?'

'H'm.' I wrinkled my brow a moment in concentrated thought. 'Yes, I believe I did.'

'So? What was it?'

'Hanged if I can say, exactly,' I admitted, 'but – well, it seemed – this sounds absurd, I know – but it seemed as though his hand had two backs – no palm at all – if that means anything to you.'

'It means much, my friend; it means a very great deal,' he answered with such a solemn nod that I burst into a fit of laughter. 'Believe me, it means much more than you suspect.'

It must have been some two weeks later that I chanced to remark to de Grandin, 'I saw your friend, Count Czerny, in New York yesterday.'

'Indeed?' he answered with what seemed like more than necessary interest. 'And how did he impress you at the time?'

'Oh, I just happened to pass him on Fifth Avenue,' I replied. 'I'd been up to see an acquaintance in Fifty-ninth Street and was turning into the avenue when I saw him driving away from the Plaza. He was with some ladies.'

'No doubt,' de Grandin responded dryly. 'Did you notice him particularly?'

'Can't say that I did, especially,' I answered, 'but it seems to me he looked older than the day we met him at Mrs Norman's.'

'Yes?' the Frenchman leaned forward eagerly. 'Older, do you say? *Parbleu*, this is of interest; I suspected as much!'

'Why—' I began, but he turned away with an impatient shrug.

'Pah!' he exclaimed petulantly. 'Friend Trowbridge, I fear Jules de Grandin is a fool, he entertains all sorts of strange notions.'

I had known the little Frenchman long enough to realize that he was as full of moods as a prima donna, but his erratic, unrelated remarks were getting on my nerves. 'See here, de Grandin,' I began testily, 'what's all this nonsense—'

The sudden shrill clatter of my office telephone bell cut me short. 'Dr Trowbridge,' an agitated voice asked over the wire, 'can you come right over, please? This is Mrs Norman speaking.'

'Yes, of course,' I answered, reaching for my medicine case; 'what is it – who's ill?'

'It's – it's Guy Eckhart, he's been taken with a fainting fit, and we don't seem to be able to rouse him.'

'Very well,' I promised, 'Dr de Grandin and I will be right over.'

'Come on, de Grandin,' I called as I shoved my hat down over my ears and shrugged into my overcoat, 'one of Mrs Norman's house guests has been taken ill; I told her we were coming.'

'*Mais oui*,' he agreed, hurrying into his outdoors clothes. 'Is it a man or a woman, this sick one?'

'It's a man,' I replied, 'Guy Eckhart.'

'A man,' he echoed incredulously. 'A man, do you say? No, no, my friend, that is not likely.'

'Likely or not,' I rejoined sharply, 'Mrs Norman says he's been seized with a fainting fit, and I give the lady credit for knowing what she's talking about.'

'*Eh bien*,' he drummed nervously on the cushions of the automobile seat, 'perhaps Jules de Grandin really is a fool. After all, it is not impossible.'

'It certainly isn't,' I agreed fervently to myself as I set the car in motion.

Young Eckhart had recovered consciousness when we arrived, but looked like a man just emerging from a lingering fever. Attempts to get a statement from him met with no response, for he replied slowly, almost incoherently, and seemed to have no idea concerning the cause of his illness.

Mrs Norman was little more specific. 'My son Ferdinand found him lying on the floor of his bath with the shower going and the window wide open, just before dinner,' she explained. 'He was totally unconscious, and remained so till just a few minutes ago.'

'Ha, is it so?' de Grandin murmured half heedlessly, as he made a rapid inspection of the patient.

'Friend Trowbridge,' he called me to the window, 'what do you make of these objective symptoms: a soft, frequent pulse, a fluttering heart, suffused eyes, a hot, dry skin and a flushed, hectic face?'

'Sounds like an arterial hemorrhage,' I answered promptly, 'but there's been no trace of blood on the boy's floor, nor any evidence of a stain on his clothing. Sure you've checked the signs over?'

'Absolutely,' he replied with a vigorous double nod. Then to the young man: 'Now, *mon enfant*, we shall inspect you, if you please.'

Quickly he examined the boy's face, scalp, throat, wrists and calves, finding no evidence of even a pinprick, let alone a wound capable of causing syncope.

'*Mon Dieu*, this is strange,' he muttered; 'of a surety, it has the queerness of the devil! Perhaps the bleeding is internal, but – ah, *regardez vous*, Friend Trowbridge!'

He had turned down the collar of the youngster's pajama jacket, more in idle routine than in hope of discovering anything tangible, but the livid spot to which he pointed seemed the key to our mystery's outer door. Against the smooth, white flesh of the young man's left breast there showed a red, angry patch, such as might have resulted from a vacuum cup being held some time against the skin, and in the center of the discoloration was a double row of tiny punctures scarcely larger than needle-pricks, arranged in horizontal divergent arcs, like a pair of parentheses laid sidewise.

'You see?' he asked simply, as though the queer, blood-infused spot explained everything.

'But he couldn't have bled much through that,' I protested. 'Why, the man seems almost drained dry, and these wounds wouldn't have yielded more than a cubic centimeter of blood, at most.'

He nodded gravely. 'Blood is not entirely colloidal, my friend,' he responded. 'It will penetrate the tissues to some extent, especially if sufficient force is applied.'

'But it would have required a powerful suction—' I replied, when his rejoinder cut me short:

'Ha, you have said it, my friend. Suction – that is the word!'

'But what could have sucked a man's blood like this?' I was in a near-stupor of mystification.

'What, indeed?' he replied gravely. 'That is for us to find out. Meantime, we are here as physicians. A quarter-grain morphine injection is indicated here, I think. You will administer the dose; I have no license in America.'

When I returned from my round of afternoon calls next day I found de Grandin seated on my front steps in close conference with Indian John.

Indian John was a town character of doubtful lineage who performed odd jobs of snow shoveling, furnace tending and grass cutting, according to season, and interspersed his manual labors with brief incursions into the mercantile field when he peddled fresh vegetables from door to door. He also peddled neighborhood gossip and retailed local lore to all who would listen, his claim to being a hundred years old giving him the standing of an indisputable authority in all matters antedating living memory.

'*Pardieu*, but you have told me much, *mon vieux*,' de Grandin declared as I came up the porch steps. He handed the old rascal a handful of silver and rose to accompany me into the house.

'Friend Trowbridge,' he accused as we finished dinner that night, 'you had not told me that this town grew up on the site of an early Swedish settlement.'

'Never knew you wanted to know,' I defended with a grin.

'You know the ancient Swedish church, perhaps,' he persisted.

'Yes, that's old Christ Church,' I answered. 'It's down in the east end of town; don't suppose it has a hundred communicants today. Our population has made some big changes, both in complexion and creed, since the days when the Dutch and Swedes fought for possession of New Jersey.'

'You will drive me to that church, right away, at once, immediately?' he demanded eagerly.

'I guess so,' I agreed. 'What's the matter now; Indian John been telling you a lot of fairy-tales?'

'Perhaps,' he replied, regarding me with one of his steady, unwinking stares. 'Not all fairy-tales are pleasant, you know. Do you recall those of *Chaperon Rouge* – how do you say it, Red Riding Hood? – and Bluebeard?'

'Huh!' I scoffed; 'they're both as true as any of John's stories, I'll bet.'

'Undoubtlessly,' he agreed with a quick nod. 'The story of Bluebeard, for instance, is unfortunately a very true tale indeed. But come, let us hasten; I would see that church tonight, if I may.'

*

Christ Church, the old Swedish place of worship, was a combined demonstration of how firmly adzhewn pine and walnut can resist the ravages of time and how nearly three hundred years of weather can demolish any structure erected by man. Its rough-painted walls and short, firm-based spire shone ghostly and pallid in the early spring moonlight, and the cluster of broken and weather-worn tombstones which staggered up from its unkempt burying ground were like soiled white chicks seeking shelter from a soiled white hen.

Dismounting from a car at the wicket gate of the churchyard, we made our way over the level graves, I in a maze of wonderment, de Grandin with an eagerness almost childish. Occasionally he flashed the beam from his electric torch on some monument of an early settler, bent to decipher the worn inscription, then turned away with a sigh of disappointment.

I paused to light a cigar, but dropped my half-burned match in astonishment as my companion gave vent to a cry of excited pleasure. '*Triomphe!*' he exclaimed delightedly. 'Come and behold, Friend Trowbridge. Thus far your lying friend, the Indian man, has told the truth. *Regardez!*'

He was standing beside an old, weather-gnawed tomb-stone, once marble, perhaps, but appearing more like brown sandstone under the ray of his flashlight. Across its upper end was deeply cut the one word:

SARAH

while below the name appeared a verse of half-obliterated doggerel:

Let nonne difturb her deathleffe fleepe
Abote ye tombe wilde garlick keepe
For if fhee wake much woe will boaft
Prayfe Faither, Sonne & Holie Goaft.

'Did you bring me out here to study the orthographical eccentricities of the early settlers?' I demanded in disgust.

'Ah bah!' he returned. 'Let us consult the *ecclésiastique*. He, perhaps, will ask no fool's questions.'

'No, you'll do that,' I answered tartly as we knocked at the rectory door.

'Pardon, *Monsieur*,' de Grandin apologized as the white-haired old minister appeared in answer to our summons, 'we do not wish to disturb you thus, but there is a matter of great import on which we would consult you. I would that you tell us what you can, if anything, concerning a certain grave in your churchyard. A grave marked "Sarah", if you please.'

'Why' – the elderly cleric was plainly taken aback – 'I don't think there is anything I can tell you about it, sir. There is some mention in the early parish records, I believe, of a woman believed to have been a murderess being buried in that grave, but it seems the poor creature was more sinned against than sinning. Several children in the neighborhood died mysteriously – some epidemic the ignorant physicians failed to understand, no doubt – and Sarah, whatever the poor woman's surname may have been, was accused of killing them by witchcraft. At any rate, one of the bereft mothers took vengeance into her own hands, and strangled poor Sarah with a noose of well-rope. The witchcraft belief must have been quite prevalent, too, for there is some nonsense verse on the tombstone concerning her "deathless sleep" and an allusion to her waking from it;

also some mention of wild garlic being planted about her.'

He laughed somewhat ruefully. 'I wish they hadn't said that,' he added, 'for, do you know, there are garlic shoots growing about that grave to this very day. Old Christian, our sexton, declares that he can't get rid of it, no matter how much he grubs it up. It spreads to the surrounding lawn, too,' he added sadly.

'*Cordieu!*' de Grandin gasped. 'This is of the importance, sir!'

The old man smiled gently at the little Frenchman's impetuosity.

'It's an odd thing,' he commented, 'there was another gentleman asking about that same tomb a few weeks ago; a – pardon the expression – a foreigner.'

'So?' de Grandin's little, waxed mustache twitched like the whiskers of a nervous tom-cat. 'A foreigner, do you say? A tall, rawboned, fleshless living skeleton of a man with a scar on his face and a white streak in his hair?'

'I wouldn't be quite so severe in my description,' the other answered with a smile. 'He certainly was a thin gentleman, and I believe he had a scar on his face, too, though I can't be certain of that, he was so very wrinkled. No, his hair was entirely white, there was no white streak in it, sir. In fact, I should have said he was very advanced in age, judging from his hair and face and the manner in which he walked. He seemed very weak and feeble. It was really quite pitiable.'

'*Sacre nom d'un fromage vert!*' de Grandin almost snarled. 'Pitiable, do you say, *Monsieur*? *Pardieu*, it is damnable, nothing less!'

He bowed to the clergyman and turned to me. 'Come, Friend Trowbridge, come away,' he cried. 'We must go to Madame Norman's at once, right away, immediately.'

'What's behind all this mystery?' I demanded as we left the parsonage door.

He elevated his slender shoulders in an eloquent shrug. 'I only wish I knew,' he replied. 'Someone is working the devil's business, of that I am sure; but what the game is, or what the next move will be, only the good God can tell, my friend.'

I turned the car through Tunlaw Street to effect a short-cut, and as we drove past an Italian greengrocer's, de Grandin seized my arm. 'Stop a moment, Friend Trow-bridge,' he asked, 'I would make a purchase at this shop.'

'We desire some fresh garlic,' he informed the proprietor as we entered the little store, 'a considerable amount, if you have it.'

The Italian spread his hands in a deprecating gesture. 'We have it not, *Signor*,' he declared. 'It was only yesterday morning that we sold our entire supply.' His little black eyes snapped happily at the memory of an unexpected bargain.

'Eh, what is this?' de Grandin demanded. 'Do you say you sold your supply? How is that?'

'I know not,' the other replied. 'Yesterday morning a rich gentleman came to my shop in an automobile, and called me from my store. He desired all the garlic I had in stock – at my own price, *Signor*, and at once. I was to deliver it to his address in Rupleysville the same day.'

'Ah?' de Grandin's face assumed the expression of a cross-word fiend as he begins to see the solution of his puzzle. 'And this liberal purchaser, what did he look like?'

The Italian showed his white, even teeth in a wide grin. 'It was funny,' he confessed. 'He did not look like one of our people, nor like one who would eat much garlic. He was old, very old and thin, with a much-wrinkled face and white hair, he—'

'*Nom d'un chat!*' the Frenchman cried, then burst into a flood of torrential Italian.

The shopkeeper listened at first with suspicion, then incredulity, finally in abject terror. 'No, no,' he exclaimed. 'No, *Signor*; *santissima Madonna*, you do make the joke!'

'Do I so?' de Grandin replied. 'Wait and see, foolish one.'

'*Santo Dio* forbid!' The other crossed himself piously, then bent his thumb across his palm, circling it with his second and third fingers and extending the fore and little fingers in the form of a pair of horns.

The Frenchman turned toward the waiting car with a grunt of inarticulate disgust.

'What now?' I asked as we got under way once more; 'what did that man make the sign of the evil eye for, de Grandin?'

'Later, my friend; I will tell you later,' he answered. 'You would but laugh if I told you what I suspect. He is of the Latin blood, and can appreciate my fears.' Nor would he utter another word till we reached the Norman house.

'Dr Trowbridge – Dr de Grandin!' Mrs Norman met us in the hall; 'you must have heard my prayers; I've been phoning your office for the last hour, and they said you were out and couldn't be reached.'

'What's up?' I asked.

'It's Mr Eckhart again. He's been seized with another fainting fit. He seemed so well this afternoon, and I sent a big dinner up to him at 8 o'clock, but when the maid went in, she found him unconscious, and she declares she saw something in his room—'

'Ha?' de Grandin interrupted. 'Where is she, this servant? I would speak with her.'

'Wait a moment,' Mrs Norman answered; 'I'll send for her.'

The girl, an ungainly young Southern negress, came into

the front hall, sullen dissatisfaction written large upon her black face.

'Now, then,' de Grandin bent his steady, unwinking gaze on her, 'what is it you say about seeing someone in the young Monsieur Eckhart's room, *hein*?'

'Ah did see sumpin', too,' the girl replied stubbornly. 'Ah don' care who says Ah didn't see nothin', Ah says Ah did. Ah'd just toted a tray o' vittles up to Mistuh Eckhart's room, an' when Ah opened de do', dere wuz a woman – dere wuz a woman – yas, sar, a skinny, black-eyed white woman – a-bendin' ober 'um an' – an'—'

'And what, if you please?' de Grandin asked breathlessly.

'A-bitin' 'um!' the girl replied defiantly. 'Ah don' car whut Mis' Norman says, she wuz a-bitin' 'um. Ah seen her. Ah knows whut she wuz. Ah done hyeah tell erbout dat ol' Sarah woman what come up out 'er grave wid a long rope erbout her neck and go 'round bitin' folks. Yas, sar; an' she wuz a-bitin' 'um, too. Ah seen her!'

'Nonsense,' Mrs Norman commented in an annoyed whisper over de Grandin's shoulder.

'*Grand Dieu*, is it so?' de Grandin explained, and turning abruptly, leaped up the stairs toward the sick man's room, two steps at a time.

'See, see, Friend Trowbridge,' he ordered fiercely when I joined him at the patient's bedside. 'Behold, it is the mark!' Turning back Eckhart's pajama collar, he displayed two incised horizontal arcs on the young man's flesh. There was no room for dispute, they were undoubtedly the marks of human teeth, and from the fresh wounds the blood was flowing freely.

As quickly as possible we staunched the flow and applied restoratives to the patient, both of us working in silence, for my brain was too much in a whirl to permit the formation of intelligent questions, while de Grandin remained dumb as an oyster.

'Now,' he ordered as we completed our ministrations, 'we must get back to that cemetery, Friend Trowbridge, and once there, we must do the thing which must be done!'

'What the devil's that?' I asked as we left the sickroom.

'*Non, non*, you shall see,' he promised as we entered my car and drove down the street.

'Quick, the crank-handle,' he demanded as we descended from the car at the cemetery gate, 'it will make a serviceable hammer.' He was prying a hemlock paling from the graveyard fence as he spoke.

We crossed the unkempt cemetery lawn again and finally paused beside the tombstone of the unknown Sarah.

'Attend me, Friend Trowbridge,' de Grandin commanded, 'hold the searchlight, if you please.' He pressed his pocket flash into my hand. 'Now—' He knelt beside the grave, pointing the stick he had wrenched from the fence straight downward into the turf. With the crank of my motor he began hammering the wood into the earth.

Farther and farther the rough stake sank into the sod, de Grandin's blows falling faster and faster as the wood drove home. Finally, when there was less than six inches of the wicket projecting from the grave's top, he raised the iron high over his head and drove downward with all his might.

The short hair at the back of my neck suddenly started upward, and little thrills of horripilation chased each other up my spine as the wood sank suddenly, as though driven from clay into sand, and a low hopeless moan, like the wailing of a frozen wind through an ice-cave, wafted up to us from the depths of the grave.

'Good God, what's that?' I asked, aghast.

For answer he leaned forward, seized the stake in both

hands and drew suddenly up on it. At his second tug the wood came away. 'See,' he ordered curtly, flashing the pocket lamp on the tip of the stave. For the distance of a foot or so from its pointed end the wood was stained a deep, dull red. It was wet with blood.

'And now forever,' he hissed between his teeth, driving the wood into the grave once more, and sinking it a full foot below the surface of the grass by thrusting the crank-handle into the earth. 'Come, Friend Trowbridge, we have done a good work this night. I doubt not the young Eckhart will soon recover from his malady.'

His assumption was justified. Eckhart's condition improved steadily. Within a week, save for a slight pallor, he was, to all appearances, as well as ever.

The pressure of the usual early crop of influenza and pneumonia kept me busily on my rounds, and I gradually gave up hope of getting any information from de Grandin, for a shrug of the shoulders was all the answer he vouchsafed to my questions. I relegated Eckhart's inexplicable hemorrhages and the bloodstained stake to the limbo of never-to-be-solved mysteries. But—

2

'Good mornin', gentlemen,' Detective Sergeant Costello greeted as he followed Nora, my household factorum, into the breakfast room, 'it's sorry I am to be disturbin' your meal, but there's a little case puzzlin' th' department that I'd like to talk over with Dr de Grandin, if you don't mind.'

He looked expectantly at the little Frenchman as he finished speaking, his lips parted to launch upon a detailed description of the case.

'*Parbleu*,' de Grandin laughed, 'it is fortunate for me that I have completed my breakfast, *cher Sergent*, for a riddle of crime detection is to me like a red rag to a bullfrog – I must needs snap at it, whether I have been fed or no. Speak on, my friend, I beseech you; I am like Balaam's ass, all ears.'

The big Irishman seated himself on the extreme edge of one of my Heppelwhite chairs and gazed deprecatingly at the derby he held firmly between his knees. 'It's like this,' he began, "tis one o' them mysterious disappearance cases, gentleman an' whilst I'm thinkin' th' young lady knows exactly where she's at an' why she's there, I hate to tell her folks about it.

'All th' high-hat folks ain't like you two gentlemen, askin' your pardon, sors – they mostly seems to think that a harness bull's unyform is sumpin' like a livery – like a shofur's or a footman's or sumpin', an' that a plainclothes man is just a sort o' inferior servant. They don't give th' police credit for no brains, y'see, an' when one o' their darters gits giddy an' runs off th' reservation, if we tells 'em th' gurrl's run away of her own free will an' accord they say we're a lot o' lazy, good-fer-nothin' bums who are tryin' to dodge our laygitimate jooties by castin' mud on th' young ladies' char-ac-ters, d'ye see? So, when this Miss Esther Norman disappears in broad daylight – leastwise, in th' twilight – o' th' day before her dance, we suspects right away that th' gurrl's gone her own ways into th' best o' intentions, y'see; but we dasn't tell her folks as much, or they'll be hollerin' to th' commissioner fer to git a bran' new set o' detectives down to headquarters, so they will.

'Now, mind ye, I'm not sayin' th' young lady *mightn't* o' been kidnapped, y'understand, gentlemen, but I do be sayin' 'tis most unlikely. I've been on th' force, man an' boy, in unyform and in plain clothes fer th' last twenty-five years, an' th' number of laygitimate kidnapin's o' young women over ten years of age I've seen can be counted on th' little finger o' me left hand, an' I ain't got none there, at all, at all.'

He held the member up for our inspection, revealing the fact that the little finger had been amputated close to the knuckle.

De Grandin, elbows on the table, pointed chin cupped in his hands, was puffing furiously at a vile-smelling French cigarette, alternately sucking down great drafts of its acrid smoke and expelling clouds of fumes in double jets from his narrow, aristocratic nostrils.

'What is it you say?' he demanded, removing the cigarette from his lips. 'Is it the so lovely *Mademoiselle* Esther, daughter of that kind Madame Tuscarora Avenue Norman, who is missing?'

'Yes, sor,' Costello answered, ''tis th' same young lady's flew the coop, accordin' to my way o' thinkin'.'

'*Mordieu!*' the Frenchman gave the ends of his blond mustache a savage twist; 'you intrigue me, my friend. Say on, how did it happen, and when?'

''Twas about midnight last night th' alarm came into headquarters,' the detective replied. 'Accordin' to th' facts as we have 'em, th' young lady went downtown in th' Norman car to do some errands. We've checked her movements up, an' here they are.'

He drew a black-leather memorandum book from his pocket and consulted it.

'At 2:45 or thereabouts, she left th' house, arrivin' at th' Ocean Trust Company at 2:55, five minutes before th' instytootion closed for th' day. She drew out three hundred an' thirty dollars an' sixty-five cents, an' left th' bank, goin' to Madame Gerard's, where she tried on a party dress for th' dance which was bein' given at her house that night.

'She left Madame Gerard's at 4:02, leavin' orders for th' dress to be delivered to her house immeejately, an' dismissed her sho-fur at th' corner o' Dean an' Tunlaw Streets, sayin' she was goin' to deliver some vegytables an' what-not to a pore family she an' some o' her friends was keepin' till their oldman gits let out o' jail – twas meself an' Clancey, me buddy, that put him there when we caught him red-handed in a job o' housebreakin', too.

'Well, to return to th' young lady, she stopped at Pete Bacigalupo's store in Tunlaw Street an' bought a basket o' fruit an' canned things, at 4:30, an'—' He clamped his long-suffering derby between his knees and spread his hands emptily before us.

'Yes, "and"—?' de Grandin prompted, dropping the glowing end of his cigarette into his coffee cup.

'An' that's all,' responded the Irishman. 'She just walked off, an' no one ain't seen her since, sor.'

'But – *cordieu!* – such things do not occur, my friend,' de Grandin protested. 'Somewhere you have overlooked a factor in this puzzle. You say no one saw her later? Have you nothing whatever to add to the tale?'

'Well' – the detective grinned at him – 'there are one or two little incidents, but they ain't of any importance in th' case, as far as I can see. Just as she left Pete's store an old gink tried to "make" her, but she give him th' air, an' he went off an' didn't bother her no more.

'I'd a' liked to seen th' old boy, at that. Day before yesterday there was an old felly hangin' 'round by the silk mills, annoyin' th' gurrls as they come off from work. Clancey, me mate, saw 'im an' started to take 'im up, an' darned if th' old rummy wasn't strong as a bull. D'ye know, he broke clean away from Clancey an' darn near broke his arm, in th' bargain? Belike 'twas th' same man accosted Miss Norman outside Pete's store.'

'Ah?' de Grandin's slender, white fingers began beating a devil's tattoo on the tablecloth. 'And who was it saw this old man annoy the lady *hein?*'

Costello grinned widely, ''Twas Peter Bacigalupo himself, sor,' he answered. 'Pete swore he recognized th' old geezer as havin' come to his store a month or so ago in an autymobile an bought up all his entire stock o' garlic. Huh! Th' fool dago said he wouldn't a gone after th' felly for a hundred dollars – said he had th' pink-eye, or th' evil eye, or some such thing. Them wops sure do burn me up!'

'*Dieu et le diable!*' de Grandin leaped up, oversetting his chair in his mad haste. 'And we sit here like three *poissons d'avril* – like poor fish – while he works his devilish will on her! Quick, Sergeant! Quick, Friend Trowbridge! Your hats, your coats; the motor! Oh, make haste, my friends, fly, fly, I implore you; even now it may be too late!'

As though all the fiends of pandemonium were at his heels he raced from the breakfast room, up the stairs, three steps at a stride, and down the upper hall toward his bedroom. Nor did he cease his shouted demands for haste throughout his wild flight.

'Cuckoo?' The sergeant tapped his forehead significantly.

I shook my head as I hastened to the hall for my driving clothes. 'No,' I answered, shrugging into my topcoat, 'he's got a reason for everything he does; but you and I can't always see it, Sergeant.'

'You said a mouthful that time, doc,' he agreed, pulling his hat down over his ears. 'He's the darndest, craziest Frog I ever seen, but, at that, he's got more sense than nine men out o'ten.'

'To Rupleysville, Friend Trowbridge,' de Grandin shouted

as he leaped into the seat beside me. 'Make haste, I do implore you. Oh, Jules de Grandin, your grandfather was an imbecile and all your ancestors were idiots, but you are the greatest zany in the family. Why, oh, why, do you require a sunstroke before you can see the light, foolish one?'

I swung the machine down the pike at highest legal speed, but the little Frenchman kept urging greater haste. '*Sang de Dieu, sang de Saint Denis, sang du diable!*' he wailed despairingly. 'Can you not make this abominable car go faster, Friend Trowbridge? Oh, ah, *helas*, if we are too late! I shall hate myself, I shall loathe myself – *pardieu*, I shall become a Carmelite friar and eat fish and abstain from swearing!'

We took scarcely twenty minutes to cover the ten-mile stretch to the aggregation of tumbledown houses which was Rupleysville, but my companion was almost frothing at the mouth when I drew up before the local apology for a hotel.

'Tell me, *Monsieur*,' de Grandin cried as he thrust the hostelry's door open with his foot and brandished his slender ebony cane before the astonished proprietor's eyes, 'tell me of *un vieillard* – an old, old man with snow-white hair and an evil face, who has lately come to this so detestable place. I would know where to find him, right away, immediately, at once!'

'Say,' the boniface demanded truculently, 'where d'ye git that stuff? Who are you to be askin'—'

'That'll do' – Costello shouldered his way past de Grandin and displayed his badge – 'you answer this gentleman's questions, an' answer 'em quick an' accurate, or I'll run you in, see?'

The innkeeper's defiant attitude melted before the

detective's show of authority like frost before the sunrise. 'Guess you must mean Mr Zerny,' he replied sullenly. 'He come here about a month ago an' rented the Hazeltown house, down th' road about a mile. Comes up to town for provisions every day or two, and stops in here sometimes for a—' He halted abruptly, his face suffused with a dull flush.

'Yeah?' Costello replied. 'Go on an' say it; we all know what he stops here for. Now listen, buddy' – he stabbed the air two inches before the man's face with a blunt forefinger – 'I don't know whether this here Zerny felly's got a tellyphone or not, but if he has, you just lay off tellin' 'im we're comin'; git me? If anyone's tipped him off when we git to his place I'm comin' back here and plaster more padlocks on this place o' yours than Sousa's got medals on his blouse. Savvy?'

'Come away, *Sergent*; come away, Friend Trowbridge,' de Grandin besought almost tearfully. 'Bandy not words with the *cancre*; we have work to do!'

Down the road we raced in the direction indicated by the hotelkeeper, till the picket fence and broken shutters of the Hazelton house showed among a rank copse of second-growth pines at the bend of the highway.

The shrewd wind of early spring was moaning and soughing among the black boughs of the pine trees as we ran toward the house, and though it was bright with sunshine on the road, there was chill and shadow about us as we climbed the sagging steps of the old building's ruined piazza and paused breathlessly before the paintless front door.

'Shall I knock?' Costello asked dubiously, involuntarily sinking his voice to a whisper.

'But no,' de Grandin answered in a low voice, 'what we have to do here must be done quietly, my friends.'

He leaned forward and tried the doorknob with a light,

tentative touch. The door gave under his hand, swinging inward on protesting hinges, and we tiptoed into a dark, dust-carpeted hall. A shaft of sunlight, slanting downward from a chink in one of the window shutters, showed innumerable dust-motes flying lazily in the air, and laid a bright oval of light against the warped floor-boards.

'Huh, empty as a pork-butcher's in Jerusalem,' Costello commented disgustedly, looking about the unfurnished rooms, but de Grandin seized him by the elbow with one hand while he pointed toward the floor with the ferrule of his slender ebony walking stick.

'Empty, perhaps,' he conceded in a low, vibrant whisper, 'but not recently, *mon ami*.' Where the sunbeam splashed on the uneven floor there showed distinctly the mark of a booted foot, two marks – a trail of them leading toward the rear of the house.

'Right y'are,' the detective agreed. 'Someone's left his track here, an' no mistake.'

'Ha!' de Grandin bent forward till it seemed the tip of his highbridged nose would impinge on the tracks. 'Gentlemen,' he rose and pointed forward into the gloom with a dramatic flourish of his cane, 'they are here! Let us go!'

Through the gloomy hall we followed the trail by the aid of Costello's flashlight, stepping carefully to avoid creaking boards as much as possible. At length the marks stopped abruptly in the center of what had formerly been the kitchen. A disturbance in the dust told where the walker had doubled on his tracks in a short circle, and a ringbolt in the floor gave notice that we stood above a trap-door of some sort.

'Careful, Friend Costello,' de Grandin warned, 'have ready your flashlight when I fling back the trap. Ready? *Un – deux – trois!*'

He bent, seized the rusty ringbolt and heaved the trap-door back so violently that it flew back with a thundering crash on the floor beyond.

The cavern had originally been a cellar for the storage of food, it seemed, and was brick-walled and earth-floored, without window or ventilation opening of any sort. A dank, musty odor assaulted our nostrils as we leaned forward, but further impressions were blotted out by the sight directly beneath us.

White as a figurine of carven alabaster, the slender, bare body of a girl lay in sharp reverse silhouette against the darkness of the cavern floor, her ankles crossed and firmly lashed to a stake in the earth, one hand doubled behind her back in the position of a wrestler's hammerlock grip, and made firm to a peg in the floor, while the left arm was extended straight outward, its wrist pinioned to another stake. Her luxuriant fair hair had been knotted together at the ends, then staked to the ground, so that her head was drawn far back, exposing her rounded throat to its fullest extent, and on the earth beneath her left breast and beside her throat stood two porcelain bowls.

Crouched over her was the relic of a man, an old, old, hideously wrinkled witch-husband, with matted white hair and beard. In one hand he held a long, gleaming, double-edged dirk while with the other he caressed the girl's smooth throat with gloating strokes of his skeleton fingers.

'Howly Mither!' Costello's County Galway brogue broke through his American accent at the horrid sight below us.

'My God!' I exclaimed, all the breath in my lungs suddenly seeming to freeze in my throat.

'*Bonjour, Monsieur le Vampire!*' Jules de Grandin greeted nonchalantly, leaping to the earth beside the pinioned girl and waving his walking stick airily. 'By the horns of the devil, but you have led us a merry chase, Baron

Lajos Czuczron of Transylvania!'

The crouching creature emitted a bellow of fury and leaped toward de Grandin, brandishing his knife.

The Frenchman gave ground with a quick, catlike leap and grasped his slender cane in both hands near the top. Next instant he had ripped the lower part of the stick away, displaying a fine, three-edged blade set in the cane's handle, and swung his point toward the frothing-mouthed thing which mouthed and gibbered like a beast at bay. 'A-ah?' he cried with a mocking, upward-lilting accent. 'You did not expect this, eh, Friend Blood-drinker? I give you the party-of-surprize, *n'est-ce-pas*? The centuries have been long, *mon vieux;* but the reckoning has come at last. Say, now will you die by the steel, or by starvation?'

The aged monster fairly champed his gleaming teeth in fury. His eyes seemed larger, rounder, to gleam like the eyes of a dog in the firelight, as he launched himself toward the little Frenchman.

'*Sa-ha!*' the Frenchman sank backward on one foot, then straightened suddenly forward, stiffening his sword-arm and plunging his point directly into the charging beastman's distended, red mouth. A scream of mingled rage and pain filled the cavern with deafening shrillness, and the monster half turned, as though on an invisible pivot, clawed with horrid impotence at the wire-fine blade of de Grandin's rapier, then sank slowly to the earth, his death cry stilled to a sickening gurgle as his throat filled with blood.

'*Fini!*' de Grandin commented laconically, drawing out his handkerchief and wiping his blade with meticulous care, then cutting the unconscious girl's bonds with his pocket-knife. 'Drop down your overcoat, Friend Trowbridge,' he added, 'that we may cover the poor child's nudity until we can piece out a wardrobe for her.'

'Now, then' – as he raised her to meet the hands Costello and I extended into the pit – 'if we clothe her in the motor rug, your jacket, *Sergent*, Friend Trowbridge's topcoat and my shoes, she will be safe from the chill. *Parbleu*, I have seen women refugees from the Boche who could not boast so complete a toilette!'

With Esther Norman, hastily clothed in her patchwork assortment of garments, wedged in the front seat between de Grandin and me, we began our triumphant journey home.

'An' would ye mind tellin' me how ye knew where to look for th' young lady, Dr de Grandin, sor?' Detective Sergeant Costello asked respectfully, leaning forward from the rear seat of the car.

'Wait, wait, my friend,' de Grandin replied with a smile. 'When our duties are all performed I shall tell you such a tale as shall make your two eyes to pop outward like a snail's. First, however, you must go with us to restore this *pauvre enfant* to her mother's arms; then to the headquarters to report the death of that *sale bête*. Friend Trowbridge will stay with the young lady for so long as he deems necessary, and I shall remain with him to help. Then, this evening – with your consent, Friend Trowbridge – you will dine with us, *Sergent*, and I shall tell you all, everything, in total. Death of my life, what a tale it is! *Parbleu*, but you shall call me a liar many times before it is finished!'

Jules de Grandin placed his demitasse on the tabouret and refilled his liqueur glass. 'My friends,' he began, turning his quick, elfish smile first on Costello, then on me, 'I have promised you a remarkable tale. Very well, then, to begin.'

He flicked a wholly imaginary fleck of dust from his dinner jacket sleeve and crossed his slender, womanishly small feet on the hearth rug.

'Do you recall, Friend Trowbridge, how we went, you and I, to the tea given by the good Madame Norman! Yes? Perhaps, then, you will recall how at the entrance of the ballroom I stopped with a look of astonishment on my face. Very good. At that moment I saw that which made me disbelieve the evidence of my own two eyes. As the gentleman we later met as Count Czerny danced past a mirror on the wall I beheld – *parbleu!* what do you suppose? – the reflection only of his dancing partner! It was as if the man had been non-existent, and the young lady had danced past the mirror by herself.

'Now, such a thing was not likely, I admit; you, *Sergent*, and you, too, Friend Trowbridge, will say it was not possible; but such is not the case. In certain circumstances it is possible for that which we see with our eyes to cast no shadow in a mirror. Let that point wait a moment; we have other evidence to consider first.

'When the young man told us of the count's prowess in battle, of his incomparable ferocity, I began to believe that which I had at first disbelieved, and when he told us the count was a Hungarian, I began to believe more than ever.

'I met the count, as you will remember, and I took his hand in mine. *Parbleu*, it was like a hand with no palm – it had hairs on both sides of it! You, too, Friend Trowbridge, remarked on that phenomenon.

'While I talked with him I managed to manoeuver him before a mirror. *Morbleu*, the man was as if he had not been; I could see my own face smiling at me where I knew I should have seen the reflection of his shoulder!

'Now, attend me: The *Sûreté Générale* – what you call the Police Headquarters – of Paris is not like your English and American bureaus. All facts, no matter however seemingly absurd, which come to that office are carefully noted down for future reference. Among other histories I have read in the archives of that office was that of one Baron Lajos Czuczron of Transylvania, whose actions had once been watched by our secret agents.

'This man was rich and favored beyond the common run of Hungarian petty nobles, but he was far from beloved by his peasantry. He was known as cruel, wicked and implacable, and no one could be found who had ever one kind word to say for him.

'Half the countryside suspected him of being a *loup-garou*, or werewolf, the others credited a local legend that a woman of his family had once in the olden days taken a demon to husband and that he was the offspring of that unholy union. According to the story, the progeny of this wicked woman lived like an ordinary man for one hundred years, then died on the stroke of the century *unless his vitality was renewed by drinking the blood of a slaughtered virgin!*

'Absurd? Possibly. An English intelligence office would have said "bally nonsense" if one of its agents had sent in such a report. An American bureau would have labeled the report as being the sauce-of-the-apple; but consider this fact: in six hundred years there was no single record of a Baron Czuczron having died. Barons grew old – old to the point of death – but always there came along a new baron, a man in the prime of life, not a youth, to take the old baron's place, nor could any say when the old baron had died or where his body had been laid.

'Now, I had been told that a man under a curse – the werewolf, the vampire, or any other thing in man's shape who lives more than his allotted time by virtue of wickedness – can not cast a shadow in a mirror; also that those accursed ones have hair in the palms of their hands. *Eh bien,* with this foreknowledge, I engaged this man who called himself Count Czerny in conversation concerning Transylvania. *Parbleu*, the fellow denied all knowledge of the country. He denied it with more force than was necessary. "You are a liar, *Monsieur le Comte*," I tell him, but I say it to myself. Even yet, however, I do not think what I think later.

'Then came the case of the young Eckhart. He loses blood, he can not say how or why, but Friend Trowbridge and I find a queer mark on his body. I think to me, "if, perhaps, a vampire – a member of that accursed tribe who leave their graves by night and suck the blood of the living – were here, that would account for this young man's condition. But where would such a being come from? It is not likely."

'Then I meet that old man, the one you call Indian John. He tells me much of the history of this town in the early days, and he tells me something more. He tells of a man, an old, old man, who has paid him much money to go to a certain grave – the grave of a reputed witch – in the old cemetery and dig from about it a growth of wild garlic. Garlic, I know is a plant intolerable to the vampire. He can not abide it. If it is planted on his grave he can not pass it.

'I ask myself, "Who would want such a thing to be, and why?" But I have no answer; only, I know, if a vampire have been confined to that grave by planted garlic, then liberated when that garlic is taken away, it would account for the young Eckhart's strange sickness.

'*Tiens*, Friend Trowbridge and I visit that grave, and on its tombstone we read a verse which makes me believe the tenant of that grave may be a vampire. We interview the good minister of the church and learn that another man, an old, old man, have also inquired about that strange grave.

"Who have done this?" I ask me; but even yet I have no definite answer to my question.

'As we rush to the Norman house to see young Eckhart I stop at an Italian green grocer's and ask for fresh garlic, for I think perhaps we can use it to protect the young Eckhart if it really is a vampire which is troubling him. *Parbleu*, some man, an old, old man, have what you Americans call "cornered" the available supply of garlic. "*Cordieu*," I tell me, "this old man, he constantly crosses our trail! Also he is a very great nuisance."

'The Italian tell me the garlic was sent to a house in Rupleysville, so I have an idea where this interfering old rascal may abide. But at that moment I have greater need to see our friend Eckhart than to ask further questions of the Italian. Before I go, however, I tell that shopkeeper that his garlic customer has the evil eye. *Parbleu, Monsieur* Garlic-Buyer you will have no more dealings with that Italian! He knows what he knows.

'When we arrive at the Norman house we find young Eckhart in great trouble, and a black serving maid tells of a strange-looking woman who bit him. Also, we find tooth-marks on his breast. "The vampire woman, Sarah, is, in the very truth, at large," I tell me, and so I hasten to the cemetery to make her fast to her grave with a wooden stake, for, once he is staked down, the vampire can no longer roam. He is finished.

'Friend Trowbridge will testify he saw blood on the stake driven into a grave dug nearly three hundred years ago. Is it not so, *mon ami?*'

I nodded assent, and he took up his narrative:

'Why this old man should wish to liberate the vampire-woman, I know not; certain it is, one of that grisly guild, or one closely associated with it, as this "Count Czerny" undoubtedly was, can tell when another of the company is in the vicinity, and I doubt not he did this deed for pure malice and deviltry.

'However that may be, Friend Trowbridge tells me he have seen the count, and that he seems to have aged greatly. The man who visited the clergyman and the man who bought the garlic was also much older than the count as we knew him. "Ah ha, he is coming to the end of his century," I tell me; "now look out for devilment, Jules de Grandin. Certainly, it is sure to come."

'And then, my *Sergent*, come you with your tale of *Mademoiselle* Norman's disappearance, and I, too, think perhaps she has run away from home voluntarily, of her own free will, until you say the Italian shopkeeper recognized the old man who accosted her as one who has the evil eye. Now what old man, save the one who bought the garlic and who lives at Rupleysville, would that Italian accuse of the evil eye? *Pardieu*, has he not already told you the same man once bought his garlic? But yes. The case is complete.

'The girl has disappeared, an old, old man has accosted her; an old, old man who was so strong he could overcome a policeman; the count is nearing his century mark when he must die like other men unless he can secure the blood of a virgin to revivify him. I am more than certain that the count and baron are one and the same and that they both dwell at Rupleysville. *Voilà*, we go to Rupleysville, and we arrive there not one little minute too soon. *N'est-ce-pas, mes amis?*'

'Sure,' Costello agreed, rising and holding out his hand in farewell, 'you've got th' goods, doc. No mistake about it.'

To me, as I helped him with his coat in the hall, the detective confided, 'An' he only had one shot o' licker all evenin'! Gosh, doc, if one drink could fix me up like that I wouldn't care how much prohibition we had!'

The Bloodsucker of Portland Place

SYDNEY HORLER

Vampire hunter: Dr Paul Metternich
Locality of case: London
Time: 1935
Author: English mystery novelist, Sydney Horler (1888–1954) was for a time in the thirties the main rival to Edgar Wallace as Britain's best-selling thriller writer. Initially a journalist, he became famous for his characters Tiger Standish, a tough superhero in the same mould as Bulldog Drummond, and the occult detective with a name very similar to the previous contributor, Sebastian Quin. Horler – whose books all carried the slogan, 'Horler for Excitement' – wrote several short stories about vampires as well as a novel, *The Vampire*, published in 1935, which allegedly sold over 100,000 copies – although it is very difficult to find today. The story concerns the pursuit by three men – neurologist Dr Martin Kent, Assistant Commissioner Sir Harold Lellant and vampire expert Dr Paul Metternich – of the mysterious Count Ziska who is the mastermind behind a 'hideous conspiracy which has for its object the slaying of human souls'. After many exciting incidents the trio finally trace the Count to his hiding place in London and demand that the Home Secretary take action. But convincing top government officials that the man is a vampire proves quite another matter . . .

The Home Secretary turned uneasily in his chair.

'I will be frank, Lellant,' he said: 'If I had not known you ever since we were at Harrow together, I should say you were stark, raving mad.'

'Completely tile-less,' supported His Majesty's Secretary of State for Foreign Affairs, whose weakness for slangy expressions was a perpetual thorn in the side of Sir Andrew McTaggart, the Premier, on the occasion of cabinet meetings.

'But, as it is, I'm prepared to go on listening,' resumed the first speaker.

'D'ye mind if I have a drink?' interrupted his colleague in the Cabinet. 'Perhaps you'd like one too, Lellant?'

'I should,' stated the Assistant Commissioner.

The man whom *The Times* had recently declared to be the best controller of British foreign policy for the past fifty years, poured out three stiff whiskies and added a little soda in perfunctory fashion.

'Now get on with your 'orrible story. I'm interested,' he said.

'The position is this,' said the Assistant Commissioner. 'Professor Metternich continues to receive threatening letters bearing the London postmark, and has come definitely to the opinion that this fiend Ziska—'

'Sounds like a saxophone player in a jazz orchestra,' drawled the Foreign Secretary, holding up his glass to the light.

'Please, sir!' pleaded Lellant.

'Yes – to the devil with your alleged humour!' growled the other Cabinet Minister, and, snatching a loose cushion, hurled it at the other's head. 'Go on, Lellant,' he urged.

'Metternich is pretty certain Ziska has his hide-away at the Sovranian Embassy.'

'"The Bloodsucker of Portland Place",' quoted the

SYDNEY HORLER

Foreign Secretary, picking up a newspaper and reading an imaginary headline. 'That ought to send the sales up. Make a good placard too – bit of a change, moreover, from all this Abyssinian stuff.' The speaker finished his drink, set down the glass and became serious.

'Well, Lellant, what do you propose?' he said. 'Assuming (*a*) that this fellow Ziska is a vampire, (*b*) that he has done all the things you say he has, and (*c*) that he's got to have a steel stake pushed through his what-not, with all the rest of the trimmings to follow, how can we help you? If he really does tuck himself away in Portland Place, may I remind you that his corporeal body is on Sovranian soil and that I have quite enough worry on my hands at the present time, thank you?' The Foreign Secretary brushed his fingers together as though rubbing them clean of dirt.

'Traynor is taking horse-sense, Lellant,' said Wadey, the Home Secretary. 'So long as this fellow is attached to the Sovranian Embassy, he can claim diplomatic privilege and is therefore above arrest. Virtually he cannot be touched.'

'My dear boy,' now drawled Traynor, 'how can you possibly arrest a bloke who – according to our policeman pal here – has the power of dissolving himself into a cloud of dust whenever he wants to save a taxi fare home late at night? No, Lellant' – returning to his serious mood – 'if you want to lay this nasty piece of work by the heels (although God only knows how you're going to do it), you'll have to find your own ways and means: Wadey and I cannot help you. And please understand that whatever you do must be done entirely on your own responsibility – heaven's blessings upon you if you pull it off, but don't expect any mercy if you fail! That's a sound rule of politics.' With a negligent wave of the hand, the Foreign Secretary lounged out of the room.

THE BLOODSUCKER OF PORTLAND PLACE

147

'Sorry, Lellant – but he's right: we can't go outside the regulations, you know.'

The Assistant Commissioner laughed.

'What's the matter?' enquired the Cabinet Minister. 'You used to be such a stickler for regulations yourself.'

'Yes,' replied the other slowly, 'only what I've seen recently rather puts me off the orthodox. All right, Wadey' – holding out his hand. 'Thanks for listening and being so patient.'

The Home Secretary frowned.

'There's something strange about you, Lellant – you've changed. There's no need for me to tell you, I suppose, that it would be silly for a man occupying your position to do anything – well . . .'

'Unorthodox? Outside the regulations?' supplied his listener.

'Damn it, Lellant – what *is* the matter with you?' demanded the politician.

'Ever read Shakespeare?' was the reply. 'That bit about "There are more things in heaven and earth" – I don't know if I'm quoting correctly, Horatio, but look it up for yourself.'

'I was right after all,' declared Wadey, after staring incredulously: 'you're as crazy as a loon.'

But the only answer he got was a puzzling grin.

For some after the Assistant Commissioner had gone, Wadey continued to frown. The story Lellant had just told him and Traynor with a wealth of circumstantial detail had been startling enough in all conscience, but what worried him almost as much was the peculiar manner of the man he had known intimately for the past thirty years. During the whole of that time Harold Lellant had been known as a martinet for discipline (and this included himself), a stickler for duty, and a fervent upholder of established rules and regulations – really a bit of a prig, if anything, when it came down to it. And yet here he was hinting that the very official gods he had worshipped and obeyed for so long ought to be dethroned and smashed into a thousand pieces! ... Queer; very queer.

Lellant walked quickly across the Green Park, cut up Dover Street, and let himself into a small service flat in Welbeck Street.

Paul Metternich rose to greet him.

'Your news?' asked the scientist anxiously.

The Assistant Commissioner flung his hat and gloves on to a table.

'It was as I had expected,' he replied. 'Both were afraid to take a chance. That's the worst of these confounded politicians – thinking of their jobs before anything else. That's unfair perhaps,' he amended quickly, 'but I'm sick with disappointment, Paul.'

The Professor took the other's arm.

'It is for my sake that you are saying this, my dear friend,' he said, 'and I thank you from the bottom of my heart. Did you tell them everything?' he enquired after a pause.

'Everything! I said that you had been receiving letters threatening your life and the lives of Kent and Miss Rodney practically every day, that you were certain these were being sent by Ziska, that you wished them to give me permission to demand the surrender of his body from the Sovranian Ambassador, as you believed he was hiding in the Embassy ... but it was no good, Paul; they told me that if I did anything it would have to be done entirely on my own responsibility.'

'I wouldn't ask you to do that, my friend.'

'But I'm *going* to do it!' declared the Assistant Commissioner. 'I feel I shouldn't be carrying out my job properly if I didn't. You have convinced me, Paul, that— Are you expecting anybody?' he asked, as the front door of the flat was heard to close.

'Only Martin,' replied the Professor, and the next moment Kent himself walked into the room. He was holding an envelope in his hand.

'Hullo, Sir Harold!' he said in greeting. 'I found this on the mat, Paul,' he went on.

The two other men noticed that Metternich turned pale as he tore open the envelope and read what was on the paper inside.

Without a word of explanation he handed it to the Assistant Commissioner.

Lellant read out the few typewritten words:

Tonight! The third check! – Ziska.

It was twenty minutes past nine by the BBC clock, Martin noticed, as the car passed Broadcasting House. Somewhere inside that great building an announcer was starting to tell millions of listeners the night's news. He wondered if this robot's voice would undergo any appreciable change if he knew that passing within a comparatively few yards of him at that moment was a small body of men who had pledged themselves to the committing of an act which would stagger the world by its audacity were it only to become known. These same men had sworn to commit murder, even if it was the most justifiable killing that history had ever known.

The car, the windows of which were screened by curtains, drew up at the end of Hallam Street, and the driver, having already received his instructions, turned.

Sir Harold Lellant gave a few last whispered instructions to his companions.

'Directly anyone comes, you others rush through the door. Barty, you will deal with the flunkey. As quickly as you can do it, gag and bind him and then join us. Above all, no shooting – that would be disastrous. I don't know how many men there will be in the place, but we ought to manage them if they become difficult. In any case, I dared not take anyone else into my confidence.'

Martin Kent listened like a man who was living through a dream; even now he found it difficult to believe that what had been so carefully planned would shortly happen. When Sir Harold Lellant had first outlined his plan in Paul Metternich's Welbeck Street flat only a few hours before, he had imagined for a moment that the Assistant Commissioner could not be serious: the whole thing sounded like the wildest melodrama. Lellant must have sensed this, for he suddenly stopped and said sternly: 'If you can think of a better way, Kent, please tell me – I am in your hands.'

He had protested vehemently against the suggestion at once; and Metternich, when his opinion was asked, had given unqualified approval to the scheme.

'It is audacious – but perhaps it will succeed through its very audacity,' he said; 'in any case, it is our last hope.'

No time had been lost after that. Two telephone messages were sent by Lellant. One brought Detective-Inspector Barty, and the other an elderly man carrying what appeared at first sight to be a small suitcase. The man himself looked completely nondescript.

'This is a very good friend of mine, Mr Albert Winson,' stated Sir Harold Lellant briefly. 'Winson, my three friends and I are going to a – well, a fancy-dress ball tonight, and it is vitally important that none of us should be recognized.

We want you to make the necessary alterations in our appearance.'

'Very good, Sir Harold.' Whatever private feelings the man may have had, he did not allow them to show either in his face or in his manner. Kent, watching him closely, felt that his discretion must have been tested before by the Assistant Commissioner.

It took the 'disguiser' a matter of two and a half hours to complete his work, and when he had finished he announced himself, in a quiet, laconic way, as pleased with his handi-work. Certainly the four members of the party which was shortly to undertake what Lellant (perhaps to quieten any doubts Winson may have had) once referred to as a 'gorgeous lark', when they looked in the glass, failed to recognize either themselves or any of their companions. Metternich looked at least twenty years younger, Lellant twenty years older than his actual age, whilst the normal appearances of Kent and Barty had both been transformed in distinctive ways.

And now, here they were, standing twenty yards or so from the mansion which was their objective.

Suddenly Lellant shot ahead; the three others closed quietly but swiftly behind him whilst he rang the bell of the Sovranian Embassy.

It was well that they did so, for the summons was answered within a couple of seconds by the appearance of a gorgeously uniformed footman.

Kent heard Lellant say: 'I am from the Foreign Office – I must see His Excellency the Ambassador immediately' – and then Kent, rushing forward, dived straight for the flunkey's legs. It was not until the fellow had been dragged into a room off the spacious hall and had been effectually gagged and his wrists and ankles bound with cord that

Martin remembered he had taken on Barty's duties instead of his own!

He was reassured by a voice at the door.

'Come on, Mr Kent – *I've* cut the telephone wires (as many as I could find, anyway), and now we're going through the house. Bit of luck for us that the place is practically deserted – all the staff seem to be having a night out – but then, I reckon the A.C. knew a thing or two about that before we started. He's a wise old bird is the A.C. – sometimes. Anyway, there's no sign of the Ambassador yet – he's the fellow we want to see. Next to His Nibs, that is, of course.'

The homely words of the detective-inspector, uttered in an excited whisper, brought a sense of reality back to Kent. He remembered the mission which had brought him and his three companions there that night, and, after making sure that his revolver was safe after the scuffle, he followed Barty out of the big room.

A curious sight met him: three men, obviously servants, had been dealt with in exactly the same way as the unfortunate footman. Paul Metternich, his eyes glowing, rose from the task of binding the ankles of the last man.

'See to the door,' Lellant now ordered, and Barty ran back through the length of the hall and drew the great bolts at the top and bottom, after turning the huge key.

He had scarcely finished when a man was seen running wildly down the broad staircase. He was dressed in a neat, dark suit, and Kent imagined him to be some type of secretary.

Lellant took command. As the man, staring goggle-eyed at the four strangers, practically took the last few stairs at a leap, the disguised Assistant Commissioner rapped out a command.

'Your hands over your head, please!' he ordered in French.

The man, after uttering a squeak like that of a frightened animal, obeyed.

The following interrogatory ensued.

'Where is His Excellency the Ambassador?'

The man choked.

'I do not know – and who are you?'

'That does not concern you.'

'But it *does* concern me; I am His Excellency's principal secretary … I must request you to oblige me with an explanation of your presence here; otherwise I shall be compelled to telephone for the police.'

'You will not find that possible. You need not be alarmed – we have no desire to do any injury to His Excellency. But you must tell us where he is – and quickly, please!'

'I have said I do not know where His Excellency is. I have been looking for the Ambassador in order that he may sign some important documents. But he does not appear to be in the Embassy – I was beginning to be afraid that something had happened to him. You—?' And a fresh wave of apprehension passed over the pale face.

'I can assure you that none of us has even seen His Excellency, although we urgently want to do so. Tell me, what is your name?'

'Nagy.'

'Do you know the Baron Ziska, Herr Nagy?'

Fear now gave way to loathing.

'That unspeakable scoundrel!' he cried. 'Yes – I know him.'

'Baron Ziska is attached to the staff of the Embassy, I believe?'

'That is so. But His Excellency has tried many times to

get rid of him. Only last night I heard him telephoning to Marke.'

Another voice broke in.

'Herr Nagy, will you be good enough to tell me if the Embassy has extensive underground quarters?' It was Paul Metternich who asked the question, and Martin Kent, standing by his side, saw his body stiffen.

The secretary expressed the surprise he must have felt by the glance he gave the speaker.

'Yes, there are several large cellars beneath the Embassy,' he replied, 'but I do not think they are used. Is it possible,' he went on, with a faint suggestion of humour, 'that you are British Secret Service agents and that you suspect the Sovranian Embassy of having a secret arsenal?'

Lellant cut in.

'Such a remark is ridiculous, Herr Nagy. My friend – this gentleman here – had a good reason for asking this question. Tell me, has the Baron Ziska a bedroom in the Embassy?'

'Yes – but—'

'We will see it,' declared the other promptly.

The inspection proved profitless – nothing was gained by a look at that small, sparsely furnished room on the third floor. All the time Metternich had been fretting impatiently, and now he could not restrain his eagerness any longer.

'The cellars!' he said.

Lellant caught hold of the secretary's arm.

'You will show us these cellars, please. And, by the way, when did you see the Baron Ziska last?'

'I have not seen him for some time – I had hoped that he had left London.'

'*Quickly!*' urged Metternich.

Martin Kent, too, was eager to get this grisly hunt over.

So far their luck had held good; but suppose the Ambassador, or some other highly placed official of the Embassy, returned and, finding such a gross liberty had been taken, rang up Scotland Yard or complained to the Foreign Office? The position then would be devilishly awkward for all of them – but more especially for Lellant.

The cellars beneath this Portland Place mansion which, until his death in 1896, had been the town residence of the fabulously wealthy and eccentric Earl of Dunheved, were certainly extensive. There were three of them altogether, and it was not until they came to the last that the bewildered-looking Nagy began to understand the reason for this strange exploration.

Then he noticed the man who had evidenced such an eager and curious interest in the underground quarters of the Embassy spring forward.

'You see that?' Metternich asked Lellant almost stridently. He pointed downwards with a quivering finger.

Martin Kent and Detective-Inspector Barty nudged each other. What Metternich's finger pointed out were distinct traces of blood scattered round what looked like a trap-door – which, judging by the dust dislodged, had recently been used!

Barty answered the summons of his superior before the words could leave Sir Harold Lellant's mouth: he seized the iron ring and, with a tremendous effort, pulled the trap-door up.

A snarl immediately sounded from below – a man-hunting animal trapped in its lair might have made such a sound.

Stooping below Paul Metternich's extended arm, Kent stared down into a black void lit only by a fitfully burning oil-lamp. At first he could not distinguish anything else, and, indeed, his senses were mainly concerned with fighting the nausea caused by the sickening reek that rose from the space beneath. It was a mixture of many noxious odours, but what the different constituents were he could not decide, beyond the fact that he thought he caught the smell of freshly turned earth.

Paul Metternich's eyes must have been keener than his.

'In the name of God the Father, God the Son, and God the Holy Ghost – *stop!*' he called, in a ringing voice.

By the time he had come to the end of that exhortation, Kent had leapt. He had intended to fall on the shoulders of the monster and thus stop him, perhaps, from completing his devil's work – if that had not already been done; but the sound of Metternich's voice had disturbed Ziska, and he had jumped clear, crouching like a beast, as Martin landed on the slimy floor of his secret den.

Kent knew he would never forget the horror of that moment. In an instant he had been able to visualize everything: the prone figure of the man in evening clothes, from whose body blood was flowing, the crouching figure of mankind's most deadly enemy regarding him with a cold, terrible malignancy, the cheeks full and ruddy as though his dreadful vampire's appetite had recently been satisfied, the lips drawn back from the cruel, pointed teeth, now showing themselves as abnormally long – the whole picture of Ziska so inhuman, so bestial, so abnormal that—

As he put his hands up to shut out the sight which was numbing and paralysing his nerve-centres, the *thing* sprang. He felt cold tentacles that seemed made of steel close round his neck, felt a rank, miasmic breath on his face – and then heard the voice of Paul Metternich speaking as from a great distance.

'Your time is finished, Ziska! For centuries you have lived and wrought your evil, but tonight you die! Yes, die in truth, so that mankind shall no longer be tortured by your attacks upon it.'

Kent opened his eyes. He could not believe he was still alive – alive, and unharmed so far as he could tell.

It was Barty who gave him reassurance by a touch of the arm.

He followed the detective-inspector's look. Still crouched like a vicious beast, Ziska, the vampire, was snarling his defiance at the Viennese scientist, who, with crucifix upheld in his left hand and a long-bladed sword-stick in his right, was advancing upon his enemy.

That Ziska was afraid was plain: his snarls changed to squeals as Metternich drew nearer.

'You thought you would frighten me by your threats, no doubt, but, instead, I was determined to seek you out, enemy of the world, worshipper of Satan, disciple of Lucifer, and destroy you.' Metternich's voice rang with an awe-inspiring sincerity; it was majestic with a righteous indignation and an unshakable courage.

'We did not come to this fight armed only with earthly weapons, Ziska: we came with spiritual shields. What my friend holds in that small box is holy water, consecrated only an hour ago.' Passing the sword-stick to Lellant, he took the box and threw the contents over the convulsed figure.

What followed Kent could never afterwards sort out with any degree of clarity – he heard Ziska scream, saw Paul Metternich, looking more than ever an embodiment of biblical vengeance, take the thin-bladed swordstick from Lellant and make a lunge with it. He watched the steel enter Ziska's body – and before his eyes the flesh, which such a short time before had been so repulsive, but so human, crumbled into dust . . .

'O God of Hosts, we thank Thee for helping us to vanquish our enemy!' cried Paul Metternich in a loud, clear voice.

Paul Metternich looked across at his listeners.

'Our work is done, my friends; we have suffered much, but gained the final victory – thanks to the help of God, Who has watched over us all through the battle, vouchsafed to us.'

Detective-Inspector Barty coughed.

'You wish to make an observation, my good Barty?' said the scientist, with a smile. He might have been addressing a favourite but somewhat backward pupil.

'I'd like to ask a question, if it's the same thing,' was the answer.

'Ask it, my friend.'

'Well,' said the detective-inspector, choosing his words carefully and speaking slowly, 'from what I read at the Metropolitan Library, and from what you told me when we were waiting outside Pit House that night, I had understood that a vampire had the power after sunset of changing himself into different things – a cloud of dust, a rat, a bat. Why didn't Ziska, when he knew he was up against it, as he must have known, try to pull off some of that magic stuff?'

'A shrewd question, Barty, and I am glad you asked it, for it shows that your mind works logically. Perhaps that explains why you are such a good detective . . . Now what you have said is true: according to all the information we possess on the subject, vampires do have such powers bestowed upon them by the Evil One' (here the speaker crossed himself), 'but that power, in the case of the infamous Ziska, was neutralized by the holy water. Once that had touched him, the Devil, his master and protector, was forced to retreat, leaving the servant who had served him for so many centuries defenceless . . .'

Metternich sighed.

'Now that my work here is done, I must think about returning to Vienna immediately – the Vienna, alas, that is only a mockery of what it was once.'

After he had seen his two visitors off, the Professor returned to the sitting-room of the small flat and sank heavily into a chair. In this, the greatest moment of his life, he felt unbelievably weary; reaction had come, and he was scarcely strong enough to stand it.

The Last Grave of Lill Warran

MANLY WADE WELLMAN

Vampire hunter: John Thunstone
Locality of case: Sandhill, North Carolina
Time: 1951
Author: Part American Indian, mystery novelist Manly Wade Wellman (1905–86), was born in Angola – where his father was then serving as a medical missionary – but returned to America for his education and later became noted for his historical works and stories based on folklore. His early fiction appeared in the pages of *Weird Tales*, *Unknown* and *Wonder Stories* and among his most popular characters werè David Return, a policeman on the reserve of the fictional Tsichah tribe, whom Ellery Queen called 'the first truly American detective'; Judge Keith Pursuivant who made a speciality of tracking down werewolves; and the intrepid John Thunstone, described by Dorothy McIlwraith as 'America's most popular vampire hunter in the 1940s and 50s'. According to friends of Wellman, Thunstone was based on the big, hulking author himself, while a number of the vampire cases the investigator encountered were drawn from real-life accounts of supernatural occurrences that had taken place in North Carolina and Connecticut. In introducing the following story, Wellman wrote 'It harks back to a long-ago newspaper I read, which told of such things apparently happening ...'

The side road became a rutted track through the pines, and the track became a trail. John Thunstone reflected that he might have known his car would not be able to travel the full distance, and in any case a car seemed out of place in these ancient and uncombed woods. A lumber wagon would be more in keeping; or a riding mule, if John Thunstone were smaller and lighter, a fair load for a mule. He got out of the car, rolled up the windows, and locked the door. Ahead of him a path snaked through the thickets, narrow but well marked by the feet of nobody knew how many years of tramping.

He set his own big feet upon it. His giant body moved with silent grace. John Thunstone was at home in woods, or in wilder places.

He had dressed roughly for this expedition. He had no intention of appearing before the Sandhill woods people as a tailored and foreign invader. So he wore corduroys, a leather jacket that had been cut for him from deer hides of his own shooting, and a shabby felt hat. His strong-boned, trim-mustached face was sober and watchful. It did not betray excitement, or any advance on the wonder he expected to feel when he finished his quest. In his big right hand he carried a walking stick of old dark wood.

'Yep, yep,' the courthouse loafers at the town back on the paved road had answered his questions. 'Lill Warran – that's her name, Lill, not Lily. Not much lily about her, nothin' so sweet and pure. She was a witch, all right, mister. Sure she was dug out of her grave. Nope, we wasn't there, we just heard about the thing. She was buried, appears like, in Beaver Dam churchyard. And somebody or several some-bodies, done dug her up outa there and flung her body clear of the place. Old-time folks believe it's poison bad luck to bury a witch in church ground. You do that and leave her, you might's well forget the church 'cause it won't be blessed no more. Ain't saying we believe that personal; it's country belief.'

But the courthouse loafers had not denied the belief in the necessity of digging up a witch. One or two of them contributed tales of Lill Warran. How she was no dry, stooped, gnarled old crone, but a 'well-growed' woman, tall and fully and finely made, with a heavy massive wealth of black hair. She wore it knotted into a great loaf at her nape, they said, and that hair shone like fresh-melted tar. Her eyes, they said, were green as green glass, in a brown face, and her mouth—

'Huh!' they'd agreed to Thunstone. 'You've come a far piece, and it's like you seen a many fine-looking women. But, mister, ain't no possible argument, you seen Lill Warran and that red mouth she had on her, you'd slap a mortgage on your immortal soul to get a kiss of it.'

And the inference was, more than one man had mortgaged his immortal soul for a kiss of Lill Warran's mouth. She was dead now. How? Bullet, some said. Accident, said others. But she was dead, and she'd been buried twice over, and dug up the both times.

Gathering this and other information, John Thunstone was on the trail of the end of the story. For it has been John Thunstone's study and career to follow such stories to their end. His story-searches have brought him into adventures of which only the tenth part has been told, and that tenth part the simplest and most believable. His experiences in most cases he has kept to himself. Those experiences have helped, perhaps, to sprinkle gray in his smooth black hair, to make somber his calm, strong face.

The trail wound, and climbed. Here the wooded land sloped upward. And brush of a spiny species grew under the pines, encroaching so that John Thunstone had to force his way through, like a bull in a swamp. The spines plucked at his leather-clad arms and flanks, like little detaining fingers.

At the top of the slope was the clearing he sought.

It was a clearing in the strictest sense of the word. The tall pines had been axed away, undoubtedly their strong, straight trunks had gone to the building of the log house at the center. And cypress, from some swamp near by, had been split for the heavy shingles on the roof. All around the house was bare sand. Not a spear of grass, not a tuft of weed, grew there. It was as naked as a beach by the sea. Nobody moved in that naked yard, but from behind the house came a noise. *Plink, plink,* rhythmically. *Plink, plink.* Blows of metal on something solid, like stone or masonry.

Moving silently as an Indian, John Thunstone rounded the corner of the log house, paused to make sure of what was beyond, then moved toward it.

A man knelt there, of a height to match John Thunstone's own, but lean and spare, after the fashion of Sandhills brush dwellers. He wore a shabby checked shirt and blue dungaree pants, worn and frayed and washed out to the blue of a robin's egg. His sleeves were rolled to the biceps, showing gaunt, pallid arms with sharp elbows and knotty hands. His back was toward Thunstone. The crown of his head was beginning to be bald. Before him on the ground lay a flat rectangle of liver-colored stone. He held a short-handled, heavy-headed hammer in his right hand, and in his left a narrow-pointed wedge, such as is used to split sections of log into fire wood. The point of the wedge he held set against the face of the stone, and with the hammer he tapped the wedge butt. *Plink, plink.* He moved the point. *Plink.*

Still silent as a drifting cloud, Thunstone edged up

　　　　　　　　　　　　　　MANLY WADE WELLMAN

behind him. He could see what the gaunt man was chiseling upon the stone. The last letter of a series of words, the letters irregular but deep and square:

HERE LIES
LILL   WARRAN
TWICE BURIED AND TWICE DUG UP
BY FOOLS AND COWARDS
NOW SHE MAY
REST IN PEACE
SHE WAS A ROSE OF SHARON
A LILY OF THE VALLEY

John Thunstone bent to read the final word, and the bright afternoon sun threw his shadow upon the stone. Immediately the lean man was up and his whole body whipped erect and away on the other side of his work, swift and furtive as a weasel. He stood and stared at John Thunstone, the hammer lowered, the lean-pointed wedge lifted a trifle.

'Who you?' the gaunt man wheezed breathily. He had a sharp face, a nose that projected like a pointed beak, with forehead and chin sloping back from it above and below. His eyes were dark, beady, and close-set. His face was yellow and leathery, and even the whites of the eyes looked clouded, as with biliousness.

'My name is John Thunstone,' Thunstone made reply, as casually as possible. 'I'm looking for Mr Parrell.'

'That's me. Pos Parrell.'

Pos . . . It was plain to see where the name suited the man. That lean, pointed snout, the meager chin and brow, the sharp eyes, looked like those of an opossum. A suspicious, angry, dangerous opossum.

'What can I do for you?' demanded Pos Parrell. He sounded as if he would like to do something violent.

'I want to ask about Miss Lill Warran,' said Thunstone, still quietly, soothingly, as he might speak to a restive dog or horse. 'I see you're making a gravestone for her.' He pointed with his stick.

'And why not?' snapped Pos Parrell. His thin lips drew back from lean, strong teeth, like stained fangs. 'Ain't she to be allowed to rest peacefully in her grave some time?'

'I hope she will,' said Thunstone. 'I heard at the county seat about how she'd been dragged out of her grave at the churchyard.'

Pos Parrell snorted. His hands tightened on hammer and wedge. 'Now, mister, what almighty pick is it of yours? Listen, are you the law? If you are, you just trot your law back to the county seat. I'm not studying to hear any law. They won't let her stay buried at Beaver Dam, I've buried her here, and here she'll stay.'

'No,' Thunstone assured him. 'I'm not the law.'

'Then what are you? One of them reporters from the newspapers? Whatever you are, get off my place.'

'Not until we've talked a bit, Mr Parrell.'

'I'll put you off. I got a right to put you off my place.'

Thunstone smiled his most charming. 'You do have the right. But could you put me off?'

Pos Parrell raked him with the beady eyes. 'You about twice as big as me, but—'

He dropped the hammer. It struck the sand with a grim thud. He whipped the lean wedge over to his right hand, holding it daggerwise.

'Don't try that,' warned Thunstone, and his walking stick lifted in his own hand.

Pos Parrell took a stamping stride forward. His left hand

clutched at the tip of Thunstone's stick, the wedge lifted in his right.

But Thunstone drew back on the stick's handle. There was a metallic whisper. The lower part of the stick, clamped in Parrell's grasp, stripped away like the sheath of a sword, revealing a long, straight skewer of gleaming blade that set in the handle as in a heft. As Parrell drove forward with his wedge, Thunstone delicately flicked the point of his sword cane across the back of Parrell's fist. Parrell squeaked with pain, and the wedge fell beside the hammer. Next instant Parrell was backing away hurriedly. Thunstone moved lightly, calmly after him, the sword point quivering inches from Parrell's throat.

'Hey!' protested Parrell. 'Hey!'

'I'm sorry, but you'll have to listen to me.'

'Put that thing down. I quit!'

Thunstone lowered the point, and smiled.

'Let's both quit. Let's talk.'

Parrell subsided. He still held the hollow lower length of the stick. Thunstone took it from him and sheathed his blade.

'You know what?' said Parrell, rather wearily. 'That's about the curiousest place I ever seen a man carry a stab weapon.'

'It's a sword cane,' explained Thunstone, friendly again. 'It was made hundreds of years ago. The man who gave it to me said it was made by Saint Dunstan.'

'Who was that?'

'He was an Englishman.'

'Foreigner, huh?'

'Saint Dunstan was a silversmith,' Thunstone told Parrell. 'This blade in my stick is made out of silver. Among other things, Saint Dunstan is said to have twisted the devil's nose.'

'Lemme see that thing again,' Parrell said, and again Thunstone cleared the blade. 'Huh!' grunted Parrell. 'It got words on it. I can't make 'em out.'

Thunstone's big finger tapped the engraved lettering. '*Sic pereant omnes inimici tui, Domine*,' He read aloud. 'That means, "So perish all thine enemies, O God."'

'Bible words or charm words?'

'Perhaps both,' said Thunstone. 'Now, Parrell, I want to be your friend. The people in town are pretty rough in their talk about you.'

'And about Lill,' said Parrell, so faintly that Thunstone could hardly hear. 'But I loved her. Lots of men has loved her, but I reckon I was the only one loving her when she died.'

'Tell me,' urged Thunstone.

Parrell tramped back toward the cabin, and Thunstone followed. Parrell sat on the door sill and scuffed the dirt with his coarse shoes. He studied the back of his right hand, where Thunstone's skilful flick of the silver blade had raised a thin wale and shed a drop of blood.

'You know, you could have hurt me worse if you'd had a mind,' he said.

'I didn't have a mind,' Thunstone told him.

Again the shoes scuffed the sand. 'I prized up my door stoop stone to make that marker for Lill's grave.'

'It's a good one.'

Parrell gestured to the edge of the clearing. There, in the shade of the pines, showed a mound of sand, dark with fresh digging, the size and shape of a body.

'I buried her there,' he said, 'and there she'll stay. At the last end, I reckon, she knowed I loved her and nothing could change it.'

A rose of Sharon, a lily of the valley. Lill Warran had been

MANLY WADE WELLMAN

no sweet lily, the court house loafers had insisted. Thunstone squatted on his heels.

'You know,' he said, 'you'll feel better if you talk about it
to somebody who will listen.'

'Reckon I will.'

And Poss Parrell talked.

Later Thunstone wrote down Parrell's story from memory, as a most interesting record of belief in the supernatural, and also belief in a most beautiful and wilful
woman.

Lill Warran was called a witch because her mother had been
one, and her grandmother had been one. Folks said she
could curse pigs thin, and curse hens out of laying, and make
trees fall on men cutting them. They wouldn't hear of things
like that happening by chance. The preacher at Beaver Dam
had sworn she said the Lord's Prayer wrong – 'Our Father,
who *wert* in heaven.' Which meant Satan, who'd fallen from
the Pearly Gates, the way it says in the book of Isaiah. No,
the preacher hadn't read Lill Warran out of church, but she
stopped coming, and laughed at the people who mumbled.
The old folks hated her, the children were afraid, and the
women suspicious. But the men!

'She could get any man,' said Parrell. 'She got practically
all of them. A hunter would leave his gun, a drinker would
leave his bottle of stump-hole whiskey, a farmer would leave
his plough standing in the field. There was a many wives
crying tears because their husbands were out at night,
following after Lill Warran. And Nobe Filder hanged
himself, everybody knows, because he was to meet Lill and
she didn't come, but went that night to a square dance with
Newton Henley. And Newton grew to hate her, but he took
sick and when he was dying he called on her name.'

Pos Parrell had just loved her. She never promised to meet him, she tossed him smiles and chance words, like so many table scraps to a dog. Maybe it was as well. Those who were lovers of Lill Warran worshipped her, then feared and hated her.

That, at least, was witch history as Thunstone had read it and researched it. The old books of the old scholars were full of evidence about such seductive enchantresses, all the way back to the goddesses of dark love – Ishtar, Ashtoreth, Astarte, various names for the same force, terrible in love as the God of War is terrible in battle. To Thunstone's mind came a fragment of the Epic of Gilgamesh, lettered on a Chaldean tablet of clay five millennia ago. Gilamesh had taunted Ishtar's overtures:

> Thou fellest in love with the herdsman
> Who ever scattered grain for thee,
> And daily slaughtered a kid for thee;
> Thou smotest him,
> Turned him into a wolf . . .

'It didn't prove nothing,' Parrell was protesting. 'Only that she was easy to fall in love with and hard to keep.'

'What did she live on?' asked Thunstone. 'Did her family have anything?'

'Shucks, no. She was orphaned. She lived by herself – they've burned the cabin now. People said she knew spells, so she could witch meat out of smokehouse into her pot, witch meal out of pantries onto her table.'

'I've heard of people suspecting that of witches,' nodded Thunstone, careful to keep his manner sympathetic. 'It's an easy story to make yourself believe.'

'I never believed it, not even when—'

MANLY WADE WELLMAN

Parrell told the climax of the sorry, eerie tale. It had happened a week ago. It had to do with a silver bullet.

For silver bullets are sure death to demons, and this was known to a young man by the name of Taylor Howatt, the latest to flutter around the fascinating flame that was Lill Warran. His friends warned him about her, and he wouldn't listen. Not Taylor! Not until there was prowling around his cabin by something that whined and yelped like a beast-varmint – a wolf, the old folks would say, except that wolves hadn't been seen in those parts since the old frontier days. And Taylor Howatt had glimpsed the thing once or twice by moonlight. It was shaggy, it had pointy ears and a pointy muzzle, but it stood up on its two legs, part of the time at least.

'The werewolf story,' commented Thunstone, but Parrell continued.

Taylor Howatt knew what to do. He had an old, old deer rifle, the kind made by country gunsmiths as long back as the War with the North. He had the bullet mould, too, and he'd melted down half a silver dollar and cast him a bullet. He'd loaded the deer rifle ready, and listened for several nights to the howls. When the thing came peeking close to an open window, he caught its shape square against the rising moon and fired.

Next day, Lill Warran was found dead on the foot path leading to her own home, and her heart was shot through.

Of course, there'd been a sheriff deputy down. Taylor Howatt was able to claim it was accidental. The people had gathered at Lill's cabin, and there they'd found stuff, they said. One claimed a side of bacon he said had hung in his smokehouse. And another found a book.

'Book?' said John Thunstone quickly. For books are

generally interesting properties in stories like the story of Lill Warran.

'I've been told about it by three folks who swore they seen it,' replied Parrell. 'Me myself, I didn't see it, so I hold I ain't called on to judge of it.'

'What did those three people tell you about it?'

'Well – it was hairy like. The cover all hairy and dark, like the skin of a black bear. And inside it had three parts.'

'The first part,' said Thunstone, 'was written with red ink on white paper. The second part, with black ink on red paper. And the third, black paper, written on with—'

'You been talking to them other folks!' accused Parrell, half starting up.

'No. Though I heard the book mentioned at the court house. It's just that I've heard of such books before. The third part of the book, black paper, is written on with white ink that will shine in the dark, so that it can be read without light.'

'Then them folks mocking me heard what you heard about the like of the book. They made it up to vex my soul.'

'Maybe,' agreed Thunstone, though he doubted that the people of the Sandhills brush would have so much knowledge of classical and rare grimoires. 'Go on.'

The way Parrell had heard the book explained, the first part – red ink on white paper – was made up of rather simple charms, to cure rheumatism or sore eyes, with one or two more interesting spells that concerned the winning of love or the causing of a wearisome lover to depart. The second, the black ink on red, had the charm to bring food from the stores of neighbors, as well as something that purported to make the practitioner invisible, and something else that aided in the construction of a mirror in which one could see far away scenes and actions.

MANLY WADE WELLMAN

'And the black part of the book?' asked Thunstone, more calmly than he felt.

'Nobody got that far.'

'Good,' said Thunstone thankfully. He himself would have thought twice, and more than twice, before reading the shiny letters in the black third section of such a book.

'The preacher took it. Said he locked it in his desk. Next day it was gone. Folks think it went back to Satan himself.'

Folks might not be far wrong, thought Thunstone, but did not say as much aloud.

Parrell's voice was wretched as he finished his narrative. Lill Warran had had no kinsmen, none who would claim her body at least. So he, Parrell, had claimed it – bought a coffin and paid for a plot in Beaver Dam churchyard. He and an undertaker's helper had been alone at the burying of Lill Warran.

'Since nobody wanted to be Christian, nothing was said from the Bible at the burying,' Parrell told Thunstone. 'I did say a little verse of a song I remembered, I always remembered, when I thought of her. This is what it was.'

He half-crooned the rhyme:

'The raven crow is a coal, coal black,
The jay is a purple blue,
If ever I forget my own fair love,
Let my heart melt away like dew.'

Thunstone wondered how old the song was. 'Then?' he prompted.

'You know the rest. The morning after, they tore her up out of the grave and flung her in my yard. I found her lying near to my doorstep, the one I just now cut for her gravestone.' Parrell nodded toward where it lay. 'I took her and buried her again. And this morning it was the same. There she lay. So let them all go curse. I buried her yonder, and yonder she'll stay, or if anybody says different I'll argue with something more than a law book. Did I do wrong, mister?'

'Not you,' said Thunstone. 'You did what your heart told you.'

'Thanks. Thank you kindly. Like you said, I do feel better for talking it over.' Parrell rose. 'I'm going to set up that stone.'

Thunstone helped him. The weight of the slab taxed their strength. Parrell drove it into the sand at the head of the grave. Then he looked to where the sun was sinking behind the pines.

'You won't be getting back away from here before it's dark and hard to pick the way. I'll be honored if you stopped here tonight. Not much of a bed or supper doings, but if you'll so be kind—'

'Thank you,' said Thunstone, who had been wondering how to manage an overnight stay.

They entered the front room of the little cabin. Inside it was finished in boards, rough sawn but evenly fitted into place. There was an old table, old chairs, a very old cook stove, pans hanging to nails on the walls. Parrell beckoned Thunstone to where a picture was tacked to a wall.

'It's her,' he said.

The photograph was cheap, and some slipshod studio artist had touched it up with colors. But Thunstone could see what sort of woman Lill Warran had been. The picture was half length, and she wore a snug dress with large flower figuring. She smiled into the camera, with the wide full mouth of which he had heard. Her eyes were slanting, mocking, and lustrous. Her head was proud on fine

MANLY WADE WELLMAN

shoulders. Round and deep was the bosom into which a silver bullet had been sent by the old deer rifle of Taylor Howatt.

'You see why I loved her,' said Parrell.

'I see,' Thunstone assured him.

Parrell cooked for them. There was corn bread and syrup, and a plate of rib meat, hearty fare. Despite his sorrow, Parrell ate well of his own cooking. When the meal was finished, Parrell bowed and mumbled an old country blessing. They went out into the yard. Parrell walked slowly to the grave of Lill Warran and gazed down at it. Thunstone moved in among the trees, saw something that grew, and stooped to gouge it out.

'What you gathering?' called Parrell.

'Just an odd little growth,' Thunstone called back, and pulled another. They were the roots called throughout the south by the name of John the Conqueror, great specifics against enchantment. Thunstone filled his pockets with them, and walked back to join Parrell.

'I'm glad you came along, Mr Thunstone,' said Parrell. His opossum face was touched with a shy smile. 'I've lived alone for years, but never so lonely as the last week.'

Together they entered the house. Parrell found and lighted an oil lamp, and immediately Thunstone felt the impact of eyes from across the room. Swiftly facing that way, he gazed into the face of the portrait of Lill Warran. The pictured smile seemed to taunt and defy him, and to invite him as well. What had the man leered at the court house? *You'd slap a mortgage on your immortal soul to get a kiss.* That picture was enough to convince Thunstone that better men than pitiful, spindling Pos Parrell could find Lill Warran herself irresistible.

'I'll make you up a pallet bed here,' offered Parrell.

'You needn't bother for me,' Thunstone said, but Parrell opened a battered old wooden chest and brought out a quilt, another. As he spread them out, Thunstone recognized the ancient and famous patterns of the quilt work. Kentucky Blazing Star, that was one of them. Another was True Love Fancy.

'My old mamma made them,' Parrell informed him.

Parrell folded the quilts into a pallet along the wall. 'Sure you'll be all right? You won't prefer to take my bed.'

'I've slept a lot harder than what you're fixing for me,' Thunstone quickly assured him.

They sat at a table and talked. Parrell's thoughts were still for his lost love. He spoke of her, earnestly, revealingly. Once or twice Thunstone suspected him of trying for poetic speech.

'I would look at her,' said Parrell, 'and it was like hearing, not seeing.'

'Hearing what?'

'Hearing – well, more than anything else it was like the sound of a fiddle, played prettier than you ever heard. Prettier than I can ever play.'

Thunstone had seen the battered fiddlecase on a hand-hewn shelf beside the door of the rear room which was apparently Parrell's sleeping quarters, but he had not mentioned it. 'Suppose you play us something now,' he suggested.

Parrell swallowed. 'Play music? With her lying out there in her grave?'

'She wouldn't object, if she knew. Playing the fiddle gives you pleasure, doesn't it?'

Parrell seemed to need no more bidding. He rose, opened the case, and brought out the fiddle. It was old and dark, and he tuned it with fingers diffidently skilful. Thunstone looked at him. 'Where did you get it? The fiddle, I mean.'

'Oh, my granddaddy inherited it to me. I was the onliest grandboy he had cared to learn.'

'Where did he get it?'

'I don't rightly know how to tell you that. I always heard a foreigner fellow – I mean a sure-enough foreigner from Europe or some place, not just somebody from some other part of the country – gave it to my granddaddy, or either traded it to him.'

Thunstone knew something about violins, and judged that this one was worth a sum that would surprise Parrell, if no more than mentioned. Thunstone did not mention any sum. He only said, 'Play something, why not?'

Parrell grinned, showing his lean teeth. He tucked the instrument against his jowl and played. He was erratic but vigorous; with training, he might have been brilliant. The music soared, wailed, thundered, and died down. 'That was interesting,' said Thunstone. 'What was it?'

'Just something I sort of figured out for myself,' said Parrell apologetically. 'I do that once in a while, but not lots. Folks would rather hear the old songs – things they know, like 'Arkansaw Traveller' and 'Fire In the Mountains'. I generally play my own stuff to myself, alone here in the evenings.' Parrell laid down the instrument. 'My fiddle's kept me company, sometimes at night when I wished Lill was with me.'

'Did you ever know,' said Thunstone, 'why we have so many fiddles in the American country localities?'

'Never heard that I recollect.'

'In the beginnings of America,' Thunstone told him, 'frontier homes were lonely and there were wild beasts around. Wolves, mostly.'

'Not now,' put in Parrell. 'Remember that crazy yarn Taylor Howatt told about shooting at a wolf, and there hasn't been a wolf around here since I don't know when.'

'Maybe not now, but there were wolves in the old days. And the strains of fiddle music hurt the ears of the wolves and kept them away.'

'There may be a lot in what you say,' nodded Parrell, and put his instrument back into its box. 'Listen, I'm tired. I've not slept fit for a dog these past six nights. But now, with you here, talking sense like you have—' Parrell paused, stretched and yawned. 'If it's all right with you, I'll go sleep a while.'

'Good-night, Parrell,' said Thunstone, and watched his host go into the rear room and close the door.

Then Thunstone went outside. It was quiet and starry, and the moon rose, half of its disk gleaming pale. He took from his pockets the roots of John the Conqueror, placing one on the sill above the door, another above the front window and so on around the shanty. Returning, he entered the front room again, turned up the lamp a trifle, and spread out a piece of paper. He produced a pen and began to write:

My Dear de Grandin:

I know your own investigations kept you from coming here with me, but I wonder if this thing isn't more interesting, if not more important, than what you chose to stay and do in New Jersey.

The rumors about Lill Warran, as outlined to you in the letter I wrote this morning, are mostly confirmed. Here, however, are the new items I've uncovered:

Strong evidence of the worst type of grimoire. I refer to one with white, red and black sections. Since it's men-

tioned in this case, I incline to believe there was one –
these country folk could hardly make up such a grimoire
out of their heads. Lill Warran, it seems, had a copy,
which later vanished from a locked drawer. Naturally! Or,
super-naturally!

Presence of a werewolf. One Taylor Howatt was sure
enough to make himself a silver bullet, and to use it
effectively. He fired at a hairy, point-eared monster, and
it was Lill Warran they picked up dead. This item
naturally suggests the next.

*Nobody knows the person or persons who turned Lill
Warran twice out of her grave.* Most people of the region
are rather smugly pleased at the report that Lill Warran
wasn't allowed rest in consecrated churchyard soil, and
Pos Parrell, grief-stricken, has buried her in his yard,
where he intends that she will have peace. But, de
Grandin, you will already have guessed the truth they
have failed even to imagine: if Lill Warran was indeed a
werewolf – and the black section of the grimoire
undoubtedly told her how to be one at will – if, I say, Lill
Warran was a werewolf...

Thunstone sat up in the chair, the pen in his fingers.
Somebody, or something, moved stealthily in the darkness
outside.

There was a tapping whisper at the screen Pos Parrell had
nailed over the window. Thunstone grimly forebore to
glance. He made himself yawn, a broad hand covering his
mouth – the reflex gesture, he meditated as he yawned, born
of generations past who feared lest the soul might be
snatched through the open mouth by a demon. Slowly he
capped his pen, and laid it upon the unfinished letter to de
Grandin. He rose, stretched, and tossed aside his leather

jacket. He stopped and pretended to untie his shoes, but did not take them off. Finally, cupping his palm around the top of the lamp chimney, he blew out the light. He moved to where Parrell had spread the pallet of quilts and lay down upon them. He began to breathe deeply and regularly. One hand, relaxed in its seeming, rested within an inch of the sword cane.

The climax of the adventure was upon him, he knew very well; but in the moments to follow he must possess himself with calm, must appear to be asleep in a manner to deceive the most skeptical observer.

Thus determined, he resolutely relaxed, from the toe-joints up. He let his big jaw go slack, his big hands curl open. He continued to breathe deeply and regularly, like a sleeper. Hardest of all was the task of conquering the swift race of heart and pulse, but John Thunstone had learned how to do that, too, because of necessity many times before. So completely did he contrive to pretend slumber that his mind went dreamy and vague around the edges. He seemed to float a little free of the pallet, to feel awareness at not too great a distance of the gates of dreamland.

But his ears were tuned to search out sounds. And outside in the dark the unknown creature continued its stealthy round.

It paused – just in front of the door, as John Thunstone judged. It knew that the root of John the Conqueror lay there, an obstacle; but not an obstacle that completely baffled. Such an herb, to turn back what Thunstone felt sure was besieging the dark cabin, would need to be wolfbane or garlic: or, for what grew naturally in these parts of the world, French lilac. John the Conqueror – Big John or Little John, as woodland gatherers defined the two varieties – was only 'used to win', and might not assure victory. All it could do, certainly, was slow up the advance of the besieger.

Under his breath, very soft and very low, John Thunstone began to mutter a saying taught him by a white magician in a far-away city, half a prayer and half a spell against evil enemies:

'Two wicked eyes have overshadowed us, but two holy eyes are fixed upon us; the eyes of Saint Dunstan, who smote and shamed the devil. Beware, wicked one; beware twice, wicked one; beware thrice . . .'

In the next room, Thunstone could hear sounds. They were sounds as of dull, careful pecking. They came from the direction in which, as he had seen, was set the closed casement window of Pos Parrell's sleeping chamber.

With the utter silence he knew how to keep, Thunstone rolled from his pallet, lying for a moment face down on the floor. He drew up one knee and both hands, and rose to his full height. In one hand he brought along the sword cane.

The pecking sound persisted as he slid one foot along the rough planks of the floor, praying that no creak would sound. He managed a step, another, a third. He was at the door leading to the next room.

His free hand groped for a knob. There was none, only a latch string. Thunstone pulled, and the door sagged silently open.

He looked into a room, the dimness of which was washed by light from the moon outside. In the window, silhouetted against the four panes, showed the outline of head and shoulders. A tinkling whisper, and one of the panes fell inward, to shatter musically on the boards below. Something had picked away the putty. A dark arm crept in, weaving like a snake, to fumble at the catch. A moment later the window was open, and something thrust itself in, made the passage and landed on the floor.

The moonlight gave him a better look at the shape as it rose from all fours and faced toward the cot where Pos Parrell lay, silent and slack as though he were drugged.

John Thunstone knew that face from the picture in the room where he had slept. It had the slanted, lustrous eyes, the cloud of hair – not clubbed, but hanging in a great thunder cloud on either side of the face. And the wide, full mouth did not smile, but quivered as by some over-whelming pulse.

'Pos,' whispered the mouth of Lill Warran.

She wore a white robelike garment, such as is put on dead women in that country. Its wide, winglike sleeves swaddled her arms, but it fell free of the smooth, pale shoulders, the fine upper slope of the bosom. Now as in life, Lill Warran was a forbiddingly beautiful creature. She seemed to sway, to float toward Parrell.

'You love me,' she breathed at him.

The sleeper stirred for the first time. He turned toward her, a hand moved sleepily, almost as though it beckoned her. Lill Warran winnowed to the very bedside.

'Stop where you are!' called John Thunstone, and strode into the room, and toward the bed.

She paused, a hand on the blanket that covered Parrell. Her face turned toward Thunstone, the moonlight playing upon it. Her mocking smile possessed her lips.

'You were wise enough to guess most of me,' she said. 'Are you going to be fool enough to try to stop what is bound to happen?'

'You won't touch him,' said Thunstone.

She chuckled. 'Don't be afraid to shout. You cannot waken Pos Parrell tonight – not while I stand here. He loves me. He always loved me. The others loved and then hated. But he loves – though he thinks I am dead—'

She sounded archaic, she sounded measured and stilted, as though she quoted ill-rehearsed lines from some old play. That was in order, Thunstone knew.

'He loves you, that's certain,' agreed Thunstone. 'That means you recognize his helplessness. You think that his love makes him your easy prey. You didn't reckon with me.'

'Who are you?'

'My name is John Thunstone.'

Lill Warran glared, her lips writhed back. She seemed as though she would spit.

'I've heard that name. John Thunstone! Shall I not dispose of you, right now and at once, you fool?'

She took a step away from the bed. Her hands lifted, the winglike sleeves slipped back from them. She crooked her fingers, talon fashion, and Thunstone saw the length and sharpness of her nails.

Lill Warran laughed.

'Fools have their own reward. Destruction!'

Thunstone stood with feet apart. The cane lay across his body, its handle in his right fist, the fingers of his left hand clasping around the lower shank that made a sheath.

'You have a stick,' said Lill Warran. 'Do you think you can beat me away, like a dog?'

'I do.'

'You cannot even move, John Thunstone!' Her hands weaved in the air, like the hands of a hypnotist. 'You're a toy for me! I remember hearing a poem once: "A fool there was—"' She paused, laughing.

'Remember the title of that poem?' he said, almost sweetly, and she screamed, like the largest and loudest of bats, and leaped.

In that instant, Thunstone cleared the long silver rapier

from its hiding, and, as swiftly as she, extended his arm like a fencer in riposte.

Upon the needle-pointed blade, Lill Warran skewered herself. He felt the point slip easily, smoothly, into the flesh of her bosom. It grated on a bone somewhere, then slid past and through. Lill Warran's body slammed to the very hilt, and for a moment she was no more than arm's length from him. Her eyes grew round, her mouth opened wide, but only a whisper of breath came from it.

Then she fell backward, slack as an empty garment, and as Thunstone cleared his blade she thudded on the floor and lay with her arms flung out to right and left, as though crucified.

From his hip pocket Thunstone fished a handkerchief and wiped away the blood that ran from point to base of the silver weapon forged centuries before by Saint Dunstan, patron of those who face and fight creatures of evil.

To his lips came the prayer engraved upon the blade, and he repeated it aloud: '*Sic pereant omnes inimici, tui, Domine. . . .* So perish all thine enemies, O God.'

'Huh?' sleepily said Pos Parrell, and sat up on his cot. He strained his eyes in the dimness. 'What you say, Mister? What's happened?'

Thunstone moved toward the bureau, sheathing his silver blade. He struck a match, lifted the chimney from the lamp on the bureau, and lighted it. The room filled with the warm glow from the wick.

Parrell sprang out of bed. 'Hey, look. The window's open – it's broke in one pane. Who done that?'

'Somebody from outside,' said Thunstone, standing still to watch.

Parrell turned and stared at what was on the floor. 'It's Lill!' he bawled in a quivering voice. 'Sink their rotten souls

MANLY WADE WELLMAN

to hell, they come dug her up again and throwed her in here!'

'I don't think so,' said Thunstone, and lifted the lamp. 'Take a good look.'

Moving, he shed light down upon the quiet form of Lill Warran. Parrell knelt beside her, his trembling hands touching the dark stain on her bosom.

'Blood!' he gulped. 'That's fresh blood. Her wound was bleeding, right now. She wasn't dead down there in the grave!'

'No,' agreed Thunstone quietly. 'She wasn't dead down there in the grave. But she's dead now.'

Parrell examined her carefully, miserably. 'Yes, sir. She's dead now. She won't rise up no more.'

'No more,' agreed Thunstone again. 'And she got out of her grave by her own strength. Nobody dug her up, dead or alive.'

Parrell stared from where he knelt. Wonder and puzzlement touched his grief-lined, sharp-snouted face.

'Come out and see,' invited Thunstone, and lifted the lamp from where it stood on the bureau. He walked through the front room and out of the door. Parrell tramped at his heels.

The night was quiet, with so little breeze that the flame of the lamp barely flickered. Straight to the graveside Thunstone led Parrell, stopped there and held the lamp high over the freshly opened hole.

'Look, Parrell,' Thunstone bade him. 'That grave was opened from inside, not outside.'

Parrell stooped and stared. One hand crept up and wiped the low, slanting brow.

'You're right, I guess,' said Parrell slowly. 'It looks like what a fox does when he breaks through at the end of his digging – the dirt's flung outward from below, only bigger'n a fox's hole.' Parrell straightened up. His face was like sick tallow in the light of the lamp. 'Then it's true, though it looks right pure down impossible. She was in there, alive, and she got out tonight.'

'She got out the other two nights,' said Thunstone. 'I don't think I can explain to you exactly why, but night time was the time of her strength. And each time she came here to you – walked or crept all the way. Each time, again, she could move no more when it was dawn.'

'Lill came to me!'

'You loved her, didn't you? That's why she came to you.'

Parrell turned toward the house. 'And she must have loved me,' he whispered, 'to come to me out of the grave. Tonight, she didn't have so far to go. If she'd stayed alive –'

Thunstone started back to the house. 'Don't think about that, Parrell. She's certainly dead now, and what she would have done if she'd stayed alive isn't for us to think about.'

Parrell made no reply until they had once more entered the front door and walked through to where Lill Warran lay as they had left her. In the light of the lamp Thunstone carried her face was clearly defined.

It was a calm face, a face at peace and a little sorrowful. Yes, a sweet face. Lill Warran may not have looked like that in life, or in life-in-death, but now she was completely dead, she was of a gentle, sleeping beauty. Thunstone could see how Parrell, or any other man, might love a face like that.

'And she came to me, she loved me,' breathed Parrell again.

'Yes, she loved you,' nodded Thunstone. 'In her own way she did love you. Let's take her back to her grave.'

Between them they carried her out and to the hole. At its

MANLY WADE WELLMAN

bottom was the simple coffin of pine planks, its lid thrown outward and upward from its burst fastenings. Thunstone and Parrell put the body into the coffin, straightened its slack limbs, and lowered the lid. Parrell brought a spade and a shovel, and they filled and smoothed the grave.

'I'm going to say my little verse again,' said Parrell. Standing with head bowed, he mumbled the lines:

'The raven crow is a coal, coal black,
The jay is a purple blue,
If ever I forget my own fair love,
Let my heart melt away like dew.'

He looked up at Thunstone, tears streaming down his face. 'Now she'll rest in peace.'

'That's right. She'll rest in peace. She won't rise again.'

'Listen, you mind going back to the house? I'll just watch here till morning. You don't think that'll hurt, do you?'

Thunstone smiled.

'No, it won't hurt. It will be perfectly all right. Because nothing whatever will disturb you.'

'Or her,' added Parrell.

'Or her,' nodded Thunstone. 'She won't be disturbed. Just keep remembering her as somebody who loved you, and whose rest will never be interrupted again.'

Back in the house, Thunstone brought the lamp to the table where he had interrupted his letter to de Grandin. He took his pen and began writing again:

I was interrupted by events that brought this adventure to a good end. And maybe I'll wait until I see you before I tell you that part of it.

But, to finish my earlier remarks:

If Lill Warran was a werewolf, and killed in her werewolf shape, it follows as a commonplace that she became a vampire after death. You can read as much in Montague Summers, as well as the work of your countryman, Cyprien Robert.

And as a vampire, she would and did return, in a vampire's travesty of affection, to the one living person whose heart still turned to her.

Because I half suspected all this from the moment I got wind of the story of Lill Warran, I brought with me the silver blade forged for just such battles by Saint Dunstan, and it was my weapon of victory.

He finished and folded the letter. Outside, the moon brightened the quiet night, in which it seemed no evil thing could possibly stir.

The Beefsteak Room

PETER HAINING

Vampire hunter: Professor Abraham Van Helsing
Locality of case: London
Time: 1960s
Author: English novelist and editor Peter Haining (1940–)
was a Fleet Street journalist and publishing executive
before becoming a full-time writer in the early seventies.
A decade before, he had become an enthusiast of the
series of Dracula films started by Hammer Films in 1958
and this led to friendships with the two stars, Christopher
Lee and Peter Cushing, who were responsible for creating
a whole new wave of interest in the horror classics.
Subsequently, Peter co-authored books with both actors,
Christopher Lee's New Chamber of Horrors and *Peter
Cushing's Movie Monsters*, in which they revealed
secrets of their careers and selected favourite horror
stories. Peter Cushing's portrayal of Professor Van Helsing also inspired the following short story, the first to
come from Peter Haining's pen . . .

The old man leaned heavily on his walking-stick as he turned out of the Strand and into Wellington Street. Before him loomed the colonnaded front of the Lyceum Theatre, which was at once so intriguing and yet so mysterious to him. He had been in London before, of course, but then he had had urgent business to attend to and no time for frivolous pursuits like going to the theatre. Now it was different and he at last had the time to satisfy one of his longest standing curiosities.

For a moment the bent figure stopped, pushed back the brim of his felt hat and adjusted his glasses. His rheumy eyes moved slowly up the features of the building, a thin smile crossing his deeply-lined face. In his mind, the old memories began to stir once again.

He moved on slowly, scarcely aware of the people hurrying by intent on their afternoon business, and turned into the theatre's vaulted foyer. A solitary figure was just visible behind the box-office grille. The old man spoke in a voice that was little more than a whisper.

'Excuse, I wonder might I have a ticket for this evening's performance, please?' His English was still as halting as it had always been.

'Stalls or circle?' the reply from behind the grille was flat, disinterested.

'Oh, the circle, I think. What time am I coming for the performance?'

'Eight o'clock.'

A single yellow ticket appeared beneath the grille. The old man slowly took out his wallet and paid without another word. If the ticket-seller had been more communicative he might have asked his opinion about the production ... but then that was the least important element of his visit to the theatre. He was getting very old now and travel was becoming increasingly difficult.

Doctor Abraham Van Helsing had come for just one last look at London – and especially at the place where Bram Stoker had first heard about vampires . . .

The huddled figure in the circle seat might have been asleep for all the notice he seemed to take of the performance. In truth, Van Helsing's thoughts were far away, searching with his mind's eye beyond the walls of the auditorium, hoping that his researches into where the Beefsteak Room might be would prove correct. That famous room where the great Sir Henry Irving had often entertained his guests at dinner after a performance at what was so eloquently known as 'The Sublime Society of Beefsteaks'.

Van Helsing, however, had learned the value of patience many years ago and was content to remain in his seat until the performance was over. He was not even tempted to leave it during the interval. Then he politely joined in the applause with the rest of the audience and rose to make his way to the stairs at the rear. As he was about to leave the auditorium, his pace quickened for the first time that day and his eyes grew brighter with expectancy.

Outside in the passageway with its ornate decor and framed posters, Van Helsing saw a door marked 'Staff Only'. If his calculations were correct, a corridor lay behind that door which would lead him directly to the room he was seeking. The room where, on a certain night in April 1890, a Romanian expert on folklore, Arminius Vambery, from the University of Budapest had regaled Irving and Bram Stoker – then the actor's manager – with stories of the Undead in his native Transylvania.

Deliberately holding back until the last member of the audience had disappeared, Van Helsing placed his hand on the handle of the door and turned. It was unlocked. He stepped quickly inside and silently closed the door behind him. For a moment he remained without moving to make sure no one had seen or heard him and also to let his eyes grow more accustomed to the darkness. Then he took a small flashlight from the pocket of his coat and switched it on.

The beam of light revealed a corridor just as Van Helsing had expected. He stepped forward purposefully. Around a corner the torch picked out another door. It was grimy and showed all the signs of not having been opened for years.

Van Helsing lifted the arm of his coat and, with his sleeve, brushed away a layer of dust. There, still unmistakable but very faded, were the words 'Beefsteak Room – Private'. The old man allowed himself a little sigh of pleasure.

The handle of this door also gave way under his touch, the hinges screeching from lack of use as they slowly swung open. Inside the darkness was almost tangible.

Van Helsing's light cut into a room that had obviously once been richly ornamented and hung with costly furnishings. Even the few remaining tables and chairs which were smothered in dust and hung with cobwebs bore the hallmarks of quality.

A smile lit up the intruder's face. His mind was now working quickly as he started to conjure up what the room must have looked like when it was full of lights and music, people and conversation, and tables groaning with fine food and wine . . .

He had not moved more than a few steps into the room when a noise in the darkness interrupted his thoughts. It sounded almost like another door being opened. But not quite. More like a lid being raised, he thought, puzzled at why he should think so.

Van Helsing's eyes narrowed in the gloom, and although he felt his pulse begin to race, he was not afraid. He had already braved so much during his long and active life.

Suddenly, he was aware of a figure in the shadows. The figure of a large, bulky man with a beard. A man dressed in an immaculate evening suit.

Van Helsing was hardly conscious of the figure moving, but almost at once the man had glided in front of him.

'Welcome to the Beefsteak Room, Doctor Van Helsing!' The voice seemed to be dredged up from deep inside the man, as if the vocal chords had not been in use for years. There was just the hint of a brogue in the accent, too. 'I have been waiting a long time for *you!*'

Now fear suddenly replaced the quickening pulse in Van Helsing's body. He stumbled backwards and involuntarily raised the hand which clasped the torch. In its beam he now saw that the beard was red while in the man's huge hands he was carrying a wooden stake and an iron hammer. The tools of his own profession. They were the last things that old vampire hunter ever saw as the ancient voice spoke again.

'My name is Bram,' it growled, 'Bram Stoker . . .'

The Night Stalker

JEFF RICE

Vampire hunter: Carl Kolchak
Locality of case: Las Vegas, Nevada
Time: 1970
Author: American novelist and screenwriter Jeff Rice (1944–) grew up in Beverley Hills but moved to Las Vegas in 1955 where his early career as a reporter won him the citation of Outstanding Young Journalist of Nevada in 1968. This led to scriptwriting for Hollywood, appearances in several movies, and the writing of the groundbreaking story of 'The Night Stalker' – a Las Vegas newspaperman on the trail of a modern day vampire which became one of the most successful TV series of the seventies, attracting an audience of 75 million people in 1972 – one third of American viewers – a television record that stood unchallenged for more than a decade. Carl Kolchak, the reporter-turned-vampire-hunter, was first introduced in an hour-long TV special and played by Darren McGavin, with Simon Oakland as his highly sceptical newspaper boss, Tony Vincenzo. Such was the show's success that Kolchack returned the following year to track down another monster in Seattle, and was then turned into a 20-part series, *Kolchak: The Night Stalker* in 1974 with McGavin now narrating his own stories of tracking down supernatural monsters. The programme was shown on both sides of the Atlantic and left an enduring memory with countless viewers. Here is the opening episode which began that unique TV legend . . .

Tony Vincenzo is a small, dried-out Brooklyn-born Sicilian of such commanding presence and warmth that for years he has been totally disregarded by the Cosa Nostra, the Knights of Columbus *and* the Italian-American club.

Vincenzo of the rapier wit: 'Where else would you put a "discard" but in a trash can?'

Vincenzo didn't think it was worth speculation even though a police coverup was as plain as flies in a pail of milk.

By the end of the fourth day, after getting my fill of cold stares from Chief Butcher, Sheriff Reese Lane and the d.a. himself, I *knew* something was up. Fortunately, I still had friends among the undertaking trade who would, for a generous stipend, look the other way while I performed some mild necrophilic investigations.

I first saw what was left of Cheryl Ann Hughes late Wednesday afternoon, April 29, in the cold room of The Willows, one of our town's 'leading' undertaking establishments. At first, I, too, in my untrained way, saw nothing remarkable about the reasonably attractive young woman who had been neatly opened by the coroner's scalpel and then, just as neatly, stitched closed. It is usually best when examining four-day-old corpses to take as impersonal an attitude as possible. So I didn't really look at her face until I was through inspecting the body and was replacing the sheet.

Then I saw the two little holes.

At first I couldn't figure out what they might be. Largely, because I didn't try. They didn't register at all until I was sliding her back into her icy little nook. Then, some little ghost of a thought flitted through my mind and without thinking I pulled her back out and took a second look. I called in my well-bribed contact man and asked him what the holes were.

'Funny, I never noticed those,' he said.

Bullshit! He's a professional and he'd notice something like that right away. From his deliberately obtuse manner and his sudden myopia I gathered I was really on to something . . . but what? A girl who died under mysterious circumstances. A murder. No clues. No motive. But not just written off. Oh no! Written off and swept under the rug by the very people who should have been running around in a sweat trying to solve the crime.

With my usual tact, I managed to receive a 'first warning' from Vincenzo before the week was out: 'Quit bugging the PD. When something breaks, they'll let us know. Meanwhile, use your head and lay off. Whatever they're up to, they don't want any help from amateur bloodhounds like you. And neither does the boss.'

Marvelous! Vincenzo never ceases to amaze me. I have never figured out just why he became a newsman, and I use that term loosely. He's been one since '46 and has never had the ambition or curiosity to look outside to see if it was raining. We have locked horns so many times I've lost count. And it's sad because he is basically a decent, honest, hardworking man. But he plods! He toes the mark. He never crosses the line *or* the publisher, even if it means a scoop. I suppose some of this is unfair because, all in all, he has been a friend at times. OK. I'm unfair. But I can still smell out a story. Vincenzo's sinuses are perpetually blocked. He has all the news sense of a tree stump.

Add it up: dead girl in a garbage can; two puncture marks on her neck; no known enemies; money in her purse; not sexually assaulted; no established motive; no clues.

The night before the second victim, Bonnie Reynolds,

was discovered, I sniffed out the startling information from a County General intern that the Hughes girl 'didn't bleed at all during the autopsy. *All* corpses bleed.'

I was just formulating my 'crazy theory' when Mrs Reynolds was found and was alert for new developments on the Hughes thing when the call came in over the police radio.

MONDAY, MAY 4, 1970

I got there probably less than fifteen minutes after the first squad car. I got a good look – if anything like the sight of Bonnie Reynolds' crumpled form could be called a 'good' look. Of course, having to write it up before the autopsy, I was in no position to know that she, too, was found drained of every drop of blood. Nor could I, with any grain of common sense, openly speculate on that, especially since I hadn't been given any clearance to report the speculations and rumors about the first death.

Vincenzo made one mistake. He let me print the fact that there were two puncture marks in her neck even though he wouldn't let me link that fact with the similar marks on Miss Hughes. The public wasn't treated to that little bit of information until Carol Hanochek was found, clad in a see-through shortie nightgown and panties, the following Monday morning around nine, on the kitchen floor of her ground-level apartment on Ida Street, behind the Bird of Paradise Hotel.

MONDAY, MAY 11, 1970

Carol Hanochek was crumpled up in a corner between the stove and the kitchen wall. Her roommate, Sandi Jensen, a brokerage house receptionist between jobs, had gotten up, wandered into the kitchen and discovered Carol whom she thought had fainted or fallen. She spent a few anxious minutes trying to revive her, not noticing the neat puncture marks under her right jaw. Finally, she summoned an ambulance and the crew, knowing a 'dead one' on sight, made no further attempt to find the cause, but notified the sheriff's office.

Carol, a swing-shift cocktail waitress in the Bird of Paradise's show lounge, had gotten home (guesswork, here) around 2:15–2:30, poured herself a glass of milk, and had opened the back door of the kitchen for reasons unknown. (Fingerprints were later found on the outside knob that, while smudged, didn't belong to either girl.)

She had opened the door, and died. Suddenly, quietly, without disturbing her sleeping roommate only a few feet away.

Like Cheryl Ann Hughes, Carol was a blond, twenty-three, and just a bit over five foot five, though somewhat chunkier, weighing in at 130 or thereabouts. Like Cheryl Ann, she lived within walking distance of her job and had no car. Unlike either of the first two victims, Carol Hanochek had never been married and had never (Regenhaus' examination later revealed) borne children. She was described by co-workers and the lounge's bar manager to be gregarious, efficient and 'straight', with no steady boyfriends and no record of any trouble either at work or (to their knowledge) in her private life.

Something of a pattern had started to form and it was ugly. Young girls, all engaged in casino-oriented jobs and all working after dark, were dead. All were seen more or less frequently with men, none of whom were then (or later) very good suspects.

I was certain it was the work of one individual and assumed him to be a male, well over 200 pounds (he would need size and strength to accomplish his gruesome tasks quickly and silently) and definitely of doubtful emotional stability.

I also decided he was a white man. I'll explain that in a minute. I further decided that the individual involved got some kind of twisted sexual thrill from the killings, and the way they were performed.

None of the three women died from heart failure, burst blood vessels, crushed larynxes or broken necks. There were few bruises except just under the throat in both the first and third cases, indicating little if any struggle. Discount the badly bruised body of Bonnie Reynolds in this context because the bruises did not kill her (though it was revealed in her autopsy her right arm was dislocated, most likely in the fight).

No. They all died, Regenhaus said (later) from 'shock induced by massive loss of blood'.

How the blood was lost was where my theory differed from the professional investigators'. And why I must now digress once more to tell something of myself and my background. It will be dull but brief.

My given name is Karel but no one has ever managed to spell it correctly, hence the use of 'Carl'. In the course of my work I've been called worse names. I'm forty-seven, a second-generation American, old enough to get 'blooded' in Europe by almost two years of combat (most of it behind a typewriter) and lucky enough to have a trick knee left over from that war to miss out on that little 'police action' in Korea. I managed to graduate from Columbia University with a B.A. in journalism in 1948 without any distinction unless being near the bottom of my class qualifies in that respect.

My grandparents were immigrants. Pop grew up a hesitant agnostic and superstitious. Mom was a believer in people. My grandmother was a shadowy figure in my life as she died of heart failure two years after Pop was born. I was closest to my grandpop, Anton, a cabinetmaker from Rumania with a penchant for telling his young grandson endless folktales in the dark of night. But always with a grain of salt included, or a few historical facts as footnotes, such as his disclosure to me that there really was a 'Count Dracula', a fifteenth-century warlord known as 'The Impaler' because he used to pin his enemies to the ground with stakes for entertainment. It was said he often drank the blood of his victims at dinner, his cup a human skull. These were the fairy-tales of *my* childhood. They led me to the movie house on Saturdays and kept me up half the night afterwards. Then I grew up and forgot all about my fairy-tales when Adolph Hitler proved to the world that whole-sale horror could never be safely tucked away between the covers of a work of fiction.

Out of this kind of background, plus a slight knowledge of abnormal psychology acquired along the way from college to newspapering, I developed my initial theory, to wit: we had a nut running around who had taken all that bloodsucking stuff in movies too seriously. At least (I thought then) he had taken it enough to heart to use some kind of an instrument to puncture the carotid arteries of three women while somehow keeping them absolutely still and quiet. Somehow this character had managed to draw off ten to twelve pints of blood from each victim and, after due consideration, I surmised that, in his twisted logic, he *drank* the blood. This, as you will discover later, is not such a fantastic idea as you might think. And, he was very neat. Not a trace of blood was ever found except on Bonnie, around her abrasions.

He had to be big. That was obvious. And, as I contended earlier, white. By and large, if Vegas isn't a segregated community, it certainly isn't a fully integrated one. Ask the Westside residents if you don't want to take my word for it. It's called 'de facto segregation' when all the minorities (in this case, blacks) live in one part of town, even after most real-estate barriers are supposedly down.

Well, anyhow, he had to be white. Police in Vegas are ever vigilant for three things: narcotics; youths; and blacks. Preferably black youths involved with narcotics. Harsh judgement? Ask Municipal Judge Howard 'Buzz' Sawyer. He came out of the Vegas ghetto. Ask Police Detective Sergeant Roy Frisbee, also black, why a shooting in a residence near Huntridge is an assault with a deadly weapon while the same thing at a home near D and Monroe streets is a 'family disturbance'. The unofficial policy is that 'black people just act that way – you know, like animals.' It's changing, but very slowly.

So, I believed (without too much brilliance) that this faceless murderer's invisibility was due in part to the fact he was white. A black man would be much more noticeable in an almost ninety-nine-percent-white neighborhood like the one around Vegas High School, or the area around Ida, Winnick and Albert streets where they intersect Audree Lane (where Carol Hanochek was found).

But a white man, moving quietly about in the night might well *not* be considered suspicious in a viewer's mind. After all, Vegas is a twenty-four-hour town and nearly a fourth of its work force is up at what most people consider 'ungodly' hours. It is not at all unusual to see pale, distinguished-looking men in tuxedos carrying around lumpy sacks (that turn out to contain laundry) at 3:00 A.M. They are captains and *maître d*'s and baccarat dealers and musicians getting off late shifts. Women in bikinis and thongs doing their weekly marketing just before sunrise are common sights in Vegas.

No, he had to be white. And probably well-dressed. Possibly with a late-model car. A very middle-class type of character, not a sneaking, second-story type with turtleneck sweater, mask and tennis shoes.

Having spoken of my theory to Vincenzo and having met with his usual stone wall of resistance, I kicked it on up to the managing editor, Llewellyn Cairncross, who looked at me out of his one good eye and said with his customary tact, 'Bullshit! Kolchak, for years I have suspected you were mentally deranged and now I have confirmation of that suspicion. Why don't you go to Alaska or Florida or *anywhere* and plague somebody else for a change?'

So, very patiently, while jamming his office door shut so he couldn't throw me out, I went over everything I had come up with including the tight-lipped comments from the police department and the sheriff's office.

'OK, Lew. What conclusion do *you* come to?'

He started to fire off one of his legendary put-downs but it died before it ever rolled off his tongue. He slammed his mouth shut and glared at me with that bloodshot eye. Then he called the boss, Jacob E. 'Jake' Herman, editor and publisher. Herman the Heinous. Herman the Magnificent. Part crusader. Part charlatan. Once the scourge of crooked politicians; now a political king-maker. Before Howard Hughes came to our fair city, he was one of the state's biggest wheeler-dealers. And I suspect he could still teach the 'bashful billionaire' a few tricks. And probably will.

I went to sit with Jake's assistant, Bess Melvin, a truly lovely person who could smell a news item through two feet of reinforced concrete. The fifteen years she'd devoted to

Jake Herman showed in the frustration and tiny crowsfeet on her thin, attractive face. I've always thought it too bad that she didn't own and run the *Daily News*. Too bad for the public. And, as it turned out later, too bad for me.

The phone rang. Bess picked it up and handed it to me. The receiver growled with electronic venom. 'Kolchak, you miserable sonofabitch, if you ever, *ever* go over Vincenzo's head again . . .' I let him sputter on. When he paused for breath I got in my two cents' worth and he surprised me by telling me to write 'the goddamned piece' any way I saw fit. He told me to have Lew come into his office. I motioned to our distinguished managing editor and he entered the sanctum sanctorum.

I returned to my typewriter and explained to the public all the things I have just explained to you, put the words in United Press' best recommended style and headed for home in the sure and certain belief that on May 12 I would either be well on my way to a Nevada State Press Association award for the best crime story of the year, or out of town on a rail.

My story ran the next day with all my pet theories deleted. So much for Jake's much vaunted 'word'. It was not a propitious start at all. Later that day the district attorney called to inquire whether I might not be better used by the *Daily News* in preparing an in-dept study of the treatment of the mentally ill – from personal experience – up in Sparks, Nevada, the Bedlam of the Golden West.

TUESDAY, MAY 12, 1970

I sulked in my apartment off Karen Court until I got a tip from an informant that Parkway Hospital had just been 'knocked over'.

'Fine,' I said. 'Knocked over for what? Cash? Drugs? Equipment?'

'Blood,' said my informant.

'Blood?'

'Blood. Every damn container in the place. Clean sweep. They've had the sheriff's people out here all morning and have sent to the blood bank and to County General for some fill-in stock until they can get stores flown up from California.'

I hung up and just sat there, looking out of my living-room window at the gaudy, concrete, candy-stripe tent of the Circus a half-mile away on the Strip.

Man! I thought. You *couldn't* be this right! There really *is* a guy running around who thinks he's a . . . I couldn't bring myself to finish the thought. Parkway is less than a mile from my apartment – or where it was when I lived there. (I keep slipping. Can't help it.) So, I threw on some clothes and hied on over to talk with the chief resident, Dr Stoddard Welles. He confirmed what I'd been told on the phone.

'Everything, Kolchak. Seems blood type and Rh factor didn't matter. Every ounce we had. Why? I can't imagine. Stuff won't keep without refrigeration and even then, not forever. And there's no black market for the stuff that I know of. So why? Who knows?'

Dr Welles' question was largely rhetorical and it was clear he wanted to be off on his rounds.

I headed back to my place and my upstairs den. Unlike many of my trade, I am not – or should say – *was* not a clannish sort, never a joiner, and was neither a member of the Las Vegas Press Club nor a regular at any of the local bars and lounges (though I soon changed my ways, as you can see). When something takes hold of me I don't know, and if I can't think where to go with it (the 'something'), then I prefer to hole up in familiar surroundings and brood on it. That could be called laziness by some, and they'd be right. I *am* physically lazy. I'm about five feet ten, weigh about one hundred and eighty-five pounds going on two hundred, am going bald, and look a great deal like a boozy ex-prizefighter. My idea of exercise – lifting weights for example – is to lift one hundred and eighty-five pounds just once a day: when I hoist myself out of bed. I like to do my legwork on the phone as much as possible, at least in the preliminary stages of gathering data on a beat. But I surprise even myself when I've got my teeth into something solid because then I can go without sleep for three days and not even notice the meals I've missed.

I lay on my L-shaped couch for the better part of two hours while the sun moved past its zenith and began to dip towards the Charleston Mountain area. Then, as the sun eased below the top edge of my west-facing window and threw a little gleam in my eye, the idea came to me that FBI Special Agent Bernie Fain might be in a good enough humor to listen to me. So I slapped my half-empty Coors can on the coffee table and gave him a ring. He was in, and, for once, not busy, so I invited him up and thirty minutes later, over beer and pretzels, I went over what I had with him.

His interest was rewarding.

'You're nuts!' he opined.

I pressed on. 'We have three murders; we have a guy, at least one, maybe more, who goes around grabbing young girls – so far all casino employees – and draining them of their blood.'

'You're not supposed to know about that – much less talk about it.'

'Well, I do. What about your people, Bernie?'

'This is nothing for the Bureau to mess with at this stage.'

'True, but you could make some "unofficial" inquires for me ...'

'Like? ...'

'Like to other police departments in the cities where we get our greatest flow of tourist traffic: LA, Frisco, Denver, Chicago, St. Louis, Dallas, Miami, Boston and New York.

'Like check the hospitals in those cities, particularly the mental hospitals. Find out if there have been any other corpses like the ones found here – you know, bloodless and all that and not necessarily women. Also find out if there are any guys in these bug houses who think they're Count Dracula, even if they haven't done anything to prove it.'

Bernie just looked at me. 'You believe in vampires, little boy?'

'Very funny,' I said. 'Will you do it or are you just going to sit there like a cheap *gonif* and drink my beer?'

'I'll think about it. Repeat: *think* about it.' He glared at me. Everybody had taken to glaring at me. 'Vampires! Jesus H. Christ!'

I just sat there staring at the painting over my desk: a Transylvanian village street at night with the wind blowing sheets of rain into the face of a bluish, gabled building at a dirt-road intersection. I had that painting for years. It brought back the tales of my grandfather's homeland and was smuggled into this country with him when he was a lad. After this thing was all over and I had left Vegas, looking at it made me uneasy. I have since burned it.

I regarded Bernie with a sideways glance as he gnawed on a pretzel. 'You know about the blood stolen from Parkway Hospital?' I asked him.

'Ummhmm.'

'Know how much?'

'Ummhmm.'

'And the three dead girls. . . .'

'Ummhmm.'

'How much blood do you figure the average, adult-type girl has in her body?'

''Bout ten, maybe twelve pints.'

'So,' I jumped in, 'if we add up what I've given you, in the past sixteen days someone, or some thing, has taken thirty to thirty-six pints of blood from three women. And somehow, just by coincidence of course, thirty pints of blood were stolen last night from Parkway. Don't you see any possible link?'

'Hmmm. Couldn't say. Maybe yes. Maybe no.'

Bernie Fain. A fund of information. A wealth of suppositions. Brother!

'Stop drinking my beer and listen to me! Add up the thirty or so pints of blood missing from the three corpses and the thirty pints from the hospital and what do you get?'

'I get thirty to thirty-six pints missing from three women's bodies. Also, I get thirty pints missing from Parkway Hospital. I do not see an implicit connection between these things and I sure don't see any vampire written into any of this.'

'OK. Fine,' I told him. 'Close your eyes and it'll go away. I'm only working on theory anyhow. But check out what you can for me, please. I want to be on top of this thing when the next one . . .'

'What next one? How come you're so sure there'll *be* a next one?'

'That is part of the old Kolchak "vampire theory". Whoever this character is, he has a lust for blood so powerful

JEFF RICE

that fear of discovery won't hold him in check for too long. He's bound to strike again.

'Sure, I know this is crazy. So was the situation where that kid shot three dozen people from a campus tower at that Texas university. But I'm sure there's a connection between the disappearance of the hospital's blood and these murders.'

Bernie gave me one of *his* sidelong glances. 'Hope it won't disillusion you to know that the local law enforcement people share your views – somewhat – and are working along those very lines. If you'd stay in your office more you might hear things on the radio. You're getting too fat and too lazy.'

'Lay off my gut and proceed with your point.'

'Well, Kolchak, you're not the only one who likes to play detective. The police and sheriff's boys think they're pretty good at it, too. They think there's a possible connection between the missing blood and the dead women. Not that they buy that vampire crap . . .'

'. . . even in the face of no other easy explanation,' I broke in.

'. . . but even so,' he continued, 'they continue to probe and ask questions. Last I heard, they were waiting for a special report from two pathology experts who were flown up from the Los Angeles police department together with a small truckload of equipment. If you want to join me at the sheriff's office, they'll be meeting at 6:30 with Chief Butcher and the d.a. to present their findings. You may still be able to get into these little sessions if you haven't worn out your welcome with this stupid vampire theory of yours.'

'Well, thanks, I'll . . .'

'One other thing, Sherlock. Scuttlebutt is: one of the Parkway nurses saw something. Told the cops she noticed an orderly near the blood storage area last night. Her name's Amanda Staley. She only noticed him because he was new.'

'And?'

'And hospital records show no new orderlies hired in the past three months.'

'Got a description?'

'Ummhmm. About six-four and skinny. Pale. Dark hair. And bad breath.'

'Whoopee! Bad breath. That ought to be a great help in finding him.'

'If *you* were a professional detective maybe you could make some sense out of it. Since you are a *writer* and *not* a detective, it might be wise for you to stick to reporting and leave the detecting to us poor benighted professionals. To know what I know, all you had to do was *ask*. See you at 6:30.'

He left me feeling like a punctured balloon.

Beyond Any Measure

KARL EDWARD WAGNER

Vampire hunter: Dr Ingmar Magnus
Locality of case: London
Time: 1982
Author: American novelist, anthologist and publisher, Karl Edward Wagner (1945–94) began his working life as a practising psychiatrist but such was his enthusiasm for horror fiction – inspired by collecting the old weird and fantasy pulp magazines and amassing a huge and near-complete library of these rare publications – that he gave up this profession and subsequently became one of the most admired names in the fantasy fiction genre. Aside from his own novels and anthologies, Wagner continued several of Robert E. Howard's series' characters, including Conan and Bran Mak Morn, as well as using the name Kane for a series of stories, which he termed 'Acid Gothics', about a warrior-necromancer whose adventures take place before recorded history began. Wagner was a regular visitor to England and had only just returned to America from this country when he died suddenly. His knowledge and appreciation of London are fully revealed in this exploit of Dr Ingmar Magnus who describes himself simply as a 'consultant' but is actually deeply versed in all elements of the supernatural – especially vampires . . .

I

'In the dream I find myself alone in a room. I hear musical chimes – a sort of music box tune – and I look around to see where the sound is coming from.

'I'm in a bedroom. Heavy curtains close off the windows and it's quite dark, but I can sense that the furnishings are entirely antique – late Victorian, I think. There's a large four-poster bed, with its curtains drawn. Beside the bed is a small night table upon which a candle is burning. It is from here that the music seems to be coming.

'I walk across the room toward the bed, and as I stand beside it I see a gold watch resting on the night table next to the candlestick. The music box tune is coming from the watch, I realize. It's one of those old pocket watch affairs with a case that opens. The case is open now, and I see that the watch's hands are almost at midnight. I sense that on the inside of the watchcase there will be a picture, and I pick up the watch to see whose picture it is.

'The picture is obscured with a red smear. It's fresh blood.

'I look up in sudden fear. From the bed, a hand is pulling aside the curtain.

'That's when I wake up.'

'Bravo!' applauded someone.

Lisette frowned momentarily, then realized that the comment was directed toward another of the chattering groups crowded into the gallery. She sipped her champagne; she must be a bit tight, or she'd never have started talking about the dreams.

'What do you think, Dr Magnus?'

It was the gala reopening of Covent Garden. The venerable fruit, flower and vegetable market, preserved from the demolition crew, had been renovated into an airy mall of expensive shops and galleries: 'London's new shopping experience'. Lisette thought it an unhappy hybrid of born-again Victorian exhibition hall and trendy 'shoppes'. Let the dead past bury its dead. She wondered what they might make of the old Billingsgate fish market, should SAVE win its fight to preserve that landmark, as now seemed unlikely.

'Is this dream, then, a recurrent one, Miss Seyrig?'

She tried to read interest or scepticism in Dr Magnus's pale blue eyes. They told her nothing.

'Recurrent enough.'

To make me mention it to Danielle, she finished in her thoughts. Danielle Borland shared a flat – she'd stopped terming it an apartment even in her own mind – with her in a row of terrace houses in Bloomsbury, within an easy walk of London University. The gallery was Maitland Reddin's project; Danielle was another. Whether Maitland really thought to make a business of it, or only intended to showcase his many friends' not-always-evident talents was not open to discussion. His gallery in Knightsbridge was certainly successful, if that meant anything.

'How often is that?' Dr Magnus touched his glass to his blond-bearded lips. He was drinking only Perrier water, and at that was using his glass for little more than to gesture.

'I don't know. Maybe half a dozen times since I can remember. And then, that many again since I came to London.'

'You're a student at London University, I believe Danielle said?'

'That's right. In art. I'm over here on fellowship.'

Danielle had modelled for an occasional session – Lisette now was certain it was solely from a desire to display her body rather than due to any financial need – and when a muttered profanity at a dropped brush disclosed a common American heritage, the two *émigrés* had rallied at a pub afterward to exchange news and views. Lisette's bed-sit near the Museum was impossible, and Danielle's roommate had just skipped to the Continent with two months' owing. By closing time it was settled.

'How's your glass?'

Danielle, finding them in the crowd, shook her head in mock dismay and refilled Lisette's glass before she could cover it with her hand.

'And you, Dr Magnus?'

'Quite well, thank you.'

'Danielle, let me give you a hand?' Maitland had charmed the two of them into acting as hostesses for his opening.

'Nonsense, darling. When you see me starting to pant with the heat, then call up the reserves. Until then, do keep Dr Magnus from straying away to the other parties.'

Danielle swirled off with her champagne bottle and her smile. The gallery, christened *Such Things May Be* after Richard Burton (*not* Liz Taylor's ex, Danielle kept explaining and got laughs each time), was ajostle with friends and well-wishers – as were most of the shops tonight: private parties with evening dress and champagne, only a scattering of displaced tourists, gaping and photographing. She and Danielle were both wearing slit-to-thigh crêpe de Chine evening gowns and could have passed for sisters: Lisette blonde, green-eyed, with a dust of freckles; Danielle light brunette, hazel-eyed, acclimated to the extensive facial make-up London women favoured; both tall without seeming coltish, and close enough of a size to wear each other's clothes.

'It must be distressing to have the same nightmare over

and again,' Dr Magnus prompted her.

'There have been others as well. Some recurrent, some not. Similar in that I wake up feeling like I've been through the sets of some old Hammer film.'

'I gather you were not actually troubled with such nightmares until recently?'

'Not recently. Being in London seems to have triggered them. I suppose it's repressed anxieties over being in a strange city.' It was bad enough that she'd been taking some of Danielle's pills in order to seek dreamless sleep.

'Is this, then, your first time in London, Miss Seyrig?'

'It is.' She added, to seem less the typical American student: 'Although my family was English.'

'Your parents?'

'My mother's parents were both from London. They emigrated to the States just after World War I.'

'Then this must have been rather a bit like coming home for you.'

'Not really. I'm the first of our family to go overseas. And I have no memory of Mother's parents. Grandmother Keswicke died the morning I was born.' Something Mother never was able to work through emotionally, Lisette added to herself.

'And have you consulted a physician concerning these nightmares?'

'I'm afraid your National Health Service is a bit more than I can cope with.' Lisette grimaced at the memory of the night she had tried to explain to a Pakistani intern why she wanted sleeping medications.

She suddenly hoped her words hadn't offended Dr Magnus; but then, he scarcely looked the type who would approve of socialized medicine. Urbane, perfectly at ease in formal evening attire, he reminded her somewhat of a blond-bearded Peter Cushing. Enter Christopher Lee, in black cape, she mused, glancing toward the door. For that matter, she wasn't at all certain just what sort of doctor Dr Magnus might be. Danielle had insisted she talk with him, very likely had insisted that Maitland invite him to the private opening: 'The man has such *insight!* And he's written a number of books on dreams and the subconscious – and not just rehashes of Freudian silliness!'

'Are you going to be staying in London for some time, Miss Seyrig?'

'At least until the end of the year.'

'Too long a time to wait to see whether these bad dreams will go away once you're back home in San Francisco, don't you agree? It can't be very pleasant for you, and you really should look after yourself.'

Lisette made no answer. *She* hadn't told Dr Magnus she was from San Francisco. So then, Danielle had already talked to him about her.

Dr Magnus smoothly produced his card, discreetly offered it to her. 'I should be most happy to explore this further with you on a professional level, should you so wish.'

'I don't really think it's worth . . .'

'Of course it is, my dear. Why otherwise would we be talking? Perhaps next Tuesday afternoon? Is there a convenient time?'

Lisette slipped his card into her handbag. If nothing else, perhaps he could supply her with some barbs or something. 'Three?'

'Three it is, then.'

II

The passageway was poorly lighted, and Lisette felt a vague sense of dread as she hurried along it, holding the hem of her nightgown away from the gritty filth beneath her bare feet. Peeling scabs of wallpaper blotched the leprous plaster, and, when she held the candle close, the gouges and scratches that patterned the walls with insane graffiti seemed disquietingly non-random. Against the mottled plaster, her figure threw a double shadow: distorted, one crouching forward, the other following.

A full-length mirror panelled one segment of the passageway, and Lisette paused to study her reflection. Her face appeared frightened, her blonde hair in disorder. She wondered at her nightgown – pale, silken, billowing, of an antique mode – not remembering how she came to be wearing it. Nor could she think how it was that she had come to this place.

Her reflection puzzled her. Her hair seemed longer than it should be, trailing down across her breasts. Her finely chiselled features, prominent jawline, straight nose – her face, except the expression was not hers: lips fuller, more sensual, redder than her lip gloss glinted; teeth fine and white. Her green eyes, intense beneath level brows, cat-cruel, yearning.

Lisette released the hem of her gown, raised her fingers to her reflection in wonder. Her fingers passed through the glass, touched the face beyond.

Not a mirror. A doorway. Of a crypt.

The mirror-image fingers that rose to her face twisted in her hair, pulled her face forward. Glass-cold lips bruised her own. The dank breath of the tomb flowed into her mouth.

Dragging herself from the embrace, Lisette felt a scream rip from her throat . . .

... And Danielle was shaking her awake.

III

The business card read *Dr Ingmar Magnus*, followed simply by *Consultations* and a Kensington address. Not Harley Street, at any rate. Lisette considered it for the hundredth time, watching for street names on the corners of buildings as she walked down Kensington Church Street from the Notting Hill Gate station. No clue as to what type of doctor, nor what sort of consultations; wonderfully vague, and just the thing to circumvent licensing laws, no doubt.

Danielle had lent her one of his books to read: *The Self Reborn*, put out by one of those miniscule scholarly publishers clustered about the British Museum. Lisette found it a bewildering *mélange* of occult philosophy and lunatic-fringe theory – all evidently having something to do with reincarnation – and gave it up after the first chapter. She had decided not to keep the appointment until her nightmare Sunday night had given force to Danielle's insistence.

Lisette wore a loose silk blouse above French designer jeans and ankle-strap sandal-toe high heels. The early summer heat wave now threatened rain, and she would have to run for it if the grey skies made good. She turned into Holland Street, passed the recently closed Equinox book-shop, where Danielle had purchased various works by Aleister Crowley. A series of back streets – she consulted her map of Central London – brought her to a modestly respectable row of nineteenth-century brick houses, now done over into offices and flats. She checked the number on the brass plaque with her card, sucked in her breath, and entered.

Lisette hadn't known what to expect. She wouldn't have

been surprised, knowing some of Danielle's friends, to have been greeted with clouds of incense, Eastern music, robed initiates. Instead she found a disappointingly mundane waiting-room, rather small but expensively furnished, where a pretty Eurasian receptionist took her name and spoke into an intercom. Lisette noted that there was no one else – patients? clients? – in the waiting-room. She glanced at her watch and noticed she was several minutes late.

'Please do come in, Miss Seyrig.' Dr Magnus stepped out of his office and ushered her inside. Lisette had seen a psychiatrist briefly a few years before at her parents' demand, and Dr Magnus's office suggested the same – from the tasteful, relaxed décor, the shelves of scholarly books, down to the traditional psychoanalyst's couch. She took a chair beside the modern, rather carefully arranged desk, and Dr Magnus seated himself comfortably in the leather swivel chair behind it.

'I almost didn't come,' Lisette began, somewhat aggressively.

'I'm very pleased that you did decide to come,' Dr Magnus smiled reassuringly. 'It doesn't require a trained eye to see that something is troubling you. When the unconscious tries to speak to us, it is foolhardy to attempt to ignore its message.'

'Meaning that I may be cracking up?'

'I'm sure that must concern you, my dear. However, very often dreams such as yours are evidence of the emergence of a new level of self-awareness – sort of growing pains of the psyche, if you will – and not to be considered a negative experience by any means. They distress you only because you do not understand them – even as a child kept in ignorance through sexual repression is frightened by the changes of puberty. With your cooperation, I hope to help you come to understand the changes of your growing self-awareness, for it is only through a complete realization of one's self that one can achieve personal fulfilment and thereby true inner peace.'

'I'm afraid I can't afford to undergo analysis just now.'

'Let me begin by emphasizing to you that I am not suggesting psychoanalysis; I do not in the least consider you to be neurotic, Miss Seyrig. What I strongly urge is an *exploration* of your unconsciousness – a discovery of your whole self. My task is only to guide you along the course of your self-discovery, and for this privilege I charge no fee.'

'I hadn't realized the National Health Service was this inclusive.'

Dr Magnus laughed easily. 'It isn't, of course. My work is supported by a private foundation. There are many others who wish to learn certain truths of our existence, to seek answers where mundane science has not yet so much as realized there are questions. In that regard I am simply another paid researcher, and the results of my investigations are made available to those who share with us this yearning to see beyond the stultifying boundaries of modern science.'

He indicated the book-lined wall behind his desk. Much of one shelf appeared to contain books with his own name prominent upon their spines.

'Do you intend to write a book about me?' Lisette meant to put more of a note of protest in her voice.

'It is possible that I may wish to record some of what we discover together, my dear. But only with scrupulous discretion, and, needless to say, only with your complete permission.'

'My dreams.' Lisette remembered the book of his that she had tried to read. 'Do you consider them to be evidence of some previous incarnation?'

KARL EDWARD WAGNER

'Perhaps. We can't be certain until we explore them further. Does the idea of reincarnation smack too much of the occult to your liking, Miss Seyrig? Perhaps we should speak in more fashionable terms of Jungian archetypes, genetic memory, or mental telepathy. The fact that the phenomenon has so many designations is ample proof that dreams of a previous existence are a very real part of the unconscious mind. It is undeniable that many people have experienced, in dreams or under hypnosis, memories that can not possibly arise from their personal experience. Whether you believe that the immortal soul leaves the physical body at death to be reborn in the living embryo, or prefer to attribute it to inherited memories engraved upon DNA, or whatever explanation – this is a very real phenomenon and has been observed throughout history.

'As a rule, these memories of past existence are entirely buried within the unconscious. Almost everyone has experienced *déjà vu*. Subjects under hypnosis have spoken in languages and archaic dialects of which their conscious mind has no knowledge, have recounted in detail memories of previous lives. In some cases these submerged memories burst forth as dreams; in these instances the memory is usually one of some emotionally laden experience, something too potent to remain buried. I believe that this is the case with your nightmares – the fact that they are recurrent being evidence of some profound significance in the events they recall.'

Lisette wished for a cigarette; she'd all but stopped buying cigarettes with British prices, and from the absence of ashtrays here, Dr Magnus was a non-smoker.

'But why have these nightmares only lately become a problem?'

'I think I can explain that easily enough. Your forebears were from London. The dreams became a problem after you arrived in London. While it is usually difficult to define any relationship between the subject and the remembered existence, the timing and the force of your dream regressions would seem to indicate that you may be the reincarnation of someone – an ancestress, perhaps – who lived here in London during this past century.'

'In that case, the nightmares should go away when I return to the States.'

'Not necessarily. Once a doorway to the unconscious is opened, it is not so easily closed again. Moreover, you say that you had experienced these dreams on rare occasions prior to your coming here. I would suggest that what you are experiencing is a natural process – a submerged part of your self is seeking expression, and it would be unwise to deny this shadow stranger within you. I might further argue that your presence here in London is hardly coincidence – that your decision to study here was determined by that part of you who emerges in these dreams.'

Lisette decided she wasn't ready to accept such implications just now. 'What do you propose?'

Dr Magnus folded his hands as neatly as a bishop at prayer. 'Have you ever undergone hypnosis?'

'No.' She wished she hadn't made that sound like two syllables.

'It has proved to be extraordinarily efficacious in a great number of cases such as your own, my dear. Please do try to put from your mind the ridiculous trappings and absurd mumbo-jumbo with which the popular imagination connotes hypnotism. Hypnosis is no more than a technique through which we may release the entirety of the unconscious mind to free expression, unrestricted by the countless artificial barriers that make us strangers to ourselves.'

'You want to hypnotize me?' The British inflection came

to her, turning her statement into both question and protest.

'With your fullest cooperation, of course. I think it best. Through regressive hypnosis we can explore the significance of these dreams that trouble you, discover the shadow stranger within your self. Remember – this is a part of *you* that cries out for conscious expression. It is only through the full realization of one's identity, of one's total self, that true inner tranquillity may be achieved. Know thyself, and you will find peace.'

'Know myself?'

'Precisely. You must put aside this false sense of guilt, Miss Seyrig. You are not possessed by some alien and hostile force. These dreams, these memories of another existence – this is *you*.'

IV

'Some bloody weirdo made a pass at me this afternoon,' Lisette confided.

'On the tube, was it?' Danielle stood on her toes, groping along the top of their bookshelf. Freshly showered, she was wearing only a lace-trimmed teddy – camiknickers, they called them in the shops here – and her straining thigh muscles shaped her buttocks nicely.

'In Kensington, actually. After I had left Dr Magnus's office.' Lisette was lounging in an old satin slip she'd found at a stall in Church Street. They were drinking Bristol Cream out of brandy snifters. It was an intimate sort of evening they loved to share together, when not in the company of Danielle's various friends.

'I was walking down Holland Street, and there was this seedy-looking creep all dressed out in punk regalia, pressing his face against the door where that Equinox bookshop used to be. I made the mistake of glancing at him as I passed, and he must have seen my reflection in the glass, because he spun right around, looked straight at me, and said: "Darling! What a lovely surprise to see you!"'

Lisette sipped her sherry. 'Well, I gave him my hardest stare, and would you believe the creep just stood there smiling like he knew me, and so I yelled "Piss off!" in my loudest American accent, and he just froze there with his mouth hanging open.'

'Here it is,' Danielle announced. 'I'd shelved it beside Roland Franklyn's *We Pass From View* – that's another you ought to read. I must remember to someday return it to that cute Liverpool writer who lent it to me.'

She settled cozily beside Lisette on the couch, handed her a somewhat smudged paperback, and resumed her glass of sherry. The book was entitled *More Stately Mansions; Evidences of the Infinite* by Dr Ingmar Magnus and bore an affectionate inscription from the author to Danielle. 'This is the first. The later printings had two of his studies deleted; I can't imagine why. But these are the sort of sessions he was describing to you.'

'He wants to put *me* in one of his books,' Lisette told her with an extravagant leer. 'Can a woman trust a man who writes such ardent inscriptions to place her under hypnosis?'

'Dr Magnus is a perfect gentleman,' Danielle assured her, somewhat huffily. 'He's a distinguished scholar and is thoroughly dedicated to his research. And besides, I've let him hypnotize me on a few occasions.'

'I didn't know that. Whatever for?'

'Dr Magnus is always seeking suitable subjects. I was fascinated by his work, and when I met him at a party I offered to undergo hypnosis.'

'What happened?'

224   KARL EDWARD WAGNER

Danielle seemed envious. 'Nothing worth writing about, I'm afraid. He said I was either too thoroughly integrated, or that my previous lives were too deeply buried. That's often the case, he says, which is why absolute proof of reincarnation is so difficult to demonstrate. After a few sessions I decided I couldn't spare the time to try further.'

'But what was it like?'

'As adventurous as taking a nap. No caped Svengali staring into my eyes. No lambent girasol ring. No swirling lights. Quite dull, actually. Dr Magnus simply lulls you to sleep.'

'Sounds safe enough. So long as I don't get molested walking back from his office.'

Playfully Danielle stroked her hair. 'You hardly look the punk rock type. You haven't chopped off your hair with garden shears and dyed the stubble green. And not a single safety pin through your cheek.'

'Actually I suppose he may not have been a punk rocker. Seemed a bit too old, and he wasn't garish enough. It's just that he was wearing a lot of black leather, and he had gold earrings and some sort of medallion.'

'In front of the Equinox, did you say? How curious.'

'Well, I think I gave him a good start. I glanced in a window to see whether he was trying to follow me, but he was just standing there looking stunned.'

'*Might* have been an honest mistake. Remember the old fellow at Midge and Fiona's party who kept insisting he knew you.'

'And who was pissed out of his skull. Otherwise he might have been able to come up with a more original line.'

Lisette paged through *More Stately Mansions* while Danielle selected a Tangerine Dream album from the stack and placed it on her stereo at low volume. The music seemed in keeping with the grey drizzle of the night outside and the coziness within their sitting-room. Seeing she was busy reading, Danielle poured sherry for them both and stood studying the bookshelves – a hodgepodge of occult and metaphysical topics stuffed together with art books and recent paperbacks in no particular order. Wedged between Aleister Crowley's *Magick in Theory and Practice* and *How I Discovered My Infinite Self* by 'An Initiate' she spotted Dr Magnus's most recent book, *The Shadow Stranger*. She pulled it down, and Dr Magnus stared thoughtfully from the back of the dust jacket.

'Do you believe in reincarnation?' Lisette asked her.

'I do. Or rather, I do some of the time.' Danielle stood behind the couch and bent over Lisette's shoulder to see where she was reading. 'Midge Vaughn assures me that in a previous incarnation I was hanged for witchcraft.'

'Midge should be grateful she's living in the twentieth century.'

'Oh, Midge says we were sisters in the same coven and were hanged together; that's the reason for our close affinity.'

'I'll bet Midge says that to all the girls.'

'Oh, I like Midge.' Danielle sipped her sherry and considered the rows of spines. 'Did you say that man was wearing a medallion? Was it a swastika or that sort of thing?'

'No. It was something like a star in a circle. And he wore rings on every finger.'

'Wait! Kind of greasy black hair slicked back from a widow's peak to straight over his collar in back? Eyebrows curled up into points like they've been waxed?'

'That's it.'

'Ah, Mephisto!'

'Do you know him, then?'

'Not really. I've just seen him a time or two at the Equinox and a few other places. He reminds me of some ham actor playing Mephistopheles. Midge spoke to him once when we were by there, but I gather he's not part of her particular coven. Probably hadn't heard that the Equinox had closed. Never impressed me as a masher; very likely he actually did mistake you for someone.'

'Well, they do say that everyone has a double. I wonder if mine is walking somewhere about London, being mistaken for me?'

'And no doubt giving some unsuspecting classmate of yours a resounding slap on the face.'

'What if I met her suddenly?'

'Met your double – your *Doppelgänger*? Remember William Wilson? Disaster, darling – *disaster!*'

V

There really wasn't much to it; no production at all. Lisette felt nervous, a bit silly, and perhaps a touch cheated.

'I want you to relax,' Dr Magnus told her. 'All you have to do is just relax.'

That's what her gynaecologist always said, too, Lisette thought with a sudden tenseness. She lay on her back on Dr Magnus's analyst's couch: her head on a comfortable cushion, legs stretched primly out on the leather upholstery (she'd deliberately worn jeans again), fingers clenched damply over her tummy. A white gown instead of jeans, and I'll be ready for my coffin, she mused uncomfortably.

'Fine. That's it. You're doing fine, Lisette. Very fine. Just relax. Yes, just relax, just like that. Fine, that's it. Relax.'

Dr Magnus's voice was a quiet monotone, monotonously

repeating soothing encouragements. He spoke to her tire-lessly, patiently, slowly dissolving her anxiety.

'You feel sleepy, Lisette. Relaxed and sleepy. Your breath-ing is slow and relaxed, slow and relaxed. Think about your breathing now, Lisette. Think how slow and sleepy and deep each breath comes. You're breathing deeper, and you're feeling sleepier. Relax and sleep, Lisette, breathe and sleep. Breathe and sleep . . .'

She *was* thinking about her breathing. She counted the breaths; the slow monotonous syllables of Dr Magnus's voice seemed to blend into her breathing like a quiet, tuneless lullaby. She *was* sleepy, for that matter. And it was very pleasant to relax here, listening to that dim, droning murmur while he talked on and on. How much longer until the end of the lecture . . .

'You are asleep now, Lisette. You are asleep, yet you can still hear my voice. Now you are falling deeper, deeper, deeper into a pleasant, relaxed sleep, Lisette. Deeper and deeper asleep. Can you still hear my voice?'

'Yes.'

'You are asleep, Lisette. In a deep, deep sleep. You will remain in this deep sleep until I shall count to three. As I count to three, you will slowly arise from your sleep until you are fully awake once again. Do you understand?'

'Yes.'

'But when you hear me say the word *amber*, you will again fall into a deep, deep sleep, Lisette, just as you are asleep now. Do you understand?'

'Yes.'

'Listen to me as I count, Lisette. One. Two. Three.'

Lisette opened her eyes. For a moment her expression was blank, then a sudden confusion. She looked at Dr Magnus seated beside her, then smiled ruefully. 'I was asleep, I'm afraid. Or was I? . . .'

'You did splendidly, Miss Seyrig.' Dr Magnus beamed reassurance. 'You passed into a simple hypnotic state, and as you can see now, there was no more cause for concern than in catching an afternoon nap.'

'But I'm sure I just dropped off.' Lisette glanced at her watch. Her appointment had been for three, and it was now almost four o'clock.

'Why not just settle back and rest some more, Miss Seyrig. That's it, relax again. All you need is to rest a bit, just a pleasant rest.'

Her wrist fell back onto the cushions, as her eyes fell shut.

'Amber.'

Dr Magnus studied her calm features for a moment. 'You are asleep now, Lisette. Can you hear me?'

'Yes.'

'I want you to relax, Lisette. I want you to fall deeper, deeper, deeper into sleep. Deep, deep sleep. Far, far, far into sleep.'

He listened to her breathing, then suggested: 'You are thinking of your childhood now, Lisette. You are a little girl, not even in school yet. Something is making you very happy. You remember how happy you are. Why are you so happy?'

Lisette made a childish giggle. 'It's my birthday party, and Ollie the Clown came to play with us.'

'And how old are you today?'

'I'm five.' Her right hand twitched, extended fingers and thumb.

'Go deeper now, Lisette. I want you to reach farther back. Far, far back into your memories. Go back to a time before you were a child in San Francisco. Far, farther back, Lisette.

I want you to go back to the time of your dreams.'

He studied her face. She remained in a deep hypnotic trance, but her expression registered sudden anxiousness. It was as if she lay in normal sleep – reacting to some intense nightmare. She moaned.

'Deeper, Lisette. Don't be afraid to remember. Let your mind flow back to another time.'

Her features still showed distress, but she seemed less agitated as his voice urged her deeper.

'Where are you?'

'I'm ... I'm not certain.' Her voice came in a well-bred English accent. 'It's quite dark. Only a few candles are burning. I'm frightened.'

'Go back to a happy moment,' Dr Magnus urged her, as her tone grew sharp with fear. 'You are happy now. Something very pleasant and wonderful is happening to you.'

Anxiety drained from her features. Her cheeks flushed; she smiled pleasurably.

'Where are you now?'

'I'm dancing. It's a grand ball to celebrate Her Majesty's Diamond Jubilee, and I've never seen such a throng. I'm certain Charles means to propose to me tonight, but he's ever so shy, and now he's simply fuming that Captain Stapledon has the next two dances. He's so dashing in his uniform. Everyone is watching us together.'

'What is your name?'

'Elisabeth Beresford.'

'Where do you live, Miss Beresford?'

'We have a house in Chelsea ...'

Her expression abruptly changed. 'It's dark again. I'm all alone. I can't see myself, although surely the candles shed sufficient light. There's something there in the candlelight. I'm moving closer.'

KARL EDWARD WAGNER

'One.'
'It's an open coffin.' Fear edged her voice.
'Two.'
'*God in Heaven!*'
'Three.'

VI

'We,' Danielle announced grandly, 'are invited to a party.'

She produced an engraved card from her bag, presented it to Lisette, then went to hang up her damp raincoat.

'Bloody English summer weather!' Lisette heard her from the kitchen. 'Is there any more coffee made? Oh, fantastic!'

She reappeared with a cup of coffee and an opened box of cookies – Lisette couldn't get used to calling them biscuits. 'Want some?'

'No, thanks. Bad for my figure.'

'And coffee on an empty tummy is bad for the nerves,' Danielle said pointedly.

'*Who* is Beth Garrington?' Lisette studied the invitation.

'Um.' Danielle tried to wash down a mouthful of crumbs with too-hot coffee. 'Some friend of Midge's. Midge dropped by the gallery this afternoon and gave me the invitation. A costume revel. Rock stars to royalty among the guests. Midge promises that it will be super fun; said the last party Beth threw was unbridled debauchery – there was cocaine being passed around in an antique snuff box for the guests. Can you imagine that much coke!'

'And how did Midge manage the invitation?'

'I gather the discerning Ms Garrington had admired several of my drawings that Maitland has on display – yea, even unto so far as to purchase one. Midge told her that she knew me and that we two were ornaments for any debauchery.'

'The invitation is in both our names.'

'Midge *likes* you.'

'Midge despises me. She's jealous as a cat.'

'Then she must have told our depraved hostess what a lovely couple we make. Besides, Midge is jealous of everyone – even dear Maitland, whose interest in me very obviously is not of the flesh. But don't fret about Midge – English women are naturally bitchy toward "foreign" women. They're oh-so proper and fashionable, but they never shave their legs. That's why I love mah fellow Americans.'

Danielle kissed her chastely on top of her head, powdering Lisette's hair with biscuit crumbs. 'And I'm cold and wet and dying for a shower. How about you?'

'A masquerade?' Lisette wondered. 'What sort of costume? Not something that we'll have to trot off to one of those rental places for, surely?'

'From what Midge suggests, anything goes so long as it's wild. Just create something divinely decadent, and we're sure to knock them dead.' Danielle had seen *Cabaret* half a dozen times. 'It's to be in some back alley stately old home in Maida Vale, so there's no danger that the tenants downstairs will call the cops.'

When Lisette remained silent, Danielle gave her a playful nudge. 'Darling, it's a party we're invited to, not a funeral. What is it – didn't your session with Dr Magnus go well?'

'I suppose it did.' Lisette smiled without conviction. 'I really can't say; all I did was doze off. Dr Magnus seemed quite excited about it though. I found it all ... well, just a little bit scary.'

'I thought you said you just dropped off. *What* was scary?'

KARL EDWARD WAGNER

'It's hard to put into words. It's like when you're starting to have a bad trip on acid: there's nothing wrong that you can explain, but somehow your mind is telling you to be afraid.'

Danielle sat down beside her and squeezed her arm about her shoulders. 'That sounds to me like Dr Magnus is getting somewhere. I felt just the same sort of free anxiety the first time I underwent analysis. It's a good sign, darling. It means you're beginning to understand all those troubled secrets the ego keeps locked away.'

'Perhaps the ego keeps them locked away for some perfectly good reason.'

'Meaning hidden sexual conflicts, I suppose.' Danielle's fingers gently massaged Lisette's shoulders and neck. 'Oh, Lisette. You mustn't be shy about getting to know yourself. *I* think it's exciting.'

Lisette curled up against her, resting her cheek against Danielle's breast while the other girl's fingers soothed the tension from her muscles. She supposed she was over-reacting. After all, the nightmares were what distressed her so; Dr Magnus seemed completely confident that he could free her from them.

'Which of your drawings did our prospective hostess buy?' Lisette asked, changing the subject.

'Oh, didn't I tell you?' Danielle lifted up her chin. 'It was that charcoal study I did of you.'

Lisette closed the shower curtains as she stepped into the tub. It was one of those long, narrow, deep tubs beloved of English bathrooms that always made her think of a coffin for two. A Rube Goldberg plumbing arrangement connected the hot and cold taps, and from the common spout was affixed a rubber hose with a shower head which one might either hang from a hook on the wall or hold in hand. Danielle had replaced the ordinary shower head with a shower massage when she moved in, but she left the previous tenant's shaving mirror – a bevelled glass oval in a heavily enamelled antique frame – hanging on the wall above the hook.

Lisette glanced at her face in the steamed-over mirror. 'I shouldn't have let you display that at the gallery.'

'But why not?' Danielle was shampooing, and lather blinded her as she turned about. 'Maitland thinks it's one of my best.'

Lisette reached around her for the shower attachment. 'It seems a bit personal somehow. All those people looking at me. It's an invasion of privacy.'

'But it's thoroughly modest, darling. Not like some topless billboard in Soho.'

The drawing was a charcoal and pencil study of Lisette, done in what Danielle described as her David Hamilton phase. In sitting for it, Lisette had piled her hair in a high chignon and dressed in an antique cotton camisole and drawers with lace insertions that she'd found at a shop in Westbourne Grove. Danielle called it 'Dark Rose'. Lisette had thought it made her look fat.

Danielle grasped blindly for the shower massage, and Lisette placed it in her hand. 'It just seems a bit too personal to have some total stranger owning my picture.' Shampoo coursed like sea-foam over Danielle's breasts. Lisette kissed the foam.

'Ah, but soon she won't be a total stranger,' Danielle reminded her, her voice muffled by the pulsing shower spray.

Lisette felt Danielle's nipples harden beneath her lips. The brunette still pressed her eyes tightly shut against the

KARL EDWARD WAGNER

force of the shower, but her other hand cupped Lisette's head encouragingly. Lisette gently moved her kisses downward along the other girl's slippery belly, kneeling as she did so. Danielle murmured, and when Lisette's tongue probed her drenched curls, she shifted her legs to let her knees rest beneath the blonde girl's shoulders. The shower massage dropped from her fingers.

Lisette made love to her with a passion that surprised her – spontaneous, suddenly fierce, unlike their usual tenderness together. Her lips and tongue pressed into Danielle almost ravenously, her own ecstasy even more intense than that which she was drawing from Danielle. Danielle gasped and clung to the shower rail with one hand, her other fist clenched upon the curtain, sobbing as a long orgasm shuddered through her.

'Please, darling!' Danielle finally managed to beg. 'My legs are too wobbly to hold me up any longer!'

She drew away. Lisette raised her face.

'Oh!'

Lisette rose to her feet with drugged movements. Her wide eyes at last registered Danielle's startled expression. She touched her lips and turned to look in the bathroom mirror.

'I'm sorry,' Danielle put her arm about her shoulder. 'I must have started my period. I didn't realize ...'

Lisette stared at the blood-smeared face in the fogged shaving mirror.

Danielle caught her as she started to slump.

VII

She was conscious of the cold rain that pelted her face, washing from her nostrils the too-sweet smell of decaying flowers. Slowly she opened her eyes onto darkness and mist. Rain fell steadily, spiritlessly, gluing her white gown to her drenched flesh. She had been walking in her sleep again.

Wakefulness seemed forever in coming to her, so that only by slow degrees did she become aware of herself, of her surroundings. For a moment she felt as if she were a chess piece arrayed upon a board in a darkened room. All about her, stone monuments crowded together, their weathered surfaces streaming with moisture. She felt neither fear nor surprise that she stood in a cemetery.

She pressed her bare arms together across her breasts. Water ran over her pale skin as smoothly as upon the marble tombstones, and though her flesh felt as cold as the drenched marble, she did not feel chilled. She stood barefoot, her hair clinging to her shoulders above the low-necked cotton gown that was all she wore.

Automatically, her steps carried her through the darkness, as if following a familiar path through the maze of glistening stone. She knew where she was: this was Highgate Cemetary. She could not recall how she knew that, since she had no memory of ever having been to this place before. No more could she think how she knew her steps were taking her deeper into the cemetery instead of toward the gate.

A splash of colour trickled onto her breast, staining its paleness as the rain dissolved it into a red rose above her heart.

She opened her mouth to scream, and a great bubble of unswallowed blood spewed from her lips.

'Elisabeth! Elisabeth!'
    'Lisette! Lisette!'
    Whose voice called her?
    'Lisette! You can wake up now, Lisette.'

KARL EDWARD WAGNER

Dr Magnus's face peered into her own. Was there sudden concern behind that urbane mask?

'You're awake now, Miss Seyrig. Everything is all right.'

Lisette stared back at him for a moment, uncertain of her reality, as if suddenly awakened from some profound nightmare.

'I . . . I thought I was dead.' Her eyes still held her fear.

Dr Magnus smiled to reassure her. 'Somnambulism, my dear. You remembered an episode of sleepwalking from a former life. Tell me, have you yourself ever walked in your sleep?'

Lisette pressed her hands to her face, abruptly examined her fingers. 'I don't know. I mean, I don't think so.'

She sat up, searched in her bag for her compact. She paused for a moment before opening the mirror.

'Dr Magnus, I don't think I care to continue these sessions.'

She stared at her reflection in fascination, not touching her make-up, and when she snapped the case shut, the frightened strain began to relax from her face. She wished she had a cigarette.

Dr Magnus sighed and pressed his fingertips together, leaning back in his chair; watched her fidget with her clothing as she sat nervously on the edge of the couch.

'Do you really wish to terminate our exploration? We have, after all, made excellent progress during these last few sessions.'

'Have me?'

'We have, indeed. You have consistently remembered incidents from the life of one Elisabeth Beresford, a young English lady living in London at the close of the last century. To the best of your knowledge of your family history, she is not an ancestress.'

Dr Magnus leaned forward, seeking to impart his enthusiasm. 'Don't you see how important this is? If Elisabeth Beresford was not your ancestress, then there can be no question of genetic memory being involved. The only explanation must therefore be reincarnation – proof of the immortality of the soul. To establish this I must first confirm the existence of Elisabeth Beresford, and from that demonstrate that no familial bond exists between the two of you. We simply must explore this further.'

'Must we? I meant what progress have we made toward helping me, Dr Magnus? It's all very good for you to be able to confirm your theories of reincarnation, but that doesn't do anything for me. If anything, the nightmares have grown more disturbing since we began these sessions.'

'Then perhaps we dare not stop.'

'What do you mean?' Lisette wondered what he might do if she suddenly bolted from the room.

'I mean that the nightmares will grow worse regardless of whether you decide to terminate our sessions. Your unconscious self is struggling to tell you some significant message from a previous existence. It will continue to do so no matter how stubbornly you will yourself not to listen. My task is to help you listen to this voice, to understand the message it must impart to you – and with this understanding and self-awareness, you will experience inner peace. Without my help . . . Well, to be perfectly frank, Miss Seyrig, you are in some danger of a complete emotional breakdown.'

Lisette slumped back against the couch. She felt on the edge of panic and wished Danielle were here to support her.

'Why are my memories always nightmares?' Her voice shook, and she spoke slowly to control it.

'But they aren't always frightening memories, my dear. It's just that the memory of some extremely traumatic experience often seeks to come to the fore. You would expect some tremendously emotional laden memory to be a potent one.'

'Is Elisabeth Beresford . . . dead?'

'Assuming that she was approximately twenty years of age at the time of Queen Victoria's Diamond Jubilee, she would have been past one hundred today. Besides, Miss Seyrig, her soul has been born again as your own. It must therefore follow . . .'

'Dr Magnus. I don't *want* to know how Elisabeth Beresford died.'

'Of course,' Dr Magnus told her gently. 'Isn't that quite obvious?'

VIII

'For a wonder, it's forgot to rain tonight.'

'Thank God for small favours,' Lisette commented, thinking July in London had far more to do with monsoons than the romantic city of fogs celebrated in song. 'All we need is to get these rained on.'

She and Danielle bounced about on the back seat of the black Austin taxi, as their driver democratically seemed as willing to challenge lorries as pedestrians for the right of way on Edgeware Road. Feeling a bit self-conscious, Lisette tugged at the hem of her patent leather trench coat. They had decided to wear brightly embroidered Chinese silk lounging pyjamas that they'd found at one of the vintage clothing shops off the Portobello Road – gauzy enough for stares, but only a demure trouser-leg showed beneath their coats. 'We're going to a masquerade party,' Lisette had felt obliged to explain to the driver. Her concern was needless, as he hadn't given them a second glance. Either he was used to the current Chinese look in fashion, or else a few seasons of picking up couples at discos and punk rock clubs had inured him to any sort of costume.

The taxi turned into a series of side streets off Maida Vale and eventually made a neat U-turn that seemed almost an automotive pirouette. The frenetic beat of a new wave rock group clattered past the gate of an enclosed courtyard: something Mews – the iron plaque on the brick wall was too rusted to decipher in the dark – but from the lights and noise it must be the right address. A number of expensive-looking cars – Lisette recognized a Rolls or two and at least one Ferrari – were among those crowded against the curb. They squeezed their way past them and made for the source of the revelry, a brick-fronted townhouse of three or more storeys set at the back of the courtyard.

The door was opened by a girl in an abbreviated maid's costume. She checked their invitation while a similarly clad girl took their coats, and a third invited them to select from an assortment of masks and indicated where they might change. Lisette and Danielle chose sequined domino masks that matched the dangling scarves they wore tied low across their brows.

Danielle withdrew an ebony cigarette holder from her bag and considered their reflections with approval. 'Divinely decadent,' she drawled, gesturing with her black-lacquered nails. 'All that time for my eyes, and just to cover them with a mask. Perhaps later – when it's cock's-crow and all unmask . . . Forward, darling.'

Lisette kept at her side, feeling a bit lost and out of place. When they passed before a light, it was evident that they wore nothing beneath the silk pyjamas, and Lisette was grateful for the strategic brocade. As they came upon others of the newly arriving guests, she decided there was no danger of outraging anyone's modesty here. As Midge had promised, anything goes so long as it's wild, and while their costumes might pass for street wear, many of the guests need avail themselves of the changing rooms upstairs.

A muscular young man clad only in a leather loin cloth and a swordbelt with broadsword descended the stairs leading a buxom girl by a chain affixed to her wrists; aside from her manacles she wore a few scraps of leather. A couple in punk rock gear spat at them in passing; the girl was wearing a set of pasties with dangling razor blades for tassels and a pair of black latex tights that might have been spray paint. Two girls in vintage Christian Dior New Look evening gowns ogled the semi-nude swordsman from the landing above; Lisette noted their pronounced shoulders and Adam's apples and felt a twinge of jealousy that hormones and surgery could let them show a better cleavage than she could.

A new wave group called the Needle was performing in a large first floor room – Lisette supposed it was an actual ballroom, although the house's original tenants would have considered tonight's ball a *danse macabré*. Despite the fact that the decibel level was well past the threshold of pain, most of the guests were congregated here, with smaller, quieter parties gravitating into other rooms. Here, about half were dancing, the rest standing about trying to talk. Marijuana smoke was barely discernible within the harsh haze of British cigarettes.

'There's Midge and Fiona,' Danielle shouted in Lisette's ear. She waved energetically and steered a course through the dancers.

Midge was wearing an elaborate medieval gown – a heavily brocaded affair that ran from the floor to midway across her nipples. Her blonde hair was piled high in some sort of conical headpiece, complete with flowing scarf. Fiona waited upon her in a page boy's costume.

'Are you just getting here?' Midge asked, running a deprecative glance down Lisette's costume. 'There's champagne over on the sideboard. Wait, I'll summon one of the cute little French maids.'

Lisette caught two glasses from a passing tray and presented one to Danielle. It was impossible to converse, but then she hadn't anything to talk about with Midge, and Fiona was no more than a shadow.

'Where's our hostess?' Danielle asked.

'Not down yet,' Midge managed to shout. 'Beth always waits to make a grand entrance at her little dos. You won't miss her.'

'Speaking of entrances . . .' Lisette commented, nodding toward the couple who were just coming onto the dance floor. The woman wore a Nazi SS officer's hat, jackboots, black trousers and braces across her bare chest. She was astride the back of her male companion, who wore a saddle and bridle in addition to a few other bits of leather harness.

'I can't decide whether that's kinky or just tacky,' Lisette said.

'Not like your little sorority teas back home, is it?' Midge smiled.

'Is there any coke about?' Danielle interposed quickly.

'There was a short while ago. Try the library – that's the room just down from where everyone's changing.'

Lisette downed her champagne and grabbed a refill before following Danielle upstairs. A man in fishnet tights, motorcycle boots and a vest comprised mostly of chain and bits of Nazi medals caught at her arm and seemed to want to dance. Instead of a mask he wore about a pound of eye shadow and black lipstick. She shouted an inaudible excuse, held a finger to her nostril and sniffed and darted after Danielle.

'That was Eddie Teeth, lead singer for the Trepans, whom you just cut,' Danielle told her. 'Why didn't he grab *me!*'

'You'll get your chance,' Lisette told her. 'I think he's following us.'

Danielle dragged her to a halt halfway up the stairs.

'Got toot right here, loves.' Eddie Teeth flipped the silver spoon and phial that dangled amidst the chains on his vest.'

'Couldn't take the noise in there any longer,' Lisette explained.

'Needle's shit.' Eddie Teeth wrapped an arm about either waist and propelled them up the stairs. 'You gashes sisters? I can dig incest.'

The library was pleasantly crowded – Lisette decided she didn't want to be cornered with Eddie Teeth. A dozen or more guests stood about, sniffling and conversing energetically. Seated at a table, two of the ubiquitous maids busily cut lines onto mirrors and set them out for the guests, whose number remained more or less constant as people wandered in and left. A cigarette box offered tightly rolled joints.

'That's Thai.' Eddie Teeth groped for a handful of the joints, stuck one in each girl's mouth, the rest inside his vest. Danielle giggled and fitted hers to her cigarette holder. Unfastening a silver tube from his vest, he snorted two thick lines from one of the mirrors. 'Toot your eyeballs out, loves,' he invited them.

One of the maids collected the mirror when they had finished and replaced it with another – a dozen lines of cocaine neatly arranged across its surface. Industriously she began to work a chunk of rock through a sifter to replenish the empty mirror. Lisette watched in fascination. This finally brought home to her the wealth this party represented: all the rest simply seemed to her like something out of a movie, but dealing out coke to more than a hundred guests was an extravagance she could relate to.

'Danielle Borland, isn't it?'

A man dressed as Mephistopheles bowed before them. 'Adrian Tregannet. We've met at one of Midge Vaughn's parties, you may recall.'

Danielle stared at the face below the domino mask. 'Oh, yes. Lisette, it's Mephisto himself.'

'Then this is Miss Seyrig, the subject of your charcoal drawing that Beth so admires.' Mephisto caught Lisette's hand and bent his lips to it. 'Beth is so much looking forward to meeting you both.'

Lisette retrieved her hand. 'Aren't you the . . .'

'The rude fellow who accosted you in Kensington some days ago,' Tregannet finished apologetically. 'Yes, I'm afraid so. But you really must forgive me for my forwardness. I actually did mistake you for a very dear friend of mine, you see. Won't you let me make amends over a glass of champagne?'

'Certainly.' Lisette decided that she had had quite enough of Eddie Teeth, and Danielle was quite capable of fending for herself if she grew tired of having her breasts squeezed by a famous pop star.

Tregannet quickly returned with two glasses of champagne. Lisette finished another two lines and smiled appreciatively as she accepted a glass. Danielle was trying to shotgun Eddie Teeth through her cigarette holder, and Lisette thought it a good chance to slip away.

'Your roommate is tremendously talented,' Tregannet suggested. 'Of course, she chose so charming a subject for her drawing.'

Slick as snake oil, Lisette thought, letting him take her arm. 'How very nice of you to say so. However, I really feel a bit embarrassed to think that some stranger owns a portrait of me in my underwear.'

'Utterly chaste, my dear – as chaste as the "Dark Rose" of its title. Beth chose to hang it in her boudoir, so I hardly think it is on public display. I suspect from your garments in the drawing that you must share Beth's appreciation for the dress and manners of this past century.'

Which is something I'd never suspect of our hostess judging from this party, Lisette considered. 'I'm quite looking forward to meeting her. I assume that Ms is a bit too modern for one of such quiet tastes. Is it Miss or Mrs Garrington?'

'Ah, I hadn't meant to suggest an impression of a genteel dowager. Beth is entirely of your generation – a few years older than yourself, perhaps. Although I find Ms too suggestive of American slang, I'm sure Beth would not object. However, there's no occasion for such formality here.'

'You seem to know her well, Mr Tregannet.'

'It is an old family. I know her aunt, Julia Weatherford, quite well through our mutual interest in the occult. Perhaps you, too? . . .'

'Not really; Danielle is the one you should chat with about that. My field is art. I'm over here on fellowship at London University.' She watched Danielle and Eddie Teeth toddle off for the ballroom and jealously decided that Danielle's taste in her acquaintances left much to be desired. 'Could I have some more champagne?'

'To be sure. I won't be a moment.'

Lisette snorted a few more lines while she waited. A young man dressed as an Edwardian dandy offered her his snuff box and gravely demonstrated its use. Lisette was struggling with a sneezing fit when Tregannet returned.

'You needn't have gone to all the bother,' she told him. 'These little French maids are dashing about with trays of champagne.'

'But those glasses have lost the proper chill,' Tregannet explained. 'To your very good health.'

'Cheers.' Lisette felt light-headed and promised herself to go easy for a while. 'Does Beth live here with her aunt, then?'

'Her aunt lives on the Continent; I don't believe she's visited London for several years. Beth moved in about ten years ago. Theirs is not a large family, but they are not without wealth, as you can observe. They travel a great deal as well, and it's fortunate that Beth happened to be in London during your stay here. Incidently, just how long will you be staying in London?'

'About a year is all.' Lisette finished her champagne. 'Then it's back to my dear, dull family in San Francisco.'

'Then there's no one here in London? . . .'

'Decidedly not, Mr Tregannet. And now if you'll excuse me, I think I'll find the ladies'.'

Cocaine might well be the champagne of drugs, but cocaine and champagne didn't seem to mix well, Lisette mused, turning the bathroom over to the next frantic guest. Her head felt really buzzy, and she thought she might do better if she found a bedroom somewhere and lay down for a moment. But then she'd most likely wake up and find some man on top of her, judging from this lot. She decided she'd lay off the champagne and have just a line or two to shake off the feeling of having been sandbagged.

The crowd in the study had changed during her absence. Just now it was dominated by a group of guests dressed in

KARL EDWARD WAGNER

costumes from *The Rocky Horror Show*, now closing out its long run at the Comedy Theatre in Piccadilly. Lisette had grown bored with the fad the film version had generated in the States, and pushed her way past the group as they vigorously danced the Time Warp and bellowed out songs from the show.

'Give yourself over to absolute pleasure,' someone sang in her ear as she industriously snorted a line from the mirror. 'Erotic nightmares beyond any measure,' the song continued.

Lisette finished a second line and decided she had had enough. She straightened from the table and broke for the doorway. The tall transvestite dressed as Frankie barred her way with a dramatic gesture, singing ardently: 'Don't dream it – be it!'

Lisette blew him a kiss and ducked around him. She wished she could find Danielle first – if she could handle the ballroom that long.

The dance floor was far more crowded than when they'd come in. At least all these jostling bodies seemed to absorb some of the decibels from the blaring banks of amplifiers and speakers. Lisette looked in vain for Danielle amidst the dancers, succeeding only in getting champagne sloshed on her back. She caught sight of Midge, recognizable above the mob by her conical medieval headdress, and pushed her way toward her.

Midge was being fed caviar on bits of toast by Fiona while she talked with an older woman who looked like the pictures Lisette had seen of Marlene Dietrich dressed in men's formal evening wear.

'Have you seen Danielle?' Lisette asked her.

'Why, not recently, darling,' Midge smiled, licking caviar from her lips with the tip of her tongue. 'I believe she and the rock singer were headed upstairs for a bit more privacy. I'm sure she'll come collect you once they're finished.'

'Midge, you're a cunt,' Lisette told her through her sweetest smile. She turned away and made for the doorway, trying not to ruin her exit by staggering. Screw Danielle – she needed to have some fresh air.

A crowd had gathered at the foot of the stairway, and she had to push through the doorway to escape the ballroom. Behind her, the Needle mercifully took a break. 'She's coming down!' Lisette heard someone whisper breathlessly. The inchoate babel of the party fell to a sudden lull that made Lisette shiver.

At the top of the stairway stood a tall woman, enveloped in a black velvet cloak from her throat to her ankles. Her blonde hair was piled high in a complex variation of the once-fashionable French twist. Strings of garnets entwined in her hair and edged the close-fitting black mask that covered the upper half of her face. For a hushed interval she stood there, gazing imperiously down upon her guests.

Adrian Treganett leapt to the foot of the stairway. He signed to a pair of maids, who stepped forward to either side of their mistress.

'Milords and miladies!' he announced with a sweeping bow. 'Let us pay honour to our bewitching mistress whose feast we celebrate tonight! I give you the lamia who haunted Adam's dreams – Lilith!'

The maids smoothly swept the cloak from their mistress's shoulders. From the multitude at her feet came an audible intake of breath. Beth Garrington was attired in a strapless corselette of gleaming black leather, laced tightly about her waist. The rest of her costume consisted only of knee-length, stiletto-heeled tight boots, above-the-elbow gloves, and a spiked collar around her throat – all of black leather

KARL EDWARD WAGNER

that contrasted starkly against her white skin and blonde hair. At first Lisette thought she wore a bull-whip coiled about her body as well, but then the coils moved, and she realized that it was an enormous black snake.

'Lilith!' came the shout, chanted in a tone of awe. 'Lilith!'

Acknowledging their worship with a sinuous gesture, Beth Garrington descended the staircase. The serpent coiled from gloved arm to gloved arm, entwining her clinched waist; its eyes considered the revellers imperturbably. Champagne glasses lifted in a toast to Lilith, and the chattering voice of the party once more began to fill the house.

Tregannet touched Beth's elbow as she greeted her guests at the foot of the stairway. He whispered into her ear, and she smiled graciously and moved away with him.

Lisette clung to the staircase newel, watching them approach. Her head was spinning and she desperately needed to lie down in some fresh air, but she couldn't trust her legs to carry her outside. She stared into the eyes of the serpent, hypnotized by its flickering tongue.

The room seemed to surge in and out of focus. The masks of the guests seemed to leer and gloat with the awareness of some secret jest; the dancers in their fantastic costumes became a grotesque horde of satyrs and wanton demons, writhing about the ballroom in some witches' sabbat of obscene mass copulation. As in a nightmare, Lisette willed her legs to turn and run, realized that her body was no longer obedient to her will.

'Beth, here's someone you've been dying to meet,' Lisette heard Tregannet say. 'Beth Garrington, allow me to present Lisette Seyrig.'

The lips beneath the black mask curved in a pleasurable smile. Lisette gazed into the eyes behind the mask, and discovered that she could no longer feel her body. She thought she heard Danielle cry out her name.

The eyes remained in her vision long after she slid down the newel and collapsed upon the floor.

IX

The Catherine Wheel was a pub on Kensington Church Street. They served good pub lunches there, and Lisette liked to stop in before walking down Holland Street for her sessions with Dr Magnus. Since today was her final such session, it seemed appropriate that they should end the evening here.

'While I dislike repeating myself,' Dr Magnus spoke earnestly, 'I really do think we should continue.'

Lisette drew on a cigarette and shook her head decisively. 'No way, Dr Magnus. My nerves are shot to hell. I mean, look – when I freak out at a costume party and have to be carted home to bed by my roommate! It was like when I was a kid and got hold of some bad acid: the whole world was some bizarre and sinister freak show for weeks. Once I got my head back on, I said: no more acid.'

'That was rather a notorious circle you were travelling in. Further, you were, if I understand you correctly, over-indulging a bit that evening.'

'A few glasses of champagne and a little toot never did anything before but make me a bit giggly and talkative.' Lisette sipped her half of lager; she'd never developed a taste for English bitter, and at least the lager was chilled. They sat across from each other at a table the size of a hubcap; she in the corner of a padded bench against the wall, he at a chair set out into the room, pressed in by a wall of standing bodies. A foot away from her on the padded bench, three young men huddled about a similar table, talking animatedly. For all that, she and Dr Magnus might have been all alone in the room. Lisette wondered if the psychologist who had coined the faddish concept of 'space' had been inspired in a crowded English pub.

'It isn't just that I fainted at the party. It isn't just the nightmares.' She paused to find words. 'It's just that everything somehow seems to be drifting out of focus, out of control. It's . . . well, it's frightening.'

'Precisely why we must continue.'

'Precisely why we must not.' Lisette sighed. They'd covered this ground already. It had been a moment of weakness when she agreed to allow Dr Magnus to buy her a drink afterward instead of heading back to the flat. Still, he had been so distressed when she told him she was terminating their sessions.

'I've tried to cooperate with you as best I could, and I'm certain you are entirely sincere in your desire to help me.' Well, she wasn't all *that* certain, but no point in going into that. 'However, the fact remains that since we began the sessions, my nerves have gone to hell. You say they'd be worse without the sessions, I say the sessions have made them worse, and maybe there's no connection at all – it's just that my nerves have gotten worse, so now I'm going to trust my intuition and try life without these sessions. Fair enough?'

Dr Magnus gazed uncomfortably at his barely tasted glass of sherry. 'While I fully understand your rationale, I must in all conscience beg you to reconsider, Lisette. You are running risks that . . .'

'Look. If the nightmares go away, then terrific. If they don't, I can always pack up and head back to San Francisco. That way I'll be clear of whatever it is about London that disagrees with me, and if not, I'll see my psychiatrist back home.'

'Very well, then.' Dr Magnus squeezed her hand. 'However, please bear in mind that I remain eager to continue our sessions at any time, should you change your mind.'

'That's fair enough, too. And very kind of you.'

Dr Magnus lifted his glass of sherry to the light. Pensively, he remarked: 'Amber.'

X

'Lisette?'

Danielle locked the front door behind her and hung up her inadequate umbrella in the hallway. She considered her face in the mirror and grimaced at the mess of her hair. 'Lisette? Are you here?'

No answer, and her rain things were not in the hallway. Either she was having a late session with Dr Magnus, or else she'd wisely decided to duck under cover until this bloody rain let up. After she'd had to carry Lisette home in a taxi when she passed out at the party, Danielle was starting to feel real concern over her state of health.

Danielle kicked off her damp shoes as she entered the living-room. The curtains were drawn against the greyness outside, and she switched on a lamp to brighten the flat a bit. Her dress clung to her like a clammy fishskin; she shivered and thought about a cup of coffee. If Lisette hadn't returned yet, there wouldn't be any brewed. She'd have a warm shower instead, and after that she'd see to the coffee – if Lisette hadn't returned to set a pot going in the meantime.

'Lisette?' Their bedroom was empty. Danielle turned on the overhead light. Christ, it was gloomy! So much for long English summer evenings – with all the rain, she couldn't remember when she'd last seen the sun. She struggled out of her damp dress, spread it flat across her bed with the vague hope that it might not wrinkle too badly, then tossed her bra and tights onto a chair.

Slipping into her bathrobe, Danielle padded back into the living-room. Still no sign of Lisette, and it was past nine. Perhaps she'd stopped off at a pub. Crossing to the stereo, Danielle placed the new Blondie album on the turntable and turned up the volume. Let the neighbours complain – at least this would help dispel the evening's gloom.

She cursed the delay needed to adjust the shower temperature to satisfaction, then climbed into the tub. The hot spray felt good, and she stood under it contentedly for several minutes – initially revitalized, then lulled into a delicious sense of relaxation. Through the rush of the spray, she could hear the muffled beat of the stereo. As she reached for the shampoo, she began to move her body with the rhythm.

The shower curtain billowed as the bathroom door opened. Danielle risked a soapy squint around the curtain – she knew the flat was securely locked, but after seeing *Psycho* ... It was only Lisette, already undressed, her long blonde hair falling over her breasts.

'Didn't hear you come in with the stereo going,' Danielle greeted her. 'Come on in before you catch cold.'

Danielle resumed lathering her hair as the shower curtain parted and the other girl stepped into the tub behind her. Her eyes squeezed shut against the soap, she felt Lisette's breasts thrust against her back, her flat belly press against her buttocks. Lisette's hands came around to cup her breasts gently.

At least Lisette had gotten over her silly tiff about Eddie Teeth. She'd explained to Lisette that she'd ditched that greasy slob when he'd tried to dry hump her on the dance floor, but how do you reason with a silly thing who faints at the sight of a snake?

'Jesus, you're chilled to the bone!' Danielle complained with a shiver. 'Better stand under the shower and get warm. Did you get caught in the rain?'

The other girl's fingers continued to caress her breasts, and instead of answering, her lips teased the nape of Danielle's neck. Danielle made a delighted sound deep in her throat, letting the spray rinse the lather from her hair and over their embraced bodies. Languidly she turned about to face her lover, closing her arms about Lisette's shoulders for support.

Lisette's kisses held each taut nipple for a moment, teasing them almost painfully. Danielle pressed the other girl's face to her breasts, sighed as her kisses nibbled upward to her throat. She felt weak with arousal, and only Lisette's strength held her upright in the tub. Her lover's lips upon her throat tormented her beyond enduring; Danielle gasped and lifted Lisette's face to meet her own.

Her mouth was open to receive Lisette's red-lipped kiss, and it opened wider as Danielle stared into the eyes of her lover. Her first emotion was one of wonder.

'You're not Lisette!'

It was nearly midnight when Lisette unlocked the door to their flat and quietly let herself in. Only a few lights were on, and there was no sign of Danielle – either she had gone out, or more likely had gone to bed.

Lisette hung up her raincoat and wearily pulled off her shoes. She'd barely caught the last train. She must have been crazy to let Dr Magnus talk her into returning to his office for another session that late, but then he was quite right: as serious as her problems were, she really did need all the help he could give her. She felt a warm sense of gratitude to Dr Magnus for being there when she so needed his help.

The turntable had stopped, but a light on the amplifier indicated that the power was still on. Lisette cut it off and closed the lid over the turntable. She felt too tired to listen to an album just now.

She became aware that the shower was running. In that case, Danielle hadn't gone to bed. She supposed she really ought to apologize to her for letting Midge's bitchy lies get under her skin. After all, she had ruined the party for Danielle; poor Danielle had had to get her to bed and had left the party without ever getting to meet Beth Garrington, and she was the one Beth had invited in the first place.

'Danielle? I'm back.' Lisette called through the bathroom door. 'Do you want anything?'

No answer. Lisette looked into their bedroom, just in case Danielle had invited a friend over. No, the beds were still made up; Danielle's clothes were spread out by themselves.

'Danielle?' Lisette raised her voice. Perhaps she couldn't hear over the noise of the shower. 'Danielle?' Surely she was all right.

Lisette's feet felt damp. She looked down. A puddle of water was seeping beneath the door. Danielle must not have the shower curtain closed properly.

'Danielle! You're flooding us!'

Lisette opened the door and peered cautiously within. The curtain was closed, right enough. A thin spray still reached through a gap, and the shower had been running long enough for the puddle to spread. It occurred to Lisette that she should see Danielle's silhouette against the translucent shower curtain.

'Danielle!' She began to grow alarmed. 'Danielle! Are you all right?'

She pattered across the wet tiles and drew aside the curtain. Danielle lay in the bottom of the tub, the spray falling on her upturned smile, her flesh paler than the porcelain of the tub.

XI

It was early afternoon when they finally allowed her to return to the flat. Had she been able to think of another place to go, she probably would have gone there. Instead, Lisette wearily slumped onto the couch, too spent to pour herself the drink she desperately wanted.

Somehow she had managed to phone the police, through her hysteria make them understand where she was. Once the squad car arrived, she had no further need to act out of her own initiative; she simply was carried along in the rush of police investigation. It wasn't until they were questioning her at New Scotland Yard that she realized she herself was not entirely free from suspicion.

The victim had bled to death, the medical examiner ruled, her blood washed down the tub drain. A safety razor used for shaving legs had been opened, its blade removed. There were razor incisions along both wrists, directed lengthwise, into the radial artery, as opposed to the shallow, crosswise cuts utilized by suicides unfamiliar with human anatomy. There was in addition an incision in the left side of the throat. It was either a very determined suicide, or a skilfully concealed murder. In view of the absence of any signs of forced entry or of a struggle, more likely the former. The victim's roommate did admit to a recent quarrel. Laboratory tests would indicate whether the victim might have been drugged or rendered unconscious through a blow. After that, the inquest would decide.

KARL EDWARD WAGNER

Lisette had explained that she had spent the evening with Dr Magnus. The fact that she was receiving emotional therapy, as they interpreted it, caused several mental notes to be made. Efforts to reach Dr Magnus by telephone proved unsuccessful, but his secretary did confirm that Miss Seyrig had shown up for her appointment the previous afternoon. Dr Magnus would get in touch with them as soon as he returned to his office. No, she did not know why he had cancelled today's appointments, but it was not unusual for Dr Magnus to dash off suddenly when essential research demanded immediate attention.

After a while they let Lisette make phone calls. She phoned her parents, then wished she hadn't. It was still the night before in California, and it was like turning back the hands of time to no avail. They urged her to take the next flight home, but of course it wasn't all that simple, and it just wasn't feasible for either of them to fly over on a second's notice, since after all there really was nothing they could do. She phoned Maitland Reddin, who was stunned at the news and offered to help in any way he could, but Lisette couldn't think of any way. She phoned Midge Vaughn, who hung up on her. She phoned Dr Magnus, who still couldn't be reached. Mercifully, the police took care of phoning Danielle's next of kin.

A physician at New Scotland Yard had spoken with her briefly and had given her some pills – a sedative to ease her into sleep after her ordeal. They had driven her back to the flat after impressing upon her the need to be present at the inquest. She must not be concerned should any hypothetical assailant yet be lurking about, inasmuch as the flat would be under surveillance.

Lisette stared dully about the flat, still unable to comprehend what had happened. The police had been thorough –

measuring, dusting for fingerprints, leaving things in a mess. Bleakly Lisette tried to convince herself that this was only another nightmare, that in a moment Danielle would pop in and find her asleep on the couch. Christ, what was she going to do with all of Danielle's things? Danielle's mother was remarried and living in Colorado; her father was an executive in a New York investment corporation. Evidently he had made arrangements to have the body shipped back to the States.

'Oh, Danielle.' Lisette was too stunned for tears. Perhaps she should check into a hotel for now. No, she couldn't bear being all alone with her thoughts in a strange place. How strange to realize now that she really had no close friends in London other than Danielle – and what friends she did have were mostly people she'd met through Danielle.

She'd left word with Dr Magnus's secretary for him to call her once he came in. Perhaps she should call there once again, just in case Dr Magnus has missed her message. Lisette couldn't think what good Dr Magnus could do, but he was such an understanding person and she felt much better whenever she spoke with him.

She considered the bottle of pills in her bag. Perhaps it would be best to take a couple of them and sleep around the clock. She felt too drained just now to have energy enough to think.

The phone began to ring. Lisette stared at it for a moment without comprehension, then lunged up from the couch to answer it.

'Is this Lisette Seyrig?'

It was a woman's voice – one Lisette didn't recognize. 'Yes. Who's calling, please?'

'This is Beth Garrington, Lisette. I hope I'm not disturbing you.'

'That's quite all right.'

'You poor dear! Maitland Reddin phoned to tell me of the tragedy. I can't tell you how shocked I am. Danielle seemed such a dear from our brief contact, and she had such a great talent.'

'Thank you. I'm sorry you weren't able to know her better.' Lisette sensed guilt and embarrassment at the memory of that brief contact.

'Darling, you can't be thinking about staying in that flat alone. Is there someone there with you?'

'No, there isn't. That's all right. I'll be fine.'

'Don't be silly. Listen, I have enough empty bedrooms in this old barn to open a hotel. Why don't you just pack a few things and come straight over?'

'That's very kind of you, but I really couldn't.'

'Nonsense! It's no good for you to be there all by yourself. Strange as this may sound, but when I'm not throwing one of these invitational riots, this is a quiet little backwater and things are dull as church. I'd love the company, and it will do you a world of good to get away.'

'You're really very kind to invite me, but I . . .'

'Please, Lisette – be reasonable. I have guest rooms here already made up, and I'll send the car around to pick you up. All you need do is say yes and toss a few things into your bag. After a good night's sleep, you'll feel much more like coping with things tomorrow.'

When Lisette didn't immediately reply, Beth added carefully: 'Besides, Lisette. I understand the police haven't ruled out the possibility of murder. In that event, unless poor Danielle simply forgot to lock up, there is a chance that whoever did this has a key to your flat.'

'The police said they'd watch the house.'

'He might also be someone you both know and trust, someone Danielle invited in.'

Lisette stared wildly at the sinister shadows that lengthened about the flat. Her refuge had been violated. Even familiar objects seemed tainted and alien. She fought back tears. 'I don't know what to think.' She realized she'd been clutching the receiver for a long silent interval.

'Poor dear! There's nothing you need think about! Now listen. I'm at my solicitor's tidying up some property matters for Aunt Julia. I'll phone right now to have my car sent around for you. It'll be there by the time you pack your toothbrush and pyjamas, and whisk you straight off to bucolic Maida Vale. The maids will plump up your pillows for you, and you can have a nice nap before I get home for dinner. Poor darling, I'll bet you haven't eaten a thing. Now, say you'll come.'

'Thank you. It's awfully good of you. Of course I will.'

'Then it's done. Don't worry about a thing, Lisette. I'll see you this evening.'

XII

Dr Magnus hunched forward on the narrow seat of the taxi, wearily massaging his forehead and temples. It might not help his mental fatigue, but maybe the reduced muscle tension would ease his headache. He glanced at his watch. Getting on past ten. He'd had no sleep last night, and it didn't look as if he'd be getting much tonight. If only those girls would answer their phone!

It didn't help matters that his conscience plagued him. He had broken a sacred trust. He should never have made use of post-hypnotic suggestion last night to persuade Lisette to return for a further session. It went against all principles, but there had been no other course: the girl was adamant, and he had to know – he had been so close to establishing final proof. If only for one final session of regressive hypnosis . . .

Afterward he had spent a sleepless night, too excited for rest, at work in his study trying to reconcile the conflicting elements of Lisette's released memories with the historical data his research had so far compiled. By morning he had been able to pull together just enough facts to deepen the mystery. He had phoned his secretary at home to cancel all his appointments, and had spent the day at the tedious labour of delving through dusty municipal records and newspaper files, working feverishly as the past reluctantly yielded one bewildering clue after another.

By now Dr Magnus was exhausted, hungry, and none too clean, but he had managed to establish proof of his theories. He was not elated. In doing so he had uncovered another secret, something undreamt of in his philosophies. He began to hope that his life work was in error.

'Here's the address, sir.'

'Thank you, driver.' Dr Magnus awoke from his grim revery and saw that he had reached his destination. Quickly he paid the driver and hurried up the walk to Lisette's flat. Only a few lights were on, and he rang the bell urgently – a helpless sense of foreboding making his movements clumsy.

'Just one moment, sir!'

Dr Magnus jerked about at the voice. Two men in plain clothes approached him briskly from the pavement.

'Stand easy! We're police.'

'Is something the matter, officers?' Obviously something was.

'Might we ask what your business here is, sir?'

'Certainly. I'm a friend of Miss Borland and Miss Seyrig. I haven't been able to reach them by phone, and as I have some rather urgent matters to discuss with Miss Seyrig, I thought perhaps I might try reaching her here at her flat.' He realized he was far too nervous.

'Might we see some identification, sir?'

'Is there anything wrong, officers?' Magnus repeated, producing his wallet.

'Dr Ingmar Magnus.' The taller of the pair regarded him quizzically. 'I take it you don't keep up with the news, Dr. Magnus.'

'Just what is this about!'

'I'm Inspector Bradley, Dr Magnus, and this is Detective Sergeant Wharton. CID. We've been wanting to ask you a few questions, sir, if you'll just come with us.'

It was totally dark when Lisette awoke from troubled sleep. She stared wide-eyed into the darkness for a moment, wondering where she was. Slowly memory supplanted the vague images of her dream. Switching on a lamp beside her bed, Lisette frowned at her watch. It was close to midnight. She had overslept.

Beth's Rolls had come for her almost before she had had time hastily to pack her overnight bag. Once at the house in Maida Vale, a maid – wearing a more conventional uniform than those at her last visit – had shown her to a spacious guest room on the top floor. Lisette had taken a sedative pill and gratefully collapsed onto the bed. She'd planned to catch a short nap, then meet her hostess for dinner. Instead she had slept for almost ten solid hours. Beth must be convinced she was a hopeless twit after this.

As so often happens after an overextended nap, Lisette now felt restless. She wished she'd thought to bring a book. The

KARL EDWARD WAGNER

house was completely silent. Surely it was too late to ring for a maid. No doubt Beth had meant to let her sleep through until morning, and by now would have retired herself. Perhaps she should take another pill and go back to sleep herself.

On the other hand, Beth Garrington hardly seemed the type to make it an early night. She might well still be awake, perhaps watching television where the noise wouldn't disturb her guest. In any event, Lisette didn't want to go back to sleep just yet.

She climbed out of bed, realizing that she'd only half undressed before falling asleep. Pulling off bra and panties, Lisette slipped into the antique nightdress of ribbons and lace she'd brought along. She hadn't thought to pack slippers or a robe, but it was a warm night, and the white cotton gown was modest enough for a peek into the hall.

There was a ribbon of light edging the door of the room at the far end of the hall. The rest of the hallway lay in darkness. Lisette stepped quietly from her room. Since Beth hadn't mentioned other guests and the servant's quarters were elsewhere, presumably the light was coming from her hostess's bedroom and indicated she might still be awake. Lisette decided she really should make the effort to meet her hostess while in a conscious state.

She heard a faint sound of music as she tiptoed down the hallway. The door to the room was ajar, and the music came from within. She was in luck; Beth must still be up. At the doorway she knocked softly.

'Beth? Are you awake? It's Lisette.'

There was no answer, but the door swung open at her touch.

Lisette started to call out again, but her voice froze in her throat. She recognized the tune she heard, and she knew this room. When she entered the bedroom, she could no more alter her actions than she could control the course of her dreams.

It was a large bedroom, entirely furnished in the mode of the late Victorian period. The windows were curtained, and the room's only light came from a candle upon a night table beside the huge four-poster bed. An antique gold pocket watch lay upon the night table also, and the watch was chiming an old music box tune.

Lisette crossed the room, praying that this was no more than another vivid recurrence of her nightmare. She reached the night table and saw that the watch's hands pointed toward midnight. The chimes stopped. She picked up the watch and examined the picture that she knew would be inside the watchcase.

The picture was a photograph of herself.

Lisette let the watch clatter onto the table, stared in terror at the four-poster bed.

From within, a hand drew back the curtains.

Lisette wished she could scream, could awaken.

Sweeping aside the curtains, the occupant of the bed sat up and gazed at her.

And Lisette stared back at herself.

'Can't you drive a bit faster than this!'

Inspector Bradley resisted the urge to wink at Detective Sergeant Wharton. 'Sit back, Dr Magnus. We'll be there in good time. I trust you'll have rehearsed some apologies for when we disrupt a peaceful household in the middle of the night.'

'I only pray such apologies will be necessary,' Dr Magnus said, continuing to sit forward as if that would inspire the driver to go faster.

It hadn't been easy, Dr Magnus reflected. He dare not tell

them the truth. He suspected that Bradley had agreed to making a late night call on Beth Garrington more to check out his alibi than from any credence he gave to Magnus's improvised tale.

Buried all day in frenzied research, Dr Magnus hadn't listened to the news, had ignored the tawdry London tabloids with their lurid headlines: 'Naked Beauty Slashed in Tub', 'Nude Model Slain in Bath', 'Party Girl Suicide or Ripper's Victim?' The shock of learning of Danielle's death was seconded by the shock of discovering that he was one of the 'important leads' police were following.

It had taken all his powers of persuasion to convince them to release him – or at least, to accompany him to the house in Maida Vale. Ironically, he and Lisette were the only ones who could account for each other's presence elsewhere at the time of Danielle's death. While the CID might have been sceptical as to the nature of their late night session at Dr Magnus's office, there were a few corroborating details. A barman at the Catherine Wheel had remembered the distinguished gent with the beard leaving after his lady friend had dropped off of a sudden. The cleaning lady had heard voices and left his office undisturbed. This much they'd already checked in verifying Lisette's whereabouts that night. Half a dozen harassed records clerks could testify as to Dr Magnus's presence for today.

Dr Magnus grimly reviewed the results of his research. There was an Elisabeth Beresford, born in London in 1879, of a well-to-do family who lived in Cheyne Row on the Chelsea Embankment. Elisabeth Beresford married a Captain Donald Stapledon in 1899 and moved to India with her husband. She returned to London, evidently suffering from consumption contracted while abroad, and died in 1900. She was buried in Highgate Cemetery. That much Dr

Magnus had initially learned with some difficulty. From that basis he had pressed on for additional corroborating details, both from Lisette's released memories and from research into records of the period.

It had been particularly difficult to trace the subsequent branches of the family – something he must do in order to establish that Elisabeth Beresford could not have been an ancestress of Lisette Seyrig. And it disturbed him that he had been unable to locate Elisabeth Stapledon, née Beresford's tomb in Highgate Cemetery.

Last night he had pushed Lisette as relentlessly as he dared. Out of her resurfacing visions of horror he finally found a clue. These were not images from nightmare, not symbolic representations of buried fears. They were literal memories.

Because of the sensation involved and the considerable station of the families concerned, public records had discreetly avoided reference to the tragedy, as had the better newspapers. The yellow journals were less reticent, and here Dr Magnus began to know fear.

Elisabeth Stapledon had been buried alive.

At her final wishes, the body had not been embalmed. The papers suggested that this was a clear premonition of her fate, and quoted passages from Edgar Allan Poe. Captain Stapledon paid an evening visit to his wife's tomb and discovered her wandering in a dazed condition about the graves. This was more than a month after the entombment.

The newspapers were full of pseudo-scientific theories, spiritualist explanations, and long accounts of Indian mystics who had remained in a state of suspended animation for weeks on end. No one seems to have explained exactly how Elisabeth Stapledon escaped from both coffin and crypt, but

KARL EDWARD WAGNER

it was supposed that desperate strength had wrenched loose the screws, while providentially the crypt had not been properly locked after a previous visit.

Husband and wife understandably went abroad immediately afterward in order to escape publicity and for Elisabeth Stapledon to recover from her ordeal. This she very quickly did, but evidently the shock was more than Captain Stapledon could endure. He died in 1902, and his wife returned to London soon after, inheriting his extensive fortune and properties, including their house in Maida Vale. When she later inherited her own family's estate – her sole brother fell in the Boer War – she was a lady of great wealth.

Elisabeth Stapledon became one of the most notorious hostesses of the Edwardian era and on until the close of the First World War. Her beauty was considered remarkable, and men marvelled while her rivals bemoaned that she scarcely seemed to age with the passing years. After the War she left London to travel about the exotic East. In 1924 news came of her death in India.

Her estate passed to her daughter, Jane Stapledon, born abroad in 1901. While Elisabeth Stapledon made occasional references to her daughter, Jane was raised and educated in Europe and never seemed to have come to London until her arrival in 1925. Some had suggested that the mother had wished to keep her daughter pure from her own Bohemian lifestyle, but when Jane Stapledon appeared it seemed more likely that her mother's motives for her seclusion had been born of jealously. Jane Stapledon had all her mother's beauty – indeed, her older admirers vowed she was the very image of Elisabeth in her youth. She also had inherited her mother's taste for wild living; with a new circle of friends from her own age group, she took up where her mother had left off. The newspapers were particularly scandalized by her association with Aleister Crowley and others of his circle. Although her dissipations bridged the years of Flaming Youth to the Lost Generation, even her enemies had to admit she carried her years extremely well. In 1943 Jane Stapledon was missing and presumed dead after an air raid levelled and burned a section of London where she had gone to dine with friends.

Papers in the hands of her solicitor left her estate to a daughter living in America, Julia Weatherford, born in Miami in 1934. Evidently her mother had enjoyed a typical whirlwind resort romance with an American millionaire while wintering in Florida. Their marriage was a secret one, annulled following Julia's birth, and her daughter had been left with her former husband. Julia Weatherford arrived from the States early in 1946. Any doubts as to the authenticity of her claim were instantly banished, for she was the very picture of her mother in her younger days. Julia again seemed to have the family's wild streak, and she carried on the tradition of wild parties and bizarre acquaintances through the Beat Generation to the Flower Children. Her older friends thought it amazing that Julia in a minidress might easily be mistaken as being of the same age group as her young pot-smoking hippie friends. But it may have been that at last her youth began to fade, because since 1967 Julia Weatherford had been living more or less in seclusion in Europe, occasionally visited by her niece.

Her niece, Beth Garrington, born in 1950, was the orphaned daughter of Julia's American half-sister and a wealthy young Englishman from Julia's collection. After her parents' death in a plane crash in 1970, Beth had become her aunt's protégée and carried on the mad life in London. It was apparent that Beth Garrington would inherit her aunt's property as well. It was also apparent that she was the spitting image of her Aunt Julia when the latter was her age. It would be most interesting to see the two of them together. And that, of course, no one had ever done.

At first Dr Magnus had been unwilling to accept the truth of the dread secret he had uncovered. And yet, with the knowledge of Lisette's released memories, he knew there could be no other conclusion.

It was astonishing how thoroughly a woman who thrived on notoriety could avoid having her photographs published. After all, changing fashions and new hair styles, careful adjustments with cosmetics, could only do so much, and while the mind's eye had an inaccurate memory, a camera lens did not. Dr Magnus did succeed in finding a few photographs through persistent research. Given a good theatrical costume and make-up crew, they all might have been taken of the same woman on the same day.

They might also all have been taken of Lisette Seyrig.

However, Dr Magnus knew that it *would* be possible to see Beth Garrington and Lisette Seyrig together.

And he prayed he would be in time to prevent this.

With this knowledge tormenting his thoughts, it was a miracle that Dr Magnus had held onto sanity well enough to persuade New Scotland Yard to make this late night drive to Maida Vale – desperate, in view of what he knew to be true. He had suffered a shock as severe as any that night when they told him at last where Lisette had gone.

'She's quite all right. She's staying with a friend.'

'Might I ask where?'

'A chauffered Rolls picked her up. We checked registration, and it belongs to a Miss Elisabeth Garrington in Maida Vale.'

Dr Magnus had been frantic then, had demanded that they take him there instantly. A telephone call informed them that

Miss Seyrig was sleeping under sedation and could not be disturbed; she would return his call in the morning.

Controlling his panic, Dr Magnus had managed to contrive a disjointed tangle of half-truths and plausible lies – anything to convince them to get over to the Garrington house as quickly as possible. They already knew he was one of those occult kooks. Very well, he assured them that Beth Garrington was involved in a secret society of drug fiends and satanists (all true enough), that Danielle and Lisette had been lured to their most recent orgy for unspeakable purposes. Lisette had been secretly drugged, but Danielle had escaped to carry her roommate home before they could be used for whatever depraved rites awaited them – perhaps ritual sacrifice. Danielle had been murdered – either to shut her up or as part of the ritual – and now they had Lisette in their clutches as well.

All very melodramatic, but enough of it was true, Inspector Bradley knew of the sex and drugs orgies that took place there, but there was firm pressure from higher up to look the other way. Further, he knew enough about some of the more bizarre cult groups in London to consider that ritual murder was quite feasible given the proper combination of sick minds and illegal drugs. And while it hadn't been made public, the medical examiner was of the opinion that the slashes to the Borland girl's throat and wrists had been an attempt to disguise the fact that she had already bled to death from two deep punctures through the jugular vein.

A demented killer, obviously. A ritual murder? You couldn't discount it just yet. Inspector Bradley had ordered a car.

'Who are you, Lisette Seyrig, that you wear my face?'

Beth Garrington rose sinuously from her bed. She was dressed in an off-the-shoulder nightgown of antique lace, much the same as that which Lisette wore. Her green eyes – the eyes behind the mask that had so shaken Lisette when last they'd met – held her in their spell.

'When first faithful Adrian swore he'd seen my double, I thought his brain had begun to reel with final madness. But after he followed you to your little gallery and brought me there to see your portrait, I knew I had encountered something beyond even my experience.'

Lisette stood frozen with dread fascination as her nightmare came to life. Her twin paced about her, appraising her coolly as a serpent considers its hypnotized victim.

'Who are you, Lisette Seyrig, that yours is the face I have seen in my dreams, the face that haunted my nightmares as I lay dying, the face that I thought was my own?'

Lisette forced her lips to speak. '*Who* are you?'

'My name? I change that whenever it becomes prudent for me to do so. Tonight I am Beth Garrington. Long ago I was Elisabeth Beresford.'

'How can this be possible?' Lisette hoped she was dealing with a mad-woman, but knew her hope was false.

'A spirit came to me in my dreams and slowly stole away my mortal life, in return giving me eternal life. You understand what I say, even though your reason insists that such things cannot be.'

She unfastened Lisette's gown and let it fall to the floor, then did the same with her own. Standing face to face, their nude bodies seemed one a reflection of the other.

Elisabeth took Lisette's face in her hands and kissed her full on the lips. The kiss was a long one; her breath was cold in Lisette's mouth. When Elisabeth released her lips and gazed longingly into her eyes, Lisette saw the pointed fangs that now curved downward from her upper jaw.

'Will you cry out, I wonder? If so, let it be in ecstasy and not in fear. I shan't drain you and discard you as I did your silly friend. No, Lisette, my new-found sister. I shall take your life in tiny kisses from night to night – kisses that you will long for with your entire being. And in the end you shall pass over to serve me as my willing chattel – as have the few others I have chosen over the years.'

Lisette trembled beneath her touch, powerless to break away. From the buried depths of her unconscious mind, understanding slowly emerged. She did not resist when Elisabeth led her to the bed and lay down beside her on the silken sheets. Lisette was past knowing fear.

Elisabeth stretched her naked body upon Lisette's warmer flesh, lying between her thighs as would a lover. Her cool fingers caressed Lisette; her kisses teased a path from her belly across her breasts and to the hollow of her throat.

Elisabeth paused and gazed into Lisette's eyes. Her fangs gleamed with a reflection of the inhuman lust in her expression. 'And now I give you a kiss sweeter than any passion your mortal brain dare imagine, Lisette Seyrig – even as once I first received such a kiss from a dream-spirit whose eyes stared into mine from my own face. Why have you haunted my dreams, Lisette Seyrig?'

Lisette returned her gaze silently, without emotion. Nor did she flinch when Elisabeth's lips closed tightly against her throat, and the only sound was a barely perceptible tearing, like the bursting of a maidenhead, and the soft movement of suctioning lips.

Elisabeth suddenly broke away with an inarticulate cry of pain. Her lips smeared with scarlet, she stared down at Lisette in bewildered fear. Lisette, blood streaming from the wound on her throat, stared back at her with a smile of unholy hatred.

'*What* are you, Lisette Seyrig?'

'I am Elisabeth Beresford.' Lisette's tone was implacable. 'In another lifetime you drove my soul from my body and stole my flesh for your own. Now I have come back to reclaim that which once was mine.'

Elisabeth sought to leap away, but Lisette's arms embraced her with sudden, terrible strength – pulling their naked bodies together in a horrid imitation of two lovers at the moment of ecstasy.

The scream that echoed into the night was not one of ecstasy.

At the sound of the scream – afterward they never agreed whether it was two voices together or only one – Inspector Bradley ceased listening to the maid's outraged protests and burst past her into the house.

'Upstairs! On the double!' he ordered needlessly. Already Dr Magnus had lunged past him and was sprinting up the stairway.

'I think it came from the next floor up! Check inside all the rooms!' Later he cursed himself for not posting a man at the door, for by the time he was again able to think rationally, there was no trace of the servants.

In the master bedroom at the end of the third floor hallway, they found two bodies behind the curtains of the big four-poster bed. One had only just been murdered; her nude body was drenched in the blood from her torn throat – seemingly far too much blood for one body. The other body was a desiccated corpse, obviously dead for a great many years. The dead girl's limbs obscenely embraced the mouldering cadaver that lay atop her, and her teeth, in final spasm, were locked in the lich's throat. As they gaped in horror, clumps of hair and bits of dried skin could be seen to drop away.

Detective Sergeant Wharton looked away and vomited on the floor.

'I owe you a sincere apology, Dr Magnus.' Inspector Bradley's face was grim. 'You were right. Ritual murder by a gang of sick degenerates. Detective Sergeant! Leave off that and put out an all points bulletin for Beth Garrington. And round up anyone else you find here! Move, man!'

'If only I'd understood in time,' Dr Magnus muttered. He was obviously at the point of collapse.

'No, *I* should have listened to you sooner,' Bradley growled. 'We might have been in time to prevent this. The devils must have fled down some servant's stairway when they heard us burst in. I confess I've bungled this badly.'

'She was a vampire, you see,' Dr Magnus told him dully, groping to explain. 'A vampire loses its soul when it becomes one of the undead. But the soul is deathless; it lives on even when its previous incarnation has become a soulless demon. Elisabeth Bereford's soul lived on, until Elisabeth Beresford found reincarnation in Lisette Seyrig. Don't you see? Elisabeth Beresford met her own reincarnation, and that meant destruction for them both.'

Inspector Bradley had been only half listening. 'Dr Magnus, you've done all you can. I think you should go down to the car with Detective Sergeant Wharton now and rest until the ambulance arrives.'

'But you must see that I was right!' Dr Magnus pleaded. Madness danced in his eyes. 'If the soul is immortal and infinite, then time has no meaning for the soul. Elisabeth Beresford was haunting herself.'

KARL EDWARD WAGNER

The Undead

ROBERT BLOCH

Vampire hunter: Professor Abraham Van Helsing
Locality of case: California
Time: 1984
Author: Chicago-born Robert Bloch (1917–94), who was
an enthusiastic reader of *Weird Tales* and a fan of the great
H. P. Lovecraft, has a world-wide reputation as one of the
masters of horror fiction. Inspired and instructed by
Lovecraft, Bob poured out a stream of macabre short
stories and novels which reached their apogee with
Psycho which Alfred Hitchcock made into probably his
best film in 1959. A number of Bloch's subsequent works
have also been adapted for the screen and he had written
scripts for many more. Vampirism was a constant theme
in his work – he had produced over twenty short stories
and three novels on the theme – the most recent of these
being 'The Undead'. This was inspired by the startling
revelation in 1984 that a copy of Bram Stoker's manuscript for *Dracula*, complete with his annotations, corrections and revisions in holograph, had come to light in
America. It was to be sold in California and bids were
being invited for what was described as the original typed
manuscript of 'the ultimate archetypal fantasy of death
and immortality'. Upon hearing the news, Bob, with his
unfailing ingenuity and ability to give a grim twist to even
the most everyday situation, sat down at his own typewriter and produced the following little masterpiece of
terror...

Every evening at six Carol took off her glasses, but it didn't seem to help. In the old movie reruns on TV, Cary Grant was always there to exclaim – with a mixture of surprise and gentlemanly lust – 'Why, you're beautiful without your glasses!'

No one had ever told Carol that, even though she really was beautiful, or almost so. With her light auburn hair, fair skin, regular features and sapphire-blue eyes, she needed only the benefit of contact lenses to perfect her image.

But why bother, when Cary Grant wasn't around? The bookshop's customers for first editions and rare manuscripts seemed more interested in caressing parchment than fondling flesh.

And by nightfall the place was empty; even its owner had departed, leaving Carol to shut up shop, lock the doors and set the alarms. With a valuable stock on hand she was always mindful of her responsibility.

Or almost always.

Tonight, seated in the rear office and applying her lipstick preparatory to departure, she was surprised to hear footsteps moving across the uncarpeted floor in the hall beyond.

Carol frowned and put her compact down on the desktop. She distinctly recalled turning out the shop lights, but in her preoccupation with self-pity could she have forgotten to lock the front entrance?

Apparently so, because now the footsteps halted and a figure appeared in the office doorway. Carol blinked at the black blur of the body, surmounted by a white blob of head and hair.

Then she put on her glasses and the black blur was transformed into a dark suit, the white blob became the face of an elderly gentleman with a receding hairline. Both his suit and his face were wrinkled, but the old man's dignified bearing overshadowed sartorial shortcomings and the onslaughts of age. And when he spoke his voice was resonant.

'Good evening. Are you the proprietor of this establishment?'

'I'm sorry,' Carol said. 'He's already left. We're closed for the night.'

'So I see.' The stranger nodded. 'Forgive me for intruding at this late hour, but I have traveled a long way and hoped I might still find him here.'

'We open tomorrow at ten. He'll be here then. Or if you'd like to leave a message—'

'It is a matter of some urgency,' the old man said. 'Word has reached me that your firm recently came into the possession of a manuscript – a manuscript which supposedly disappeared over seventy years ago.'

Carol nodded. 'That's right. The *Dracula* original.'

'You know the novel?'

'Of course. I read it years ago.'

Reaching into his pocket the stranger produced an old-fashioned calling-card and handed it to her. 'Then perhaps you will find this name familiar.'

Carol peered at the lettering. The Gothic typescript was difficult to decipher and she repeated aloud what she read.

'Abraham Van Helsing?'

'Correct.' The old man smiled.

Carol shook her head. 'Wait a minute. You don't expect me to believe—'

'That I am the namesake of my great-grandfather, Mynheer Doctor-Professor Van Helsing of Amsterdam?' He nodded. 'Oh yes, I can assure you that *Dracula* is not entirely a work of fiction. The identity of some of its characters was disguised, but others, like my illustrious ancestor, appeared under their own names. Now do you understand why I am interested in the original manuscript?' As he spoke, the old man glanced at the safe in the far corner. 'Is it too much to hope that you have it here?'

'I'm sorry,' Carol said. 'I'm afraid it's been sold.'

'Sold?'

'Yes. The day after we sent out our announcement the phones started ringing. I've never seen anything like it – just about every customer on our mailing list wanted to make a bid. And the final offer we got was simply fantastic.'

'Could you tell me who purchased the manuscript?'

'A private collector. I don't know his name, because my boss didn't tell me. Part of the deal was that the buyer would remain completely anonymous. I guess he was afraid somebody would try to steal it from him.'

The old man's frown conveyed a mingling of anger and contempt. 'How very cautious of him! But then they were all cautious – concealing something which never truly belonged to any of them. That manuscript has been hidden away all these years because it was stolen in the first place. Stolen from the man to whom the author gave it in gratitude for providing him with the basis of the novel – my own great-grandfather.' He stared at Carol. 'Who brought this to your employer?'

'He didn't tell me that, either. It's very hush-hush—'

'You see? Just as I told you. He must have known he had no right to possess it. Thieves, all of them!'

Carol shrugged. 'Really, I didn't know.'

'Of course. And I'm not blaming you, my dear young lady. But perhaps you can still be of some assistance to me. Did you happen to see the manuscript before it was sold?'

'Yes.'

'Can you describe it?'

'Well, to begin with, it wasn't called *Dracula*. The hand-written title was *The Undead*.'

'Ah, yes.' The old man nodded quickly. 'That would be the original. What else can you recall about it?'

'The cover page was in Bram Stoker's handwriting, but the manuscript was typed. The author's changes and editorial corrections were done by hand, and so were the renumbering of the pages. It looked as though a lot of pages had been omitted – almost a hundred, I'd guess.' Carol paused. 'That's really just about all I remember.'

'And more than enough. From your description there's no doubt it is the genuine manuscript.' The old man nodded again. 'You're sure about pages being omitted?'

'Yes, quite sure, because my boss commented on that. Why, is it important?'

'Very. It seems Bram Stoker was wiser than his informant. Although the published novel does refer to Count Dracula's plan to bring vampirism to England, this motive is not stressed. What the missing pages contained is what Van Helsing revealed about Dracula's ultimate goal – to spread vampirism throughout the world. They also presented factual proof of Dracula's existence, proof too convincing to be ignored. Stoker wrote down everything Van Helsing told him, but had second thoughts about including it in his final draft. I wished to make certain, however, that those pages didn't still exist in manuscript form. Now that I know, it won't even be necessary to seek out the new owner.'

'But you talk as though all this was true,' Carol said. 'It's only a novel. And Count Dracula gets killed in the end.'

'Again an example of Stoker's caution,' the old man told her. 'He had to invent a death-scene to reassure his readers. Even so, just think of the influence that novel has had on millions of people who learned of Dracula and vampirism through the book and the theatre and films. As it is, many of them still half-believe.' The resonant voice deepened. 'What do you think would have happened if Stoker hadn't novelized the story – if he'd written it for what it was, a true account of the actual experiences of Abraham Van Helsing? Even in novel form, if those missing pages still existed their message might bring a warning to the world which would endanger Dracula's plans.'

Carol glanced at her watch as he spoke. Six-thirty. She was getting hungry and the old man's hangup was getting on her nerves. She stood up, forcing a smile.

'This has been very interesting,' she said. 'But I really must close up now.'

'You have been most kind.' The old man smiled. 'It seems a pity you do not entirely believe me, but I speak the truth. Count Dracula is as real as I am.'

Carol reached for her open compact on the desk. In the oval mirror she saw her reflection, but there was none of her visitor, even though he was standing quite close. Close enough for her to smell the rank breath, see the whiteness of the pointed teeth, feel the surprising strength of the hands that rose now to imprison her in their implacable grip.

As he forced her head back Carol's glasses dislodged, clattering to the floor, and for a moment her image in the compact mirror was indeed quite beautiful. Then the bright droplets spurted down, blotting it out forever.

ROBERT BLOCH

The Master of Rampling Gate

ANNE RICE

Vampire hunter: Julie Rampling
Locality of case: Northern England
Time: 1985
Author: American novelist Jane O'Brien Rice (1941–)
was raised in New Orleans and drew heavily on her
background and strict religious upbringing for her now
world-famous first novel, *Interview With The Vampire*
(1976), which *The Catholic Herald* declared, 'must stand
alongside Bram Stoker's Dracula', and has recently been
filmed with Tom Cruise as the vampire, Lestat. This book,
like all her work, is very much in the decadent tradition of
horror fiction and it has been followed by a series of
novels about a race of the Undead living in contemporary
society which are known by the generic title 'The Vampire
Chronicles'. Anne Rice's stories are also marked by their
careful attention to authentic detail and brilliant exposition
of sexual undertones: both of which will be found in 'The
Master of Rampling Gate', one of Anne's few short
stories, in which a young woman decides to track down
the source of the mysterious evil which has been haunting
the confines of her old family home for generations . . .

Rampling Gate: It was so real to us in those old pictures, rising like a fairytale castle out of its own dark wood. A wilderness of gables and chimneys between those two immense towers, grey stone walls mantled in ivy, mullioned windows reflecting the drifting clouds.

But why had Father never gone there? Why had he never taken us? And why on his deathbed, in those grim months after Mother's passing, did he tell my brother, Richard, that Rampling Gate must be torn down stone by stone? Rampling Gate that had always belonged to Ramplings, Rampling Gate which had stood for over five hundred years.

We were in awe of the task that lay before us, and painfully confused. Richard had just finished four years at Oxford. Two whirlwind social seasons in London had proven me something of a shy success. I still preferred scribbling poems and stories in the quiet of my room to dancing the night away, but I'd kept that a good secret, and though we were not spoilt children, we had enjoyed the best of everything our parents could give. But now the carefree years were ended. We had to be careful and wise.

And our hearts ached as, sitting together in Father's booklined study, we looked at the old pictures of Rampling Gate before the small coal fire. 'Destroy it, Richard, as soon as I am gone,' Father had said.

'I just don't understand it, Julie,' Richard confessed, as he filled the little crystal glass in my hand with sherry. 'It's the genuine article, that old place, a real fourteenth-century manor house in excellent repair. A Mrs Blessington, born and reared in the village of Rampling, has apparently managed it all these years. She was there when Uncle Baxter died, and he was the last Rampling to live under that roof.'

'Do you remember,' I asked, 'the year that Father took all these pictures down and put them away?'

'I shall never forget that,' Richard said. 'How could I? It

was so peculiar, and so unlike Father, too.' He sat back, drawing slowly on his pipe. 'There had been that bizarre incident in Victoria Station, when he had seen that young man.'

'Yes, exactly,' I said, snuggling back into the velvet chair and looking into the tiny dancing flames in the grate. 'You remember how upset Father was?'

Yet it was a simple incident. In fact nothing really happened at all. We couldn't have been more than six and eight at the time and we had gone to the station with Father to say farewell to friends. Through the window of a train Father saw a young man who startled and upset him. I could remember the face clearly to this day. Remarkably handsome, with a narrow nose and well-drawn eyebrows, and a mop of lustrous brown hair. The large black eyes had regarded Father with the saddest expression as Father had drawn us back and hurried us away.

'And the argument that night, between Father and Mother,' Richard said thoughtfully. 'I remember that we listened on the landing and we were so afraid.'

'And Father said *he* wasn't content to be master of Rampling Gate anymore; *he* had come to London and revealed himself. An unspeakable horror, that is what he called it, that *he* should be so bold.'

'Yes, exactly, and when Mother tried to quiet him, when she suggested that he was imagining things, he went into a perfect rage.'

'But who could it have been, the master of Rampling Gate, if Father wasn't the master? Uncle Baxter was long dead by then.'

'I just don't know what to make of it,' Richard murmured. 'And there's nothing in Father's papers to explain any of it at all.' He examined the most recent of the pictures, a lovely tinted engraving that showed the house perfectly reflected in the azure water of its lake. 'But I tell you, the worst part of it, Julie,' he said shaking his head, 'is that we've never even seen the house ourselves.'

I glanced at him and our eyes met in a moment of confusion that quickly passed to something else. I leant forward:

'He did not say we couldn't go there, did he, Richard?' I demanded. 'That we couldn't visit the house before it was destroyed.'

'No, of course he didn't!' Richard said. The smile broke over his face easily. 'After all, don't we owe it to the others, Julie? Uncle Baxter who spent the last of his fortune restoring the house, even this old Mrs Blessington that has kept it all these years?'

'And what about the village itself?' I added quickly. 'What will it mean to these people to see Rampling Gate destroyed? Of course we must go and see the place ourselves.'

'Then it's settled. I'll write to Mrs Blessington immediately. I'll tell her we're coming and that we can not say how long we will stay.'

'Oh, Richard, that would be too marvellous!' I couldn't keep from hugging him, though it flustered him and he pulled on his pipe just exactly the way Father would have done. 'Make it at least a fortnight,' I said. 'I want so to know the place, especially if . . .'

But it was too sad to think of Father's admonition. And much more fun to think of the journey itself. I'd pack my manuscripts, for who knew, maybe in that melancholy and exquisite setting I'd find exactly the inspiration I required. It was almost a wicked exhilaration I felt, breaking the gloom that had hung over us since the day that Father was laid to rest.

'It is the right thing to do, isn't it, Richard?' I asked uncertainly, a little disconcerted by how much I wanted to go. There was some illicit pleasure in it, going to Rampling Gate at last.

'"Unspeakable horror."' I repeated Father's words with a little grimace. What did it all mean? I thought again of the strange, almost exquisite young man I'd glimpsed in that railway carriage, gazing at us all with that wistful expression on his lean face. He had worn a black greatcoat with a red woollen cravat, and I could remember how pale he had been against that dash of red. Like bone china his complexion had been. Strange to remember it so vividly, even to the tilt of his head, and that long luxuriant brown hair. But he had been a blaze against that window. And I realized now that, in those few remarkable moments, he had created for me an ideal of masculine beauty which I had never questioned since. But Father had been so angry in those moments ... I felt an unmistakable pang of guilt.

'Of course it's the right thing, Julie,' Richard answered. He was at the desk, already writing the letters, and I was at a loss to understand the full measure of my thoughts.

It was late afternoon when the wretched old trap carried us up the gentle slope from the little railway station, and we had at last our first real look at that magnificent house. I think I was holding my breath. The sky had paled to a deep rose hue beyond a bank of softly gilded clouds, and the last rays of the sun struck the uppermost panes of the leaded windows and filled them with solid gold.

'Oh, but it's too majestic,' I whispered, 'too like a great cathedral, and to think that it belongs to us.' Richard gave me the smallest kiss on the cheek. I felt mad suddenly and eager somehow to be laid waste by it, through fear or enchantment I could not say, perhaps a sublime mingling of both.

I wanted with all my heart to jump down and draw near on foot, letting those towers grow larger and larger above me, but our old horse had picked up speed. And the little line of stiff starched servants had broken to come forward, the old withered housekeeper with her arms out, the men to take down the boxes and the trunks.

Richard and I were spirited into the great hall by the tiny, nimble figure of Mrs Blessington, our footfalls echoing loudly on the marble tile, our eyes dazzled by the dusty shafts of light that fell on the long oak table and its heavily carved chairs, the sombre, heavy tapestries that stirred ever so slightly against the soaring walls.

'It is an enchanted place,' I cried, unable to contain myself. 'Oh, Richard, we are home!' Mrs Blessington laughed gaily, her dry hand closing tightly on mine.

Her small blue eyes regarded me with the most curiously vacant expression despite her smile. 'Ramplings at Rampling Gate again, I can not tell you what a joyful day this is for me. And yes, my dear,' she said as if reading my mind that very second, 'I am and have been for many years, quite blind. But if you spy a thing out of place in this house, you're to tell me at once, for it would be the exception, I assure you, and not the rule.' And such warmth emanated from her wrinkled little face that I adored her at once.

We found our bedchambers, the very finest in the house, well aired with snow white linen and fires blazing cozily to dry out the damp that never left the thick walls. The small diamond-pane windows opened on a glorious view of the water and the oaks that enclosed it and the few scattered lights that marked the village beyond.

That night, we laughed like children as we supped at the

great oak table, our candles giving only a feeble light. And afterwards, it was a fierce battle of billiards in the game room which had been Uncle Baxter's last renovation, and a little too much brandy, I fear.

It was just before I went to bed that I asked Mrs Blessington if there had been anyone in this house since Uncle Baxter died. That had been the year 1838, almost fifty years ago, and she was already housekeeper then.

'No, my dear,' she said quickly, fluffing the feather pillows. 'Your father came that year as you know, but he stayed for no more than a month or two and then went on home.'

'There was never a young man after that ...' I pushed, but in truth I had little appetite for anything to disturb the happiness I felt. How I loved the Spartan cleanliness of this bedchamber, the stone walls bare of paper or ornament, the high luster of the walnut-panelled bed.

'A young man?' She gave an easy, almost hearty laugh as with unerring certainty of her surroundings, she lifted the poker and stirred the fire. 'What a strange thing for you to ask.'

I sat silent for a moment looking in the mirror, as I took the last of the pins from my hair. It fell down heavy and warm around my shoulders. It felt good, like a cloak under which I could hide. But she turned as if sensing some uneasiness in me, and drew near.

'Why do you say a young man, Miss?' she asked. Slowly, tentatively, her fingers examined the long tresses that lay over my shoulders. She took the brush from my hands.

I felt perfectly foolish telling her the story, but I managed a simplified version, somehow, of our meeting unexpectedly a devilishly handsome young man whom my Father in anger had later called the master of Rampling Gate.

'Handsome, was he?' she asked as she brushed out the tangles in my hair gently. It seemed she hung upon every word as I described him again.

'There were no intruders in this house, then, Mrs Blessington?' I asked. 'No mysteries to be solved . . .'

She gave the sweetest laugh.

'Oh, no, darling, this house is the safest place in the world,' she said quickly. 'It is a happy house. No intruder would dare to trouble Rampling Gate!'

Nothing, in fact, troubled the serenity of the days that followed. The smoke and noise of London, and our Father's dying words, became a dream. What was real were our long walks together through the overgrown gardens, our trips in the little skiff to and fro across the lake. We had tea under the hot glass of the empty conservatory. And early evening found us on our way upstairs with the best of the books from Uncle Baxter's library to read by candlelight in the privacy of our rooms.

And all our discreet inquiries in the village met with more or less the same reply: the villagers loved the house and carried no old or disquieting tales. Repeatedly, in fact, we were told that Rampling was the most contented hamlet in all England, that no one dared – Mrs Blessington's very words – to make trouble here.

'It's our guardian angel, that old house,' said the old woman at the bookshop where Richard stopped for the London papers. 'Was there ever the town of Rampling without the house called Rampling Gate?'

How were we going to tell them of Father's edict? How were we going to remind ourselves? But we spoke not one word about the proposed disaster, and Richard wrote to his firm to say that we should not be back in London till Fall.

He was finding a wealth of classical material in the old volumes that had belonged to Uncle Baxter, and I had set up my writing in the little study that opened off the library which I had all to myself.

Never had I known such peace and quiet. It seemed the atmosphere of Rampling Gate permeated my simplest written descriptions and wove its way richly into the plots and characters I created. The Monday after our arrival I had finished my first short story and went off to the village on foot to boldly post it to the editors of *Blackwood's Magazine*.

It was a glorious morning, and I took my time as I came back on foot.

What had disturbed our father so about this lovely corner of England, I wondered? What had so darkened his last hours that he laid upon this spot his curse?

My heart opened to this unearthly stillness, to an undeniable grandeur that caused me utterly to forget myself. There were times here when I felt I was a disembodied intellect drifting through a fathomless silence, up and down garden paths and stone corridors that had witnessed too much to take cognizance of one small and fragile young woman who in random moments actually talked aloud to the suits of armour around her, to the broken statues in the garden, the fountain cherubs who had had no water to pour from their conches for years and years.

But was there in this loveliness some malignant force that was eluding us still, some untold story to explain all? Unspeakable horror . . . In my mind's eye I saw that young man, and the strangest sensation crept over me, that some enrichment of the picture had taken place in my memory or imagination in the recent past. Perhaps in dream I had reinvented him, given a ruddy glow to his lips and his cheeks.

Perhaps in my re-creation for Mrs Blessington, I had allowed him to raise his hand to that red cravat and had seen the fingers long and delicate and suggestive of a musician's hand.

It was all very much on my mind when I entered the house again, soundlessly, and saw Richard in his favourite leather wing chair by the fire.

The air was warm coming through the open garden doors, and yet the blaze was cheerful, made the vast room with its towering shelves of leatherbound volumes appear inviting and almost small.

'Sit down,' Richard said gravely, scarcely giving me a glance. 'I want to read you something right now.' He held a long narrow ledger in his hands. 'This was Uncle Baxter's,' he said, 'and at first I thought it was only an account book he kept during the renovations, but I've found some actual diary entries made in the last weeks of his life. They're hasty, almost indecipherable, but I've managed to make them out.'

'Well, do read them to me,' I said, but I felt a little tug of fear. I didn't want to know anything terrible about this place. If we could have remained here forever ... but that was out of the question, to be sure.

'Now listen to this,' Richard said, turning the page carefully. '"Fifth of May, 1938: He is here, I am sure of it. He is come back again." And several days later: "He thinks this is his house, he does, and he would drink my wine and smoke my cigars if only he could. He reads my books and my papers and I will not stand for it. I have given orders that everything is to be locked." And finally, the last entry written the morning before he died: "Weary, weary, unto death and he is no small cause of my weariness. Last night I beheld him with my own eyes. He stood in this very room.

He moves and speaks exactly as a mortal man, and dares tell me his secrets, and he a demon wretch with the face of a seraph and I a mere mortal, how am I to bear with him!"'

'Good Lord,' I whispered slowly. I rose from the chair where I had settled, and standing behind him, read the page for myself. It was the scrawl, the writing, the very last notation in the book. I knew that Uncle Baxter's heart had given out. He had not died by violence, but peacefully enough in this very room with his prayer book in his hand.

'Could it be the very same person Father spoke of that night?' Richard asked.

In spite of the sun pouring through the open doors, I experienced a violent chill. For the first time I felt wary of this house, wary of our boldness in coming here, heedful of our Father's words.

'But that was years before, Richard . . .' I said. 'And what could this mean, this talk of a supernatural being! Surely the man was mad! It was no spirit I saw in that railway carriage!'

I sank down into the chair opposite and tried to quiet the beating of my heart.

'Julie,' Richard said gently, shutting the ledger. 'Mrs Blessington has lived here contentedly for years. There are six servants asleep every night in the north wing. Surely there is nothing to all of this.'

'It isn't very much fun, though, is it?' I said timidly. 'Not at all like swapping ghost stories the way we used to do, and peopling the dark with imaginary beings, and laughing at friends at school who were afraid.'

'All my life,' he said, his eyes fixing me steadily, 'I've heard tales of spooks and spirits, some imagined, some supposedly true, and almost invariably there is some mention of the house in question feeling haunted, of having an atmosphere to it that fills one with foreboding, some sense of menace or alarm . . .'

'Yes, I know, and there is no such poisonous atmosphere here at all.'

'On the contrary, I've never been more at ease in my life.' He shoved his hand into his pocket to extract the inevitable match to light his pipe which had gone out. 'As a matter of fact, Julie, I don't know how in the world I'm going to comply with Father's last wish to tear down this place.'

I nodded sympathetically. The very same thing had been on my mind since we'd arrived. Even now, I felt so comfortable, natural, quite safe.

I was wishing suddenly, irrationally, that he had not found the entries in Uncle Baxter's book.

'I should talk to Mrs Blessington again!' I said almost crossly, 'I mean quite seriously . . .'

'But I have, Julie,' he said. 'I asked her about it all this morning when I first made the discovery, and she only laughed. She swears she's never seen anything unusual here, and that there's no one left alive in the village who can tell tales of this place. She said again how glad she was that we'd come home to Rampling Gate. I don't think she has an inkling we mean to destroy the house. Oh, it would destroy her heart if she did.'

'Never seen anything unusual?' I asked. 'That is what she said? But what strange words for her to use, Richard, when she can not see at all.'

But he had not heard me. He had laid the ledger aside and risen slowly, almost sluggishly, and he was wandering out of the double doors into the little garden and was looking over the high hedge at the oaks that bent their heavy elbowed limbs almost to the surface of the lake. There wasn't a sound at this early hour of the day, save the soft rustle of the leaves in the moving air, the cry now and then of a distant bird.

'Maybe it's gone, Julie,' Richard said, over his shoulder, his voice carrying clearly in the quiet, 'if it was ever here. Maybe there is nothing any longer to frighten anyone at all. You don't suppose you could endure the winter in this house, do you? I suppose you'd want to be in London again by then.' He seemed quite small against the towering trees, the sky broken into small gleaming fragments by the canopy of foliage that gently filtered the light.

Rampling Gate had him. And I understood perfectly, because it also had me. I could very well endure the winter here, no matter how bleak or cold. I never wanted to go home.

And the immediacy of the mystery only dimmed my sense of everything and every place else.

After a long moment, I rose and went out into the garden, and placed my hand gently on Richard's arm.

'I know this much, Julie,' he said, just as if we had been talking to each other all the while. 'I swore to Father that I would do as he asked, and it is tearing me apart. Either way, it will be on my conscience for ever, obliterating this house or going against my own father and the charge he laid down to me with his dying breath.'

'We must seek help, Richard. The advice of our lawyers, the advice of Father's clergymen. You must write to them and explain the whole thing. Father was feverish when he gave the order. If we could lay it out before them, they would help us decide.'

It was three o'clock when I opened my eyes. But I had been awake for a long time. I had heard the dim chimes of the clock below hour by hour. And I felt not fear lying here alone in the dark but something else. Some vague and relentless agitation, some sense of emptiness and need that caused me finally to rise from my bed. What was required to dissolve this tension, I wondered. I stared at the simplest things in the shadows. The little arras that hung over the fireplace with its slim princes and princesses lost in fading fibre and thread. The portrait of an Elizabethan ancestor gazing with one almond-shaped eye from his small frame.

What was this house, really? Merely a place or a state of mind? What was it doing to my soul? Why didn't the entries in Uncle Baxter's book send us flying back to London? Why had we stayed so late in the great hall together after supper, speaking not a single word?

I felt overwhelmed suddenly, and yet shut out of some great and dazzling secret, and wasn't that the very word that Uncle Baxter had used?

Conscious only of an unbearable restlessness, I pulled on my woollen wrapper, buttoning the lace collar and tying the sash. And putting on my slippers, I went out into the hall.

The moon fell full on the oak stairway, and on the deeply recessed door to Richard's room. On tiptoe I approached and, peering in, saw the bed was empty, the covers completely undisturbed.

So he was off on his own tonight the same as I. Oh, if only he had come to me, asked me to go with him.

I turned and made my way soundlessly down the long stairs.

The great hall gaped like a cavern before me, the moonlight here and there touching upon a pair of crossed swords, or a mounted shield. But far beyond the great hall, in the alcove just outside the library, I saw unmistakably a flickering light. And a breeze moved briskly through the room, carrying with it the sound and the scent of a wood fire.

I shuddered with relief. Richard was there. We could talk. Or perhaps we could go exploring together, guarding our fragile candle flames behind cupped fingers as we went from room to room? A sense of well-being pervaded me and quieted me, and yet the dark distance between us seemed endless, and I was desperate to cross it, hurrying suddenly past the long supper table with its massive candlesticks, and finally into the alcove before the library doors.

Yes, Richard was there. He sat with his eyes closed, dozing against the inside of the leather wing chair, the breeze from the garden blowing the fragile flames of the candles on the stone mantel and on the table at his side.

I was about to go to him, about to shut the doors, and kiss him gently and ask did he not want to go up to bed, when quite abruptly I saw in the corner of my eye that there was someone else in the room.

In the far left corner at the desk stood another figure, looking down at the clutter of Richard's papers, his pale hands resting on the wood.

I knew that it could not be so. I knew that I must be dreaming, that nothing in this room, least of all this figure, could be real. For it was the same young man I had seen fifteen years ago in the railway carriage and not a single aspect of that taut young face had been changed. There was the very same hair, thick and lustrous and only carelessly combed as it hung to the thick collar of his black coat, and the skin so pale it was almost luminous in the shadows, and those dark eyes looking up suddenly and fixing me with the most curious expression as I almost screamed.

We stared at one another across the dark vista of that room, I stranded in the doorway, he visibly and undeniably shaken that I had caught him unawares. My heart stopped.

And in a split second he moved towards me, closed the

gap between us, towering over me, those slender white fingers gently closing on my arms.

'Julie!' he whispered, in a voice so low it seemed my own thoughts were speaking to me. But this was no dream. He was real. He was holding on to me and the scream had broken loose from me, deafening, uncontrollable and echoing from the four walls.

I saw Richard rising from the chair. I was alone. Clutching to the door frame, I staggered forward, and then again in a moment of perfect clarity I saw the young intruder, saw him standing in the garden, looking back over his shoulder, and then he was gone.

I could not stop screaming. I could not stop even as Richard held me and pleaded with me, and sat me down in the chair.

And I was still crying when Mrs Blessington finally came.

She got a glass of cordial for me at once, as Richard begged me once more to tell him what I had seen.

'But you know who it was!' I said to Richard almost hysterically. 'It was he, the young man from the train. Only he wore a frockcoat years out of fashion and his silk tie was open at his throat. Richard, he was reading your papers, turning them over, reading them in the pitch dark.'

'All right,' Richard said, gesturing with his hand up for calm. 'He was standing at the desk. And there was no light there so you could not see him well.'

'Richard, it was he! Don't you understand? He touched me, he held my arms.' I looked imploringly to Mrs Blessington who was shaking her head, her little eyes like blue beads in the light. 'He called me Julie,' I whispered. 'He knows my name!'

I rose, snatching up the candle, and all but pushing Richard out of the way went to the desk. 'Oh, dear God,' I said, 'Don't you see what's happened? It's your letters to Dr Partridge, and Mrs Sellers, about tearing down the house!'

Mrs Blessington gave a little cry and put her hand to her cheek. She looked like a withered child in her nightcap as she collapsed into the straight-backed chair by the door.

'Surely you don't believe it was the same man, Julie, after all these years . . .'

'But he had not changed, Richard, not in the smallest detail. There is no mistake, Richard, it was he, I tell you, the very same.'

'Oh, dear, dear . . .' Mrs Blessington whispered, 'What will he do if you try to tear it down? What will he do now?'

'What will who do?' Richard asked carefully, narrowing his eyes. He took the candle from me and approached her. I was staring at her, only half realizing what I had heard.

'So you know who he is!' I whispered.

'Julie, stop it!' Richard said.

But her face had tightened, gone blank and her eyes had become distant and small.

'You knew he was here!' I insisted. 'You must tell us at once!'

With an effort she climbed to her feet. 'There is nothing in this house to hurt *you*,' she said, 'nor any of us.' She turned, spurning Richard as he tried to help her, and wandered into the dark hallway alone. 'You've no need of me here any longer,' she said softly, 'and if you should tear down this house built by your forefathers, then you should do it without need of me.'

'Oh, but we don't mean to do it, Mrs Blessington!' I insisted. But she was making her way through the gallery back towards the north wing. 'Go after her, Richard. You heard what she said. She knows who he is.'

'I've had quite enough of this tonight,' Richard said

almost angrily. 'Both of us should go up to bed. By the light of day we will dissect this entire matter and search this house. Now come.'

'But he should be told, shouldn't he?' I demanded.

'Told what? Of whom do you speak!'

'Told that we will not tear down this house!' I said clearly, loudly, listening to the echo of my own voice.

The next day was indeed the most trying since we had come. It took the better part of the morning to convince Mrs Blessington that we had no intention of tearing down Rampling Gate. Richard posted his letters and resolved that we should do nothing until help came.

And together we commenced a search of the house. But darkness found us only half finished, having covered the south tower and the south wing, and the main portion of the house itself. There remained still the north tower, in a dreadful state of disrepair, and some rooms beneath the ground which in former times might have served as dungeons and were now sealed off. And there were closets and private stairways everywhere that we had scarce looked into, and at times we lost all track of where precisely we had been.

But it was also quite clear by supper time that Richard was in a state of strain and exasperation, and that he did not believe that I had seen anyone in the study at all.

He was further convinced that Uncle Baxter had been mad before he died, or else his ravings were a code for some mundane happening that had him extraordinarily over-wrought.

But I knew what I had seen. And as the day progressed, I became ever more quiet and withdrawn. A silence had fallen between me and Mrs Blessington. And I understood only too well the anger I'd heard in my father's voice on that long-ago night when we had come home from Victoria Station and my mother had accused him of imagining things.

Yet what obsessed me more than anything else was the gentle countenance of the mysterious man I had glimpsed, the dark almost innocent eyes that had fixed on me for one moment before I had screamed.

'Strange that Mrs Blessington is not afraid of him,' I said in a low distracted voice, not longer caring if Richard heard me. 'And that no one here seems in fear of him at all . . .' The strangest fancies were coming to me. The careless words of the villagers were running through my head. 'You would be wise to do one very important thing before you retire,' I said. 'Leave out in writing a note to the effect that you do not intend to tear down the house.'

'Julie, you have created an impossible dilemma,' Richard demanded. 'You insist we reassure this apparition that the house will not be destroyed, when in fact you verify the existence of the very creature that drove our father to say what he did.'

'Oh, I wish I had never come here!' I burst out suddenly.

'Then we should go, both of us, and decide this matter at home.'

'No, that's just it. I could never go without knowing . . . "his secrets" . . . "the demon wretch". I could never go on living without knowing now!'

Anger must be an excellent antidote to fear, for surely something worked to alleviate my natural alarm. I did not undress that night, nor even take off my shoes, but rather sat in that dark hollow bedroom gazing at the small square of diamond-paned window until I heard all of the house fall quiet. Richard's door at last closed. There came those distant echoing booms that meant other bolts had been put in place.

And when the grandfather clock in the great hall chimed the hour of eleven, Rampling Gate was as usual fast asleep.

I listened for my brother's step in the hall. And when I did not hear him stir from his room, I wondered at it, that curiosity would not impel him to come to me, to say that we must go together to discover the truth.

It was just as well. I did not want him to be with me. And I felt a dark exultation as I imagined myself going out of the room and down the stairs as I had the night before. I should wait one more hour, however, to be certain. I should let the night reach its pitch. Twelve, the witching hour. My heart was beating too fast at the thought of it, and dreamily I recollected the face I had seen, the voice that had said my name.

Ah, why did it seem in retrospect so intimate, that we had known each other, spoken together, that it was someone I recognized in the pit of my soul?

'What is your name?' I believe I whispered aloud. And then a spasm of fear startled me. Would I have the courage to go in search of him, to open the door to him? Was I losing my mind? Closing my eyes, I rested my head against the high back of the damask chair.

What was more empty than this rural night? What was more sweet?

I opened my eyes. I had been half dreaming or talking to myself, trying to explain to Father why it was necessary that we comprehend the reason ourselves. And I realized, quite fully realized – I think before I was even awake – that *he* was standing by the bed.

The door was open. And he was standing there, dressed

exactly as he had been the night before, and his dark eyes were riveted on me with that same obvious curiosity, his mouth just a little slack like that of a schoolboy, and he was holding to the bedpost almost idly with his right hand. Why, he was lost in contemplating me. He did not seem to know that I was looking at him.

But when I sat forward, he raised his finger as if to quiet me, and gave a little nod of his head.

'Ah, it is you!' I whispered.

'Yes,' he said in the softest, most unobtrusive voice.

But we had been talking to each other, hadn't we, I had been asking him questions, no, telling him things. And I felt suddenly I was losing my equilibrium or slipping back into a dream.

No. Rather I had all but caught the fragment of some dream from the past. That rush of atmosphere that can engulf one at any moment of the day following when something evokes the universe that absorbed one utterly in sleep. I mean I heard our voices for an instant, almost in argument, and I saw Father in his top hat and black overcoat rushing alone through the streets of the West End, peering into one door after another, and then, rising from the marble-top table in the dim smoky music hall you ... your face.

'Yes ...'

Go back, Julie! It was Father's voice.

'... to penetrate the soul of it,' I insisted, picking up the lost thread. But did my lips move? 'To understand what it is that frightened him, enraged him. He said, "Tear it down!"'

'... you must never, never, can't do that.' His face was stricken, like that of a schoolboy about to cry.

'No, absolutely, we don't want to, either of us, you know

it . . . and you are not a spirit!' I looked at his mud-spattered boots, the faintest smear of dust on that perfect white cheek.

'A spirit?' he asked almost mournfully, almost bitterly. 'Would that I were.'

Mesmerized, I watched him come towards me and the room darkened, and I felt his cool silken hands on my face. I had risen. I was standing before him, and I looked up into his eyes.

I heard my own heartbeat. I heard it as I had the night before, right at the moment I had screamed. Dear God, I was talking to him! He was in my room and I was talking to him! And I was in his arms.

'Real, absolutely real!' I whispered, and a low zinging sensation coursed through me so that I had to steady myself against the bed.

He was peering at me as if trying to comprehend something terribly important to him, and he didn't respond. His lips did have a ruddy look to them, a soft look for all his handsomeness, as if he had never been kissed. And a slight dizziness had come over me, a slight confusion in which I was not at all sure that he was even there.

'Oh, but I am,' he said softly. I felt his breath against my cheek, and it was almost sweet. 'I am here, and you are with me, Julie . . .'

'Yes . . .'

My eyes were closing. Uncle Baxter sat hunched over his desk and I could hear the furious scratch of his pen. 'Demon wretch!' he said to the night air coming in the open doors.

'No!' I said. Father turned in the door of the music hall and cried my name.

'Love me, Julie,' came that voice in my ear. I felt his lips against my neck. 'Only a little kiss, Julie, no harm . . .' And the core of my being, that secret place where all desires and all commandments are nurtured, opened to him without a struggle or a sound. I would have fallen if he had not held me. My arms closed about him, my hands slipping into the soft silken mass of his hair.

I was floating, and there was as there had always been at Rampling Gate an endless peace. It was Rampling Gate I felt around me, it was that timeless and impenetrable soul that had opened itself at last . . . A power within me of enormous ken . . . To see as a god sees, and take the depth of things as nimbly as the outward eyes can size and shape pervade . . . Yes, I whispered aloud, those words from Keats, those words . . . To cease upon the midnight without pain . . .

No. In a violent instant we had parted, he drawing back as surely as I.

I went reeling across the bedroom floor and caught hold of the frame of the window, and rested my forehead against the stone wall.

For a moment I stood with my eyes closed. There was a tingling pain in my throat that was almost pleasurable where his lips had touched me, a delicious throbbing that would not stop.

Then I turned, and I saw all the room clearly, the bed, the fireplace, the chair. And he stood still exactly as I'd left him and there was the most appalling distress in his face.

'What have they done to me?' he whispered. 'Have they played the cruellest trick of all?'

'Something of menace, unspeakable menace,' I whispered.

'Something ancient, Julie, something that defies understanding, something that can and will go on.'

'But why, what are you?' I touched that pulsing pain with the tips of my fingers and, looking down at them, gasped.

'And you suffer so, and you are so seemingly innocent, and it is as if you can love!'

His face was rent as if by a violent conflict within. And he turned to go. With my whole will, I stood fast not to follow him, not to beg him to turn back. But he did turn, bewildered, struggling and then bent upon his purpose as he reached for my hand. 'Come with me,' he said.

He drew me to him ever so gently, and slipping his arm around me guided me to the door.

Through the long upstairs corridor we passed hurriedly, and through a small wooden doorway to a screw stairs that I had never seen before.

I soon realized we were ascending the north tower of the house, the ruined portion of the structure that Richard and I had not investigated before.

Through one tiny window after another I saw the gently rolling landscape moving out from the forest that surrounded us, and the small cluster of dim lights that marked the village of Rampling and the pale streak of white that was the London Road.

Up and up we climbed until we had reached the top-most chamber, and this he opened with an iron key. He held back the door for me to enter and I found myself in a spacious room whose high narrow windows contained no glass. A flood of moonlight revealed the most curious mixture of furnishings and objects, the clutter that suggests an attic and a sort of den. There was a writing table, a great shelf of books, soft leather chairs and scores of old yellowed and curling maps and framed pictures affixed to the walls. Candles were everywhere stuck in the bare stone niches or to the tables and the shelves. Here and there a barrel served as a table, right alongside the finest old Elizabethan chair. Wax had dripped over everything, it seemed, and in the very midst of the clutter lay rumpled copies of the most recent papers, the *Mercure de Paris*, the London *Times*.

There was no place for sleeping in this room.

And when I thought of that, where he must lie when he went to rest, a shudder passed over me and I felt, quite vividly, his lips touching my throat again, and I felt the sudden urge to cry.

But he was holding me in his arms, he was kissing my cheeks and my lips again ever so softly, and then he guided me to a chair. He lighted the candles about us one by one.

I shuddered, my eyes watering slightly in the light. I saw more unusual objects: telescopes and magnifying glasses and a violin in its open case, and a handful of gleaming and exquisitely shaped sea shells. There were jewels lying about, and a black silk top hat and a walking stick, and a bouquet of withered flowers, dry as straw, and daguerreotypes and tintypes in their little velvet cases, and opened books.

But I was too distracted now by the sight of him in the light, the gloss of his large black eyes, and the gleam of his hair. Not even in the railway station had I seen him so clearly as I did now amid the radiance of the candles. He broke my heart.

And yet he looked at me as though I were the feast for his eyes, and he said my name again and I felt the blood rush to my face. But there seemed a great break suddenly in the passage of time. I had been thinking, yes, what are you, how long have you existed . . . And I felt dizzy again.

I realized that I had risen and I was standing beside him at the window and he was turning me to look down and the countryside below had unaccountably changed. The lights of Rampling had been subtracted from the darkness that lay like a vapour over the land. A great wood, far older and denser than the forest of Rampling Gate, shrouded the hills, and I was afraid suddenly, as if I were slipping into a maelstrom from which I could never, of my own will, return.

There was that sense of us talking together, talking and talking in low agitated voices and I was saying that I should not give in.

'Bear witness, that is all I ask of you . . .'

And there was in me some dim certainty that by knowledge alone I should be fatally changed. It was the reading of a forbidden book, the chanting of a forbidden charm.

'No, only what was,' he whispered.

And then even the shape of the land itself eluded me. And the very room had lost its substance, as if a soundless wind of terrific force had entered this place and was blowing it apart.

We were riding in a carriage through the night. We had long long ago left the tower, and it was late afternoon and the sky was the colour of blood. And we rode into a forest whose trees were so high and so thick that scarcely any sun at all broke to the soft leafstrewn ground.

We had no time to linger in this magical place. We had come to the open country, to the small patches of tilled earth that surrounded the ancient village of Knorwood with its gabled roofs and its tiny crooked streets. We saw the walls of the monastery of Knorwood and the little church with the bell chiming Vespers under the lowering sky. A great bustling life resided in Knorwood, a thousand hearts beat in Knorwood, a thousand voices gave forth their common prayer.

But far beyond the village on the rise above the forest stood the rounded tower of a truly ancient castle, and to that ruined castle, no more than a shell of itself anymore, as darkness fell in earnest, we rode. Through its empty chambers we roamed, impetuous children, the horse and the road quite forgotten, and to the Lord of the Castle, a gaunt and white-skinned creature standing before the roaring fire of the roofless hall, we came. He turned and fixed us with his narrow and glittering eyes. A dead thing he was, I understood, but he carried within himself a priceless magic. And my young companion, my innocent young man passed by me into the Lord's arms. I saw the kiss. I saw the young man grow pale and struggle to turn away. It was as I had done this very night, beyond this dream, in my own bedchamber; and from the Lord he retreated, clutching to the sharp pain in his throat.

I understood. I knew. But the castle was dissolving as surely as anything in this dream might dissolve, and we were in some damp and close place.

The stench was unbearable to me, it was that most terrible of all stenches, the stench of death. And I heard my steps on the cobblestones and I reached to steady myself against the wall. The tiny square was deserted; the doors and windows gaped open to the vagrant wind. Up one side and down the other of the crooked street I saw the marks on the houses. And I knew what the marks meant. The Black Death had come to the village of Knorwood. The Black Death had laid it waste. And in a moment of suffocating horror I realized that no one, not a single person, was left alive.

But this was not quite right. There was someone walking in fits and starts up the narrow alleyway. Staggering he was, almost falling, as he pushed in one door after another, and at last came to a hot, stinking place where a child screamed on the floor. Mother and Father lay dead in the bed. And the great fat cat of the household, unharmed, played with the screaming infant, whose eyes bulged from its tiny sunken face.

'Stop it,' I heard myself gasp. I knew that I was holding my head with both hands. 'Stop it, stop it please!' I was screaming and my screams would surely pierce the vision and this small crude little room should collapse around me, and I should rouse the household of Rampling Gate to me, but I did not. The young man turned and stared at me, and in the close stinking room, I could not see his face.

But I knew it was he, my companion, and I could smell his fever and his sickness, and the stink of the dying infant, and see the sleek, gleaming body of the cat as it pawed at the child's outstretched hand.

'Stop it, you've lost control of it!' I screamed surely with all my strength, but the infant screamed louder. 'Make it stop!'

'I can not ...' he whispered. 'It goes on forever! It will never stop!'

And with a great piercing shriek I kicked at the cat and sent it flying out of the filthy room, overturning the milk pail as it went, jetting like a witch's familiar over the stones.

Blanched and feverish, the sweat soaking his crude jerkin, my companion took me by the hand. He forced me back out of the house and away from the crying child and into the street.

Death in the parlour, death in the bedroom, death in the cloister, death before the high altar, death in the open fields. It seemed the Judgement of God that a thousand souls had died in the village of Knorwood – I was sobbing, begging to be released – it seemed the very end of Creation itself.

And at last night came down over the dead village and he was alive still, stumbling up the slopes, through the forest, towards that rounded tower where the Lord stood with his hand on the stone frame of the broken window waiting for him to come.

ANNE RICE

'Don't go!' I begged him. I ran alongside him crying, but he didn't hear. Try as I might, I could not affect these things.

The Lord stood over him smiling almost sadly as he watched him fall, watched the chest heave with its last breaths. Finally the lips moved, calling out for salvation when it was damnation the Lord offered, when it was damnation that the Lord would give.

'Yes, damned then, but living, breathing!' the young man cried, rising in a last spasmodic movement. And the Lord, who had remained still until that instant, bent to drink.

The kiss again, the lethal kiss, the blood drawn out of the dying body, and then the Lord lifting the heavy head of the young man to take the blood back again from the body of the Lord himself.

I was screaming again, *Do not, do not drink.* He turned and looked at me. His face was now so perfectly the visage of death that I couldn't believe there was animation left in him, yet he asked: What would you do? Would you go back to Knorwood, would you open those doors one after another, would you ring the bell in the empty church, and if you did would the dead rise?

He didn't wait for my answer. And I had none now to give. He had turned again to the Lord who waited for him, locked his innocent mouth to that vein that pulsed with every semblance of life beneath the Lord's cold and trans-lucent flesh. And the blood jetted into the young body, vanquishing in one great burst the fever and the sickness that had wracked it, driving it out with the mortal life.

He stood now in the hall of the Lord alone. Immortality was his and the blood thirst he would need to sustain it, and that thirst I could feel with my whole soul. He stared at the broken walls around him, at the fire licking the blackened stones of the giant fireplace, at the night sky over the broken roof, throwing out its endless net of stars.

And each and every thing was transfigured in his vision, and in my vision – the vision he gave now to me – to the exquisite essence of itself. A wordless and eternal voice spoke from the starry veil of heaven, it sang in the wind that rushed through the broken timbers; it sighed in the flames that ate the sooted stones of the hearth.

It was the fathomless rhythm of the universe that played beneath every surface, as the last living creature – that tiny child – fell silent in the village below.

A soft wind sifted and scattered the soil from the new-turned furrows in the empty fields. The rain fell from the black and endless sky.

Years and years passed. And all that had been Knorwood melted into the very earth. The forest sent out its silent sentinels, and mighty trunks rose where there had been huts and houses, where there had been monastery walls.

Finally nothing of Knorwood remained: not the little cemetery, not the little church, not even the name of Knorwood lived still in the world. And it seemed the horror beyond all horrors that no one anymore should know of a thousand souls who had lived and died in that small and insignificant village, that not anywhere in the great archives in which all history is recorded should a mention of that town remain..

Yet one being remained who knew, one being who had witnessed, and stood now looking down upon the very spot where his mortal life had ended, he who had scrambled up on his hands and knees from the pit of Hell that had been that disaster; it was the young man who stood beside me, the master of Rampling Gate.

And all through the walls of his old house were the stones

ANNE RICE

of the ruined castle, and all through the ceilings and floors the branches of those ancient trees.

What was solid and majestic here, and safe within the minds of those who slept tonight in the village of Rampling, was only the most fragile citadel against horror, the house to which he clung now.

A great sorrow swept over me. Somewhere in the drift of images I had relinquished myself, lost all sense of the point in space from which I saw. And in a great rush of lights and noise I was enlivened now and made whole as I had been when we rode together through the forest, only it was into the world of now, this hour, that we passed. We were flying it seemed through the rural darkness along the railway towards the London where the night time city burst like an enormous bubble in a shower of laughter, and motion, and glaring light. He was walking with me under the gas lamps, his face all but shimmering with that same dark innocence, that same irresistible warmth. And it seemed we were holding tight to one another in the very midst of a crowd. And the crowd was a living thing, a writhing thing, and everywhere there came a dark rich aroma from it, the aroma of fresh blood. Women in white fur and gentlemen in opera capes swept into the brightly lighted doors of the theatre; the blare of the music hall inundated us, then faded away. Only a thin soprano voice was left, singing a high, plaintive song. I was in his arms, and his lips were covering mine, and there came that dull zinging sensation again, that great uncontrollable opening within myself. Thirst, and the promise of satiation measured only by the intensity of that thirst. Up stairs we fled together, into high-ceilinged bedrooms papered in red damask where the loveliest women reclined on brass bedsteads, and the aroma was so strong now I could not bear it, and before me they offered themselves, they opened their arms. 'Drink,' he whispered, yes, drink. And I felt the warmth filling me, charging me, blurring my vision, until we broke again, free and light and invisible it seemed as we moved over the rooftops and down again through rain-drenched streets. But the rain did not touch us; the falling snow did not chill us; we had within ourselves a great and indissoluble heat. And together in the carriage, we talked to each other in low, exuberant rushes of language; we were lovers; we were constant; we were immortal. We were as enduring as Rampling Gate.

I tried to speak; I tried to end the spell. I felt his arms around me and I knew we were in the tower room together, and some terrible miscalculation had been made.

'Do not leave me,' he whispered. 'Don't you understand what I am offering you; I have told you everything; and all the rest is but the weariness, the fever and the fret, those old words from the poem. Kiss me, Julie, open to me. Against your will I will not take you . . .' Again I heard my own scream. My hands were on his cool white skin, his lips were gentle yet hungry, his eyes yielding and ever young. Father turned in the rain-drenched London street and cried out: 'Julie!' I saw Richard lost in the crowd as if searching for someone, his hat shadowing his dark eyes, his face haggard, old. Old!

I moved away. I was free. And I was crying softly and we were in this strange and cluttered tower room. He stood against the backdrop of the window, against the distant drift of pale clouds. The candlelight glimmered in his eyes. Immense and sad and wise they seemed, and oh, yes, innocent as I have said again and again. 'I revealed myself to them,' he said, 'Yes, I told my secret. In rage or bitterness, I know not which, I made them my dark co-conspirators and always I won. They could not move against me, and neither will you. But they would triumph still. For they torment me now with their fairest flower. Don't turn away from me, Julie. You are mine, Julie, as Rampling Gate is mine. Let me gather the flower to my heart.'

Nights of argument. But finally Richard had come round. He would sign over to me his share of Rampling Gate, and I should absolutely refuse to allow the place torn down. There would be nothing he could do then to obey Father's command. I had given him the legal impediment he needed, and of course I should leave the house to him and his children. It should always be in Rampling hands.

A clever solution, it seemed to me, as Father had not told *me* to destroy the place, and I had no scruples in the matter now at all.

And what remained was for him to take me to the little train station and see me off for London, and not worry about me going home to Mayfair on my own.

'You stay here as long as you wish, and do not worry,' I said. I felt more tenderly towards him than I could ever express. 'You knew as soon as you set foot in the place that Father was all wrong. Uncle Baxter put it in his mind, undoubtedly, and Mrs Blessington has always been right. There is nothing to harm there, Richard. Stay, and work or study as you please.'

The great black engine was roaring past us, the carriages slowing to a stop. 'Must go now, darling, kiss me,' I said.

'But what came over you, Julie, what convinced you so quickly …'

'We've been through it all, Richard,' I said. 'What matters is that we are all happy, my dear.' And we held each other close.

I waved until I couldn't see him anymore. The flickering

lamps of the town were lost in the deep lavender light of the early evening, and the dark hulk of Rampling Gate appeared for one uncertain moment like the ghost of itself on the nearby rise.

I sat back and closed my eyes. Then I opened them slowly, savouring this moment for which I had waited too long.

He was smiling, seated there as he had been all along, in the far corner of the leather seat opposite, and now he rose with a swift, almost delicate movement and sat beside me and enfolded me in his arms.

'It's five hours to London,' he whispered in my ear.

'I can wait,' I said, feeling the thirst like a fever as I held tight to him, feeling his lips against my eyelids and my hair. 'I want to hunt the London streets tonight,' I confessed, a little shyly, but I saw only approbation in his eyes.

'Beautiful Julie, my Julie . . .' he whispered.

'You'll love the house in Mayfair,' I said.

'Yes . . .' he said.

'And when Richard finally tires of Rampling Gate, we shall go home.'

A Week in the Unlife

DAVID J. SCHOW

Vampire hunter: 'The Vigilante'
Location of case: USA
Time: 1991
Author: David J. Schow (1955–), who was born in
Marburg, West Germany and lived briefly in England
before moving to America, is a novelist, short story writer
and media historian who has recently made a considerable impact in Hollywood with scripts for several very
popular horror pictures including *Leatherface: The Texas
Chainsaw Massacre III*, *Critters 3* and *4*, and the much-
admired 1994 movie, *The Crow*. His long-standing fascination with, and knowledge of, the media was first revealed
in *The Outer Limits: The Official Companion* about the
legendary TV series, and this was followed by *The Silver
Scream*, an anthology of macabre cinema stories. It is,
though, for his short stories that David – a self-confessed
'Splatter Punk' – has been most highly commended:
winning several awards and being described as 'one of
the most original stylists in the new wave of horror
writers'. There are few better examples of his original
approach to the genre than 'A Week in the Unlife' – a story
with a central character as unique as any to be found in
contemporary vampire fiction . . .

I

When you stake a bloodsucker, the heartblood pumps out thick and black, the consistency of honey. I saw it make bubbles as it glurped out. The creature thrashed and squirmed and tried to pull out the stake – they always do, if you leave on their arms for the kill – but by the third whack it was, as Stoker might say, dispatched well and duly.

I lost count a long time ago. Doesn't matter. I no longer think of them as being even *former* human beings, and feel no anthropomorphic sympathy. In their eyes I see no tragedy, no romance, no seductive pulp appeal. Merely lust, rage at being outfoxed, and debased appetite, focused and sanguine.

People usually commit journals as legacy. So be it. Call me sentry, vigilante if you like. When they sleep their comatose sleep, I stalk and terminate them. When they walk, I hide. Better than they do.

They're really not as smart as popular fiction and films would lead you to believe. They do have cunning, an animalistic savvy. But I'm an experienced tracker; I know their spoor, the traces they leave, the way their presence charges the air. Things invisible or ephemeral to ordinary citizens, blackly obvious to me.

The journal is so you'll know, just in case my luck runs out.

Sundown. Nap time.

II

Naturally the police think of me as some sort of homicidal crackpot. That's a given; always has been for my predecessors. More watchers to evade. Caution comes reflexively to me these days. Police are slow and rational; they deal in the minutiae of a day-to-day world, deadly enough without the inclusion of bloodsuckers.

The police love to stop and search people. Fortunately for me, mallets and stakes and crosses and such are not yet illegal in this country. Lots of raised eyebrows and jokes and nudging but no actual arrests. When the time comes for them to recognize the plague that has descended upon their city, they will remember me, perhaps with grace.

My lot is friendliness, solo. I know and expect such. It's okay.

City by city, I'm good at ferreting out the nests. To me, their kill-patterns are like a flashing red light. The police only see presumed loonies, draw no linkages; they bust and imprison mortals and never see the light.

I am not foolhardy enough to leave bloodsuckers lying. Even though the mean corpus usually dissolves, the stakes might be discovered. Sometimes there is other residue. City dumpsters and sewers provide adequate and fitting disposal for the leftovers of my mission.

The enemy casualties.

I wish I could advise the authorities, work hand-in-hand with them. Too complicated. Too many variables. Not a good control situation. Bloodsuckers have a maddening knack for vanishing into crevices, even hairline splits in logic.

Rule: Trust no one.

III

A female one, today. Funny. There aren't as many of them as you might suppose.

She had courted a human lover, so she claimed, like

Romeo and Juliet – she could only visit him at night, and only after feeding, because bloodsuckers too can get carried away by passion.

I think she was intimating that she was a physical lover of otherworldly skill; I think she was fighting hard to tempt me not to eliminate her by saying so.

She did not use her mouth to seduce mortal men. I drove the stake into her brain, through the mouth. She was of recent vintage and did not melt or vaporize. When I fucked her remains, I was surprised to find her warm inside, not cold, like a cadaver. Warm.

With some of them, the human warmth is longer in leaving. But it always goes.

IV

I never met one before that gave up its existence without a struggle, but today I did, one that acted like he had been expecting me to wander along and relieve him of the burden of unlife. He did not deny what he was, nor attempt to trick me. He asked if he could talk a bit, before.

In a third-floor loft, the windows of which had been spray-painted flat black, he talked. Said he had always hated the taste of blood; said he preferred pineapple juice, or even coffee. He actually brewed a pot of coffee while we talked.

I allowed him to finish his cup before I put the ashwood length to his chest and drove deep and let his blackness gush. It dribbled, thinned by the coffee he had consumed.

V

Was thinking this afternoon perhaps I should start packing a Polaroid or somesuch, to keep a visual body count, just in case this journal becomes public record someday. It'd be good to have illustrations, proof. I was thinking of that line you hear overused in the movies. I'm sure you know it: '*But there's no such THING as a vampire!*' What a howler; ranks right up there alongside '*It's crazy – but it just might work!*' and *We can't stop now for a lot of silly native superstitions!*'

Right; shoot cozy little memory snaps, in case they whizz to mist or drop apart to smoking goo. That bull about how you're not supposed to be able to record their images is from the movies, too. There's so much misleading information running loose that the bloodsuckers – the real ones – have no trouble at all moving through any urban center, *with impunity*, as they say on cop shows.

Maybe it would be a good idea to tape record the sounds they make when they die. Videotape them begging not to be exterminated. That would bug the eyes of all those monster movie fans, you bet.

VI

So many of them beleaguering this city, it's easy to feel outnumbered. Like I said, I've lost count.

Tonight might be a good window for moving on. Like them, I become vulnerable if I remain too long, and it's prudent operating procedure not to leave patterns or become predictable.

It's easy. I don't own much. Most of what I carry, I carry inside.

VII

They pulled me over on Highway Ten, outbound, for a broken left tail-light. A datafax photo of me was clipped to the visor in the Highway Patrol car. The journal book itself has been taken as evidence, so for now it's a felt-tip and high school notebook paper, which notes I hope to append to the journal proper later.

I have a cell with four bunks all to myself. The door is solid gray, with a food slot, unlike the barred cage of the bullpen. On the way back I noticed they had caught themselves a bloodsucker. Probably an accident; they probably don't even know what they have. There is no sunrise or sunset in the block, so if he gets out at night, they'll never know what happened. But I already know. Right now I will not say anything. I am exposed and at a disadvantage. The one I let slip today I can eliminate tenfold, next week.

VIII

New week. And I am vindicated at last.

I relaxed as soon as they showed me the photographs. How they managed documentation on the last few bloodsuckers I trapped, I have no idea. But I was relieved. Now I don't have to explain the journal – which, as you can see, they returned to me immediately. They had thousands of questions. They needed to know about the mallets, the stakes, the preferred method of killstrike. I cautioned them not to attempt a sweep and clear at night, when the enemy is stronger.

They paid serious attention this time, which made me feel much better. Now the fight can be mounted en masse.

They also let me know I wouldn't have to stay in the cell. Just some paperwork to clear, and I'm out among them again. One of the officials – not a cop, but a doctor – congratulated me on a stout job well done. He shook my hand, on behalf of all of them, he said, and mentioned writing a book on my work. This is exciting!

As per my request, the bloodsucker in the adjacent solitary cell was moved. I told them that to be really sure, they should use one of my stakes. It was simple vanity, really, on my part. I turn my stakes out of ashwood on a lathe. I made sure they knew I'd permit my stakes to be used as working models for the proper manufacture of all they would soon need.

When the guards come back I really must ask how they managed such crisp 8×10s of so many bloodsuckers. All those names and dates. First class documentation.

I'm afraid I may be a bit envious.

My Name Upon the Wind

PETER TREMAYNE

Vampire hunter: Professor Abraham Van Helsing
Locality of case: Kingstown, Ireland
Time: Late 1890s
Author: English novelist, short story writer and historian, Peter Tremayne (1943–) was a journalist before turning to fiction and made his literary reputation with a trilogy of novels about Dracula. His interest in the vampire Count had stemmed from reading Bram Stoker's book when he was a youth and it remains to this day his favourite horror novel. The works which comprise the trilogy are *Dracula Unborn* (1977), *The Revenge of Dracula* (1978) and *Dracula My Love* (1980), which have recently been combined in one volume as *Dracula Lives!* (1993) and optioned for filming. The books inspired the New York based Count Dracula Fan Club to make Peter a life member in 1981 for 'maintaining the image of, and creating an interest in, Bram Stoker's *Dracula*'. Of the books themselves, the author says: 'They arose from three questions I asked myself that Stoker hinted at but did not answer. How did Dracula become a vampire in the first place? Why, of all the places in the world, did he choose to come to England and was there a link? And, finally, though Dracula's women tell him he is incapable of love, what if he came up against a powerful woman who did not swoon at his approach and with whom he fell in love?' Having answered these questions in the trilogy, Peter has resisted the temptation – and the appeals of publishers and fans – to continue the saga. He has, however, produced a number of other vampire stories of which 'My Name Upon The Wind' is the latest, was written especially for this book and, as the reader will discover, brings our casebook to a most singular conclusion . . .

He lay on his back on the bed but he was not asleep. The curtains were drawn back from the dominant, leaded bay windows, showing the night sky, clear and blue-black and studded with a myriad of white, winking stars beyond. The moon was in the first quarter, not bright but drifting constantly, a pale, listless orb, behind dark, scudding clouds.

He lay bathed in sweat; the cold sweat of fear.

His lips were dry and cracked. He could only think one thought – If only *he* were here. If only . . .

He felt unable to move, unable to get up from the bed. He tried to reach out his hand to tug on the bellrope, which hung at the side of his pillow, to summon his servants to his aid. He wanted someone to secure the open windows, to draw the curtains to shut out the night sky. Its aspect seemed so forbidding and it disturbed him. There was something portentous about the doleful, hanging moon. He writhed on the bed, feeling no control over his wasted limbs. Spittle formed around his mouth as he worked his jaw in an attempt to cry out. The only sound he could make was a soft moaning, like the suppressed sobbing of a fractious child awaiting an inevitable punishment.

Then, scarcely audible against the soft sighing of the wind in the trees outside, he thought he heard his name being called.

His eyes widened fearfully.

Yes; yes! There it was – a soft whispering summons. His name! His name being called upon the wind.

Then he was aware of the figure in his bedroom. The figure standing just inside the door, looking at him. The eyes were the only part of that fearful shape that he could focus on. Eyes, red and malignant. Eyes gloating and evil. Merciless.

A throaty, voluptuous chuckle, welled from the mouth of the threatening apparition.

Slowly it moved towards him.

He tried to scream but no sound came from his restricted throat.

All he could hear now was that sighing call. His name upon the wind.

Abraham Van Helsing, even though he was now in his early sixties, had never ceased to have an eye for a pretty girl. Perhaps that was why he had never been satisfied in a single relationship; why he had never married. Women found his only dependable quality was a constant adoration of feminine beauty. Many of his fellow academics at Amsterdam's old university found this behaviour both surprising and sometimes embarrassing. Women, however, found that it was something which did not make for a durable partnership. Hence Van Helsing had remained a bachelor.

Even as Van Helsing came down the gangway of the ferry onto the granite quay of the busy Irish port of Kingstown, he noticed the girl standing alone under one of the pale, flickering gaslamps which illuminated the area. She was draped from poll to toe in a long, dark cloak. The lamps were too dim to discern its exact colour. What could be clearly seen, however, was her pale, worried face, peering anxiously up at the ship. It was a delicate face, finely shaped, which, while not exactly beautiful, was somehow beyond mere beauty; an exquisite face which made Van Helsing's breath catch in his throat. The eyes were fretful and impatient. Searching eyes. Searching for a husband? A lover? Van Helsing pursed his lips in thought.

Then, for a moment the apprehensive, somehow vulnerable eyes of the girl met Van Helsing's admiring gaze and boldly held it. Her eyes seemed to bore into him for several long seconds until it was Van Helsing who reluctantly dropped his countenance in embarrassment.

He came to the foot of the gangway and was preparing to turn into the crowd when, to his astonishment, he found the slight form of the girl barring his way.

'Are you Doctor Van Helsing from Amsterdam?' she demanded, her voice breathless and troubled.

Van Helsing showed his surprise by a slight rising of an eyebrow.

'I am he,' he replied in his oddly accented English.

The girl, to his continued wonderment, suddenly thrust out both hands impulsively and gripped his free hand in an unexpectedly strong grasp.

'Thank God, you've come! I have been waiting for you,' she said softly. Then, seeing the bewilderment on his face, she said: 'I am Sarah Mountcarbery.'

The bewilderment cleared immediately from the Dutch professor's features.

'Then you are . . . ?'

'I am the sister of Piers Mountcarbery,' she confirmed before he could finish his question. 'I am come to meet you, Doctor, and to take you straight to Castle Carbery.' She glanced down at the portmanteau he was carrying in his left hand. 'Is that all your luggage?'

Van Helsing attempted to smile. The girl's worried features seemed to forbid gaiety.

'One travels faster who is not encumbered with baggage, young miss. And when your message came to me . . . I simply picked up a bag and took the first ship to Harwich, entrained across England to Holyhead and from there . . .' He gestured to the ferry behind him.

'Then follow me,' she replied, not answering his wry smile. Her face was now a stiff, unemotional mask although Van Helsing felt it was a mask that hid a great deal.

'I have my carriage here.'

She led the way across the crowded quay to where a solitary coachman stood by a dark *calèche*, a four-wheeled, covered coach, harnessed to a pair of impatient horses. The coachmen, a tall man, with a long brown beard and a great black hat, left the horses and moved swiftly to open the door of the carriage at their approach. He did not say a word but handed up the girl and took the portmanteau from Van Helsing's hand. He waited until Van Helsing had clambered in beside Sarah Mountcarbery before closing the door. He placed the portmanteau under the seat on the driver's box, then he climbed up. With a flick of his whip, he turned the *calèche* across the stone-flagged quay and out into the dimly lit streets of Kingstown.

The coach moved at a remarkably quick pace, the only lights were the oil lamps fitted on each side of the vehicle which helped the driver keep to his road. So rapidly did the carriage proceed that they soon left all habitation behind and were deep into the darkness of the country beyond. Van Helsing was unused to such swiftness of movement but he assured himself that the coachman knew his business and eventually settled back, turning slightly in his seat so that he might view the girl's shadowy profile.

'How is your brother, Piers? In your message, you said that he was ailing and had great need of me.'

Van Helsing saw the girl bite her lip in the gloom. She hesitated a moment before replying.

'He is in very poor health, doctor.'

'I have not seen him in nearly ten years. He was a student of mine with young John Seward in Amsterdam.'

The girl shivered slightly. He felt the movement rather than saw it.

'I know. In fact, it was a letter from his friend Doctor

Seward which prompted Piers to ask me to contact you.'

'Is this so?' asked Van Helsing, his tone inviting further explanation.

'Doctor Seward wrote to Piers to say that you had been of tremendous help with some obscure virus that brought ruin to a family called Westenra in England. I do not know the details, only that Piers was very excited by what Doctor Seward wrote to him and asked me to write and plead for you to come here without delay.'

Van Helsing's face had paled slightly.

'So?' He exhaled a deep breath. 'The Westenra case. You tell me that your brother is ailing. How long has he been so?'

'For a fortnight now, for some ten days before I sent my letter to you.'

'He has seen a physician?'

'No. He lets no physician near him. He treats himself for, as you are aware, Doctor, Piers is qualified as a physician.'

Van Helsing compressed his lips.

'Ah, this I know. He was a Licentiate at the Royal College of Physicians here in Ireland before he came to study with me in Amsterdam. It was after I had read his paper in the *Dublin Journal of Medical Science* that I invited him to Amsterdam to study further various forms of obscure . . .' He hesitated and smiled. 'But you know all this. He was one of my best students. I was sad to hear from my good friend John Seward some months ago that Piers was quitting the profession of medicine. Why was this? He was not ill then, surely?'

The young girl sniffed.

'He found himself with other duties.'

'Other studies, Miss Sarah? May I call you Miss Sarah, for the sake of the friendship I hold with your brother?'

The girl grimaced, neither approving nor disapproving.

'Our father was the eleventh Earl of Mountcarbery. We have estates at Annaghdown in the Wicklow Mountains. When our father died three months ago, Piers had to forget his medical interests for he became the twelfth earl. There were new duties to consider. Our family came to this country seven hundred years ago with Strongbow and are looked to as influential in the life of the country. Piers is the twenty-eighth generation of our line to hold the estates of Annaghdown. He has a responsibility to the family, to its traditions and to the people.'

Van Helsing heard the rising pride in the girl's voice.

'And yet the vocation of a healer is an honourable profession,' he ventured mildly.

The girl made no reply. He could not see her features well in the darkness of the carriage but had a strong feeling that she disagreed with his observation.

'Tell me more about Piers' illness,' he invited, after a moment or two of silence. 'How did it start?'

The girl sniffed. He observed that she used a sniff as others used punctuation. It was part of her speech pattern. It detracted from her elegance, he thought disapprovingly.

'I do not know. I only returned to Ireland two weeks ago. I have been abroad for awhile, in Europe. When I returned to Castle Carbery, I found Piers complaining of a feeling of lassitude. He was sleeping fitfully and yet when he did sleep it was such, or so he told me, as filled with curious dreams. He found he was rising late and was still listless. He now seems so pale, almost anaemic.'

Van Helsing thrust out his lower lip, a little habit he had when he heard disturbing news.

'This is unlike the Piers Mountcarbery I knew in Amsterdam,' he remarked thoughtfully.

Indeed, Piers Mountcarbery had been a tall, well-built, red-headed Irishman with a laugh that was like the roar of an express train. If Van Helsing was to conjure the epitome of a healthy man, in the full vigour and strength of life, it would have been the image of Piers Mountcarbery who came to mind.

'The main point is . . . can you help him?' Sarah Mountcarbery suddenly turned her face to his. The cold ice-blue of the moonlight suddenly flitted into the carriage and illuminated her mask-like features for a moment. Van Helsing stared into her deep, dark eyes unable to discern the subtlety of her expression.

'I can only answer, Miss Sarah, that I shall endeavour to do so. I can say no more until I have seen my young friend again.'

The carriage swayed and rumbled along the narrow roadway through the darkened mountains. Van Helsing felt that the girl was in a state of tension and that further conversation would not ease it. So he sat in silence, meditating on what he had been told.

It had only been a few months previously that he had returned from the Carpathian mountains with his friends John Seward and Jonathan and Mina Harker. How relieved he had been to bring that extraordinary episode to an end. It had been with a sense of foreboding that he had read the hastily scrawled message from the sister of his old student Piers Mountcarbery. Why had Piers asked her to send for him after receiving a letter from John Seward? And now, as Miss Sarah described the malady from which Piers was suffering, he found a clammy coldness on the nape of his neck, a sense of *déjà vu*.

He reached up a hand and ran a finger around the inside of his starched collar as if to ease the sudden constriction he felt in his throat.

They had been travelling several hours. Van Helsing realized that it must be approaching dawn. He was about to ask how much further the Mountcarbery estate was when the driver suddenly pulled rein on the horses and Van Helsing heard a shouting in a language he did not understand.

'What . . . ?' he began.

The girl stirred at his side.

'We are at the gates of Annaghdown, our estate.'

'Ah,' Van Helsing suddenly remembered that he was in a land where two languages were spoken. 'And your coachman calls his instructions in the Irish language, is this not so?'

The girl nodded affirmatively.

'Most people in the country still speak the old tongue,' she conceded. 'He simply tells the gate keeper to open the gates so that we may proceed.'

The *calèche* was rumbling forward again. To Van Helsing's surprise it was a further half-hour before the girl suddenly pointed towards the window on his side of the carriage.

'That's Castle Carbery. Yet I do not understand why there are so many lights on.'

To call the house a castle was a wild overstatement, thought Van Helsing, as he viewed the dark outlines of the building. Castle Carbery was not, and never had been, a castle. It was a sedate Georgian country mansion, fit to be inhabited by people of moderate fortune. Van Helsing had yet to learn that most of the Anglo-Irish aristocracy were impecunious with only their dignity and their pretensions to supply a subsistence. Their old castles, from which they had set forth to conquer Ireland and carve their own initial fortunes, had generally fallen into ruin and neglect. The continuing wars of conquests, confiscations of estates, and wave after wave of new colonists from England, had not given the old Anglo-Irish the peace and security to grow rich and prosper, any more than it had done for the long-suffering native Irish aristocracy, who had been forcibly dispersed to France, Spain and Austria.

After the devastating conquests of William of Orange, those Anglo-Irish who survived had found it necessary to leave their crumbling castles and move into more modest houses. Because they still clung to their tastes for the grandiose they considered it undignified to live in simple houses or mansions and thus called them castles still.

Such was Castle Carbery, home of the earls of Mountcarbery and barons of Annaghdown.

The main thing Van Helsing noticed, which the girl had drawn attention to, was that several windows of the house shone with light as the carriage approached the house along the broad, curving driveway which would bring it to halt before the main arched doorway. There was a tall woman standing at the door, obviously awaiting the approach of the carriage.

The driver pulled rein outside and at once a harsh female voice cried out in the same language that Van Helsing had previously heard.

'What is the matter?' he demanded.

The coachman was helping Sarah Mountcarbery down from the carriage.

The tall, hard-faced woman came hurrying forward. She spoke rapidly in her own language to the girl. Van Helsing, as he clambered down after the girl, noticed that the woman's eyes held a cold glint as she spoke, staring surreptitiously towards the Dutchman while addressing the girl. She spoke in staccato tones in Irish to which the girl responded shortly and with a sharpness in her voice. Then the woman spoke more slowly and Sarah Mountcarbery's response was a small cry of anguish, a hand going to her cheek.

Van Helsing instinctively knew what the news would be even before the girl turned to translate the harsh tones of the woman.

'Piers is dead,' she said in a choking voice.

Then the girl's eyes rolled back and she fell into a faint. Only his quick response prevented her from falling to the ground. He caught her in his arms, for Van Helsing was a powerful man in spite of his advancing years.

'Where may I put her?' he snapped at the anxious servant, at the same time striding towards the house.

The tall, raw-boned woman hurried at his side.

'Oh, sir ... sir ... place her in the library. There is a fire there. Ah, ah, *a chailín bhocht!*'

Van Helsing glanced at her in irritation.

'Where is the library?' he demanded.

She bobbed and weaved before him, ushering him into the house, while muttering asides in her own tongue. She led the way into a room leading off the large hallway.

There was a *chaise-longue* in the library and he laid the girl upon it, checking her pulse and respiration.

'I am a doctor,' he explained to the woman, who hovered at his side, anxiety on her face. 'Your mistress has only fainted. Do you have smelling-salts?'

The woman nodded reluctantly.

'Then get them. She will revive presently. In the meantime, get someone to show me his lordship's room?'

'His lordship's room?' the woman looked startled.

'Lord Mountcarbery,' snapped Van Helsing.

'Oh, Master Piers.'

'Very well, Master Piers' room. Has any other doctor been called for?'

The woman shook her head.

'Master Piers forbade any doctor to attend him. We knew that Miss Sarah had gone to meet you from Kingstown and would return soon. We heard her say that you were a doctor, so thought it best to wait your arrival.'

'When did his lordship's . . . Master Piers' death occur?'

'I can't say exactly, sir. It was sometime after Miss Sarah had left to meet you. Just after midnight, I went to take Master Piers a drink. He usually became thirsty in the night, sir. That's when I discovered him. I . . .'

Her eyes widened suddenly as she glanced at someone entering the room behind him. Van Helsing swung round. It was the tall, brown-bearded coachman, now divested of his driving coat. He and the woman exchanged a half-dozen rapid fire sentences in their native tongue before the man turned to Van Helsing.

'I am Draigen, sir,' he said.

'You are the coachman?' queried Van Helsing in bemusement, for usually a coachman did not make so free of the interior domain of his master's house.

The man did not smile.

'I am also the factor of the estate. I have many responsibilities at Annaghdown.'

'And who are you?' Van Helsing turned to the woman who had secured a phial of smelling-salts from a cupboard and was about to apply them to the young unconscious girl's nostrils.

'I am Mrs Bebinn, sir. The housekeeper.'

Van Helsing sighed.

'Very well, Mrs Bebinn. Revive Miss Sarah and give her

what comfort you can. And now, Draigen – is that your name? – you may take me to Master Piers' bedchamber. What does your name mean, by the way? It has a familiar ring.'

'In our Irish language, it means a blackthorn tree, sir.'

Draigen, the factor, turned and led the way into the hall. There were no other servants about. The factor was a powerfully-built man whose pale face lay hidden behind his beard. He took an already lighted lamp from a side table and began to ascend the stairs. Van Helsing clambered after the man's broad-shouldered form, having to quicken his pace to keep up. The tall man had a long stride.

As he ascended, Van Helsing pulled forth his Hunter gold watch and flicked open the lid. It was four o'clock in the morning.

'Would you know if anything has been touched? I mean, has the corpse been touched since the discovery?'

Draigen shook his head, glancing at Van Helsing with a curious light in his eye.

'Everything has been left as it was, Doctor,' he said without emotion. 'Or so I am informed.'

They had ascended the broad oak-wood stair to a main landing. Holding the lamp high, Draigen turned and hesitated before a door. Then, as if summoning some resolve, he bent and unlocked it from the key that was in the lock.

Van Helsing raised an eyebrow.

The man saw the gesture and shrugged.

'Mrs Bebinn thought it better to secure the room until you arrived, sir. Until we know...' He gave a grimace. 'Until we know what virus the young master died of.'

He pushed open the door and stood aside to let Van Helsing enter, holding the lamp high.

Van Helsing hesitated on the threshold.

'Will you want me to come in, sir?'

He caught a curious tone in Draigen's voice. He reached out a hand for the lamp and shook his head.

'No, my friend. You may wait outside. I will only be a short while.'

Van Helsing entered the room and, closing the door behind him, he stood with his back to it, surveying the room.

It was a large bedchamber. There were heavy curtains at the windows but they were not drawn. One of the windows was open to the chill night air, giving a view of the dark mountains outside and the pale sky which precedes dawn. It was cold and Van Helsing, shivering slightly, went to shut the window. Something on the window sill caught his eye. It was a small circular wafer which had been broken in half. Frowning he picked it up and peered closely at it.

'*Myn God!*' he whispered. 'This surely is a piece of the Sacred Host.'

Carefully, he took out his wallet and placed it inside.

Turning, he saw the large four-poster, an old-fashioned style bed, that dominated the room. There were two candles burning on either side of the bed and there was an overpowering smell of camphor.

Van Helsing walked slowly towards the still figure that lay in the bed. He halted beside it and placed the lamp on a side table.

In life Piers Mountcarbery had been, as Van Helsing remembered, a tall, large-boned, red-haired man of considerable vitality and well-proportioned muscles. In death, he lay white and shrunken, with a terrible expression on his waxing features. It was an expression of utter terror. No one had thought to close the eyelids and hide that awesome stare of death.

Van Helsing shivered slightly and cast a glance around as if to observe if any danger threatened. Then he slipped a hand inside his pocket and drew out a silver crucifix, attached to a long silver chain, and this he hung around his neck.

He stood for a moment before the corpse and took a deep breath. He reached forward with his hands and, with difficulty, he manipulated the lids into position. Then he drew back the stiffening flesh around the mouth, peering at the elongated incisors with a sickening feeling of resignation. He examined the neck. The wounds were blue-black and ugly, two rounded discoloured mounds above the jugular vein. He exhaled sharply.

'*God in de bemel*!' he muttered. 'Again! Is there no end to this evil?'

He took a mirror and wiping clean the surface, held it above the corpse's mouth for a while, staring at its bland unreflective surface. Then, with his mouth compressed more tightly, he drew back the covers and made a careful examination of the body before he finally stood upright again, staring down at the face.

'Ah, poor Piers. You knew . . . yet you could do nothing.' Van Helsing's voice was a whisper. 'With all your knowledge and strength . . . yet you were still powerless. Why?'

He was about to draw the sheet back over the body when his eyes caught sight of a scrap of paper half-hidden under the hand of the corpse. He carefully prized it from the stiffening fingers and smoothed the crumpled sheet.

He had no difficulty recognizing the scrawled hand-writing of his former student.

It was a poem:
I see black dragons mount the sky,
I see earth yawn beneath my feet—

I feel within the asp, the worm
That will not sleep and cannot die,
Fair though may show the winding-sheet!
I hear all night as through a storm
Hoarse voices calling, calling
My name upon the wind—
All omens monstrous and appalling
Afright my guilty mind.

Van Helsing blinked, took out his wallet and carefully placed the paper inside it.

He looked back down at the corpse.

'Fear not, young friend, for the peace of your soul,' he murmured. 'I am here now. You shall find peace. You shall!'

He replaced the crucifix beneath his shirt, picked up the lamp and turned from the room.

Draigen was waiting outside with troubled eyes. The servant took the lamp from Van Helsing's hand. For a moment his hand touched Van Helsing's own, cold and corpse-like. The Dutchman tried to repress a shudder and cursed himself for his imagination.

'There is much to be done,' Van Helsing said. 'Can a priest be sent for?'

The man looked startled.

'Why so?'

'A funeral must be arranged as soon as possible. The virus that he died from may well be contagious. Where will he be interred?'

Draigen looked worried.

'All the Mountcarberys are buried in the old castle chapel about a mile from here. I can send for the minister as soon as it is light.' He paused and added. 'The Mountcarberys were Protestant folk, sir, unlike the natives hereabouts.'

Van Helsing turned towards a window where the first pale streaks of light were now heralding the dawn. He was frowning.

'Protestants, you say? Master Piers had no dealings with the Catholic Church?'

Draigen shook his head.

'None, sir.'

'We are nearly at sunrise.' Van Helsing sighed after a moment. 'Let the arrangements be carried out quickly. The medical responsibility shall be mine.'

'With due respect, sir, I have to take my orders from Miss Sarah.'

Van Helsing suppressed a sigh. The man was right, of course.

'Very well, I will ask her consent.'

They went downstairs to where Mrs Bebinn was waiting in the hallway.

'And how is the young miss?' demanded Van Helsing. 'Have you deserted her?'

'Oh no, sir. She sent me to discover what was happening.' The woman was clearly indignant.

'Then I will go in and speak with her,' replied Van Helsing. 'And if there is some tea to be had and something to ease the discomfiture of hunger, I would be grateful.'

Mrs Bebinn went off to perform her task, followed by Draigen. Van Helsing paused outside the library door, knocked and hearing a sound, entered.

The girl was still on the *chaise-longue* but was in a more upright position. The smelling-salts lay on her lap. She had recovered her senses.

'Doctor . . . is it true?'

There was no hope in her eyes and he decided simple truth the only way to deal with her.

'Oh!' The syllable was a soft sigh in response to his news.

'I am afraid the, er, virus has proved fatal, my poor young miss. I must, therefore, seek the origins of it and so destroy it. Yet to prevent further spread, our poor dead friend, Piers, must be laid to rest without delay.'

She stared at him in incomprehension.

'The sooner his body can be interred, the sooner we may cease our concerns for contagion.'

'Is the disease then so contagious?'

'Unless prevented, poor miss, it is very contagious, this is so bad a virus.' In his excitement, Van Helsing always found the constructions of his own language tended to dominate his English.

'Then it shall be as you say.' The girl shivered suddenly. 'I am so fatigued, Doctor, and the shock has so distressed me that I must retire awhile. Please treat the house as if it were your own. I will go to my bed now and join you later in the day when I have rested.'

She rang a bell which was immediately answered by Mrs Bebinn.

'If you need anything, Doctor, simply ask Mrs Bebinn or Draigen, who is also the factor of the estate ... he manages everything,' she added. 'You will give him your instructions concerning the arrangements for my brother's funeral. They will be carried out as if I gave them myself.'

She paused at the doorway and looked back at Van Helsing.

'Do you have any objections if I pay my respects to my brother?'

Van Helsing compressed his lips a moment.

'You must swear that you will stand only in the open doorway and not go near the body.'

She gazed at him in perplexity a moment, then sighed and

nodded as she presumed that he feared that she might contract the virus.

After she had left, Mrs Bebinn said, 'Will you take breakfast in the dining-room, sir?'

'You must tell me where it is,' smiled Van Helsing.

Mrs Bebinn did not answer his smile, but conducted him to another doorway leading off the main hall which led into a large dining-room.

'I will eat here,' Van Helsing said solemnly. 'Send Draigen to me again, telling him of what Miss Sarah has said, that my orders are her orders.'

A moment later the tall, bearded man entered.

'I have already dispatched a stable boy for Mister Bell, the local minister.'

'And is there a coffin maker in these parts?'

'There is.'

'Then you may convey the importance to him, as well as the minister, that the interment should be not later than sundown today.'

Draigen's eyebrows shot up.

'Sundown *today*, sir?'

'Precisely so. Now, there are two things I would like to see,' Van Helsing said, as Mrs Bebinn entered with a tray. Van Helsing wrinkled his nose at the plate of greasy bacon and eggs under the silver cover. He settled for the tea, toast and honey.

'Two things you wish to see, sir?' prompted Draigen as Van Helsing busied himself over breakfast.

'Yes. I would like to see the place of interment and then I would like to meet your local Catholic priest.'

'But Master Piers was not a Catholic, sir,' protested Draigen. 'I have already told you this. Mister Bell was his minister.'

'I do not question your information. Nevertheless, I would like to see the priest.'

Draigen bit his lower lip to suppress a sigh. His expression betrayed his opinion of this officious, interfering Dutchman.

One of the stable lads, a fair-headed youth named Enda, conducted Van Helsing to the old, deserted chapel, which was the burial place of many generations of Mountcarberys. The chapel was surrounded by an assortment of tombs and crypts. One of these impressive vaults was a recent marble construction bearing a dedication to the eleventh earl, who had been Piers' father.

Having examined the strong, iron gates which barred the entrance to the tomb, watched by the curious eyes of the stable lad, Van Helsing indicated that he was ready to move on to see the parochial house where the priest dwelt.

Father MacCarthy, the priest, was a surprisingly youthful-looking man. He was of powerful build and of a vigorous disposition, although something seemed to be wrong with his eyes for he wore tinted glasses, such as the blind affected to wear, and was sitting in a shaded room when the housekeeper showed Van Helsing into the man's study and announced him.

'Forgive me greeting you in near darkness, sir,' the priest rose to shake his hand with so firm a grip that Van Helsing almost winced. 'I had an accident.'

He gestured to the wall where, to Van Helsing's surprise, a bow and a quiver of arrows was hanging on a hook.

'My hobby, sir. I like to play the archer, but a few days ago the bow broke as I was stringing an arrow and the flight scratched my eye. I need to rest it from harsh light.'

He paused and smiled thinly.

'What can I do for you, sir? You are a stranger to our

district? I don't think I caught your name properly ... Doctor Halse?'

Van Helsing reintroduced himself and told the priest briefly of his reasons for visiting Castle Carbery. The priest's face whitened.

'Dead, you say? And it was only two days ago that I was speaking with Piers. He was looking forward to your coming. I know your name now. Your reputation is well-known to me through Piers.'

'So you knew Piers well?'

'Well enough. I was a fellow student with him at the Royal College in Dublin. Then I found my vocation. I went to study at the Irish College in Rome and after ordination I spent two years doing missionary work in Constanta.'

Van Helsing was thoughtful.

'That's a port on the Black Sea coast, is it not?'

'It is. I am but recently returned home to Ireland where coincidence has made me curate of this parish. But tell me, Doctor, of what did Piers die?'

'Of as terrible a disease as can be conceived by man, Father.'

Father MacCarthy stared at him a moment.

Van Helsing opened his wallet and carefully extracted the piece of the Sacred Host. He laid it down on the desk between them.

'This, I imagine, was your doing?'

'What makes you say so?' Father MacCarthy seemed to avert his gaze from the sacrificial office.

'Piers was not a Catholic. Why would he defend his bedchamber window with fragments of a Sacred Host? The origin of this wafer is clearly a Catholic one.'

Father MacCarthy pressed his lips into a thin line.

'The Host is the Body of Christ. It is not to be used in any fashion that degrades it no matter how laudable the cause.'

'Then only in an extreme would you have sought to protect your friend – our friend – by this means. You knew what Piers suspected was happening to him?'

'What did he suspect, Doctor?' the priest countered.

'That he was being attacked by the UnDead.'

Father MacCarthy's face went white.

'I know of no such thing,' he whispered.

'I have reason to believe that my young friend Piers has fallen victim to an UnDead. We both know what that means. His soul cannot rest in peace. Before midnight, he will walk abroad again. He will walk abroad, damned to spread the vile contamination further.'

'Sacred Heart of Jesus!' breathed the young priest, his features were screwed up in agony.

'I have come to you, Father, because I have need of you. As soon as Piers is interred I need to visit the grave and . . . well, there is much I must do to prevent this evil contagion. I, too, have need of a sanctified host.'

Father MacCarthy's face was white.

'Do you know what you ask?' he whispered. 'I cannot sanction it.'

'It will not be degraded but will protect perhaps countless souls from everlasting hell.'

'I must think on this.'

'And while you think, let me ask you what Piers confided to you about his illness and anxiety?'

Father MacCarthy tugged at his lower lip.

'I knew that he was ill.'

'When did you discover this?'

'Soon after Sarah and I arrived back at Annaghdown.'

'When you *and* Sarah arrived back?' snapped Van Helsing in surprise.

'Sarah had been abroad a year or so. By coincidence, she joined the ship I was taking passage on at Piraeus. From there we journeyed home together.'

Van Helsing recalled that the girl had told him that she had only just returned to Ireland after being away in Europe.

'Go on, Father. What did you know of Piers' mental state?'

'I knew that he was fearful. He had come to fear an old family legend.'

Van Helsing eased forward in his chair, frowning.

'A legend?'

'Yes. But there are many such legends in Ireland.'

'Tell me this one.'

'It is just a legend.'

'In legend may be found many truths. You found it so compelling that you supplied him with a Host. So tell me. Are we not fighting evil together?'

The priest thought a moment or two and then shrugged.

'When Strongbow, the Earl of Pembroke, landed with his Anglo-Norman knights in Ireland, to conquer this land, he had a knight called Walter FitzWilliam under his command. This Walter was the founder of the house of Mountcarbery for he took the daughter of King Carbery of Annaghdown as his wife. Like most Norman knights of the time he was a cruel man who seized what he wanted and held on to it. He claimed the kingship of Annaghdown by killing all of Carbery's family except his daughter, Béfind, whom he forced to marry him. By Béfind he begot his children. The accounts say that she would not give in to him and each time he forced her by rape, keeping her imprisoned in his castle.

'It was said that Béfind became demented and renounced

the living God in whose name these Norman plunderers acted. The Normans had received the blessings of the Popes in their invasion and despoilment of Ireland . . .'

Van Helsing looked astonished.

Father MacCarthy nodded grimly.

'Oh yes, both Pope Adrian IV and Pope Alexander III urged and approved the invasion of Ireland. So Béfind, daughter of Carbery, disowned the living God and ritually cursed her husband with all the dark powers of the pagan priests of the Druids. Every seventh generation would be damned – utterly damned.'

Father MacCarthy's voice had risen with a strange vehemence. He cut off abruptly.

'Piers was worried because he was the twenty-eighth generation in descent from Walter and had learnt that every seven generations, the head of the Mountcarbery family, the title taken by the descendants of Walter FitzWilliam and the poor Lady Béfind, had died or disappeared in mysterious circumstances. I thought that it was this which was making him ill.'

Van Helsing looked unhappy.

'You do not believe in this curse?'

'I have said that there are many such tales in Ireland. You cannot go to a country which has been conquered in the manner that Ireland has and not expect to hear stories of curses, massacres and killings. Of cruel men and wrongs that need to be avenged.'

'Do you say that you do not believe in the curse of evil, in the curse of the UnDead?'

Father MacCarthy looked uncomfortable.

'If I believe in good then it follows that I must believe in evil.'

'Then let me tell you this, my friend, I have seen such evil

PETER TREMAYNE

walking abroad. Evil clad in rotting flesh, spreading like a disease among the living. It was something that I had hoped never to encounter again.'

The sun was setting when the small circle of mourners gathered in the private cemetery before the vaulted crypt of the last earl of Mountcarbery. Van Helsing was astonished that only the small band of servants had come to carry the coffin and pay their last respects. Mrs Bebinn had told him that Miss Sarah was feeling too unwell to attend and that she had to stay with her. And Draigen was not there but had, apparently, been sent thither on some mission. Of all those attending, only Van Helsing and the hawk-like minister were not members of the Mountcarbery household.

The Minister was a short, angular man, pale of skin and a shock of brilliant white hair which fell to his shoulders. He looked like some patriarch of old. His beak-like nose and thin red lips, and eyes that burnt with some strange pale fire, added to an otherworldly impression as he stabbed at the air above the coffin with a skeletal hand.

'Grant this man eternal peace, great Creator!' he called in a reedy, thin voice. 'Forgive his sins which are many and save him from eternal damnation, from the everlasting and consuming fires of hell, from the horrors of eternal purgatory!'

Van Helsing winced at the icy vehemence in the man's voice. Even in asking for forgiveness and compassion, the minister made it sound like an invocation to punishment.

'He sinned! Aye, we all sin! But he pandered to the scarlet harlot of Rome. He suffered Papishers into his house and sought their friendship. Heretics they are who will burn for all eternity! I know them!'

Suddenly, the minister threw out a hand, stabbing into

the oncoming gloom of the evening with a sharp forefinger. He pointed upwards.

'I see you! Heretic! You are doomed to suffer the everlasting torments of damnation.'

Van Helsing found himself turning in the direction in which the minister was pointing. To his surprise he saw a figure standing on a little mound overlooking the cemetery but outside its walls; a great cloak was flapping around it in the evening breeze. Van Helsing narrowed his eyes. It was silhouetted against the lowering sun. It was difficult to recognize but Van Helsing was sure that it was Father MacCarthy.

'Begone, heretic, harbinger of the evil one. I recognize you for what you are!' screamed the minister.

Van Helsing saw the figure of the priest hesitate as if he would dispute with him.

Minister Bell raised his Bible and held it aloft.

'I need no Popish images to challenge you,' he yelled, spittle at his mouth. 'I need only the true Word of God!'

Father MacCarthy turned abruptly on his heel and disappeared from sight.

The minister then turned to the huddled group of servants who were muttering uneasily among themselves.

'Ah, children, children! I know you stumble in the ways of Roman ignorance. Repent. Repent before the dead body of your master . . .'

Van Helsing bit his lip in annoyance.

'Surely, minister, this is not the time or place to preach conversion. We are here to lay to rest our young friend, Piers Mountcarbery.'

Minister Bell spun round, his eyes glowing.

'Rest? Lay to rest, you say? This young man goes into damnation for his sins . . .' The old minister's wild eyes abruptly widened to stare over Van Helsing's shoulder. Did Van Helsing see some strange, terrible expression in them?

The old man's arm raised upwards again, jabbing into the oncoming gloom:

'I see him. I see him, spawn of the devil. Only the fires of damnation will expedite his sin.'

Van Helsing turned his head.

On the rise behind the graveyard, where the tack from Castle Carbery wound its way down to the chapel and its grounds, stood a *calèche*. The tall, brown-bearded man was seated on the driver's box. The setting sun shone and its amber rays bathed the carriage in a curious brown rust-red so that it seemed that the entire *calèche* was drenched in blood.

'Evil stalks Annaghdown. Only when Castle Carbery is no more will life return to this land of death which is yet undeath.'

Without another word, the old minister turned and clambered into a trap drawn by a single horse and whipped it into a canter away from the cemetery.

Van Helsing swallowed hard. It was the most astonishing funeral service he had ever attended.

The servants stood silent a moment, their heads staring towards the parked *calèche* on the hillside. Then the tall man on the driver's box seemed to flick the reins and it moved off into the gloom. Several of the stable lads moved hurriedly forward now and lifted the coffin. Van Helsing noticed that one or two of them swiftly genuflected before the act. Then the coffin was taken with almost indecent haste into the crypt and left.

It was just after midnight. Van Helsing crouched uncomfortably beside one of the tombs in the grounds of the old castle chapel and burial ground. He had borrowed a horse from the stables at Castle Carbery and, with his worn leather medical bag which he had extracted from his portmanteau, he had ridden to this place an hour before midnight. Now he shifted uneasily and peered at his Hunter fob-watch again. Such a vigil was better shared with friends, but there was no one he could trust in this strange land. He was hoping that he could have trusted Father MacCarthy. How strange that the minister, Mister Bell, could rebuke him so publicly and call him evil. What did he mean by that?

There was a slight change in the atmosphere which suddenly caught his attention. He felt a distinct chill and shivered violently.

He glanced towards the crypt in which Piers Mountcarbery had been laid that late afternoon.

A white, ethereal mist seemed to be drifting under the metal door.

Van Helsing compressed his lips into a thin line. He had been right. It was happening as he had said it must.

The mist rose, forming and reforming until it resolved itself and vanished. In its place stood the tall, unmistakable figure of Piers Mountcarbery, clad as he had been dressed for his coffin.

The figure cocked an ear and, two bright eyes burning like coals from the fires of hell, stared straight towards Van Helsing. The Dutch professor eased himself up, realizing that further concealment was useless.

'Why, Doctor,' Piers' voice was smooth and cajoling. 'It is good to see you here. I have felt your presence for some hours. I am honoured that you have come to see me. To see me and perhaps to join me . . . ?'

The tall figure began to walk, no – more glide – yes, it seemed to slide without movement across the overgrown cemetery towards him.

Van Helsing pulled aside his coat and revealed the silver crucifix at his neck.

'Ah, I should have known.'

The figure of Piers stopped its motion, the face was momentarily baffled and annoyed.

Van Helsing took a step forward. He cleared his throat.

'I am speaking to the spirit that was once Piers Mountcarbery, a young man of noble thought and deed who was once my friend. Piers, young friend, if your soul still lingers in this vile shell, tell me what evil was responsible for this. Piers, can you tell me?'

The figure began to chuckle.

'I am Piers, good Doctor. I am Piers for all eternity now!'

'What great UnDead has severed you from real life?' cried Van Helsing.

'One who called my name upon the wind,' sneered the creature, making a dart forward towards him.

Van Helsing raised his crucifix and began to intone a Latin prayer. With a grimace of disgust the spectre reduced itself to elemental mist and began to retreat towards the crypt.

Undaunted by the sight, Van Helsing hurried swiftly towards the crypt. The door was easily opened. He was in time to see the opaque mist vanishing into the new coffin which had been laid inside.

Van Helsing had gambled. He had gambled that the new UnDead form of Piers Mountcarbery was weakened by its first movement abroad, for the corpse had not suckled its first blood as yet. It had none of the vile nourishment needed to sustain such long periods of activity without rest. Van Helsing unscrewed the lid of the coffin as quickly as he dared.

The corpse lay there with a strangely somnambulant expression on its face.

Van Helsing bent over it, making sure the crucifix was at his throat.

'Is the spirit called Piers Mountcarbery within this shell?' he called softly.

The eyes blinked. They were not alive, neither did they glow, as in the chapel yard, with that strange red vehemence. The mouth did not move but a strange whisper seemed to echo from the body.

'I am . . . still here. Help me! Help me!'

Van Helsing gave a sharp intake of breath.

'I am here, Piers,' he said triumphantly. 'I have come to help you. Before I do so, my young friend, you must tell me . . . tell me if you have the strength . . . name the Great Undead who has done this evil thing to you.'

'Help me, Professor!' The voice was a moan of pain. 'Do not let me succumb to . . . to this . . . It grows stronger every moment, have a care!'

'The name of the UnDead, Piers. Then you may rest in peace.'

'The UnDead . . . it is . . .'

Van Helsing heard the movement a second before a heavy hand sent him flying across the crypt, cannoning into a pillar. As he sought to regain his balance, he heard a terrible cry of pain.

Blinking, Van Helsing recovered his balance and stared back towards the coffin.

Father MacCarthy was bending over the corpse chanting in Latin.

With a suppressed exclamation, Van Helsing moved forward.

The priest was still gripping with both hands the wooden shaft of an arrow which he had driven directly through the heart of the corpse. Blood was bubbling up, black and thick, all around it.

'You damned fool!' cried the professor in agitation. 'You fool! You have prevented him revealing the name of the source of this evil!'

The priest shook his head fiercely.

'I have destroyed the devil's spawn. This thing was not living. It was a creature of Satan. I did what I had to do.'

He threw back his head and began to laugh uncontrollably. The priest was hysterical.

Van Helsing leaned forward and slapped the priest across the cheek. The laughter stopped at once. Father MacCarthy staggered backwards and stared at him in astonishment.

Van Helsing ignored him, turning back to the coffin and gazing down. There was no doubt that Piers Mountcarbery was in peace now. Yet there was one or two things left to do. He looked at Father MacCarthy.

'Did you come prepared to finish this night's work, Father?'

The priest shook his head, hanging it before the older man like an intractable schoolboy.

'I do not know what you mean.'

'You knew enough to realize that a wooden stake must be driven through the heart of a vampire.'

MacCarthy blinked rapidly but did not reply.

Van Helsing sighed in irritation.

'Very well. I am prepared.'

From his small doctor's bag he selected a scalpel.

'What do you intend to do?' whispered the priest.

'Give my poor friend eternal rest,' replied Van Helsing shortly, and, turning, he drew the scalpel swiftly across the throat of the corpse.

'Blasphemers! Spawn of Satan!'

The old, cracked voice shrieked through the stillness of

the crypt, reverberating in its intensity.

Van Helsing glanced towards the door, the scalpel still held in his hand. He froze momentarily over the coffin.

The thin, angular figure of the old minister Bell stood at the entrance, clutching his Bible.

'Back, dogs of the evil one! Back, I say!'

He advanced with his Bible upheld.

'Wait!' cried Van Helsing. 'You do not know what you have intruded upon.'

'I do not know? I have come across blasphemy and sacrilege! You, sir, are hand in glove with the devil's spawn, with the scarlet harlot of Rome! What Papish blasphemy are you at?'

The pale, cold eye of the minister suddenly fell on the silver crucifix at Van Helsing's neck.

To the Dutchman's surprise, the pale-faced man flinched as if in physical pain and backed away.

At once suspicion shot through the professor and he suddenly advanced a pace holding up the crucifix before him as a talisman.

'Do you abjure the devil and all his works?' he demanded. 'Do you acknowledge Christ as the living God and Mary as His Mother?' he demanded.

The minister closed his eyes and moaned, holding his hands to his ears.

'I will never acknowledge heresy!' he cried.

Van Helsing moved quickly across the crypt to the old man and laid the crucifix upon his forehead in one swift motion.

The old minister screamed and with a surprising twist of strength he grabbed Van Helsing's arm and flung him backwards.

Van Helsing rolled over on the floor, managing to regain his hold on the crucifix, and he stared up at the minister. To his utter astonishment there was no imprint of burnt flesh on the forehead of the man. The crucifix had not left a mark as he had believed it would.

'You ... but you are not an UnDead!' breathed Van Helsing in bewilderment.

'Heretics! Blasphemers!' screamed the old man. 'I shall return and drive you out of this land.'

He turned and vanished with surprising swiftness for one so aged, vanished rapidly into the night.

As Van Helsing picked himself up from the floor, he heard a sobbing chuckle and turned round.

Father MacCarthy was standing in the back of the crypt, his shoulders heaving.

'You poor fool,' breathed the priest, catching his breath. 'The old man is a Protestant, a die-hard who abjures the symbols of our faith. He was reacting to the crucifix as a symbol, in his eyes, of idolatry. You thought he was reacting from fear of it as a symbol of good ...'

Van Helsing exhaled in annoyance and began to dust himself down.

'I have little understanding of the ways of this land. I did not expect to encounter such fanaticism among priests.'

Father MacCarthy seemed to recover his equilibrium and he shook his head sadly.

'We are all entitled to some prejudice, I suppose.'

Van Helsing returned to the corpse and bent over it once more with his surgical implements.

'Is this truly necessary?' demanded the priest, peering over his shoulder with distaste as the Dutchman severed the head from the body.

'To ensure that the body is never reanimated by the UnDead, the head must be severed,' nodded Van Helsing dispassionately. 'Then the flowers of wild garlic, which I have brought, must be placed into its mouth. But no word of this must ever be revealed outside this crypt.'

He took some wild garlic flowers from his bag.

'Not from my mouth, Doctor,' agreed Father MacCarthy. 'Ah, but I wish that you had arrived sooner and prevented this tragedy.'

'Let us now be honest with each other,' Van Helsing said, as he motioned Father MacCarthy to help him lift the coffin lid back into place. 'Did you know that Piers had fallen prey to the UnDead?'

The priest shrugged.

'How is one to know such things? I knew only what I told you earlier of my friend's fears. I knew of the curse of the Mountcarberys and that some evil had gripped this house. That is all I knew.'

Van Helsing finished screwing back the coffin lid.

'There, now he is the true dead of Christ,' he breathed, standing back. 'Perhaps you will say a prayer?'

The priest hesitated.

'I do not think that it is proper.'

Van Helsing frowned, puzzled.

'Not proper when we have released his soul into merciful rest?'

'How can you be so sure . . . ?'

'Believe me, Father. I am sure and have no regrets for my work this night. The only thing I do regret is that you dispatched his soul before he could identify the great UnDead who attempted this evil.'

He broke off abruptly as his ears caught a faint sound in the night air. There was a flapping sound, a soft noise like the gentle beat of wings, slowly and rhythmically pulsating against the air.

Van Helsing felt a momentary chill.

He turned slowly towards the door of the crypt.

A figure was forming as if from a mist. A tall figure. A tall man with a large brown beard. The eyes glowed malignant and red into the darkness.

'Draigen!' breathed Van Helsing.

The man stood still, arms folded across his broad chest. His expression was filled with hatred.

'You have destroyed him! For that I will take my revenge. You think you can destroy us. We are legion and the earth is ours to inherit.'

The great vampire leapt towards Van Helsing, who stumbled back and fell, the crucifix flying from his hand even as he attempted to raise it in an effort to protect himself and ward off the attack. It vanished into the dim recess behind one of the coffins. Van Helsing lay stunned a moment, unable to move as the UnDead thing towered over him with a sneer of triumph.

'Stop!' Van Helsing was aware of Father MacCarthy almost screaming the word. 'In the name of Christ, I command you . . .'

The priest had pushed his way past Van Helsing and placed himself before the man. He barred Draigen's path, holding up his hand. The massive form did not halt. One giant hand came up and seized the priest by the throat, in spite of MacCarthy's youth and strength, and held him at arm's length, a good foot above the ground. The priest struggled, desperate for air. Then the vampire threw him across the crypt as if he had been no more than a rag doll.

There was a sickening impact of flesh against stone as the priest hit the wall and slithered down to the floor like a broken toy.

With his mouth working, the specks of blood flying from his lips which were drawn back over the yellowing teeth, the vampire turned towards Van Helsing. The professor had scrambled to his knees, realizing that he had stumbled backwards over a discarded spade left by some lazy workman. For want of any other weapon, he seized it and swung it with all his might as Draigen came at him. The edge of the spade caught against the neck of the creature and, to his amazement, the pure iron of the working edge sliced into the creature's neck.

With a scream of agony, Draigen's charge was halted and he stumbled back.

Van Helsing seized the spade with both hands and clambered to his feet, advancing on the creature and swinging again with all his might.

Iron was pure. He dimly recalled that fact. Evil could not stand against purity. He felt the blade cut into Draigen. The creature went down before him and, standing over the writhing form of the UnDead, Van Helsing brought the spade down with all the force that he could muster directly into the heart of the thing. One long agonized cry assailed his ears and then the body started to waxen in death.

Van Helsing stared at it in surprise. He had expected the flesh to fall away, the bones begin to crumble until nothing but dust lay on the floor of the crypt. But Draigen's corpse remained. With growing horror, Van Helsing realized that Draigen could only recently have been seduced to the ranks of the UnDead. He was not the source, not the great UnDead that he sought! If he had been, then the body would have withered. Then who . . . ?

Van Helsing stared down, shivering a little.

A groan caused him to raise his head.

Van Helsing limped to the side of the body of Father MacCarthy. There was nothing he could do and yet . . . yet the priest was still alive. He coughed blood and tried to speak. Van Helsing bent forward trying to catch the words that strangled in the man's throat.

'Miss Sarah . . . danger . . . you must get to her . . . save her . . . Piers feared the curse . . . the curse of the UnDead! Miss Sarah too is . . . of the seventh generation! Béfind's curse is on her now!'

'But if Draigen is not the UnDead,' frowned Van Helsing, 'who then?'

'The creature who haunted the family . . . the creature who cursed the family . . . creature was Béfind . . . Béfind who cursed the seed of . . . of Walter Fitzwilliam.'

Van Helsing was agitated.

'What are you saying?'

'Another form . . . of rendering Béfind . . . Bebinn. Go, save Miss Sarah . . . from Bebinn!'

Father MacCarthy fell back, the last strength of his body being expended in his effort.

Van Helsing started up, a coldness within him as he rose to his feet. Mrs Bebinn! Béfind was Mrs Bebinn, a great UnDead who fed off her own children, every seventh generation since . . . If the priest was right, then Miss Sarah was in terrible danger as her brother had been. And she was alone at Castle Carbery with this fiend. He had not a moment to lose.

Van Helsing found his horse standing patiently where he had tethered it. He mounted and, crouching low along its neck, dug his heels firmly into its ribs, riding as he had never ridden in his life. It was more due to the horse's good sense than Van Helsing's uninspired horsemanship that the beast sped straight along the tortuous trackway, through the moonlit woods towards Castle Carbery.

The Georgian mansion stood in darkness as he approached the front of the building. Reining in a flurry of flying gravel, Van Helsing almost fell from the beast and stumbled to the door. To his surprise, he found it open and burst into the house. It seemed deserted, although a single lamp burnt in the hallway.

God! If he were too late! If the fiend Bebinn had reached young Sarah already . . .

He grabbed the lamp and sped up the stairs, two at a time.

A shadow stirred on the landing.

A shriek of rage rang out as the figure of the transformed housekeeper came rushing towards him. Blood was flecking at her mouth where her teeth gnashed against her lips.

Van Helsing drew out his crucifix while feeling in his pocket for the phial of holy water he carried.

'Back, I order, in the name of the living God!' he thundered.

The malevolent creature came to a halt, hands before her eyes as the light reflected on the silver of the cross.

Van Helsing moved resolutely forward onto the main landing.

'Miss Sarah, where are you?' he called. 'It is I, Van Helsing.'

The door of one of the rooms opened a fraction. He saw the pale, slight form of the girl framed in the doorway.

'Professor! Thank goodness . . .'

'Are you all right?' asked Van Helsing, not taking his eyes from the creature Bebinn, who had backed into a darkened corner of the landing.

'Yes, yes. What is happening? Why . . . what is the matter with Mrs Bebinn . . . ?'

Van Helsing moved swiftly across to the girl.

'Stay by me for safety's sake. This Bebinn is a creature of death . . . It was the priest who made me realize it. In his dying breath he . . .'

'Father MacCarthy is dead?' She interrupted in a shocked and horrified voice.

'Yes, I am afraid so,' nodded Van Helsing, his eyes not leaving the angry but baffled figure of the housekeeper, who now and then attempted to move in half-hearted threatening fashion towards them. Van Helsing took out the phial of holy water and told Sarah to move back in her room. Then he bent down and allowed the water to spill along the threshold of the bedroom door, knowing that the UnDead creature would not be able to pass over it. He pushed Sarah back inside the bedchamber and followed her beyond the protection of the door. Bebinn's scream of baffled rage followed them.

'What do you intend to do?' demanded the girl.

'Do? Ah, about that creature?' Van Helsing jerked his head towards the door. 'We'll wait until dawn and then I will track her to her resting place and destroy her.'

He suddenly frowned as the thought struck him.

'Yet if Bebinn was UnDead, and Draigen as well, how did they function in this house as servants when they had to rest from sunrise to sunset. How . . . ?'

He heard Sarah's sharp intake of breath behind him. He was about to turn when he felt something hard knock into him. The crucifix went flying out of his hand through the doorway into the hall beyond, sliding out of reach.

Van Helsing stumbled and when he regained his balance, he turned with a growing feeling of apprehension.

Sarah Mountcarbery stood transformed. Her eyes were twin pools of malignant fire, red and flickering. The teeth had grown longer, great yellowing fangs from which the lips were pulled back to show the white decaying gums.

'Puny, foolish man!' the voice was venomous. 'You thought to outwit me as you outwitted my lover. You never had a chance.'

Van Helsing blinked, his mind working desperately, trying to adjust to events that moved too fast for him to understand.

'Your lover?' His voice strangled in his dry throat.

The creature which the girl had become gave a sneering laugh.

'Had you pursued your inquiries a little more vigorously you would have known that two years ago I left for a tour of the east, travelling to Turkey. My way lay through the beautiful Carpathians. There I met *him* . . . *he* taught me . . . nurtured me . . . and then bade me return here while *he* prepared to follow. I was to join him at Carfax . . . then I heard how you and your friends thwarted and destroyed him.'

Van Helsing swallowed hard.

'Carfax? Then you speak of . . . ?'

'Of Count Dracula. When he died, I was reborn. I became complete as he had been; just as he had intended. By coincidence I learnt from my brother that you had been his teacher once. How prosaic! It was I who proselytised Draigen and Bebinn to my cause, and my puny brother . . . we were going to wreak such vengeance on those who destroyed my Dracula . . . but I still shall. The plan to send for you was easy to make . . . You swallowed the bait. You came to rescue my brother. And you have had some luck. That is now ended. There is no one to rescue you from my revenge!'

Van Helsing felt utterly helpless as this beautiful creature of the night threw back her slender white throat and gave vent to the most hideous laughter that he had ever heard. With anguish he realized that Father MacCarthy had been wrong about the ancient curse of the Mountcarberys. It had been no more than a legend. This was the new reality. His mind thought frantically for a way out, for some means of protection. He saw Bebinn beyond the door, her fangs bared in something meant as a smile of triumph. His path to his crucifix was obstructed. He glanced desperately around. He was aware of her voice, whispering his name gently. Sighing his name, as if it were the sound of a faint breeze; his name upon the wind.

He felt a bitter irony; a mocking resignation. He had been confounded by this slip of a girl.

Abraham Van Helsing, even though he was now in his early sixties, had never ceased to have an eye for a pretty girl. Perhaps that was why he had never been satisfied with a single relationship. Women found his only dependable quality was a constant adoration of feminine beauty. Many of his fellow academics at Amsterdam's old university found that both surprising and sometimes embarrassing. One of them once sagely remarked that women would eventually be the death of old Bram Van Helsing!